The BOOK *of* LOST HOURS

The
BOOK
of
LOST
HOURS

A Novel

HAYLEY GELFUSO

ATRIA BOOKS

New York Amsterdam/Antwerp London
Toronto Sydney/Melbourne New Delhi

An Imprint of Simon & Schuster, LLC
1230 Avenue of the Americas
New York, NY 10020

This book is a work of fiction. Any references to historical events, real people, or real places are used fictitiously. Other names, characters, places, and events are products of the author's imagination, and any resemblance to actual events or places or persons, living or dead, is entirely coincidental.

Simon & Schuster strongly believes in freedom of expression and stands against censorship in all its forms. For more information, visit BooksBelong.com.

For information about special discounts for bulk purchases, please contact Simon & Schuster Special Sales at 1-866-506-1949 or business@simonandschuster.com.

The Simon & Schuster Speakers Bureau can bring authors to your live event. For more information or to book an event, contact the Simon & Schuster Speakers Bureau at 1-866-248-3049 or visit our website at www.simonspeakers.com.

Interior design by Esther Paradelo

Manufactured in the United States of America

1   3   5   7   9   10   8   6   4   2

Library of Congress Control Number: 2024044145

ISBN 978-1-6680-7634-7
ISBN 978-1-6680-7636-1 (ebook)

For Ernest,
whose memory I would visit every day if I could

1

―――――――――

1938, Nuremberg, Germany

IN THE CITY OF Nuremberg in 1938, a man told his daughter a bedtime story. The man was a clockmaker, the son in a long line of clockmakers who lived in the city's Jewish neighborhood. Keeping time as his ancestors had for two centuries.

"Time for bed, Lisavet. You've had enough stories for tonight," the clockmaker said when his daughter asked him, for the third time that night, for another story.

Out the window, the streets had long since gone dark and chill with November winds. The clockmaker's mind was on the work he had to finish downstairs in the shop. And more specifically on the letter from America that sat on his desk, delivered earlier that morning.

"I'm not tired," Lisavet pouted. "I want to stay up until Klaus comes home."

"Your brother won't be home until late," the clockmaker scolded.

The smile on his face foiled his attempts at discipline. He ran a hand through her hair, already knowing that she would wear him down. His daughter was his late wife reborn, with golden hair and caramel brown eyes.

When she was alive, his wife had often teased that they had replicated themselves into two miniature versions, him in their son and her in their daughter. It was true in the physical sense but beyond that, Ezekiel Levy and his son, Klaus, could not be more different. Klaus was like his mother with his high society taste and dreams of attending school in the capital. It was Lisavet who was most like Ezekiel. She could often be found perched on the stool beside him in his workshop, watching him coax the gears and springs of old broken watches until they shuddered back into life. She was the one who wound the clocks in the front of the shop each morning, watching with quiet reverence as the wood and metal masterpieces sang to the tune of time. And she was the one who would one day inherit his shop and the family secrets that came with it.

"Tell me about the magic watch again," Lisavet said, clutching his wrist tightly as he tried to stand.

At eleven years old, Lisavet was almost too old for bedtime stories at all, and the clockmaker knew it wouldn't be long before she stopped asking. He settled himself on the edge of the bed.

"Once upon a time in Germany, a clockmaker named Ezekiel lived with his two children in their happy little home above the shop that his family had owned for generations," he began in a deep voice that crackled like flames in a hearth. "The family were world-renowned for the magnificent clocks that they sold in their store, made from the finest materials. Gold and gems and carved wood that gleamed in the candlelight by which they did their work. Large grandfather clocks, small table clocks, and everything in between. But among all these wondrous masterpieces was the most precious timepiece of all. A simple brass pocket watch, passed from father to son for over a hundred years. That watch was not special because it was laden with silver or gold, but because—" He broke off, bushy eyebrows raised, waiting for his daughter to finish the line. It was a game they played with all his stories, but especially this one.

"Because it let them talk to Time itself," Lisavet said in a hushed voice.

"That's right." Ezekiel smiled and tapped her on the nose. "Time is the axis on which the world spins. Humans count their lives in months and weeks, as if calculating the cumulative measure of their existence will somehow earn them more of it. Accidents occur in three clicks of the second hand. Hearts stop in a moment of time. But there are things that happen in the space between seconds. Worlds are built. Planets burn. Souls fade into the space between one instant and the next and memories fall to depths, lost to the silence and flames."

He dropped his voice lower, hissing like the shadows. Lisavet's eyes went wide.

"It was not always this way. Centuries ago, the things that fell from our world and into the silence were hidden. Closed off to humanity. Unwitnessed. Unknown. The most devoted sensed something more, seeking it in meditations, brushing against it in dreams, never fully grasping what it was they were reaching for. As Time became more tangible, more precious, so did the shadows. With the invention of sundials came the ability to count the hours, and with clocks, the seconds. What can be counted can be mastered, and soon the veil between our world and what falls beyond it became thinner. Those who learned the language of Time called themselves timekeepers."

The clockmaker whispered the word *timekeeper* with a devotee's reverence. Outside the window, the winds began to blow.

"Like Ezekiel," Lisavet said, right on cue. "He was a timekeeper."

"That's right. It was a secret that the family had carried for decades. Until one day, things started to change . . ."

"A storm was coming," Lisavet prompted.

Ezekiel furrowed his brow, his tone deepening. "A storm was coming. The world began to grow darker and in crept a cold fierce enough to blow out every hearth. People stopped coming to buy clocks from their shop. Ezekiel could feel the darkness lurking out on the streets, advancing. The men who brought the storm were ruthless, full of hate and fire. Some came to Ezekiel's shop one evening in the summer and asked him about his secret. They wanted the power for themselves. They demanded that he give them the watch that let him speak to Time."

"But Ezekiel tricked them," Lisavet said, full of pride.

"Yes, he did. It was his job to protect the secret, so he gave them a fake. They left his shop alone then, but Ezekiel knew that they would be back as soon as they discovered his deception. Time was in danger, and so was the clockmaker's family. So he wrote a letter to an old friend. Another timekeeper who might be able to help him."

"Why didn't they just leave?" Lisavet asked, frowning slightly.

He bit his lip, thinking. "Because the men who had brought the storm might catch them. So Ezekiel asked his friends to help his family escape by other means. You see, the timekeepers knew of a place hidden in the folds of Time where they could disappear. A place where his family could hide, and with the help of another timekeeper, where they could escape into other lands far away from the storm."

"And did it work? Did they help him?" Lisavet asked with a sleepy yawn.

Every other time he'd told this story, Ezekiel had ended it with a promise to tell the rest of the story another night. But tonight, there was a letter on his desk from his friend in America. Tonight, he kissed Lisavet on the forehead and smiled.

"Yes, they did. His friends wrote back and promised him help. Ezekiel and his family waited for the right moment. They talked to their closest friends and neighbors about the dangers of the coming darkness and brought as many of them with them as they could. It took some convincing. Not everyone believed in this tunnel through Time, and many were afraid of it. Still others didn't want to leave home no matter how strong the winds got. Those who would come settled on a day: the first night of Hanukkah when they would all be together with their families." Here the clockmaker paused. Lisavet had begun to close her eyes. The last part of his story came in a whisper. "So by the light of the full moon in December, they escaped through the shadows and into freedom."

As soon as he said it, two dozen grandfather clocks in the shop below all chimed eleven o'clock. Ezekiel fell silent, listening. As the chimes faded, echoing deep into the night, another sound met his ears. Shouting out on the streets, followed by the crash of breaking glass.

"What was that?" Lisavet asked, eyes wide open once more.

He went to the window, pulling aside the curtains. On the cobblestones below, coming up the street like a gale, a mob of angry faces was blowing in with the wind. Shattering glass drew his attention to another shop down the street and he watched in horror as his neighbors rushed out of their apartments, the children barefoot in their nightgowns.

"Papa, what's happening?" Lisavet said. She was climbing out of bed.

"Put on your shoes, Lisavet," he said. "I'll be right back."

He ignored her cries for him to stay and bolted down the stairs to his shop. The crowd was drawing nearer. He could hear the pounding of their hands against the doors. The crunch of glass underfoot. He had seen such sights and heard such sounds carried in the memories of the dead. He knew what happened next. First came the shouting, the breaking, the anger. Then came the fire, the fighting, the killing.

The last clock in the shop let out a final chime, sounding like a name. *Klaus*. Ezekiel's heart rose to his throat as he thought of his son down at the synagogue. He stood frozen on the last step, panicked.

"Papa?" Lisavet's voice came from the top of the stairs.

"Stay up there!"

They were coming. The first of them was at his shop, beating on the door. They locked eyes through the window, steel gray and ice cold. Coming for the watch. Then the knocking became kicking, and the shouting became jeering. Ezekiel rushed for the letter on the desk. He stuffed it into his pocket and emptied the drawer below of other letters. Letters that spoke of the timekeepers and those complicit in his attempts to escape. He threw them into the bucket of water he used to mop up, the soap and lye expediting their disintegration. Without bothering to shut the drawer, he reached for his coat. He had barely pulled it on when the first rock struck the window frame. Lisavet was halfway down the stairs when he returned to her, stumbling on the too-long hem of her nightgown.

"Papa!"

"Upstairs, Lisavet," he said, reaching into his coat for the pocket watch. The old familiar brass was slick in his palm.

His fingers fumbled over the crown until it clicked into place, and he flung open the door. What had once been their cozy, two-room apartment was instead a silent cavern of shadows. Lisavet clutched his arm at the sight of what lay beyond. Ezekiel gripped his daughter's shoulders tight, kneeling down to look her in the eye.

"Listen to me, Lisavet. I'm going to find your brother, okay? I want you to wait in there. Stay right there by this door. Do not move from that spot. I promise as soon as I get Klaus, we will come and find you. All right?"

"But, Papa, what is that?"

A second rock struck the shop. This one found its mark, shattering the glass on impact. "This is the tunnel through Time that I told you about," he said frantically. "The one that will take us somewhere far away."

"But that was just a story!" Lisavet exclaimed, shaking her head as he propelled her forward. On the other side of the door, she could see nothing but shadows and darkness.

"It wasn't just a story, Lisavet. Go inside. I'll be right back for you, I promise."

She dug her heels in, and he picked her up as he had when she was younger, tossing her over one shoulder. He deposited her on the other side of the door and stopped for just a moment longer to kiss her head and drape his brown coat around her tiny shoulders. It pooled on the ground at her feet.

"Be brave," he said, his words muffled against her hair.

"Papa?" she said, her voice echoing.

He pressed a finger to his lips and left her, slipping back over the threshold.

The door closed behind him and never opened again.

FOR HOURS, Lisavet waited. Everything was deathly quiet and impossibly still. She counted the seconds. At the top of every hour, she longed to hear the music of the clocks from the shop in which she'd grown up, but instead heard only silence. A silence so all-encompassing that it seemed alive, like a solid thing you could touch. Shadows obscured her vision and prevented her from seeing more than fifty feet ahead of her, but what she could see was strangely familiar.

Bookshelves. Towering on both sides and lined with leather-bound volumes of all sizes and shapes. Like a library. Lisavet took a single tentative step forward, her eyes slowly adjusting. *Library* wasn't quite the right word. Indeed there were books, their leather spines packed in neat, even rows. Sweeping archways and Roman pillars stood at intervals between the endless rows of shelves, and Lisavet's eyes followed the path of one of them all the way up. Where she expected to find a ceiling, she instead saw an inky sky filled with watery images, as though Michelangelo had painted the Sistine Chapel into the very stars themselves, each image swirling into the next like clouds drifting in the wind.

She wanted to walk among the shelves, but her father's words echoed in her head. Stay right by the door. Do not move from this spot. When she turned around to face the door once more, it had changed. Now it appeared blurry, like a watery reflection of a door more than the door itself. It began fading away, familiar planks of wood consumed by darkness. Lisavet lunged for the doorknob, but it evaporated beneath her touch, taking any chance of returning to her father away with it. Lisavet sank to the ground where she stayed huddled on the floor, sobs racking her body.

The whispering started from somewhere within the darkness. A gentle, curious jingle as the shadows sought the source of a sound they had never heard before. Lisavet dried her eyes on the back of her hand, heart thudding. She did not know it yet, but this was Time itself, that long cherished friend of her ancestors, learning to speak to her, and she, uncertain and afraid, spoke back to it.

"H-hello?" she called as loudly as she dared.

Hello, the whispers repeated, echoing her own voice back to her.

Lisavet stood up. "Who's there?" she asked.

The whispers sounded again, closer now.

Lisavet's breathing came fast and shallow. She took a few steps in the direction of the darkness, away from the place her father had left her.

"Stay right there," she said. "I'm coming to find you."

Stay, stay, stay, the whispers echoed.

Lisavet stepped farther into the shadows and darkness in search of Time.

No one was coming.

Lisavet had been trapped for two weeks and in that time, she had learned three very important things.

The first was that the laws of nature didn't seem to apply here. She never got hungry. She never got thirsty or needed to use the bathroom. Sleep was unnecessary in the traditional sense. She could sleep, and sometimes did just to pass the time, but before long she began prolonging the time she spent awake, just to see how long she could go.

Second, there were no other doors hidden away in this place, confirmed by several days of searching. No way out.

And third, Time did not live here as her father's story had suggested. Or if it did, it would offer her no help.

No one was coming. Perhaps no one even knew she was here.

The sky inside the quiet place was the most beautiful thing Lisavet had ever seen. Filled with swirling colors that moved and shifted like aqueous stars. For what must have been days, she lay on the floor between two bookshelves, staring up at it. She relied on it, its immensity and its mystery, to remind herself that she was alive. As she lay on the floor, she sometimes thought she saw her father's face conjured in the swirling colors overhead but as soon as she focused her eyes on it, the picture vanished.

When she wasn't hiding away among the shelves, she wandered up and down the stacks, singing in hopes that the sound might reach back through the disappearing door to her father, or that Time might finally take heed and come for her. One day she took to screaming her way up and down the shelves. Louder and louder, hoping someone would hear. Eventually, someone did. Or rather, something did.

"Why in heaven are you screaming like that?" a voice said, sharp and irritated.

Lisavet spun around to see the ill-rendered figure of a man emerging from the bookshelves. His image dragged through the air before joining with the rest of him, like ink dragging through water, distorted and semitransparent. He wore a white powdered wig, a set of purple tails, and spoke in strangely accented German.

"I-I'm looking for my father," Lisavet stuttered, too shocked by his sudden appearance to be afraid.

"Can't you see he's not here, girl? Good thing too. You should consider yourself lucky."

"Lucky?"

"Most of the people here are dead. Only the dead live in this godforsaken place."

"But I'm not dead. And I'm here."

The man looked her up and down, assessing her claims. "So you are. Are you a timekeeper?"

"A what?"

"A timekeeper," the man repeated impatiently.

"N-no," Lisavet said tentatively.

"If you aren't a timekeeper, who are you?"

"My name is Lisavet Levy," she told him.

The man didn't respond. He was listening intently to something in the distance.

"Shhh!" he pressed a finger to his lips. "Hear that?"

Lisavet listened. The soft sound of whispers met her ears. "Time!" she exclaimed. "It's back!"

"Time?" The gentleman raised an eyebrow at her foolishness. "Is that what you call that demon thing? Well, I suppose that's as good an explanation for it as any. Time is the beast that makes mortals of all one way or another. It takes everything, heedless of wealth or status." The man curled his lip bitterly as he said this, and Lisavet got the impression that he had once had both wealth and status before Time took them away. "If you're not careful, it will take you, too, before you're ready."

"Take me where?"

That was what she wanted after all. Perhaps it would take her out of this place. To America, like in the story.

But the man shook his head. "Nowhere you want to go. Believe me."

Lisavet's eyes grew wide as the gentleman's image ebbed away into nothing. The whispers became louder, calling out in formless echoes, hissing like water on hot coals. Lisavet ran from it, though she wasn't sure exactly what she was running from. She took refuge in a particularly dark corner where the books on the shelves were dustiest. No more singing. Only silence.

Soon Lisavet went off in search of the ghost again. This time, instead of screaming, she whispered, walking slowly down each row of books.

"Hello?" she said quietly, careful not to wake the sounds from before.

No answer. She remembered that the man had seemed to come from out of the books on the shelves. As her fingers brushed one of the dusty leather spines, another voice spoke.

"Be careful doing that," it said.

Lisavet drew her hand back in alarm. "Who said that?"

"This section is for medieval England," the voice said. "You're far too young for that."

On her left, a watery image shifted into focus. Fragments of light and color pulled together to take the form of a man. This one was younger than the last, wearing robes of coarse gray fabric. He had a hand pressed to his chin, contemplating.

"You'd be better off avoiding all of medieval Europe if I'm being honest. Though there are a few things that might be all right. Royals perhaps, or . . ." His eyes flicked in her direction. "Maybe you'd prefer the Romantic period instead. Do you like poetry?"

Lisavet mumbled something incoherent.

"You're a bit young for love poems, I suppose. Tell me, are you set on England or are you open to somewhere else? Italy perhaps? Oh, Italy in summer. The Renaissance period. You would love it."

"What are you talking about?"

"The memories."

"Memories?"

"Yes. Memories in the books. Normally I don't care what you time-keepers start with, but . . ." He turned to face her, his watery image shifting as he did so. "You're just so young. I would hate for you to encounter something dreadful on your first go at it."

"I'm not a timekeeper," Lisavet protested.

"You're not? Oh. How disappointing. And here I thought they were finally being progressive and appointing a girl. It really is a shame, you know . . . but I suppose it can't be helped." He seemed not to notice her growing alarm as he lamented her existence. "What are you doing here then?"

"I'm trapped. My father left me here and now I can't find my way back out."

"I see," the man said, looking concerned but offering no other help or solution.

"Well . . . is there?" Lisavet prompted.

"Is there what?"

"A way out? A door or a . . .'"

"Oh. No. 'Fraid not."

Lisavet felt her whole body deflate. "Then can you at least tell me what this place is?"

"It isn't a place. It's more . . . a concept. You are in the space between the past and present. Everywhere and nowhere at all. This is the place where Time ends. The place where consciousness drifts when bodies die. It exists in the space between the fabric of tangible things, one moment to the next. Here, all things that happened on Earth linger in the form of memories."

"So you're a memory?" Lisavet asked, frowning.

"Unfortunately yes."

"Am I . . . dead?" She didn't know if she wanted the answer.

"People are always so worried about death. As if it is the end."

Lisavet could only stare at him.

He sighed. "No, you are not dead."

"Am I dreaming?"

"Not dreaming either. I assure you this is all very real."

"But you just said that you're a memory. You can't be real."

"Why not? Memories are the realest thing any of us have, Lisavet."

Lisavet took a step back. "You know my name?"

"Yes, of course," the man said with a slight smirk. "I found it in your memories. You know. Those things you insist aren't real."

Lisavet bit her lip sheepishly. "What's your name?"

"Me? Oh, I don't have one. Well. Not anymore anyway. It's been Forgotten." He gave a small shudder at the word.

"Forgotten?" Lisavet repeated.

He flinched again. "Yes, by a timekeeper who didn't want the world to remember me."

"I don't understand," Lisavet said.

The man turned toward the books again, a wistful expression on his inky face. "These books hold the memories of every person who has ever lived or died. Before the timekeepers they used to just hang around here in the time space, unattended. Not like it is now, all neat and tidy, filed away in books."

Lisavet thought of her father. His bedtime story. Noticing her confused expression, the memory of the man offered her a blurry hand, his features fixed in a kind smile.

"If you'd like, I can show you Italy now. It's really quite lovely, and I know the perfect memory to take you to."

Sound erupted the moment they settled into the memory. It came from all over. The earth, the buildings, the streets, the very sky. After so much silence, the sudden cacophony was more than just a flood, it was a hurricane, enveloping every inch of Lisavet's body. The warm sun shone on her face, a breeze lifted her hair. Warmth! Movement! They were standing on the edge of a parapet, watching a festival down below. People laughing and singing. Lisavet almost cried at the sight of it. It felt almost real . . . almost.

"How do you know how to do this?" Lisavet asked.

Beside her, the memory of the man was smiling, watching her reaction. "I was a timekeeper," he said.

"You were?"

"The very first. Before the Romans conquered my people, I had found the time space through sundials and meditations. I am the one they stole the secrets from."

He took her down from the parapet, pointing out the young girl whose memory they were walking in. She looked to be about Lisavet's age, sitting above the crowd in a dress of fine silk.

"One of the Medici daughters," the man told her. "Very wealthy and important."

Lisavet didn't know much about the Medicis and their supposed wealth. To her, the girl just looked bored, like she wanted to join the festival but couldn't. As they walked through the crowd, Lisavet started to understand how she felt. She, too, was there, but not really there. She wanted to taste the delicacies sold from carts. Wanted to play with the other children darting through the crowd. Everything she touched passed through her hands. Eyes passed over her, seeing only blank space where she stood.

Lisavet turned her attention to the one person she could talk to. "Can I ask a question?"

"If you'd like."

"If you've been . . . Forgotten . . ." Lisavet said this as delicately as she could, but he still flinched. ". . . why can I still see you?"

"Oh, they didn't erase me completely. If they did that, they'd be erasing their own knowledge of the time space. And so what little of my memory that remains stays as it is. In the time space."

"That's confusing."

"It is, isn't it?" He frowned, looking just as puzzled as she felt. "Even so I'm glad for it. It allows me to provide assistance to other timekeepers when they need it. I show them how things work if they're struggling."

"If you don't have a name, what should I call you?"

The memory shrugged. "Whatever you like, I suppose."

Lisavet considered him. She had never named anything before. Aside from her dolls, but that was different. He was a person. Or at least he had been once. She couldn't quite tell where he was from. His skin was neither particularly pale nor particularly dark but a warm olive color. Maybe he was Italian? That would explain his love of Italy. His head was shaven. The robes he wore offered no hints, either. They were plain and old, like something worn by a monk, but having never met a monk before, she couldn't be certain.

"Azrael," she said after a moment.

The man looked amused. "Azrael? The Judeo-Christian angel of death? Bit on the nose, isn't it?"

Lisavet blushed. "Or we can pick something else."

"No, no. Azrael is fine." He said the name aloud a few times as if trying it on. "I rather think it suits me."

They stayed a little longer, listening to the music, until the edges of the world started to fade, crinkling and rippling like water. Lisavet looked up at Azrael in alarm. He shook his head.

"Worry not. The memory is ending." He pointed back up at the parapet where the girl was being led away by her nurse. "Let's return to the time space for now." He held out a hand.

"I don't want to go back there."

Azrael frowned slightly. "You don't have to stay for long. Now that you know how to time walk, you can go wherever you'd like. But . . ." He tilted his head, squinting at her. "Do be careful. There is more evil in the world than you've been yet made aware of."

Lisavet promised she would, mind racing with possibility. She thought about all the things she'd learned about history in school. Ancient Egypt. Germany before it was Germany. The Great War her father had so often talked about. All of it at her fingertips. She slipped her

hand into Azrael's, and they left the memory. Silence hit her like a wall
the moment they returned. Gone was the sun. Gone was the breeze and
the music and the smells. They had returned to the unmoving darkness.
Lisavet was surprised to feel a small sense of relief at the absence of so
much stimulus.

"Do you think you could show me your book next?" she asked, pointing up at the shelves.

Azrael winced slightly. "I would if I could; however, I don't have a
book myself. Any specter you see in the time space has not been 'collected,' so to speak, by a timekeeper. Meaning we have no book of memories to confine us."

"Oh. I didn't realize that—"

Azrael held up a hand, pressing a finger to his lips. His eyes were
fixed on something down the row of shelves. Lisavet followed his gaze
and saw the figure of a man passing between the rows. His shadow did
not drag the way Azrael's did. This was a real person, not a memory.

"A timekeeper," Azrael murmured.

Lisavet's eyes widened. A timekeeper? Perhaps he could help her
leave! But Azrael shook his head.

"I don't think this one would want to help you."

"Why not?"

Azrael shushed her again and beckoned her to follow him. They followed the timekeeper at a distance until they saw him slip between a row
of shelves up ahead.

"That section is Germany," Azrael said quietly. "Rather close to
modern day."

Lisavet sensed the change in his tone. Germany? Her Germany?
Ignoring his warning, she stole past him and ran for the row of shelves
that the man had gone down. She didn't stop until she'd reached the
edge of the shelf. Breathing hard, she peered around the side. The man
was standing in the center of the row. He had pulled one of the books

down from the shelves, hand tracing over the closed cover. His blond hair was cropped close in the military style and when he turned with the book in hand, Lisavet got a better look at his clothes. From the side, his black uniform was indistinguishable, but from the front she could clearly see the many silver pins and insignias. The bright red armband fixed around his bicep. A Nazi.

She watched in horror as the soldier opened the book and withdrew a pack of matches from his pocket. He held the flame to one of the pages until it caught fire. As the flames grew, he dropped the book to the ground, cover face up, spine bent.

"Timekeepers destroy the memories they don't want the world to remember."

Lisavet jumped. Azrael had caught up to her and was watching the scene over her shoulder, his expression grave.

"But why?" she asked.

Azrael shrugged. "To uphold their ideology. The past is a mirror of us. It tells us who we've been and what we have become. Some people don't like what they see in their reflection, so they change it by erasing memories from the face of the earth. By erasing people from existence."

"Erasing people?" Lisavet repeated, horror raising the pitch of her voice.

The soldier's head snapped up. "*Wer ist da?*" he demanded, reaching for his belt.

Lisavet ducked around the corner, heart thudding. Azrael stayed where he was. The soldier shouted a few angry words at him, cursing Azrael for startling him. The Nazi took something from his pocket and Lisavet squinted at it to get a better look. The glass crystal of a pocket watch caught the light of the flames, glinting at her with unmistakable familiarity. Its bronze case was worn with age, its patina a reflection of the many hands who held it before. From father to son, now soldier. Her whole body went cold with recognition.

The soldier fiddled with the watch until a door opened six feet away from him. He disappeared through it, casting one last glance at the burning heap of paper on the ground. The minute the door sealed behind him, Lisavet rushed forward. She collapsed onto her knees in front of the burning book and reached both hands into the flames to pull what remained of the leather-bound volume free. The cover was burnt at the edges. Most of the remaining pages were charred to ash that crumbled under her feet as she stamped the fire out. But a few of them, the ones closest to the beginning, remained intact. They whispered to her as she swept the soot from them with careful, flame-stung fingers. Telling her their story in a deep, crackling voice. Her father's story. Her father's voice.

Her breath came in ragged gasps and tears stung her eyes. She had forgotten Azrael was there until he spoke.

"The watch . . ." he said quietly.

Lisavet only cried harder. She didn't want to think about what it meant, even though she knew there was only one way her father would have given up his pocket watch to a Nazi soldier. Azrael said nothing but stayed by her side as she cradled what remained of her father's memories.

No one was coming.

2

1965, Boston, Massachusetts

THERE COULD BE NO mistaking the girl who stood at the edge of the grave. A forlorn, neglected thing in an oversize cardigan that puffed out from the sleeves of her coat. She was not yet sixteen, and her freckled face and limp red hair made her seem even younger. It was the hair, a luminous shade of copper, that gave her away, identifying her as the niece of the man in the casket.

Moira watched the girl through the haze of smoke from her cigarette. She stood under an umbrella as the casket was carried over the muddy ground. It was October, late enough in autumn that the leaves had begun to shake off their vibrancy. Moira tossed her spent cigarette onto the ground and withdrew another from her coat pocket. The silver lighter she carried gave a shuddering click as she lit it, carrying over the sound of the priest delivering his prayer for the fallen man in the casket. The girl looked up at the noise. Moira smiled at her, the kind of cold, thin smirk that came most naturally to her. The girl immediately looked away in discomfort. They didn't know each other, Moira and this girl, and it was clear that she wondered who Moira was. Why she was at her uncle's burial.

It had rained every day since Ernest Duquesne's death. The city was waterlogged, sidewalks brimming with mud. On the day of his funeral, it had rained so much that there had been talks of postponing, but in the end it was decided that they would go forward, leaving the procession to stamp through the muddy grass out to the gravesite. The service had been sparsely attended. Moira hadn't gone, but instead had watched from her car as mourners entered the chapel downtown, keeping stock of who was present. Neighbors. Old schoolmates. The occasional distant cousin. The moment the prayer was over, and the priest closed his book, they all filed out with great rapidity, not wanting to be seen lingering for reasons of self-preservation. Except for the girl.

In their absence, the girl stood alone at the edge of the grave with her eyes closed, head tipped slightly forward as rain fell on her head. Her red hair clung to her temples, making her look even more pitiful than she already did. Moira, who took great pride in her own appearance, had to remind herself that the girl was young, alone, and grieving, and therefore could not be expected to care about such things. She moved around the edge of the grave silently and stood beside her, raising the umbrella so it covered the child as well. At the sound of the rain hitting against the vinyl, the girl looked up in alarm.

"Amelia Duquesne?" Moira asked in a smooth, easy tone.

"Y-yes?" Amelia stuttered.

"My name is Moira Donnelly. I used to work with your uncle."

"You did?"

Moira watched as her gaze dropped down to assess Moira's outfit. A knee-length pencil skirt, black turtleneck, cap-toe heels, and an unbuttoned leather trench coat, none of which seemed appropriate for an employee of the State Department where Ernest Duquesne had worked. Add in the red lipstick, blunt bob cut, and side-swept bangs and Moira looked more like someone apt to be accused of being a beatnik than any sort of government employee.

"You and I met once," Moira informed her. "When you were about nine. Do you remember?"

"Not really," Amelia said, hands bunching around the sleeves of her cardigan. Wondering what someone from that part of her uncle's life was doing here at his funeral after all he had been accused of. She was easy to read, this girl. They would have to fix that.

"Hold this for me, will you?" Moira asked, putting the umbrella in the girl's hand. She took it without question. Moira turned toward the grave, reaching into her pocket for a second cigarette. "Funny how time works," she lamented. "We always feel as though we're standing at the precipice of our lives, all our years still stretched before us. Not realizing that at any moment, something could come along and push us over the edge. We are all immortal in our own time. Until we aren't."

There was a pause as she lit her cigarette with the silver lighter. The girl stared.

"Ernest used to talk about you a lot," Moira said offhandedly. "He was always telling us all how bright you were. You must be grieving for him now that he's gone."

Amelia's eyes clouded over and she shook her head at once. "They're saying he was selling secrets to the Russians," she said hastily.

Moira smiled faintly. That wasn't all they were saying. They were calling him a communist. Ernest Duquesne. Devoted civil servant. Distinguished war veteran. Communist. Traitor. Spy. That's what all the newspapers were writing alongside harrowing details about his death. *Shot through the head with state secrets still poised on his lips*, they wrote. He would have been arrested. Charged with treason and lit up like the Rosenbergs in '53. If it weren't for the fact that he was already dead.

"And? Why should that change what he meant to you?" Moira asked.

Amelia bristled suspiciously. "Were you close? Is that why you came today?"

"I came because there's something I wanted to ask you," she said, getting to the point at last. "Your uncle had something very important in his possession when he died. I was hoping you might be able to help me locate it."

"People have already been to our house. They searched his office . . . seized everything they could find that was at all tied to his work."

Moira nodded impatiently. She already knew that. "The thing is, I work for a special department that isn't affiliated with the agents who searched your house. What I'm looking for isn't something that they would have taken notice of. They wouldn't have known to look for it."

"What is it?"

There was a pause. Rain hitting the umbrella over their heads.

"A watch."

"A watch?"

"White dial with a gold bezel. By the watchmaker called Glashütte."

Amelia's eyes slid to the coffin. "That was the one he always wore."

Moira glanced at the puffed sleeves of the girl's sweater, noting the way she'd started tugging at the left one anxiously. "I was hoping you would know of another place where he might keep it. A relative's house, perhaps. Or a lover's?"

Amelia gestured to the empty graveyard. "Clearly not," she said, with more snark than Moira had assumed her capable of. "Maybe he was wearing it when he died."

Moira eyed Amelia for a moment, wondering how much to disclose but also wondering how much she might already know. "As you might have surmised, it's not just a normal timepiece. It has special functions that most manual watches don't, making it a very expensive asset. One we would like to recover now that he's gone."

"We?" Amelia asked.

"The department." Moira withdrew a card from a different coat pocket. It had her name embossed in red ink the same color as her lipstick, accompanied by a phone number. "If you happen to come across it, give this number a call."

Amelia pinched the card between two fingers. "Does this watch have something to do with the secrets my uncle was accused of selling to the Russians?"

Moira smiled at her grimly. "Let's just say that if it were to fall into Russian hands, we might all find ourselves living in a very different world."

"Does it have the secrets of the atom bomb engraved on the back or something?"

Moira pursed her lips. She knew there was a reason she usually steered clear of teenagers. "There is more than one way to end a war, Amelia. And there are secrets far more dangerous than weapons of mass destruction." She took a long drag on the cigarette, shielding it from the falling rain. "This is the way the world ends. Not with a bang but a whimper."

To her surprise, Amelia perked up. "T.S. Eliot," she said.

"You've read it?" Moira asked skeptically.

"My uncle gave me a book of his poems last Christmas."

Moira wasn't surprised. Ernest had always been a fanatic about poetry, able to quote the most obscure lines from memory. It stood to reason his niece would be the same.

"Then you'll recognize this line. 'Between the idea and the reality. Between the motion and the act' . . ."

"Falls the shadow," Amelia finished.

Moira studied Amelia for a long moment, cigarette dangling between two fingers. "Don't give the watch to any of the other agents. They won't know what it means. When you find it, make sure you bring it to me. And only to me. Understand?"

"If I find it, you mean," Amelia said.

"Oh, I'm sure it will turn up."

She dropped the spent cigarette into the wet grass. It fizzled out immediately, the glowing red extinguished in the muck. She pulled back the sleeve of her coat to reveal a watch of her own, a smaller model on a white gold bracelet.

"You're going to be late for school, Miss Duquesne," she warned.

At the mention of school, a look of dread swept across Amelia's face. And for good reason. Moira had been watching the girl for over a week, had dug into her records, and therefore knew all about her current situation at Pembroke Academy. Though bright, her record came with a rather long list of demerits and absent notices. As it turned out, Amelia Duquesne was quite the rebel beneath that mousy exterior. Amelia handed back the umbrella and turned to go, casting one last glance at her uncle's grave.

"Oh, and Amelia," Moira said, waiting until the girl turned to look at her. "Whatever you do, when you find the watch . . ." She paused and looked pointedly at Amelia's sleeve. ". . . don't wind it."

Amelia drew her wrist ever so slightly toward her chest, catching herself in time to pass it off by folding her arms. She turned and walked away, hurrying through the rain. Moira watched her disappear through the gates and down the street.

AMELIA WAS late to her first class of the morning, but for once, her teacher didn't seem to mind. Normally Mr. Markham was very strict about such things. Most of her many demerits for tardiness came from him. His class took place promptly at eight in the morning and Amelia found it difficult to wake any time before nine. This morning he simply waved her into the room when she opened the door. She thought perhaps he was sparing her the lecture because of the burial that morning, but then he called out as she made her way over to her desk.

"By the way, Miss Duquesne. This is your third tardy this month. Please see me after class."

Amelia's heart sank. She took her seat miserably amid the sound of snickering. Mr. Markham continued, picking up his lecture on the Civil War where he'd left off. Amelia flipped through her textbook, conscious of the many eyes on her. Her uncle's death had been the gossip of the school this past week. Rumors of his treason had followed Amelia around campus like a storm cloud.

"I heard they buried him this morning," said the girl seated in front of her, turning around to taunt her in a low whisper as Mr. Markham wrote on the chalkboard.

The girl, Rebecca, was the daughter of a congressman. One of many who attended Pembroke. The school was a popular choice for politicians to send their daughters, given its proximity to most major cities on the East Coast, as well as its track record for churning out both university candidates and well-mannered debutantes. Amelia, for whom neither path held much appeal, had always been an outsider despite her uncle's position working for the State Department. His fall from grace only served to push her further from the center of Pembroke's social circle.

"So does this mean you'll be defecting back to the motherland now that your uncle is dead?" Rebecca asked a few minutes later.

"Yup," Amelia responded dryly, head bent over her textbook. "Just waiting for Stalin to send a plane." Another student to her left let out a gasp.

"You should be careful making jokes like that," Rebecca said threateningly. "My father said that if your uncle was still alive, he would have been given the chair. He says he would have deserved it for betraying his country like that."

"That's an awful lot of gumption coming from a man who forged results of a hearing test to avoid the draft," Amelia bit back.

Mr. Markham shushed them from the front of the room, calling out Amelia's name in warning. Rebecca waited until he turned back around before striking again.

"I heard he was killed right in the act of selling secrets to the Russians. Shot in the head, wasn't he?"

Amelia tilted her book up to create a blockade, refusing to look up.

"Didn't your mother get shot in the head too? I seem to recall that's how she died. Only I suppose with her it was different. She did it to herself."

Amelia's grip on the book tightened. Her eyes slid to Mr. Markham, weighing the consequences of a demerit against the possible satisfaction of firing off a few choice curse words.

Rebecca leaned closer, putting an intrusive hand over the passage Amelia was reading. "I get it, though. I'd want to die, too, if I had a baby with a married man. Can you imagine? What would it be like to be so unwanted? Only . . . I guess you don't have to imagine, do you?"

Amelia slammed the textbook closed on Rebecca's fingers. Rebecca let out a yelp, far louder than was warranted.

"Miss Duquesne!" Mr. Markham snapped. He pointed to the door. "Out."

Amelia collected her things amid the sound of snickering. In the hall she took her seat on the bench that seemed to have been placed there exclusively for her. She glanced at the clock on the wall. Five minutes was a new record for her.

Pembroke Academy was a private, all girls' boarding school of great prestige. They had no tolerance for rule bending and little patience for snark; two things that Amelia had always had an overabundance of. Showing up late, sneaking into dining halls after curfew, and talking back to her teachers with frequency were par for the course for her. It was a defense mechanism. She'd learned early in life to recognize the look of pity in someone's eyes and hated it.

Amelia tried to swallow down the tears welling in her eyes in case anyone walked by. She wasn't sure if she was even allowed to grieve. The burial was one thing, hardly anyone had been there. But was it okay to continue crying like this after what he had done? Was it acceptable to mourn a traitor, or would people start to assume she was one too? She couldn't get the image of his coffin out of her head. The casket had been closed for the ceremony, and Amelia was glad for that at least. That she didn't have to see him that way. The uncle who had raised her when her mother had died, drained of color and life.

Amelia had been seven years old when her mother died, and Uncle Ernest, the bachelor with a busy schedule and absolutely no experience with children, had been the least likely candidate to take her in. He was, however, the only one who volunteered. For the first several months of living with him, Amelia had been so shy that she'd barely spoken, delivering head motions instead of words. He had given her a room on the second floor that had once been a small library of sorts, filled with bookshelves that reached from floor to ceiling, and a big window overlooking the oak tree in the backyard. Thick, leather-bound volumes packed to the brim with names and dates and stories of faraway countries.

"This was the European history section," he had said sheepishly as they stood in the doorway for the first time, her tiny suitcase in his hand. "I promise I'll move them out once I can find another place to put them."

Where? Amelia had thought to herself, looking around.

Uncle Ernest's house seemed at times more like a library than an actual home, with shelves lining each wall and books stacked on every space that wasn't for either eating or sleeping. In an effort to clear her room, he had another set of shelves installed in the dining room. But then Amelia had begun asking him questions about Joan of Arc and Maximilien Robespierre and King Henry VIII over breakfast and he realized that she'd been reading them on nights when dreams of her mother jerked her from sleep. The first full conversation she ever had with him was to ask him the meaning of the word *guillotine*, breaking her self-enforced fast of words after two months of saying nothing at all. So the books stayed, though he did remove a few of the more gruesome ones, replacing them with books of poetry, which she loved almost as much as the history. So much that she had memorized them so she could quote them the way he did.

As Amelia had settled in, her dreams of her mother were replaced with nightmares of waking up in this house alone, abandoned, Uncle Ernest having fled in the night and leaving her by herself.

"You're stuck with me, kiddo," he said to her on those nights, stroking her hair and holding her close. "I'm never going to abandon you."

But now here she was. Alone. He had abandoned her anyway.

As thoughts and memories tangled themselves in Amelia's head, her hand closed around the watch on her wrist. She had been lying to Moira Donnelly when she told her she didn't know where it was. It had shown up in her school mailbox three days ago, wrapped carefully in brown paper. No note. No return address. Nothing to indicate how it had come to be there, which should have alarmed her. She was far too relieved to see it to be concerned. The watch was the thing that most reminded her of Uncle Ernest. He had worn it every day for as long as she could remember. The idea of parting with it, of giving it to that woman, was unbearable.

Don't wind it, she'd said.

But why not? It was a watch. Watches were meant to be wound. Her uncle had several others he kept in a box in his bedroom, and though this one was the only one he ever wore, he still wound them daily to keep the gears from rusting. As a girl, Amelia had watched him while he did so, studying the way his hands worked to keep them moving forward. A stopped watch was a dreaded outcome. Time neglected.

"Time is an intentional thing," he told her as he worked. "You have to look after it and it will look after you."

Amelia pulled back her sleeve. Her fingers hovered over the watch's crown, wondering. Maybe Moira assumed she didn't know how to properly wind a watch. They could break if wound incorrectly. But Amelia knew how to do it right. Curiosity won out. She raised the crown of the watch with careful fingers. She spun it around a few times, first forward, then backward, but nothing happened. Amelia frowned, feeling vaguely disappointed. She pushed the crown back in. The entire watch seemed to shudder as she did so and all of a sudden, the hands on the dial stopped moving. There was a pause, barely even a second, and then it began to move again. Only this time, it was moving backward.

She sat up a little straighter.

"Amelia?" Mr. Markham had opened the door to the classroom.

She looked up, annoyed at him for interrupting. "What?"

He knitted his eyebrows in equal annoyance. "Watch your tone, Miss Duquesne. You may come back inside. I'm about to assign tonight's homework."

Amelia tucked the sleeve of her cardigan back over the watch and stood up. The words to the poem that Moira had quoted at her were suddenly in her head, as clearly as if the woman were standing beside her.

Between the idea and the reality . . .

A strange, prickling sensation traveled from the top of Amelia's head clear down her spine.

. . . falls the shadow.

She passed through the door to reenter the classroom, and then the world upended itself. At first, she heard someone shouting. Then a thousand someones, all calling out at once. Voices echoing into an abyss that she couldn't see, yet she could feel it, her whole body teetering on the edge of an invisible precipice. And then she was falling, crashing down through darkness and shadows. There was a rush of hot air and suddenly she was no longer falling. There was no impact, no abrupt stop. Her feet were back on solid ground as though they had always been.

She opened her eyes, hearing the stretch of her own breath. In front of her was a silent cavern. Two walls on either side of her, stretching up. A murky pool of shadows danced in her periphery. As her eyes adjusted, she saw that the walls were actually shelves, extending forward in a maze. She grasped desperately for the watch, spinning the crown again, palms sweating. She stepped backward and felt her foot catch on the edge of the doorframe. There was a jerking sensation along her spine, as though someone had attached a string to her waist, and then a lift until her feet hit the ground a second time.

She kept her eyes closed, afraid to open them and face whatever might be in front of her. The silence was gone, swept away as quickly as it came, and instead she heard wind brushing against fallen leaves like a whisper, a metallic click . . .

"Not so good at following instructions, I see."

Amelia's eyes flew open.

She was standing in the cemetery. The sky was overcast but bright with morning. Her uncle's grave was before her. To her left, Moira Donnelly blew a long column of smoke up into the air, eyes on her own watch.

"We'll have to work on that," she said, lowering her wrist and fixing her dark eyes on Amelia.

Amelia let out a loud, desperate breath she'd been holding since the instant she'd tipped over the edge. How long ago was that? Hours? Seconds? She wasn't sure. Everything was the same as it had been that morning. Her shoes soaked from the damp grass, the raindrops hitting her face, the open grave with the casket still visible.

"W-what's happening?" she asked, looking desperately at Moira.

A smile twinged the edges of Moira's red lips. "You tell me."

Amelia tried to breathe but every time she tried to draw a breath it stuck in her throat.

"I don't understand. Is this . . . are you . . . what *time* is it?"

Moira took a drag on her cigarette before answering. "About thirty seconds past eight in the morning."

Amelia's eyes nearly bugged out of her head. "But I . . . it was just . . ."

"I did warn you not to wind it."

"I know. But I was in the hallway, and then I went through the door and . . ." Amelia paused to draw breath. "And then . . ." She trailed off.

Moira raised her eyebrows. "And then?"

Amelia shook her head, lost for words. "I don't know."

It was a blur. The falling, the shouts, the abyss.

Moira tossed the cigarette to the ground and reached for Amelia's wrist. "Well, I suppose we'd better get you back."

"What are you talking about?"

"Back to the right time." She had begun fiddling with the crown of the watch. "When you leave here, wind the watch again and a door will appear for you that will take you back to your classroom. That should do the trick."

Amelia tried to pull away and Moira slapped her wrist sharply. "But I thought . . . Aren't you going to take it?"

"I'm afraid it's a bit late for that. We'll talk again later." There was a small snap as Moira pressed the crown into place. "Off you go then," she prompted.

"But I . . . how?"

"Any passageway will do. A door, or a gate, or—" Moira broke off, glancing around at the deserted cemetery. "Here's another poem for you, if you can guess it. Walt Whitman. 'Entering thy sovereign, dim, illimitable grounds . . . As at thy portals . . .'"

In her upturned state, it took some time for the poem to gather itself in Amelia's head. Moira had placed the lines out of order. But Walt Whitman was one of her favorites.

". . . also death," she finished.

Moria gave her a broad, catlike smile. "In many religions, graves are portals, too, my dear. Doors to a world that lies within our own, but beyond it."

Amelia made a small squeaking noise. "I don't understand."

"Watch your head," Moira said.

With one hand, she shoved Amelia backward into the open grave.

WHEN AMELIA had vanished from sight, Moira let out a sigh. This might be more complicated than she'd thought. She took her time getting to her next destination. In the parking lot, she shook out her umbrella and dusted the rain from her coat. Her car, a bright red Cadillac with a black top, was one of the many things about which she was particular, and she didn't want to track water into it. Having a car at all was a status symbol in a city like Boston. Having one so clean and cared for was another.

Above all, Moira wanted to be someone whose competence people didn't question. She was entirely self-sufficient. Her own money, her own apartment. A career with the State Department rivaling that of many men. She had earned her place, but she knew many of her colleagues still viewed her as the smiling, demure, compliant secretary to Jack Dillinger that she'd been when she'd first started ten years ago. Now she had Jack's old job and some of those same men were her subordinates. They respected her as their boss but that didn't mean they weren't still keeping an eye out. Waiting for her to slip up.

So Moira made sure never to falter. They wanted compliant so she gave them stubborn. They wanted demure so she gave them cunning. They expected smiling, so she gave them cold, impassive, blunt. Someone who did not need assistance opening her car door and who might sooner bite your hand off for getting fingerprints on the finish. Each day, she made sure her appearance was immaculate. She kept her dark hair trimmed just beneath her chin and avoided the bright dresses worn by the wives of the men she worked with. Instead, she wore trousers or pencil skirts cinched in at the waist, heels with pointed toes, and turtleneck sweaters in dark colors. And never, under any circumstances, did she go to work without applying charcoal eyeliner and curling her lashes with careful precision.

That morning, she wouldn't be seeing any of her colleagues, but still looked the part as she sat outside Pembroke Academy's main administrative building. She smoked yet another cigarette while she waited, keeping one arm propped against the open window. It was still early. From her seat, she could just make out the office where Amelia Duquesne would be meeting with the dean in a few hours. As it turned out, the only person of any real importance in Amelia's life now that Ernest was gone was the dean himself. He would decide what to do with the sad little orphan.

Moira watched him pull into the parking spot a few rows down. He was a stodgy, balding man in his late fifties, clad in tweed and elbow patches. He got out of the car, holding a stack of portfolio folders, a leather bag slung over one arm. As he shut the door, the strap of his bag slipped down to the crook of his elbow and in his effort to fix it, he lost his grip on the files. They flew out in all directions, catching in the wind and tumbling across the parking lot. He cursed loudly, dropping his bag on the ground to chase after them.

This was her opening. Taking one last drag, Moira flicked her cigarette away and began fidgeting with the crown of her watch. Just a half-quarter turn and time shuddered back. The papers sprang up from the ground back into the dean's arms. His bag affixed itself properly on his shoulder. Moira clicked the crown into place and got out of the car just as he was doing the same.

"Dean Hodgkins?" she asked, heels striking pavement as she made her way over to him.

He looked up. The bag slipped. He reached for it. But this time, Moira took the folders from his hands before they could fall.

"Let me help you with that," she said.

Moira maintained eye contact, allowing a brief pause for him to assess her, watching his expression. It was strategic as much as it was amusing for her. How he reacted now would tell her all she needed to know about how this conversation would go. After a beat she held out a hand, shifting the papers into one arm.

"So sorry to catch you like this. My name is Moira Donnelly."

Dean Hodgkins startled like a frightened bird, scrambling so he could shake her hand properly. "How do you do? I'd introduce myself but . . . well, it seems you've got the upper hand here."

Moira smiled to herself. The scene played out smoothly. Two characters in a movie meeting for the first time. She lied and said she'd tried to call his office, but no one had answered. He made a joke about his secretary's incompetence, which Moira pretended was funny. She beat around the bush as long as possible, complimenting the school, praising its reputation. All the while she maintained perfect eye contact. By the time she got to the point, she'd gathered everything she needed to know about him. He liked her. He was fooled by her false amiability. And most importantly, he was attracted to her. She could tell by the way he tucked his left hand out of sight to conceal his wedding ring, and the way he leaned forward slightly as she spoke, hinging on every word that fell from her carefully painted mouth.

This conversation was going to go just fine.

AMELIA LANDED on her back, eyes shut, in the middle of the dark, silent place. She scrambled to her feet, gasping for air, and searched wildly for this alleged door Moira had talked about. The narrow passage was before her, the walls on either side reaching up high over her head. In her panicked state, she realized the walls were actually shelves laden with old leather books. She almost stopped to investigate until she heard the sound of footsteps somewhere beyond her line of sight. She frantically spun the crown of the watch and ran for the door that appeared before her, twisting the knob without a second thought.

She fell through to the other side with a shout, gripping the sides of the frame tightly in both hands. Her body trembled and she refused to open her eyes, fearful that she might have ended up somewhere else again. Her ears barely registered the sound of snickers coming from the room until Mr. Markham said her name.

"Miss Duquesne?" he asked. Not stern but worried. "Are you all right?"

Amelia looked up at him, struggling to place herself. She scanned the classroom. The mocking faces of her classmates. She glanced at her feet to find them standing on familiar tile. Then, hesitantly, she glanced back over her shoulder, expecting to see the dark place full of bookshelves, but instead finding the hallway with its single desk. She let out a sigh of relief.

"Miss Duquesne?" her teacher asked again. "Should I call the nurse?"

"No," Amelia said breathlessly. "No, I'm fine."

She scurried to her seat and collapsed into her chair as Mr. Markham moved to the front of the room to announce the night's assignment. She looked down at the watch still bound to her wrist. It was no longer ticking backward. It must have been a dream, she told herself. She'd fallen asleep waiting out in the hallway. Maybe she had sleepwalked her way to the door, her body reacting while her mind fled reality. It had happened before. When her mother had died, she had gone through a bout of sleepwalking that lasted months. A number of times Uncle Ernest had found her, standing by the front door, eyes half closed and flickering behind her lids. Whenever he woke her, she spoke in rapid, hushed tones about walking through a narrow, shadowy hallway not unlike the one she'd seen, pursuing the faded image of her mother.

She might have convinced herself that it was all a dream. Until Moira Donnelly showed up again, standing outside the cafeteria at lunch. At first Amelia tried to ignore her.

"Amelia," Moira said loudly, drawing the attention of several others around them. "Come here, please."

Amelia stood rigid, arms braced tightly over her books, trying to decide whether or not to listen.

"If you don't come now, I'll just find you later," Moira said bluntly.
"Difficult to hide with hair like that."

Amelia let out an indignant huff and stomped her way over spite-
fully. "What do you want?"

"I told you we would talk later."

"So talk."

Moira frowned at her. "Are you always this rude or am I just getting
special treatment?" She took her car keys from her purse and held them
up. "How about lunch?"

"What?"

"So we can talk. There's a place not far from here that serves excellent
pastrami sandwiches."

"I'm not going anywhere with you. Besides, I have class after this."

"No, you don't. You have a free period after lunch."

"Why do you know that?" Amelia asked in annoyance.

"I asked the dean for your schedule."

"And he gave it to you?"

"Not at first. But then I told him that I was your distant cousin,
flown in from London to come look after you now that your uncle is
gone, and he handed it over."

"You are *not* my cousin."

"No, of course not. I am, however, your only option. Before I showed
up, that dean of yours was ready to call child services to come pick you
up and take you to a group home. So really you should be thanking me.
Now come on. If you don't want lunch, then I'm taking you home. I'll
make us some coffee and we can chat."

"Home?" Amelia repeated, exasperated.

"To your uncle's house. It's only an hour from here, right?"

Amelia started to protest again, and Moira cut her off with a wave of her hand. "Don't worry about school tomorrow. I talked to the dean, and we agreed it was best if you take some time off. To give you time to grieve. Now come on."

Amelia folded her arms stubbornly. "You pushed me into a grave."

"*You* didn't listen. I wouldn't have needed to if you hadn't wound the watch."

"So . . . that was real?" Amelia asked, curiosity getting the better of her.

"Quite."

Amelia stared at her.

"There's a lot to explain," Moira said, turning to face her on the sidewalk. "But the first thing you should know is that your uncle was not a communist."

Through all the confusion still rattling around in Amelia's head, relief came like a beam of sunlight through the clouds.

"He wasn't?"

"No. But he was murdered by one."

BY THE time they reached the house, it had started raining again. Moira pulled the car up to the curb and leaned down so she could get a better look out the passenger side, eyes scanning each gable and window. Beside her, Amelia was still sulking. Her state of shock had lasted long enough for Moira to shuffle her over to her dorm, but the attitude had resurfaced the moment Moira had begun trying to help pack her things. Amelia had declared that she needed no help, haphazardly shoving cardigans and wrinkled shirts into a bag. The only thing Amelia took any semblance of care with was the stack of poetry books she took from the shelf above the desk. Old, worn copies of Whitman, Yeats, and Byron. Those she carried tightly in both arms.

On the drive to the house, Amelia had taken up a militant silence in spite of the many questions Moira was sure she had. Amelia was proving more stubborn than Moira had anticipated. She wanted answers, but she didn't want them from *her*.

"Shall we go in?" Moira asked.

Without a word, Amelia got out of the car, slamming the door behind her. Moira rolled her eyes and followed, stopping to retrieve the bag of clothes from the back seat. By the time she reached the porch, Amelia was staring at the door.

"What's the matter?" Moira asked.

"I don't have a key," Amelia mumbled.

Moira pulled a set of keys from her pocket. She smirked triumphantly at the incredulous look Amelia gave her. Inside, all the curtains were drawn, the house shrouded in a dark cloak of mourning. Moira flipped on the hall lights, eyes sweeping the entryway. The house was as she expected. Old, but well-kept. Tidy, but overcrowded by shelf after shelf of books.

"How very . . . stuffy. Don't you ever open the windows?"

"Moisture is bad for the books," Amelia recited, sounding more like Ernest than she ever had. "Creates mold."

Moira started walking toward the kitchen. "At least open the curtains, won't you? No wonder you're so pale." In the kitchen, she made herself right at home, pouring water in the kettle on the stove. "Coffee?" she asked.

"What? No. Aren't you going to tell me what's going on?"

"Oh, are you talking to me again?"

"You said we would talk."

"And we will. Over coffee," Moira promised, holding the kettle up to show her.

"I'm not supposed to drink coffee," Amelia said defiantly. "Uncle Ernest doesn't let me."

"He's not the one offering, I am," Moira pointed out. There was a pause. "I can make you tea instead if you'd prefer, though I'd rather not. I hate tea."

Amelia exhaled in annoyance. "Coffee is fine."

Moira smiled at her. "Have a seat."

Amelia slid into the chair at the table. Moira busied herself with the kettle. As it boiled, she investigated the cupboards, which were almost completely barren. The milk in the refrigerator was spoiled. She would need to go shopping. And soon. This realization brought about her first real hesitation about the situation she had orchestrated. What did teenage girls even eat? Moira herself subsisted on a steady diet of coffee, cigarettes, and cold sandwiches. Adolescent girls needed real food. Three square meals a day. Fresh milk. Vegetables. She could feel Amelia watching her from the table as she measured out instant coffee into two mugs. Were fifteen-year-olds even supposed to drink coffee?

Moira poured equal measures of coffee into two mugs and set one down on the table. "We'll have to drink it black. Seems the milk's gone bad."

Amelia only nodded.

Moira did not sit down at the table. Instead, she leaned back against the countertop, clutching her cup of coffee. Now was the time for explaining. Sensing that Amelia was waiting for her to start things off, Moira took an extra moment to compose her thoughts before she did so.

"First things first," she began steadily. "This wasn't my idea. I'm not here to make your life miserable, so let's drop the attitude, shall we?"

"So then what are you doing here?"

"Well, first, I'm here to look after you. To protect you from things we'll discuss in a moment. And second, I was sent by my department to look into Ernest's murder."

As the mention of murder resurfaced, Amelia's careful defenses slipped again. Moira watched them crumble with a kind of perverse satisfaction.

"So he was killed by the Russians?" Amelia said in a small voice.

"That's what we believe, yes."

"How? When? I thought he was in DC."

"When you wound the watch and stepped through the doorway, you found yourself somewhere you'd never been before. Someplace dark, filled with shelves and shelves of books. Yes?"

Amelia nodded, knuckles white where she gripped the mug.

"That's called the time space. Less than one hundred people over the course of history have ever seen it. And now you're one of them."

"What is it?"

"It's the place where conscious thought becomes a memory. Where the memories of the dead, and the thoughts of those still living, become something else."

"Something else?"

Moira pursed her lips, thinking. "You've taken science classes, yes? Do you know the law of conservation of energy?"

Amelia nodded. "Energy cannot be created or destroyed. Only transferred. But thoughts aren't a form of energy."

"Aren't they? You get tired if you think too hard for too long, don't you? It costs energy to create conscious thought. So once you've done that, where does that energy go? Where do those thoughts go? If they can't be destroyed, they must go somewhere, right?"

"I suppose." A bit hesitantly.

"So if consciousness is a form of energy, and energy transfers, then where do you think it goes?"

"The time space?"

"Exactly." Moira moved over to the table and sat down.

"But what does this have to do with my uncle?"

"Ahh. First thing to know about your uncle is that he didn't work for the State Department. He worked for the CIA."

Amelia's face somehow became even paler than it already was. "So he was a spy?"

"Not exactly. Ernest was what's known as a timekeeper." Moira gestured to the watch on Amelia's wrist. "He collected memories. Uncovered the truth about things that others might have wanted to keep buried. We refer to it as temporal reconnaissance."

"And . . . the books on the shelves . . ."

"Are memories. The timekeepers of Ancient Rome began storing them that way and over time it evolved into what it is now. A library of mankind's collective memory."

Amelia rubbed at her temples, frowning. "But if that's where I went . . . how did I end up back at the cemetery with you?"

Moira frowned as well, considering how best to answer this. She wasn't sure she understood it herself. "Time works in mysterious ways. I believe what you experienced is something called temporal displacement."

"Like time travel?"

"No, you simply shifted along your own temporal plane. Your own memories. Not the same thing as time travel."

Amelia was quiet. She was still processing, caught somewhere between denial and belief. Moira knew this process well. All timekeepers went through it. But Amelia had the benefit of youth to help suspend her doubt. Her mind was more malleable, more inclined to believe seemingly impossible things. She would settle more quickly, accept this more quickly, learn more quickly.

Amelia took a deep breath. "And the Russians killed my uncle in there? In the time space?"

"Yes. It's not unusual for timekeepers of opposing ideologies to come into conflict. We've been at odds with the Russians for decades now. Ernest was head of the department that was working to improve our relationship."

"Then how did I get the watch?"

"They sent it back to us. They wanted us to know it was them who killed him. Most of the watches belong to the State Department, but your uncle's watch was a family heirloom. He left it to you in his will, so I sent it in the mail."

"So . . . you knew I had it already? Even before you asked?"

"I was trying to be polite. I didn't imagine you would lie to me."

Amelia had begun shaking her head angrily. "So all these lies about him being a communist . . . all the rumors about how he was selling secrets . . . why are you letting people believe that?"

"Because a murdered government agent would raise questions. It would draw too much attention to secrets we're trying to keep hidden. People cannot know about the time space and all the implications that it brings."

There was a pause. Moira watched Amelia closely, urging her along toward the question she knew was coming sooner or later.

"Then why are you telling *me*?"

Moira pursed her lips slightly. "That's where this gets complicated. You see, the department has been dealing with a rebellion of sorts."

"A rebellion?"

"A movement. There is a group of timekeepers, not just Americans but those of other nationalities as well, who have been interfering with our work. They are of the belief that history shouldn't be regulated by government entities and have been attempting to disrupt our efforts. Their tactics are usually subtle but lately they've gotten a bit . . . bolder. Our concern is that these rebels have formed an alliance with the Russians."

"Why would they do that?" Amelia asked with a frown.

"Because the United States timekeeper program is currently the largest, most influential government body regulating the time space. Getting rid of us stands to benefit both the rebels and the Russians in equal measure."

"I still don't see what this has to do with me."

Moira leaned forward in her chair and took hold of Amelia's wrist, gently pulling it forward so the watch was equidistant between the two of them. The girl's skin was cold and clammy to the touch.

"Because Ernest was looking for something when he was killed. Something important. A book of memories, stolen by the rebels and hidden somewhere within the time space."

"What kind of memories?"

"Dangerous ones. Memories that the rebels have taken from us over the years. Including the memory of how we make a watch like this." She tapped Amelia's wrist two times. "Before the war, there were only a few people who knew how these watches were made. Most of them German. Most of them Jewish. And most of them killed by the Nazis. When the Nazis began entering the time space, they were unfamiliar with the way things work and eradicated most of the watchmakers' memories from the time space before realizing that they needed them. The only remaining set of those memories was stolen by the rebels over a decade ago and hidden in a book of lost memories. We believe your uncle might have found this book before he died, making him a target. And now you have his watch. You've seen the time space, and you know the truth." Moira paused to draw a breath, looking Amelia squarely in the eye. "The department has asked me to garner your assistance in recovering the book."

Amelia jerked her arm back, eyes wide. "Me? Why me? Why can't you do it? Don't you have other watches?"

"We did."

"Did?"

"They were stolen. Presumably by the rebels. Which is why we need the book to create more."

Amelia scowled at her, pointing to her wrist. "What about your watch? The rebels didn't steal that one. Why can't you go instead?"

Moira made a face. "That was the plan initially. But my boss said no."

"Why?"

"The Russians already know who I am. They have profiles of every

American timekeeper and every person in the department who might come after them. But they don't know you. My superiors seem to think you would have more success."

Amelia's eyes narrowed. "I can't. I won't. If all you need is an anonymous face, then why can't you get someone else?"

Moira let out a disappointed sigh. She had expected resistance. Of course she had. But Jack had been clear in his orders. If Amelia wouldn't cooperate on her own, they had ways of forcing the matter. Moira had hoped it wouldn't come to that. People were always easier to manage when they were willing. She stood up and moved over to the sink, taking both half-empty mugs of coffee with her.

"Very well. We'll find someone else."

Amelia exhaled loudly. "Really?"

"Yes. However, if you won't help, then we will need to discuss what happens to you now." Moira dumped the contents of the mugs into the sink, idling for a moment before continuing. "It's not as simple as saying no, I'm afraid. You now know too much. Invaluable state secrets. The department won't just overlook that. And unfortunately for you, explaining away your disappearance is entirely too easy. Your uncle has been branded a communist. A traitor. How easy would it be for people to believe you're one too? The Russians are known for recruiting them young."

Amelia made a choking noise behind her. Moira didn't turn around, focusing on washing the dregs of coffee from the bottom of each mug until they sparkled.

"You'll be relocated somewhere we can keep an eye on you," she continued in a mechanical voice as she turned to look at Amelia. "Placed in an institution where anything you might let slip will be dismissed as the inane musings of an inmate."

Amelia looked as though she might liquefy. Turn to water and slip through the floorboards. They stared each other down in the silence that followed. To Moira's surprise, Amelia's expression suddenly hardened,

the fear replaced with fortitude. She saw that Moira was trying to ma-
nipulate her, that she was backing her into a corner. Moira hadn't exactly
been subtle. What kept the remnants of fear alight in Amelia's eyes, however, was not knowing how real the threat was and how much was a bluff.
For once, Moira let some of her own emotion slip through. She knew the
truth. She knew how little of what she had said was a bluff. Dragging a
child into a proxy war had not been her idea. But Jack had insisted. He
was set on it from the beginning and had sent her in, the director of the
timekeeper program, to make it happen one way or another.

"And if I agree to help?" Amelia asked in a tentative voice.

Moira recognized the look in her eyes, had seen it in the mirror more
times than she could count. A spark, a refusal to be belittled, bullied, or
coerced. A desire to be in control of her own fate as much as anyone ever
could. Suddenly all those demerits made more sense. Moira offered her
a genuine smile.

"Then you become a timekeeper."

3

1944, Somewhere in the Time Space

LISAVET LEVY MASTERED THE art of walking through time as swiftly as a child learns to crawl. Almost six years had passed since she arrived in the time space, and she spent them in Paris in the 1920s, in Morocco at the height of the Ottoman Empire, on the streets of Rome during the reign of Julius Caesar. She breathed in the scents of other times and places, letting them fill her with their splendor and their horror in equal measure. She grew up in the throes of abandoned empires and came of age in the midst of kings and queens and wars in every hemisphere. The past pulsed within her like a second heartbeat.

Azrael had become the closest thing she had to a friend. He took care of her in lieu of a parent, watching out for Nazi timekeepers heading her way, teaching her to hide in the pages of memories. He taught her how to time walk, steering her away from the uglier parts of history. It was through him that she learned the languages of other countries—Russian, English, French, and Arabic—practicing the conversations she heard in memories with him until she'd mastered their meaning. Her hours were divided into days and nights of her own making. Daytime became the time she spent reliving time passed. At night she lay on the floor between the shelves, staring up at the swirling stars. She had stopped sleeping long ago, no longer a necessity.

"What are those up there?" she asked Azrael one night.

"Those?" Azrael directed his gaze upward. He seldom looked at the strange lights floating above them. None of the dead ever did. "Those are living thoughts. Memories that are happening now at this very moment."

Lisavet was fascinated by this. The idea of things really happening. Happening now, and not in the past. She wondered what it must be like to see things as they really were, and not reflected in the memory of someone else. When they went time walking, Azrael steered her away from anything too close to the modern day.

"Best to let that lie," he told her when she asked him about the 1940s, a decade half gone before she'd known it had begun. "To know too much about the course Time is taking before it happens is to fill oneself with torment. Living is the most dangerous thing, after all. More than death. More than memories."

Azrael's words held more weight for her than any others, living or dead. So Lisavet did as he suggested and avoided the recent years, despite the pull to know what was happening.

She didn't always listen to him, though. There were certain edicts she would not obey, no matter how many times he warned her. He often hovered by her side as she stepped in to salvage the memories that timekeepers attempted to burn. After witnessing the erasure of her father's memories, she took to following timekeepers from a distance, ducking around corners and mimicking the slow movements of the dead should she ever be caught. She watched them select books from the shelves and light them on fire, the smoke blurry against the starlit ceiling. Timekeepers never stayed until the books had burned completely, and the moment they left, Lisavet would strike. She took the remnants of scorched pages and hid them away between the covers of what had once been her father's book.

"What if they find out what you're doing?" Azrael asked as she brushed away soot and ash from the remaining pages. "You'll put a target on your back." He was wearing the anxious look that Lisavet had come to recognize, his dark forehead wrinkled, his pupils large and opaque in spite of how transparent the rest of him usually was.

"There's always been a target on my back," Lisavet told him. "I'm Jewish."

He started to say something else, and she shushed him, pressing her ear close to the smoldering pages to catch whispers of the memories they contained. These memories, the ones she carried around in her book, were the most precious to her. Many of the people who owned them were Jewish, like her. Everyday memories of quiet moments that composed a life. A child's laughter. A morning walk with a loved one at dawn, cold hands entwined. A dinner shared among friends. All seemingly innocuous things that some outside force had deemed a threat. What could be so dangerous about a life that made somebody want to erase it?

At first Lisavet had merely wanted to save the memories out of principle. But over time, she noticed something strange happening among the memories she visited. They were . . . *changing*. Scenes she thought she knew would suddenly appear differently to her, the substance of them altered. Sometimes the change was subtle. A name once mentioned, glossed over. A face in a crowd erased, the space around them empty and unacknowledged. Other times, the changes were more noticeable. Entire events gone. Lives altered, memories and timelines manipulated to fill in the gaps left by someone who had been erased.

"This is what it means to be Forgotten," Azrael explained when she'd first come to him in distress over one of those lost memories. "The version of the past we remember is often very different from what actually occurred. Events, histories, entire communities . . . it's all been written and unwritten dozens of times over. Nobody knows how much has been lost. Nobody knows how much of what remains is the truth."

"Nobody?" Lisavet asked, tears shining in her eyes.

"Well . . . the timekeepers remember what it is they've erased, I suppose. But only that which they themselves have altered. The bigger picture is lost."

She came to recognize most timekeepers and knew which ones were liable to burn memories and which did their duty to save them. Most of the timekeepers she saw were white men in military uniforms. The Europeans dominated the time space, although Azrael explained that there had once been others. Timekeepers from Africa and Asia and South America who gained access to the time space, not through watches, but through deep, meditative prayer. But those people had been wiped out by imperialists years ago, leaving only a few who hid from the other timekeepers as frantically as Lisavet did whenever they saw them coming.

Then there were the Americans. They were just like the others, until one day Lisavet saw one of them do something unexpected.

She was waiting in the shadows, preparing to salvage another set of memories when she saw him. The German timekeeper burning the memories performed his task with the same efficient callousness that they all did. Experience had taught her that he would leave quickly after setting the fire, and she was ready for it, muscles tensed in anticipation. But when the moment came, someone else emerged from between the shelves, sending Lisavet scrambling backward to avoid being seen. She crouched low, peering at this new timekeeper.

A man in an American soldier's uniform took the burning bundle into his hands as she would have, as though he understood, as she did, the worth of what he was holding. He wore leather gloves, a luxury that allowed him to stamp out the fire as it still burned and rescue more of what remained. Lisavet followed him, taken aback as he carried the book carefully through the time space and hid it within another set of shelves, far from where the first timekeeper had found it.

As he turned back, passing by her hiding place so close she could have touched him, she caught a closer look at his face. He was young, younger than many of the other timekeepers she'd seen, with curly, copper-colored hair cut uncomfortably close and eyes the color of the ocean. There was something . . . different about him. And not just because he was saving memories. He had a softness in him, in spite of his uniform. A kindness to his face and features. She continued to follow him at a distance, getting closer than was advised, all the while hoping he would turn his head her way again so that she could see his face a second time. When at last he turned the crown on his watch to go, Lisavet found herself wishing that he wouldn't.

As his door sealed behind him, Lisavet felt Azrael's astral presence appear at her side. He was looking at her strangely, a wry smile curling his lips.

"What?" Lisavet asked.

Azrael was studying her as if noticing her for the first time. In the years that had passed, she had grown taller. She no longer had to look up quite so much to look him in the eye. The shabby nightdress she'd worn ever since that fateful night was tight around her chest, barely extending to her knees. Her arms fit through the sleeves of her father's coat without needing to be rolled up.

"What year is it on the outside, Lisavet?" he asked. "Do you know?"

Lisavet shook her head.

Azrael's smile grew strained. "Nineteen forty-four. February. It will be six years this November since you first came here. You are already sixteen."

Lisavet considered this with very little concern. She had long been accustomed to life inside the time space. Thoughts of leaving, though they still appeared in her daydreams, no longer occupied her every moment. How could they when she'd seen how violent the world could be on the outside? In the real world, there was no way of knowing what was real and what had been altered by timekeepers. No way to know which parts of her might have been erased. Still, there was something in the way Azrael looked at her as he said it that told her that her being here was something to grieve. That sixteen, the age she was now, was important somehow. And that being here and being sixteen together at the same time was cause for concern.

Later, when it was time for them to do their usual time walking, he put a book into her hands, opened it to a particular page, and stepped back. Lisavet waited for him to take her hand, as he usually did. She relied on his guidance to keep her out of any memories she shouldn't see. War, executions, violence . . . he kept it from her on purpose, always taking care to choose where and when they visited.

"Well?" she asked. "Aren't you going to take us there?"

Azrael shook his head. "No. This is something you should do on your own."

Without another word, he slipped back into the shadows, leaving her alone.

Lisavet looked down at the book in her hands, frowning. She heard the whispers calling out from the pages and clung to them, accepting their offered hand. The universal invitation to come closer. Around her, the familiar shift of color began. Lisavet slid between the folds of Time and found herself standing in an open field. It was night. Behind her, a line of trees cut a jagged arch across the horizon, but in front of her there was nothing but endless meadow. In her periphery, fireflies blinked in their silent light language. Overhead, the sky opened up from one end of the horizon to the other, lit by a full harvest moon. The time space had stars, thousands of them, all swirling together like paint. But the moon only existed in memories. Seeing it was her favorite part of time walking.

She heard voices. Laughter came from one end of the field and a young couple emerged from the trees, one chasing after the other. The girl had pale skin and held the skirts of her yellow dress tightly in two fists while she ran. The boy chasing her, brown skinned and dressed in a pauper's clothes, caught her around the waist as they neared the center of the field, both of them toppling into the grass. Lisavet drew closer, intrigued by their breathless laughter.

The boy had drawn the girl beneath him, one hand cupping her cheek. Their eyes shone as they gazed at each other. A light language all their own. Their lips met shyly, clumsily, and Lisavet knew this was the first time they'd dared to try it. For what felt like a long time, the two of them stayed like that, kissing under the light of the moon. Was this what Azrael had wanted her to see? Two people kissing in a field? Then the movements of the boy slowly started to change. The girl's breath became shallower, her body arched and twisted beneath his as her own hands pulled him ever closer. Their kisses grew more desperate, the two of them enveloped in passion. The boy's hand disappeared beneath the girl's skirt, and she made a different kind of sound altogether.

Lisavet couldn't look away. This was love, or at least the beginning of it. Different from the kind she thought she knew about. There was magic about it. Vulnerability. She could sense that there was something more to what they were doing. A precipice they tiptoed at the edge of but dared not jump from. There was a look in the eyes of them both that she had never seen before. It was radiant, impassioned. Full of light that burned even brighter than the moon.

LISAVET SET off in search of other memories of love. And she found them. More than she expected and far more than she'd bargained for. Two young people kissing at sunset on the coast. A girl and her husband dancing on their wedding day, eyes aglow. Two men, a musician and his muse, stealing intimate glances between acts of a performance. Lisavet longed to feel someone's lips caress hers that way. She wanted to know what it felt like to touch and to be touched in return. She wanted to be *looked* at. Seen by someone who wasn't a memory.

Lisavet was lingering in the back of a salon in France, watching a young artist paint his lover's portrait when it happened. The girl herself was half dressed, a sheet draped lazily over one shoulder, hair undone. The artist had just traced the particularly delicate line of the girl's lips and Lisavet was leaning forward to get a better look when her arm brushed against the cup full of paintbrushes. The sensation, cool glass against her skin, was so sudden and foreign to her that she didn't notice it falling until a loud crash filled the room. Both the artist and his subject jumped in alarm. The young man let out an anxious laugh as he scrambled to collect the brushes. He gathered them back into the cup, apologizing for his clumsiness. The moment passed.

Lisavet held still, too shocked to move again. She stared at the glass. The long crack in the side. Had that really happened? Had she *touched* something in a memory? That had never happened before. Normally, if she did touch something, it went straight through her, leaving only a phantom tingle. Carefully, she hovered her hand over the surface of the table and let her fingers fall. The moment her skin brushed the glossy finish, her heart plummeted. With a jerk, she fell out of the memory back into the time space.

When Azrael found her several hours later, her face was still pale from shock.

"What happened? Is everything all right?"

She explained, still scarcely believing it.

Azrael said nothing for a long while. His silence only unnerved her more. Never had Azrael not had an explanation for something. She had come to rely on it, his assuredness. They both decided it would be best if she didn't do any more time walking on her own for now.

That night, as she lay down in the center of the rows, she stretched her hands out in front of her face, studying them for signs of flickering. What if she was dying? Would she even know if she was? Her mind was already here, after all. All her memories were lived in the time space. Where else was there for her to go? Maybe she had died a long time ago,

her body abandoned somewhere in the rows of books while her mind
continued to wander. Trapped like Azrael, with no book of memories to
call her own. It wasn't death she feared most, but rather the thought of
dying without ever having known what it was to be in love.

In the world outside her own, Time spun onward.

Soon the year outside the time space was 1946. Autumn. Lisavet had
just turned nineteen years old but didn't know it. It had been months
since she had seen a Nazi timekeeper. The threat of them had gone from
the time space at least, but fewer Nazis didn't necessarily mean fewer
burned memories. In fact, there had been a steady uptick in burnings
from the Russians and the Americans specifically. Lisavet grew bolder
in her salvaging attempts, sometimes swooping in before the timekeeper
had even gone. She had begun time walking again without Azrael, drawn
to the memories in spite of her concerns. Her days were spent traipsing
through time like a shadow, dancing through dinner parties and festivals
or climbing onto the roofs of houses at night to drink in the sight of the
full moon overhead, as if it was made only for her. The moon, which borrowed its light from the sun the way she borrowed life from memories
to fill her own.

She had begun to take things from memories, too, always careful
to avoid anything that looked important. The first was a dress made
of pale blue fabric left behind by a vacationer in a hurry, taken to re-
place her own tattered nightgown. Wearing it, she looked grown-up,
the new curves of her body filling out the fabric, a girl no longer. She
took other things too. A brush for her hair that had grown long and
straight, like spun gold. A pair of shoes tossed on the rubble heap
outside the cobblers. Gloves, like the American soldier had worn, so
she could stamp out flames just as he had. This method was particularly effective, and her book was becoming overfull. The contents burst

through the binding, necessitating the need for a new cover. She began
to keep a closer eye on what the timekeepers were destroying, searching for the right one.

One night, when following a Russian timekeeper from a distance,
she found just the thing she was looking for. The memory he'd chosen
was a thick volume belonging to someone a hundred years old or more.
Instead of burning the book in one piece, he removed its blue leather
cover and cast it aside. Lisavet watched him light the fire, noticing how
disinterested he seemed in the whole process. He was a soldier following
orders, not caring about the outcome. He left quickly, not bothering to
see the process all the way through and Lisavet leapt for the book. Pages
first, she told herself, donning her gloves. She quickly extinguished the
flames, salvaging a large chunk of the center pages. Enough to be a book
all on its own. She pulled her gloves off with her teeth, letting the pages
whisper to her. As she turned around to retrieve the discarded cover,
she was arrested by the sight of another person, a timekeeper, lifting the
cover off the ground.

She recognized him in an instant. The copper-haired American she'd
caught rescuing memories. It had been two years since she'd last seen
him. He wasn't wearing a uniform anymore, dressed instead in a white
buttoned shirt and charcoal trousers.

"Hello there," he said quietly, as though addressing a frightened animal.

His water-blue eyes seemed to pierce right through her. The first set
of living eyes to look at her in eight years. Instead of being excited by it,
she found the vulnerability of being looked at terrifying. She wanted to
run, but curiosity stilled her feet.

"You were awfully quick getting that book," he said, unperturbed by
her silence. "You beat me to it." He smiled. Straight, white teeth behind
rose-colored lips. The two years had changed him. Some of the softness
of early youth had gone from his features.

"Are you from Russia?" he asked.

"Germany," Lisavet said at last. Her voice sounded cagey and frightened.

"You speak English?" he said, delighted. "I'm sorry, I didn't mean to startle you. I didn't realize anyone else was here."

"You were following the Russian, too?"

"Yeah." He gave a small grimace.

He rubbed the back of his head and Lisavet realized that he had grown out his hair. The loose copper curls suited him more than the buzz cut.

"I've never seen someone else trying to save the books before," he said.

"Me either," Lisavet said, giddy at the knowledge that they were talking. Two living people having a conversation. "Besides you, I mean."

"You've seen me before?"

"Once."

He both smiled and frowned at this. "And you didn't say hello?"

"Well, I . . . no. I don't talk to . . ." She paused, realizing she shouldn't say timekeepers, but not really knowing why, then finished, ". . . strangers."

"Well, let's fix that." He stepped forward and extended a hand. "My name is Ernest. Ernest Duquesne."

Lisavet stared at his hand. She wanted to take it but found herself hesitating. What if she passed right through him? At last, she reached for it. Their palms slid together, one warm from the gloves and flames, one cool to the touch. Lisavet felt the sensation clear down to her toes.

"Ernest," she repeated.

"Well? Aren't you going to tell me your name?"

Another round of panic. She hadn't said it out loud or heard it spoken by anyone but Azrael in eight years.

She shook her head. "No."

Ernest's eyebrows lifted. "Oh? Why not?"

"Because you're a timekeeper."

Ernest laughed at this. "And you aren't?"

Lisavet didn't answer. Ernest stopped laughing. He looked down at their joined hands and then at her left wrist that clutched the salvaged pages to her chest. He let go in alarm.

"Oh. I'm sorry, I . . . you're not . . . dead, are you?"

"No! At least, I don't think I am."

Ernest's expression grew more and more quizzical. Lisavet began to wonder if she should have lied. Something had shifted in the air between them, and she hadn't experienced enough of human interaction to know what it was. She stepped back and pointed to the book cover still dangling from his hand.

"Can I have that?"

He looked down at it as though he'd forgotten it was there. "This? It's just an empty binding."

"I know. I need it."

His blue eyes passed between her and the cover several times. "Only if you give me that," he said, gesturing to the papers.

"What do you want them for?"

"I need them," he said with a slight shrug of the shoulders. "It's an even trade. The pages for the cover."

Lisavet hesitated. "Are you going to burn them?"

"Does it matter?"

"Yes."

Ernest squinted at her. "What does a German girl want with the memories of an American?"

"I didn't know they belonged to an American," Lisavet said, mirroring his body language.

"Then why did you save them?"

"Because they're memories."

"So?"

"So they were worth saving."

This struck him in a way that told her she'd caught him off guard. He took a small step forward and she prepared to step back, but he was just leaning, one arm draped against the shelves beside her.

"Well, Germany, I guess we're at an impasse," he said.

"Guess so."

"That's a shame. And here I thought Versailles really meant something."

What did France have to do with anything? She was about to ask when suddenly he lunged forward. He stole the pages right out of her hands, quicker than lightning. She cried out in surprise, the sound piercing the time space and echoing. He ran from her. She tried to follow but he quickly outpaced her and disappeared around the corner. When she finally caught up, he was gone. Disappeared into the shadows. She looked down to find the empty cover of the book at her feet. She bent down to pick it up, examining the flower stamped into its center, certain he'd dropped it on purpose. An even trade.

Moments later, Azrael appeared at her side. "Are you all right? I heard you shout." She nodded and he looked down at the empty book in her hands. "Where did that come from?"

Lisavet shrugged carelessly. The way Ernest had. "An American time-keeper dropped it."

"An American? You should be careful with them. They seem to be on the verge of war with the whole world these days. Very dangerous."

Dangerous, Lisavet repeated in her head. Over the years, she'd begun to realize that Azrael used that word to describe just about anything outside of the time space. Thoughts, feelings, emotions, even Time itself were all dangerous. She began to wonder if what danger really was, if what it really meant, was living. Maybe the only truly safe thing was death.

Ernest Duquesne was alive, she thought, a small thrill running through her. His lungs drew breath, same as hers. His hand was solid and pulsing with life. His eyes full. As deep as oceans, as alive as an entire lifetime's worth of moons. If living was dangerous, then he was the most dangerous thing there was.

4

1965, *Boston, Massachusetts*

THERE WAS NO HANDBOOK on how to turn a rebellious teenager into a timekeeper. It was no simple task. Normally, the people who worked for the Temporal Reconnaissance Program (TRP) were highly vetted CIA operatives who had already undergone extensive training in other areas. Amelia, however, was untrained and seemed determined to make this as difficult as possible. She slumped in her seat, sighing loudly and fidgeting as Moira attempted to explain the purpose of timekeepers as it had first been explained to her years ago. The storage of important memories throughout history was the responsibility of the timekeepers of the present day. They chose which memories got cataloged and which ones did not.

"How do they choose which ones are important?" Amelia asked.

"Historically it was up to their own discretion," Moira said, pleased the young teen was, for once, paying attention. "But now it's determined by government programs like the TRP."

"The TRP. That's who my uncle worked for?"

Moira tilted her head from side to side. "At one point, after he left the military. The Temporal Reconnaissance Program, or TRP, was founded by your grandfather and was brought under the purview of the CIA in 1947. That's how Ernest got his start."

"And that's where you met him?"

"Yes. Back then, I was just a secretary for our boss, Jack Dillinger, but when Jack became director of the CIA, he named me as his successor, and your uncle was tapped to lead a new program focused on diplomacy inside the time space. Another branch of the CIA called the Office of Temporal Diplomacy."

"The OTD?"

"We don't call it that. But now we're getting off topic."

Moira continued. She explained to Amelia what the book she'd be searching for looked like: dark blue leather, composed of mismatched pages of varying shades of yellow and white, a single five-petaled flower stamped into its center. Around the time she began explaining what to do if she encountered another timekeeper, Amelia started to waver, much less inclined to listen to things that scared her. Moira sensed another bout of attitude and sent her upstairs.

"There's only so much I can do to prepare you for what you'll find in there," Moira said before Amelia left the room. "At some point, you'll have to go back in."

The following days went no better. Amelia showed no sign of re-entering the time space. Silence was her newest combat tactic. She stayed shut up in her room except for when Moira dragged her down for meals.

In her updates to Jack, Moira told him that she was the one delaying things. She needed more time, she told him, to prepare Amelia for what she was going to do. As the director of the TRP, the time space was Moira's domain, but Jack was still her boss. Her excuses wouldn't hold much longer.

On Friday morning, Moira went to the grocery store, leaving Amelia alone on the sofa in the living room. It was her second trip in two days. She had underestimated just how much such a thin girl could eat.

"You should try to go in while I'm gone," she called over her shoulder as she shut the door, fully expecting to find Amelia in the exact same spot when she returned.

However, when she opened the front door, Amelia was no longer on the sofa. Moira left the bag of groceries in the kitchen and listened closely for the sound of footsteps upstairs. The house was perfectly still. She called out Amelia's name. No response. She checked her room. Empty. Her poetry books sat on the unmade bed, her backpack was on the chair. Moira's eyes fell on the sock drawer, slightly ajar. When she opened it, she found the watch nestled carefully between rolled-up stockings. Abandoned. Moira seized it and slammed the drawer shut in frustration. She'd been patient long enough. It was time for more drastic measures. She grabbed her car keys from the table in the foyer and set out in search of Amelia.

AMELIA HAD gone to the library two blocks down the street. She'd wanted to be rid of the house, which no longer felt like her home with Moira living in it. Having her there, someone so feminine and aloof in the house that had belonged to Uncle Ernest, was an intrusion. She noticed everything. Heard everything. Even when Amelia was in her room, it seemed like Moira was right there watching her. It was unnerving.

Amelia sat on the top floor of the library next to a window overlooking the courtyard. The window was flung ajar to let the air circulate, taking advantage of what was sure to be one of the last warm days of autumn. Books of poetry were stacked all around her. Around the corner, coming from a nearby table, she could hear the whispers of public school students who frequented this library. She bristled on instinct. They weren't talking about her, why would they be? They didn't know who she was. No longer was she plagued by the terms *communist* or *traitor*. Instead, a new set of words rang inside her head, echoing in Moira's voice. *Murdered. Victim. Russian target.* Amelia tried to read, to take refuge in poems the way she often did but couldn't focus. Frustrated, she stood up and moved over to the window to look out, taking the book with her. She closed her eyes, feeling the breeze on her face, wishing she could simply turn her mind off.

"If it's peace and quiet you're looking for, I can think of a place where you might find it."

Amelia's eyes flew open. Behind her, Moira was leaning against one of the shelves, book in hand, casually flipping through the pages as though she'd been there all along.

"What are you doing here?" Amelia demanded in a sharp whisper.

Moira took her sweet time answering. "There is no frigate like a book, is there?" she said with a contented sigh.

She was quoting a poem by Emily Dickinson. Amelia didn't feel like playing Moira's game today. She repeated her question a little louder.

"What the *hell* are you doing here?"

Moira raised an eyebrow. "My, my, what a temper. I guess it is true what they say about redheads."

She came to stand beside her at the window. She was wearing a black dress that skimmed the length of her body and cut a straight line over her collarbone. Today her lipstick wasn't red, but a slightly darker shade of mauve that made her features appear more somber. *This* ensemble would have been more appropriate for a burial, Amelia thought.

"You didn't tell me you were coming here," Moira said, giving her a look.

Amelia didn't answer. She folded her arms over the book of poetry and focused all her energy on willing Moira's head to spontaneously combust.

"And you're not wearing the watch," Moira said.

"I took it off."

"You shouldn't do that. It's not smart to leave something like that lying around."

"I didn't leave it lying around," Amelia said indignantly. "I put it somewhere safe."

Moira snorted. She turned to face her and held something up a few inches away from her face. The watch, dangling from its black leather strap.

"Safe like in your sock drawer?" Moira taunted.

"You went through my room?"

"You didn't leave a note," Moira fired back.

She reached for Amelia's arm and strapped the watch onto her wrist. Her grip was firm, her lips pressed into an angry line. Amelia had never seen Moira angry and the idea of it made her nervous.

"Time to stop stalling, Amelia. You're going in one way or another. I've already wound it for you. All you have to do is walk."

She let go of her arm and stepped back expectantly.

Amelia's eyes darted around the library. "Now?"

"Now would be ideal. Don't worry about them, they won't notice."

"But I . . . I'm not ready," Amelia protested, feeling her palms begin to sweat.

"It's okay to be frightened," Moira said in a slightly softer tone. "But you can't let it stop you."

Amelia glared at her. "I'm not afraid," she said, a bit louder than she intended. Someone down the row of books shushed them. She lowered her voice, dropping her eyes to the floor. "I . . . it's just . . . he died in there. What if his body is still there? What if I find it? What if I can't do this?"

There was a pause and Moira laid a hand on her arm. "You can do this, Amelia."

"How would you know? You don't know me."

"I don't. But Ernest did. I told you, he left that watch to *you*. That must mean something."

Amelia shook her head. "You don't know what he was thinking when he did that."

Moira let out a sigh of barely concealed exasperation. "Then why don't you go find out what he was thinking?"

Amelia blinked at her. "What?"

"If you're so worried that he's made a mistake, go find his memories. They must be somewhere in the time space. Finding them will make your search for the book that much easier."

Amelia swallowed hard, her eyes widening. She looked around the room, conscious that they were alone now. The others had left.

"But . . . there are no doors to walk through," she said.

Moira hummed out a laugh that sent chills down Amelia's spine. "Oh, don't worry. We won't let that stop us."

Amelia barely had time to register the conniving look on Moira's face before Moira's hand closed around Amelia's arm and jerked her forward. She felt her feet leave the ground, felt Moira's arms around her waist before she felt herself pushed headfirst out the open window. The scream that tore from her throat barely pierced the air before the sound was silenced completely, replaced by the bone-chilling sound of darkness descending.

AMELIA'S SCREAM lasted only a millisecond before it was swallowed up by the endlessness of the time space. Moira stayed in her spot by the window, feeling satisfied even though she knew she shouldn't. The girl was just scared. Understandably so. She would be lying if she said she didn't have compassion for her. But compassion didn't yield results and with the rest of the department's watches beyond her reach, they needed the book now more than ever. Without it, the entire department was rendered useless, and the Russians could rewrite history uncontested.

"A bit harsh, don't you think?" A deep male voice came from behind her.

Moira didn't turn around. "Hello, Jack," she said, eyes on the place where Amelia had just vanished.

"Hello, Moira. I see things are going well."

Without looking at him, she clocked his location ten feet behind her, standing at the table where Amelia had piled her books. She heard him turn one of them over to look at the cover.

"She reads poetry," he said, sounding intrigued. "Just like you used to."

Moira turned to face him, arms folded. "What are you doing here?"

He let the cover of the book fall shut. Jack always wore the same gray suits cut in the modern style. His dark hair was slicked back to one side, using just enough gel to keep it in place, but not so much that it appeared greasy. A navy blue necktie was secured in place. Face neatly shaven. He was so consistent in his appearance that he was almost a caricature of himself. Like she was.

"Fred called. Told me he saw the girl leave the house alone while you were gone. So I came to make sure everything was going okay."

Moira didn't buy it. "I thought you were going to keep your distance."

Jack raised his hands in denial. "I am, I am. Hands off, just like I promised. But that doesn't mean I won't get involved if the need arises."

"The need hasn't arisen. She went to the library, not the train station."

"So you knew she was coming here?"

"Yes."

Jack cocked an eyebrow. He came to stand beside her at the window. Her spine stiffened instinctively as he got closer. She noticed he was carrying a file folder in one hand but didn't ask about it. Jack liked to make people wonder about things. It made him feel powerful to withhold information from people. To force them to ask. Moira had learned to stop playing into it years ago.

"You look tired, Jack," she said instead. "No rest for the wicked, I suppose."

"You're one to talk," he bit back.

His reply was lacking some of its usual venom, so Moira knew he must really be exhausted. Not that she could blame him. Between this investigation and his other responsibilities as head of the CIA, he was stretched thin. All the more reason to back off and let her handle things alone. Of course, he didn't see it that way.

Jack turned toward her and held up the file. "Here. Photos of all the known Russian timekeepers. Just like you asked for. The one on the top is our most likely suspect."

Moira reached for the file. He pulled it back, tauntingly out of reach.

"You know, Donnelly, it used to be that *you* were the one fetching files for *me*. Not sure I like it the other way around."

"You wanted the bigger office," Moira pointed out.

"Sure, sure," Jack said, lowering the file within her reach once more. "Still wish I could have kept the watch though."

Moira didn't respond. Given the scarcity of watches that could access the time space, Jack had been forced to give his up when he left the TRP. The day he'd handed it over to her was still one of Moira's most satisfying memories. She took the file from his hand now and flipped it open. Inside were a series of freshly printed profiles of Russian timekeepers. Names, addresses, birth dates. Last known locations. Photos were paper clipped to the top of each one. Moira looked at the face of the first one, the most likely culprit. He had a youthful face, but his eyes were hollow and haunted. The eyes of someone who had seen far too much far too soon.

"What makes you think he's the one who killed him?" she asked.

"The others said it was a boy they saw tailing Ernest. A boy, not a man. He's the only one who fits that description. Besides . . . look at the name."

Moira flipped the photograph up so she could read the document beneath. "Anton Stepanov. So this is . . ."

"Uh-huh. Anton *Vasilyevich* Stepanov. Vasily Stepanov's son. You know how the Russians like to keep it in the family."

Moira felt a cold foreboding in her chest. She had crossed paths with Vasily Stepanov once, years ago, and it had ended badly. For him at least.

And now here was his son, working for the KGB and possibly out for a little revenge. She glanced at the birth date written in text beneath the boy's name. September 1948. Seventeen. He was only seventeen. Only a year and eight months older than Amelia. She looked back at the picture for a long moment before shutting the file.

"I'll show these to her," she said, wanting Jack to go away. "Let her know who to watch out for."

He was chewing his lower lip, once again staring out the window contemplatively. "So she's scared, is she?"

"We wouldn't have this issue if you'd just let me go in to investigate myself."

"Don't start with me, Moira. You know I won't allow that."

She let out a frustrated sigh. "Then you're going to have to be patient. She'll come around, she just needs a little bit of a push."

"I suppose," Jack muttered. "Well, keep tossing her out of windows then, I guess. Whatever it takes. I want to know which Russian is responsible for this mess so we can blow his brains out."

"We have to know which brains we're looking for before you can do that," Moira said.

Jack snorted. "Or we could just shoot the lot of them. All this diplomacy is very un-American if you ask me. Do you think anyone ever stopped to make sure they were shooting the *right* German?"

"We're trying to avoid a war, Jack, not start one."

"They drew first blood," Jack said.

She shot him a look, knowing that it wasn't grief or concern over Ernest in particular that was driving his desire to strike. Jack had lost a great deal to war. His father in the first. Most of his friends in the second. He had been an officer in the navy and had watched an entire ship full of his own men burn under enemy fire after *he* had given them an order to wait. An experience that had left him with a "strike first, ask questions later" mentality that could be hard to rein in. He viewed communism and the Russians who supported it as the next great enemy, and as such, he did whatever it took to stop them.

Moira moved over to the table and began stacking Amelia's books into a neat pile. Rilke. Donne. Blake. All male poets, she noted. When she looked up, Jack was still standing there.

"Did you need something else?"

"James Gravel," Jack said.

Moira stopped shuffling books and straightened. "What about him?"

"He's still not talking."

"So send Fred after him."

"Tried that," Jack said, shaking his head. "We've twisted his arms seven ways to Sunday. The man won't budge."

Moira was only a little surprised. She had been part of the twisting, for a time. Before Ernest had died and everything came to a screeching halt. James Gravel was stubborn. Immovably so.

"And what would you like me to do about that? If you haven't noticed, I'm a little preoccupied babysitting your newest agent."

Jack ignored the subtle accusation in her tone. "He and Ernest had a rapport, right? They talked?"

"Occasionally."

Jack clicked his tongue against his teeth the way he did whenever he was scheming. "Think he'd talk to the girl? He might give something away if she's the one asking the questions."

"Finding the book is the objective," Moira said flatly. "Anything else has to be secondary."

"No. Finding the book is *one* objective," Jack said. "The other is finding the watches the rebels stole from us in the first place, and to do that, we need to find the rebels. If we root them out, we dismantle their whole movement. And James Gravel is a part of that."

Moira stiffened her jaw in resignation. She could see that Jack was set on this. "Fine. I'll take her to see him later this week."

Jack smiled. "Tomorrow. Take her tomorrow."

"Tomorrow it is."

Jack caught on to the tension in her tone and chuckled. "Attagirl." He turned to go, pausing to pat her on the shoulder as he passed. "And try to keep a closer eye on her for me, won't you? We don't want her running off all alone."

He left without another word and Moira let loose the shudder she had been suppressing ever since he appeared.

AMELIA WAS panicking. The darkness. The shadows. There was so much of it, stretching up and out and all around her. It made Amelia feel as though she was suffocating from the moment she entered the time space. The silence was a wet blanket weighing her down and stifling the air from her lungs. Her eyes scanned the row of shelves. Images of Uncle Ernest's face, bloody and lifeless, flooded her mind. The world spun around her, and she sank to the floor. She thought she heard a voice speaking to her in another language. A man's voice.

Something touched her shoulder. She let out a scream. The person standing beside her reeled back in alarm, raising up his hands in surrender. The boy was tall with a sharp jaw, hollow cheeks, and thick, regal eyebrows. He was speaking to her in a language she didn't understand, crouching low until they were at eye level.

"I ... I'm sorry. I don't ..."

Recognition registered on his face. "Ahh. American," he said in a thick accent. "Are you okay?"

Her throat was impossibly dry. "Yes. No. I don't know. I've never done this before. I can't figure out where I am and ..."

"That is no good." He held out a hand to help her up. "Come with me. I will show you the way."

Amelia took his hand, conscious of how hers was trembling and let

him pull her to her feet. He motioned for her to follow him, and she
began assessing him from behind. He had dark brown hair that fell
in waves, and he wore an ill-fitting wool coat that hung loosely on his
frame. He walked with purpose, taking long, quick strides, twisting and
turning through the maze of shelves. Soon they found themselves standing in the center of it all. A path that cut through the rows of shelves.
The boy stopped walking and pointed up.

"Look there," he said. "That will help you to breathe."

Amelia tilted her head. Instead of breathing easier, she almost stopped
breathing altogether. Swirling patterns of color and light flecked with
gold were laid against a backdrop of endless sky. Tiny beams of light shot
across the breadth of it from time to time like meteors, disappearing over
the edge. The longer she looked at it, the more her blood settled, nerves
unwinding.

"Better?" the young man asked. He was leaning back against one
of the shelves with his hands in his pockets. In this stance, he looked
younger. The sharpness in his features came more from hunger than
from age.

"Better. Thank you."

He nodded. "It was the same for me."

"How do you find your way around this place?"

"Practice. It is not so hard as you think." He gestured to the book in
her hands. She had all but forgotten it. "You are here to store the memories then?"

"Oh. No, actually I . . . do you know how I might find the memories
of a specific person?" she asked.

The young man leaned to the side, propping himself against one of
the shelves. "Which person?" he asked.

Amelia nearly told him but then reconsidered, eyeing him a bit more
closely. Maybe telling this accented stranger what she was here for was
a bad idea. After all, she didn't know where he was from. The watch

he wore was a Glashütte, like hers, but that didn't mean anything. She thought of the language he had been speaking before, wishing she'd paid more attention to it. What if he was one of the rebels Moira had mentioned? The very notion of it made her shy away from him.

"Never mind," she said, clutching the library book a bit more tightly.

"Are you sure? It is hard to find things in here. I can—"

"I can find it," Amelia said, cutting him off. "Th-thank you for your help."

He gave her a strange look and smiled at her. "You are welcome." He pointed back in the direction from which they had come. "The American section is that way. Whoever you are looking for will be over there." He nodded at the book in her hands. "If they haven't already been assimilated, you can store their memories in that."

"Assimilated?" Amelia asked in spite of her apprehension.

He chuckled at her. "They really did not tell you anything, did they? The memories appear first as ghosts until they've been stored."

"Oh . . . then how do I . . . you know?"

"Like this." He took her nonwatch wrist and opened the book, laying her hand on the pages, palm flat, like a politician taking a solemn oath. "And then they, uhh . . ." He shifted awkwardly and reached out his other hand.

Amelia jumped as he laid his palm on her cheek, warm against her clammy skin. A second ticked by and he dropped his hand abruptly.

"And that's it," he said, casting his eyes downward in embarrassment.

"That's it?"

"Well, there are the memories, of course. They play in your head like a motion picture but . . . mostly that's it." He cleared his throat. "Good luck. I hope you find what you are looking for," he said.

Amelia nodded as he turned to go, feeling her throat constrict as the silence closed in on her once more. She started back in the direction he had indicated, taking slow, careful steps as she went. Something moved in the corner of her eye, and she spun around, half expecting a Russian soldier to appear. Instead, what she saw scarcely looked real. A girl dressed in a brown dress and head covering, her body smoky and transparent. Like a ghost moving between the shelves. The thought of seeing Uncle Ernest like that made Amelia's eyes sting and for the first time, she realized that finding his memories would mean having to see the moment he had died firsthand. She wasn't ready for that, didn't know if she'd ever be ready for that.

Her eyes scanned the shelves filled with books in front of her, wondering if maybe she could find the book Moira wanted without having to look at her uncle's memories. How had she described it again? Dark blue leather with some kind of shape on the front. Why hadn't she paid more attention? She began to walk aimlessly down the rows, staring at the books. Even if she did remember the description, finding a specific book in a place filled to the brim with them felt like an impossible task. In her periphery, more of the ghostly figures appeared but she ignored them, so focused on finding her way that she almost walked right through one.

"Are you looking for someone?" the specter asked, his bright shadow dragging through the air.

Amelia jumped, whirling around to face the figure. He wore a gray robe made of simple fabric that tied at the waist. He was dressed like a monk, Amelia thought. Or maybe just someone very poor from a very long time ago.

"Sorry?" she asked.

"You're a timekeeper?"

"Oh, um. I suppose."

"A little young, aren't you?"

Amelia shifted awkwardly, wondering if he wanted her to assimilate his memories. "Do you . . . want me to . . ."

The memory waved his hand. "No, no. I'm afraid I have little left to assimilate. Any attempts would be a waste of both of our time."

Amelia frowned. If he had been assimilated, why was he still here?

"Your name is Amelia," the man said before she could ask.

"How do you know that?"

"I knew the timekeeper who wore that watch before you."

"You knew my uncle?"

"I do. Or at least I did." He leaned forward conspiratorially as though sharing some kind of secret. "I don't *normally* speak to timekeepers. He was an exception."

"But you're talking to me."

"I had to. You almost walked right through me."

"Sorry," Amelia said sheepishly.

"Quite all right. I wouldn't exactly feel it, would I?"

"I guess not." Amelia considered him for a moment. Perhaps he knew where to look. "I'm looking for a book. A blue one with some sort of engraving on the cover. A plant or . . . maybe a flower."

The figure stared at her, unblinking.

"Would you happen to know where it is?" Amelia prompted.

"Not presently."

"Oh. Well. Okay then. Thanks anyway." She started to turn away.

"You're going the wrong way," the memory said, stopping her short.

"I thought you said you didn't know where it is."

"Oh, I don't. But that's the wrong way."

"O . . . kay."

The memory stepped to the side and pointed the other direction. "That way. You'll want to go that way."

Amelia frowned at him. "And how do I know you're not leading me in the wrong direction?"

"I wouldn't do that."

"Sure, but how do I know that? You could be lying."

He stroked his chin thoughtfully. "I see your point." He pondered this for a minute, head tilted. "I am dead, you know."

"So?"

"So what would I have to gain by misleading you?"

"I guess that's . . . fair." Amelia still didn't move.

"You can go the other way if you like, it doesn't matter to me. It's just the wrong way."

Amelia frowned at him. She took a few steps in the direction he had pointed, glancing at him over her shoulder. He didn't leave right away. He was still watching her, smiling to himself in a sad sort of way.

"Was there something else you needed?" she asked.

"Oh, no. Not yet."

"Yet?"

"Later. We'll talk later."

"All right then," Amelia said.

She began walking again, shaking her head at the strangeness. Perhaps all specters were like that to some extent. She continued on, feeling less anxious now that she had somewhere to go, even if she wasn't exactly sure it was the right way. It wasn't until she'd walked for what felt like hours that she began to wonder if maybe the memory was messing with her. After all, there was nothing here but more books. None of them were blue, and in fact most of them didn't even have proper covers at all, but rather were wrapped up in old pieces of animal hide, indicating that they must be very, *very* old. She let out a sigh of frustration and looked down at her watch, alarmed to find that nearly three hours had passed since she'd entered the time space. Surely Moira wouldn't be upset if she left now?

Taking one last look at the books on the shelves, she reached for the watch and turned the crown. A door appeared, materializing out of the shadows. Amelia slipped between the silent shelves toward it, leaving the memories behind with the stars.

The sudden rush of sounds all around her shook her to her very core. She was back beside the window, the cool breeze of the autumn day trickling in behind her. Her pulse quickened, then slowed again. Her body did not feel like her own. The whole world seemed to hum around her. It took her several moments to reorient herself. She looked for Moira, but she was nowhere to be seen. Had she gone? Amelia peered down several shelves, expecting her to materialize like the memory of one of the dead. But she didn't.

Amelia returned to the table where she'd been working and found a stack of three books and a manila folder waiting for her there. A note sat on top of the file.

Amelia,

Profiles on Russian timekeepers for you to take a look at.
Particularly the first one. Dinner is at seven.

- M.

P.S. The books are poetry collections by female poets.
You really ought to diversify your reading.

Amelia made a face at the note. She looked at the books first. Elizabeth Barrett Browning. Emma Lazarus. Edna St. Vincent Millay. Tucking the books under her arm to take home, she turned her attention to the folder and flipped it open.

The first photo was of a gaunt, sharp-faced boy, with dark brown hair that fell in waves.

Anton Stepanov, seventeen years old. *Timekeeper. Russian agent. Murderer.*

5

<hr />

1947, Somewhere in the Time Space

IN 1947, MONTHS AFTER they first spoke, Lisavet began to get the sense that Ernest Duquesne was following her. She had expected not to see him again for a long time, so when he continued to show up, appearing just before she swept in to rescue another set of burned memories, she began to get suspicious.

"Stop following me," she shouted, darting around him to reach the book.

"Who says I'm following you? Maybe I'm just trying to do my job."

"And what is your job exactly?"

"Lately? It's to try and stop you from interfering."

Lisavet laughed out loud. "Interfering? What about the people destroying memories?"

"It's their *job* to decide what stays and what goes. That's the whole point of timekeepers."

"That's stupid."

"Stupid?"

"And wrong. And chauvinistic. And imperialistically minded."

"Whoa there, Merriam-Webster, calm down. English, please."

Lisavet glared at him and repeated her words in German just to make a point.

Ernest gave her a sardonic look. "Cute."

Keeping one eye on him to make sure he kept his distance, she took her book from her coat so she could file the pages away.

"So that's where you keep all the memories you steal, huh?" he asked.

"No. It's where I keep the ones I save from idiotic timekeepers like you."

"Why?"

"Because I need a place to put them."

"No, I mean, why bother saving them? Why do you care?"

Lisavet suddenly heard her father's voice in her head. The whispers of the remaining memories she carried around with her. All she had left of him. She stashed the book in the folds of her coat and stood up.

"Does it matter?" she asked.

"Kind of. What if you're saving something dangerous?"

"How could the memories of a dead person be dangerous?"

Ernest shrugged. That careless, infuriating jerk of the shoulders. "Same way the thoughts of a living person can be. They manifest. Take root. Become something bigger."

Lisavet raised an eyebrow. "I save the memories because erasing them is wrong. Dangerous or not."

She started to walk away. Ernest followed.

"Okay, well what about Hitler?"

"What about him?"

"Wouldn't it have been great if someone had erased those thoughts before they spread? Before he used them to start a war and do all those horrific things?"

Lisavet stared at him blankly. When she had entered the time space nine years ago, Hitler and the Nazis had been little more than a political movement. She knew there had been a war, but Azrael had intentionally kept her from learning too much about the outcome of it. She thought about asking Ernest but didn't want to give him the satisfaction.

"So what, you think you can just erase all the bad parts of the world? Just like that?"

"Not all of them, no. Some things spread too quickly to be stopped. Some events have too great an impact to be altered. But other ideas, sure. Why not? Even if we can't erase the event itself, we can change the way people remember it. So they remember the *right* version."

Lisavet snorted at his insolence. "And who died and put you in charge of deciding what's right?"

"My father," he said without skipping a beat.

She started to scoff at him again, then stopped. "Wait . . . you're serious?"

"As a heart attack. Which, coincidentally, is how he died."

Lisavet's lips parted in surprise. "I lost my father too," she said, the words slipping out before she could stop them. The part of her that still craved some sort of connection wouldn't be silenced.

"Oh, I'm sorry," he said, taken aback. "When?"

"A long time ago. A timekeeper erased his memories so the world would forget about him. I watched it happen."

It was Ernest's turn to be surprised. Then the surprise morphed into concern. "Wait. How long have you been in here?"

"A while."

"How long is a while?"

Lisavet took a step back. His tone had changed. Some of the edge had returned to it. An urgency that startled her. "Does it matter?"

He matched her step and followed it with another. "Well . . . yeah. This is the time space. A place where time is the only thing that exists. It can't be safe to stay here that long."

"For you maybe."

"No, listen. I know we got off on the wrong foot, but I didn't realize . . ." He came even closer, seeming intent on reaching her. "Maybe I can . . ."

"Stay back," she said, voice tightening with panic.

"No. Hang on. I can help you."

"I don't need help," Lisavet said, retreating farther and farther down the row.

"But you can't stay here. I don't think . . ."

Lisavet didn't wait to hear what he did or did not think of her life. She turned on her heel and fled.

ERNEST HAD begun to question whether what he was doing was right. It had been four months since he'd first told his boss about the German girl he'd met in the time space who was meddling in the affairs of other time-keepers. Four months since he'd started tailing her at the department's request. They wanted to know who she was, and more importantly, who she was working for. But after their last encounter, Ernest was no longer certain if she was working for anyone at all. How could she be when it sounded like she hadn't left the time space in years?

When he'd mentioned that to Jack, he'd simply waved it off.

"Nonsense. She must be working for somebody. Why else would she be interfering?"

"I don't know. She seems to be doing it on the basis of some moral high ground. She said she saw someone destroy the memories of her father. I think . . ." Ernest paused, furrowing his brow intently. "I think she's been in there for a real long time."

Jack made a disinterested humming noise. He stood up and poked his head out the door to call for his secretary to order lunch. The girl shouted back in acquiescence, her voice shrill and eager. Jack was constantly cycling through new secretaries. In his short tenure as director since the department was moved under the jurisdiction of the newly formed CIA earlier that year, he'd had at least three.

Theirs was a complicated relationship, Ernest and Jack's. As the director of the TRP, Jack was technically Ernest's superior. But Ernest, as the son of the program's founder, was the undisputed successor to Jack's job, favored by both Jack's subordinates and those further up the ladder. Ernest was smarter than Jack, more well liked than Jack, and, in his opinion, much better looking than Jack. The only reason the job wasn't his already was his age. He had only been fourteen when the second war started in 1939. Had forged his draft card in order to join the army two years later. His mother had been furious with him. His father had only just died, leaving him the man of the house. His mother wanted him to finish school, to get a good job, marry a nice girl. Since returning from war he'd done all but one of those things. He had finished school early, double majoring in history and physics, and had gotten a job in his father's old department. But he hadn't gotten married and that, he found, was more distressing to his mother than any of the rest.

"A wife would do wonders for you, Ernie," she scolded the last time he visited. "You're too much in your own head. Always reading all that poetry, always working. A wife would help you with that."

Ernest had brushed it off, as he always did. "If you're telling me that a wife will interfere with my work, I'd best avoid getting one at all costs."

"I just don't want you to be like your father. He worked too much at that job."

Ernest said nothing to this. If there was one person in the world he wanted most to be like, it was his father. Gregory Duquesne had been a great man, everyone agreed. Respected. Revered. Someone who always knew what to do and ran the TRP with unmatched steadiness. Ernest wondered what his father would have done if it were him dealing with the issue of the German girl and not Jack.

"You should get yourself a secretary, Ernest," Jack said, returning to his seat. "Free up some of that time you spend writing those reports."

"No, I'm okay. I don't mind the reports."

"Right, I forgot," Jack said with a sly grin. "You like writing those endless descriptions of the German girl. I'll tell you, that last one practically had *me* in raptures. 'Long golden hair. Big brown eyes. Legs from here to San Francisco.' She sounds like quite a looker."

"I never wrote that," Ernest protested.

"Oh right, that was my imagination filling in the blanks." He began throwing the rubber ball he kept in his desk up and down. "And you've never seen her leave the time space?"

"Not in the traditional sense. She disappears from time to time, but she doesn't have a watch."

"Maybe she's meeting with someone. Handing over the memories."

"That's not it either. She keeps all the memories in this book she carries with her."

Jack stopped throwing the ball and leaned forward. "A book? You mean she keeps it on her?"

"Yes. I've never seen her without it."

"Well, there's your solution then. Take it from her and let's see what she's been hiding all this time."

Something about this idea made Ernest uncomfortable. "I don't know . . ." he said.

"Well, why not? She could be working for God only knows who, compromising who knows what. Either you take that book from her and figure out what she's up to or you drag her out of there kicking and screaming so I can question her in person. That's always been my preference anyway."

Ernest gave him a look. Whenever Jack was presented with two options, he nearly always opted for the more violent one.

"We're not doing that," he said firmly.

"Then we need the book." Jack cocked an eyebrow. "Unless of course you'd rather I take you off the case? I'm more than happy to give it to someone else if you're not willing."

"No," Ernest said at once. "I'll take care of it."

"Excellent. Now go get 'em, soldier." Jack gave him a mock salute and sent him on his way.

Ernest thought about the German girl all night that night, staying up late to pace the hall of his DC apartment. He couldn't sleep, thinking about what it would be like to be stuck in a place like the time space. He himself couldn't stand more than a few hours at most without contracting a splitting headache and an acute case of claustrophobia. The silence and stillness, not to mention the close quarters, were positively maddening. How had she not gone crazy with loneliness?

For all he knew, she was lying about all of it. She could be a Russian agent. Or a German spy who had been forgotten when the war ended. He wanted to believe it, but deep down he knew it wasn't true. She looked about his age, twenty-two, or maybe a little younger, which wouldn't make her old enough to have gotten wrapped up in something like that.

Restless from pacing, he went to the kitchen to brew himself a cup of coffee. He stood by the sink as the coffee bubbled on the stove, staring vacantly at the brick wall opposite. The apartment he lived in while he was in DC was the same kind his fellow agents stayed in. An old building, furnished with simple furniture. Nothing particularly upscale or impressive. His mother had visited it once and then never again, lamenting to him that he could do better. They certainly had the money to fix him up someplace nicer, she told him. He should buy a house if he insisted on staying in DC so much. But Ernest didn't want that. If the agents from Brooklyn and Chicago could manage without such luxuries, then so could he.

His family did have money. A great deal of it in fact. They were the descendants of Swiss watchmakers who had made their fortune selling luxury timepieces in Europe before emigrating to the United States. His father had sold that business when he founded the TRP, and Ernest still missed the sound of watches ticking away in the workshop while an army of watchmakers worked magic to bring them to life.

When the coffee was finished, he poured himself a cup and sat down at the table. He couldn't get the girl's face out of his head. She was haunting him like a ghost. Like a memory. He pictured her as he'd seen her most often; from a distance, hunched over on the ground, tending to burned pages with gentle hands, a loving glow radiating in her eyes. He didn't think a spy of any nationality would look at the pages like that. To the timekeepers who doubled as agents, memories were just another part of the job. Another piece in the political game they were all forced to play for and against each other. She wasn't like them. There was real conviction in her voice when she spoke about the memories that wouldn't be there if she was simply carrying out an order.

A part of him wished he had never told Jack about her. He should have waited. Jack was too quick to take action.

"Always better to be the one shooting rather than the one getting shot," he said.

As a solider, Ernest was usually inclined to agree. The problem was that, when it came to the German girl, the idea of shooting at her, or of her shooting at him for that matter, did strange things to his stomach.

THE NEXT time Lisavet saw Ernest, something was different. He followed her from a distance, as he had been lately, but the way he watched her had changed. Curiosity replaced by the kind of look Lisavet saw in the eyes of all the hunters throughout history. She was being tracked. Observed. Hunted. Instead of terrifying her, this realization made her angry. Who was he to try and stop her? She wasn't like him; sometimes she wasn't even sure she was human. She was composed of all the memories she had seen, all the eras she had walked through. She was oceans and mountains and endless skies. And what was he? A man self-contained into a single strand of a life. She was eons. Light-years. He was a passing age, nothing more. Why should she be afraid of him?

Instead of running from him, she let him get closer as she lay in wait to salvage another set of memories. She shot him a glare before homing her attention in on the middle-aged Russian timekeeper in front of her.

The man was taking his time, and Lisavet could sense Ernest moving in her periphery. Preparing, not to grab the burning memories before she could reach them, but to capture *her*. As the timekeeper struck a match and tore off the cover of the book, she crouched low, holding her breath, waiting for him to drop it.

The instant the Russian started to leave, she lurched out from behind the shelves and sprinted. Behind her, Ernest cursed under his breath. The sound of her footsteps made the Russian timekeeper stop. He turned back. Saw her coming. He shouted something as she scooped the burning book off the floor with one gloved hand and turned on her heel, running back down the row.

A loud bang went off behind her. A bullet whizzed over her head, so close she felt the wind brush against her hair.

Another bang and then something large and solid struck her hard from behind. Lisavet crashed to the ground, landing on the smoldering book. Something, or rather someone, landed on top of her. She twisted around, expecting to see the Russian, but instead found herself trapped beneath Ernest's body, his arms creating a cage around her. He reached for his belt and pulled out a gun, raising himself up enough to return three shots at the Russian. The timekeeper retreated, disappearing through a door.

Lisavet let out a gasp. Ernest lowered his gun, slumping against her.

"You okay?" he asked through gritted teeth. "He didn't get you, did he?"

Lisavet shook her head, speechless.

Ernest's face was pale, drained of all color. He rolled off her, an action that seemed to require incredible effort. He pressed one hand against his side and came away with blood.

"You've been shot!" Lisavet exclaimed.

"Seems that way." He let out a ragged breath and tried to reach for his watch.

"What are you doing?"

"Have to get back." He tried to stand, wincing and gasping, but collapsed back onto the ground.

"Don't move, you'll bleed to death," Lisavet said, feeling a little nauseous.

"If I stay here, I'll bleed to death anyway," Ernest protested, reaching for the nearest shelf to try and gain some leverage.

Lisavet's eyes fell on the books near his bloody hand. An idea struck her, and she reached for one of them, flipping through the pages.

"Oh sure. Now seems like a good time to read," Ernest said.

Lisavet ignored him. She shoved the book back on the shelf and picked up another. This time, she found what she was looking for. She turned back to Ernest, book in hand, and ducked underneath his uninjured side to help him stand. He was heavy. Keeping him steady was a challenge, but hopefully she wouldn't have to for long. She let the book fall open to the page she needed.

"Hold on to me," she said.

"What are you doing?"

"Just trust me."

Ernest conceded, letting go of the shelf and leaning more heavily against her shoulder. Lisavet focused on the echoes of the book and shut her eyes.

They found themselves amid more gunfire. The sudden sound of it in the distance made them both flinch. Ernest let out an agonized groan.

"Stop moving," Lisavet said, struggling to keep her hold on him.

"Where the hell are we?"

Lisavet didn't answer. She scanned the scene for the girl whose memory she knew this was. A war nurse. She found her at the edge of the medical tent, looking out at the battle raging on the horizon as the carts brought wounded soldiers her way.

"Where . . . are we?" Ernest asked again through heavy gasps.

"Inside a memory. I need you to walk. Just a little bit."

"Inside a . . . what are you talking about?"

"We're time walking. I'll explain later."

It took five long minutes to get Ernest into the tent. Lisavet had to fight not to gag on the stench of sweat and rotting flesh. Ernest seemed not to have the same problem, and she remembered that he'd been in a uniform the first time she'd seen him. Maybe he'd experienced things like this before. All around they could hear the moans of the injured intermingling with the sounds of foreign shouting. She lowered him down onto the ground in the corner, uncertain whether he would fall right through a cot. The thought gave her pause. What if everything passed through him? She could touch things inside of a memory, but that didn't mean he could.

"What now?" Ernest asked, sensing her hesitation.

Lisavet knelt down beside him. "This is the Ukrainian war of independence, 1918. They have medical supplies here. Bandages. Medicine. I'm going to take care of your wound."

"You've done this before?"

"No. I brought us here so I could watch them do it first." She gestured to a man lying on a bed a few yards away, groaning loudly as doctors cleaned blood from a gunshot to his leg. Behind him, a nurse prepared a needle and thread.

"Oh, no," Ernest said, his face a sickly green color. "No, no, no. We're not doing that."

Lisavet ignored him and began undoing the buttons of his shirt. The entire left side was already soaked clean through with blood.

Ernest caught hold of her wrist. "What do you think you're doing?"

"I need to take off your shirt so I can see the wound."

Ernest stopped resisting, wincing in agony as she slid his arms through the sleeves. He had begun shaking even though he was glistening with sweat from the effort of walking. She needed to move quickly. She examined the bullet hole. It wasn't deep, but she could see the bullet lodged inside the wound. That was a problem. They would need to take it out. She turned around in search of supplies. She needed to test something on Ernest to make sure it wouldn't pass through him before she went any further. A half-empty bottle of pain medication was perched on a nearby shelf, and she reached for it.

"Can you take this?" she asked.

Ernest tried to grasp the bottle. He could touch it when it was in her hand, but as soon as she let go, it fell through his fingers and hit the floor. "What the . . ." he sputtered in confusion.

Lisavet cursed under her breath. She needed to think. She turned back around to watch as the nurses prepared to remove a bullet from another man's shoulder, assessing what supplies she could use that wouldn't pass through him. Metal tongs she could use so long as she didn't drop them. She had no idea what to do about disinfectant. Bandages wouldn't work. She needed something else. Without thinking about what she was doing, she shrugged off her coat and pulled the blue dress up over her head. Beneath it she still wore the remnants of her childhood nightgown, faded and shrunken as it was. She removed that, too, feeling the cold air hit her skin. She pulled the blue dress back on as quickly as she could and secured her coat around her waist. When she turned back around, Ernest had his eyes fixed pointedly on the ceiling, cheeks tinged pink even in spite of the blood loss.

"What's wrong?" she asked, worried the pain might have gotten worse.

"You could have warned me," he said uncomfortably.

"Warned you?"

"That you were going to . . . you know . . . I could have turned around or something."

Lisavet giggled. Given the circumstances, his embarrassment seemed preposterous. After a moment, he too cracked a smile.

"Glad my discomfort is amusing to you."

Lisavet began tearing her nightdress into long strips, pulling threads from along the hem to use for stitching.

"What's that for?"

"Bandages."

"Why not just use those?" He gestured to the shelf.

Lisavet hesitated. She didn't want to alarm him by saying everything here would fall right out of him if she used it. "We're in Spanish influenza time. There's a shortage of supplies and I don't trust them not to reuse bandages."

"Then why did you bring us here? All the wars in history and you pick the one in the middle of a plague?"

"You're the one who chose to get shot in the Ukrainian section," Lisavet fired back.

"Chose to get shot? I took a bullet for you! What were you doing running out in the open like that?"

"If you hadn't been following me, I wouldn't have done it at all." She handed him a piece of wadded-up fabric that had once been the neckline of her nightgown. "Here. Bite down on this."

He gave her an incredulous look. "Why?"

She lifted a pair of tongs like the ones the nurse was using to remove the bullet. "I'm going to get the bullet out."

"Like hell you are."

"You want to bleed to death? I need to stitch you up and I can't do it if there's a bullet in there."

Behind her, the man with the bullet in his arm started screaming at the most inopportune time.

Ernest's face went even paler. "Oh no. No way, crazy lady. You're not coming anywhere near me."

Lisavet dropped the tongs and held up her hands. "Fine. Die then." She started to walk away.

"Wait!" Ernest called, a little bit choked.

She turned back to look at him, meeting his eyes with unflinching steadiness. After a moment, he put the piece of fabric in his mouth and bit down in compliance. Lisavet broke away from him briefly to watch the nurse, feeling faint as she considered the reality of the situation. This man had just been shot in the stomach. He had taken a bullet for her and was lying in a makeshift medical tent in the middle of a Ukrainian battlefield. And now she was about to attempt to perform the wartime equivalent of abdominal surgery simply by mimicking the actions of a few nearby doctors. It was insane, she knew that. But it was also real. This wasn't a memory, and if she messed this up, the only person in the world who knew she existed was going to die.

She banished these thoughts from her head as she turned back to face Ernest again. He had his eyes closed, teeth clamped over the fabric. In lieu of disinfectant, Lisavet took a small bottle of vodka from the top shelf. She'd seen the nurses giving it to the patients before working on them. She doused her hands in it and then paused, looking at the wound in Ernest's side.

"This might sting a little," she warned and tipped the bottle back into her mouth.

She spit the burning alcohol directly into his wound, hoping it was strong enough to kill anything that might be festering there. Ernest screamed. Lisavet threw herself across his chest to keep him from curling in on himself.

"Don't move!" she said, panicking as blood began flowing more freely again. "Deep breaths. You have to keep your pulse down."

She demonstrated what she meant with long, deep inhales. Ernest's hand was groping the ground for something to hold on to. She grabbed it and squeezed tight while he fought to regain control of the pain. He clung to her hand like a lifeline. When he seemed to be calming, she let go and reached for the tongs. She worked as quickly as she could, but the sound of Ernest's agonized shouts made minutes feel like hours. When at last the bullet was free, Lisavet dropped it onto the ground and let out a gasp. It rolled a little away from them.

"All that for a dime," Ernest said through deep, pained breaths.

Lisavet let out a small laugh of relief. The hardest part was over. Ernest didn't scream while she stitched up his side, mimicking the pattern of the nurse. When she was finished, she secured the makeshift bandages around Ernest's abdomen, double-checking to make sure the stitches were secure.

"Not half bad, Germany," he said with an exhausted smile. His eyes were closed, swimming on the edge of consciousness.

She bit her lip. "Lisavet."

"Huh?"

"My name. It's Lisavet. Lisavet Levy."

"Lisavet. Pretty. It's French?"

"My mother was from Switzerland," she said.

Ernest made a humming noise. "So was my grandfather. And Levy . . . that's Jewish."

"Where does the name Ernest come from?"

"Oh, you know. As in 'the importance of being.' My mother is a big Oscar Wilde fan."

"Go to sleep," she said gently. "I'll take us somewhere where you can rest."

"Lisavet," he murmured again. Her name was the last thing on his mind before he slipped into dreams.

ERNEST AWOKE in a place he had never seen before. He blinked several times, adjusting to the lightening dawn streaming in from the open window. There was a tightness in his rib cage. An aching pain radiated down one side of his body. He pushed through it, forcing himself into a seated position with a soldier's determination. When he had managed this, he performed a cursory assessment of his condition. The stitches were holding firm, no more bleeding. His shirt was gone, and he wasn't sure what had happened to his gun. But the watch was still fixed to his wrist, safe and sound. In lieu of a blanket, a worn brown coat was draped over him. He recognized it as the one the German girl wore.

Lisavet, he thought to himself. The entire time he'd been tailing her, trying to gain intel for the department, he hadn't known her name. *Lisavet*. It suited her.

Satisfied that he was intact, he turned his attention back to the room. It was a hotel room, simple but comfortable. A four-poster bed. A pink settee beneath the window. The door leading out to a balcony was ajar. This must be where Lisavet had gone. Ernest struggled to his feet as silently as possible, using the walls, which were the only things he seemed able to touch, to brace himself. He took the coat in one hand and hobbled in the direction of the balcony.

Lisavet didn't notice him right away. She was standing with her arms folded on the railing. Her blue dress swayed in the breeze, the sleeves of it stained with his blood. The rising sun was striking her at just the right angle to bathe her in a halo of golden light. Ernest had never noticed how long her hair was before. She wore it loose, spilling down her back like flaxen wheat. Suddenly, unexpectedly, he found himself completely dumbstruck at the sight of her, unable to move or form proper thoughts. *Must be the blood loss*, he told himself. A moment later, she turned her head.

"Oh. You're awake." She swiped at her eyes with one hand. Had she been crying? "Are your stitches okay?"

"They're holding." Ernest took another laborious step out onto the balcony to stand beside her. "Where are we?" he asked, looking out at the street below. His eyes swept up and down the cobbled road and narrow alleys across the way. In the distance, opposite to the rising sun, snow-capped mountains stood like a wall over the city.

Lisavet turned back to the railing. "Geneva."

"Switzerland?"

She nodded. "1922."

Right. Another memory.

"How'd we get here?"

The sections for Switzerland and Ukraine weren't exactly close to-gether in the time space and he couldn't imagine this girl, who barely hit his midchest in height, carrying his unconscious form all the way there.

"It's one of my father's memories. From the book."

Ernest's eyes slid to the railing beside her. The thick leather-bound book of stolen memories sat just a few inches away from her arm. For the briefest moment, he remembered that he was a US agent with an objective from his superiors to confiscate the book. It was right there. All he had to do was reach for it. But then the breeze lifted Lisavet's hair away from her face and Ernest noticed the tearstains painted across her cheeks. She *had* been crying. He leaned against the railing beside her, using the corner to prop himself up.

"And which memory is it that we're watching?" he asked softly.

Lisavet pointed down to the street below. Two people sat next to each other at a table in the open air. A waiter was serving them coffee. The man looked nothing like Lisavet with his dark hair and glasses. The woman, however, was the spitting image.

"This is my parents' first date. They met yesterday outside the watch-makers' academy down the street. My mother lives just two blocks in the other direction. He asked her to dinner, and they had drinks." She swal-lowed and Ernest got the sense that she was holding back more tears. "They stayed out all night right here in this little square, and now they're getting breakfast together."

Ernest looked back down at the two smiling faces. Full of love, even so soon after meeting. "Do you come here a lot?"

"Sometimes. It's ... the oldest memory I have of his. Everything that came before ... his childhood, his life before this moment ... It's all burned."

Ernest didn't know what to say. He glanced sidelong at the book.

Lisavet began speaking again but it was like she was talking to herself instead of him. "My father always told the story of how they met differently. He said my mother's dress was blue, and that they drank tea. But in the actual memory, she's wearing red and they're drinking coffee. And my father used to say that the sunrise on that morning was the most beautiful the sky had ever been. But I'm looking at it, and it isn't."

Ernest looked at the sunrise again, half hidden behind Lisavet's golden hair. *It was beautiful*, he thought. But would he still think that if she weren't the one standing in it? He shook himself. He really had lost too much blood.

"Maybe it was," he said. "To him, maybe having your mother there made it that way."

"That's the problem, though, isn't it? People don't remember things the same way. Is it even possible for us to remember something as it truly happened? A memory, once it's over, is never exactly what it was when it was happening. Whatever comes later changes the meaning of it. Even if no timekeepers come along to destroy it."

"That's called nostalgia," Ernest said, ignoring her commentary about timekeepers. He was already well aware of what she thought of him.

"It's called misremembering. It's not the truth."

"And that bothers you?"

"Yes. I don't just want to remember things. I want to know what really happened. I want to know what it was like to actually be there. And the only way to do that is to see everything. Everybody's version of reality. How else will I know what it was really like?"

Ernest chewed on this for a moment. "Is that why you try so hard to stop the timekeepers from burning memories?"

"I guess that's part of it."

"And the other part?"

Lisavet placed a hand on top of the book and pulled it toward them, opening it up to show him. Ernest could hear the whispers between the pages, calling out to them both.

"When I first started saving memories, I was mostly taking them from the Nazis. That's what's in the first half of the book. I've walked through all of them hundreds of times to see why someone might want to destroy these memories, but I can't. So little of what the timekeepers are destroying is anything dangerous. Little moments. Tiny conversations. Civilian lives that contradicted what the Nazi Party was trying to do. It made me think . . . if even simple memories are so important that someone would try to destroy them . . . then maybe wasting any of them is a mistake. Maybe they're actually the most precious thing we have. And besides. What gives someone the right to decide what stays?"

"History is written by the victors," Ernest quoted, just loud enough for Lisavet to hear him.

She turned her eyes on him. Not angry, but close to it. "You say that now. But what happens if one day someone else wins? What if they decide to erase your father's memories? Like they tried to erase mine?"

"I suppose I wouldn't like it."

Lisavet bit her lip, head shaking. "But that's just it. You wouldn't even know it had happened. Your life would rearrange itself around his memory."

Ernest watched her face, transfixed as she ran one hand over the pages of the book. How was he supposed to take it from her now? There was an ache in her eyes, in every part of her being, and he was suddenly struck by the overwhelming desire to pull her into his arms. If it hadn't been for the hole in his side, he might have. Lisavet let out a sigh and turned her attention back to the couple as they got up from the table.

"The memory is ending," she said wistfully as she closed the book. "Are you strong enough to go back?"

Ernest nodded. She started to turn away and he reached for her before she could, taking her hand in his. Her eyes, when she turned them on him, made his knees go weak.

"Thank you," he said. "For stitching me up."

She gave him a half smile, the corners of her mouth barely lifting. "Thank *you*. For taking a bullet for me."

He noticed that she didn't thank him for saving her life. She didn't see it that way. They looked at each other and Ernest wished he could stop time, just for a moment. But the world around them was fading at the edges, blurring back into shadows and darkness.

"Can I see you again?" he asked as the last of the sunrise began to crack. "Like this, I mean."

Lisavet's eyes seemed to brighten. More beautiful than ever.

"You know where to find me," she said.

Their hands slid apart as the memory vanished and Lisavet was gone, walking away from him into the depths of the time space. Ernest stood still, savoring the phantom feeling of her touch long after she had gone from him.

6

1965, Boston, Massachusetts

AMELIA WAS QUIET ALL through dinner. They were having soup that night, as they had both other nights since Moira had appeared in her life. Amelia got the sense that she wasn't a very skilled cook. If she'd had the energy, Amelia might have complained about it, but a bone-deep weariness had set in, and it was all she could do to lift the spoon to her mouth and swallow.

"It's normal," Moira said after ten minutes of pure silence between them.

"What is?"

"Feeling foggy after you've been in the time space. Your consciousness is used to experiencing only one temporal reality and you've just forced it into a different one. It goes away after a night of sleep."

"Oh," Amelia said, dipping her spoon back into the bowl.

"Did everything go all right in there? You seem on edge."

"Well, maybe that's because someone pushed me out a window today."

Moira's eyes slid to her and then back to her bowl. "I'm sorry for that. I lost my temper. There's a lot riding on you finding the book and if we don't—"

"Yes, yes, the world as we know it will fall to pieces. I get it," Amelia said sharply. She didn't want excuses, she just wanted for all this to be over.

They ate in silence for a while. Amelia rubbed her arms to fight off the pervasive chill.

"Feeling cold is normal too," Moira said. "Hot baths help. If you want me to, I can draw one for you after dinner."

"No thanks."

"Are you sure? The first time is always . . ."

"I don't need you to take care of me!" Amelia snapped, throwing down her spoon. "You're not my mother, so just leave me alone!"

Moira let out an exasperated sigh and pushed back from the table. "Fine. Have it your way. We're going on a little outing tomorrow to visit a colleague of your uncle's, so be ready to go by ten a.m."

"An outing? What colleague?"

"Ten a.m.," Moira repeated. She picked up her bowl and dropped it into the sink before leaving the room.

Amelia heard the door to the first-floor guest room open and shut. She left her bowl on the table and went up to her room, slamming her own door behind her. She hugged her arms to her chest, feeling a chill settle deep into her body. *A bath* would *be nice*, she thought begrudgingly. She climbed into bed without changing out of her clothes. The hot ache of tears was building behind her eyes, but she refused to cry. As tired as she was, she couldn't sleep. Every time she closed her eyes, they popped back open. After an hour of this, she sat up and turned on the light. The house was silent. Moira must have gone to bed. Amelia reached for her backpack on the bedpost and took out the three poetry books Moira had left for her. She surveyed the covers and then selected the thickest one. *Aurora Leigh*, by Elizabeth Barrett Browning. Nestling back into the pillows, Amelia began to read until her mind quieted and she slipped into sleep with the book still propped up in her hands.

ON THEIR way into the city, Moira smoked *a lot*. Amelia kept count in her head, realizing that this was the first time she'd ever seen Moira nervous.

"So. Who is this person?" she asked.

"His name is James Gravel. He's a timekeeper."

"He works for the department too?"

Moira blew smoke out the window and tossed the butt out after it. "No. Not all timekeepers work for the government. There are a few who operate independently, using watches passed down over generations."

"But my uncle knew him?" Amelia noticed that Moira's shoulders tensed, her hands gripping the wheel of the Cadillac more tightly.

"Yes. He was in contact with James, just as he was with most of the other American timekeepers. He tried to recruit him once but . . . it didn't work out."

"Why not?"

Moira took a long time to answer her this time. She dug in her purse and lit another cigarette, steering the car with her knee. "James has a different ideology regarding the time space."

Amelia could tell there was something she wasn't saying, but she didn't know the right questions to ask. And she really wanted Moira to stop smoking. She sat back and looked out the window. When they exited the highway, Amelia sat up a little straighter. The buildings in this part of Boston were not as well kept. Peeling paint on the doors. Cracked sidewalks. Windows missing their shutters or curtains or, in some cases, glass.

"Where are we?" she asked.

Moira turned the car down a street lined with crowded brownstones and shop windows and said, "West side."

They parked in front of a pawnshop. There was black iron caging in the windows, protecting a stash of jewelry and old collectors' items.

Moira turned off the car and Amelia started to unbuckle her seat belt. Moira didn't move.

"Amelia . . . Perhaps I should warn you. Your uncle was on good terms with James but that doesn't mean all of us are."

"Oh. Are you?"

"No. In fact, I'm afraid it's rather the opposite. He and I . . . well, the department believes he is a part of the rebellion I told you about. I've been investigating him for over a year now."

Amelia looked at the pawnshop and then back at Moira. "Does he know we're coming?"

"No, he doesn't."

Encountering Moira at all was a jarring experience, but encountering her without any kind of warning, the way she herself had . . . well, that didn't feel like the wisest of decisions. They got out of the car, stepping into cool October sunshine. Moira showed no trace of nervousness now; in its place was the sharp, intimidating demeanor Amelia was more accustomed to. Eyes scanning, head held high in a manner that was almost regal. Demanding authority. She had dressed the part, too, wearing a long black coat and heels sharper than knives. Her lipstick was a deep, dangerous red.

On the steps of the building next door, two elderly men with knobbed knees and tufts of gray hair eyed them from the stoop. Amelia recognized them immediately as retired busybodies who made it their business to know exactly what was going on in the neighborhood. Their eyes glossed over Amelia, seeming to find her misplaced but nonthreatening. Moira, on the other hand . . . her they scrutinized heavily. It was clear that they recognized her, or at least knew her type, and could smell the trouble she was bringing a mile away.

"Good morning, gentlemen," Moira said, starting for the shop.

"Shop's closed on Sundays," the younger one said sharply. "Come back later."

"He's got the kids home," the older one added as if that might deter her.

Moira's lips curled. "That's all right. We're just here for a chat."

The two old men exchanged glances. Amelia followed Moira down a set of steps that dipped below the sidewalk beneath the shop.

"Are you sure we shouldn't just . . ."

Moira shushed her. "Don't worry, he'll see us."

She knocked on the door loudly and stepped back. Moments later, a woman answered, holding a small boy in her arms. She kept the chain on the door, peering out through the crack cautiously.

"Yes?"

"You must be Edith," Moira said in a honey-sweet voice. "My name is Moira Donnelly. I'm here to see your husband."

Recognition flickered in Edith's eyes. "Is he expecting you?"

"I'm afraid not. We're here to ask a few questions about the murder of Ernest Duquesne."

Moira slipped a hand into her coat pocket and withdrew a badge. Amelia was almost as surprised as Edith by its appearance. The little boy in Edith's arms began fussing and she moved him out of the line of sight.

"One moment," she said.

The door closed and there was a sound of the chain being removed before it opened to let them in. She told them to wait and went into the next room. Inside, the apartment was cramped but immaculately clean, containing two rooms and a small galley kitchen at the back. Amelia could hear hushed voices in the next room. The door opened.

James Gravel was a tall man, with dark skin and tightly coiled hair. His face carried a certain heaviness to it as he surveyed the two of them standing in his living room. He was not wearing a watch, but Amelia got the sense that this was intentional. Something seen was something that could be taken.

"Hello, Mr. Gravel," Moira said, giving him one of her conniving smiles. "Nice to see you."

"Your boys were already here last week," James said coldly. "I already told them I don't know anything about what happened to Ernest."

"Yes, I know. But unfortunately none of us believe you. Seeing as you were the last person to see him alive."

Amelia let out a small gasp. The sound drew James's attention to her.

"Who's this? Did Jack get tired of trying to indoctrinate the rest of us and start recruiting kids instead?"

"This is Amelia. She's Ernest's niece," Moira said, putting a hand on her shoulder.

James gave Amelia a look that was half bewildered, half angry. "That's real messed up," he said, glaring accusingly at Moira. "You're dragging her into this too?"

"Ernest left his watch to her," Moira said with a shrug. "He wanted her involved in this."

"Bullshit," James scoffed.

"You don't have to believe me, James. I'm not here to try and extort you for information."

"That's a first," he muttered under his breath.

Moira's arm slid from Amelia's shoulder to her waist, holding her in a half embrace. "Mr. Gravel, a man was murdered in the time space by a Russian timekeeper. Something like that is bigger than whatever beef you have with the department. You've made it clear you won't cooperate with us. But perhaps you'll set aside your prejudices long enough to help Ernest's niece." She pressed a hand between Amelia's shoulder blades, propelling her forward. "Amelia has no role in this petty feud between the department and the rebels, but if you don't talk to her ... if you don't tell her what you know about how and why Ernest Duquesne was killed ... then you're sending a child into a gunfight without a weapon."

James's eyes followed Moira out the door. As it clicked behind her, Amelia felt her heartbeat pulsing in her throat. For a moment, James stood still. Then he let out a breath that might have been a laugh and passed a tired hand over his face.

"My god, that woman is a real piece of work." His body released some of the tension he'd been holding, and he leaned against the wall. "Your uncle really left you that watch?"

Amelia nodded, swallowing hard.

"And they let you keep it?"

"Well. I wasn't supposed to wind it, but I did it anyway and so—" She broke off, hoping he'd figure out the rest.

To her surprise, he chuckled. "Ernest always did say you were a troublemaker." He said it with a levity and fondness that surprised her.

"So you knew my uncle?" she asked.

"Uh-huh." James went over to the window and pulled aside the curtains to look out, tracking Moira's movements. "I was real sorry to hear that he was gone."

There was a creaking sound as the door to the bedroom opened. Two small, curious faces appeared briefly before Edith shut it. A little girl and boy, maybe five years old.

Amelia looked back at James. "Is it true what she said? Were you really the last person to see him alive?"

He eyed her steadily, tapping his knuckles against his arm. "Look, I don't know what to tell you. He came here, yes, but whether I was the last to see him is up for debate. My guess is that the department figured out that he stopped by and are just using it as another way to harass me. I've been on their list for a long time now."

"Because you . . ." How had Moira put it? "Believe in a different ideology?"

James snorted. "Is that what they call it? I guess you could say we have different ideologies. Different ideas of what's right and what isn't."

"And they don't like you because you have a different idea of what's right?"

"They don't like me because I'm a Black man who refused to give up his watch or join their cause. Because I work to preserve the memories of *my* people, not theirs. Slaves and civil rights victims and the like. People they would sooner leave out of history altogether because they don't like what our memories say about them. They think I'm one of the rebels that have popped up these past few years, but I'm not. I'm not trying to disrupt anything, just trying to keep our version of the story alive." He glanced out the window one final time before stepping away from it at last. "So what has she got you wrapped up in this for anyway?"

Amelia shifted a little on her feet, wondering how much to say. "She wants me to find a book that my uncle was looking for. She said it's blue with a flower stamped in the center. Have you heard of it?"

She couldn't help but feel hopeful. That maybe he would just tell her where it was, and all this could be over. But then she saw his eyes glaze over in a dark, distant sort of way.

"Yeah, I've heard of it," he said cautiously.

"Do you know where it is?" she pressed.

"I'm afraid I can't help you with that," James said at once. "The book is missing. Has been for years. What's she want with it anyway?"

Amelia gave a half shrug. "She said there are stolen memories in it."

"Stolen, huh?" James said, more to himself than to her. "That's rich."

Amelia frowned at him. "Well . . . if they aren't stolen, how did they end up in the book?"

James began rubbing the back of his neck, fighting himself with each word he put forth. "Have they told you anything about someone named Lisavet Levy?"

Amelia shook her head. "Who's she?"

James took so long to answer that she was afraid he was going to ignore her question. At last, he sighed, resigning himself to whatever consequences might come from telling her all this.

"She was a Jewish girl who lived in the time space back in the forties."

Amelia's eyes went wide. "*Lived* in the time space?"

"Uh-huh. Her father was a clockmaker who made timekeeper de-vices for different government entities. His family had been doing it for generations. Which of course made him a target of the Nazi Party when they caught wind of him. They came for him on Kristallnacht, and he hid Lisavet in the time space to keep her out of harm's way. He died shortly thereafter after he refused to make new watches for them, and she was stuck."

"For how long?"

"No one is sure exactly. At least ten years, maybe longer."

Ten years. Amelia couldn't imagine what that must be like. "And what does she have to do with my uncle?"

"As she got older, she started interfering with some of the work the timekeepers were doing."

"Interfering how?"

"That's complicated. Governments try to regulate what gets remem-bered in the time space. Sometimes they destroy things that they deem as dangerous. They burn memories. Lisavet Levy tried to save them. Kept 'em all in this book she carried around with her. The one they've got you searching for."

Amelia straightened up. Timekeepers *burned* memories?

James continued. "It wasn't until 1946 that anyone even knew she was there. Ernest is the one who discovered her. It was his job to try and stop her from interfering with the US timekeepers. Eventually, other groups learned what she was doing, and she became a target, not just for the CIA, but for the Russians, the British, and just about any gov-ernment group with a stake in the game. Then suddenly, she vanished from the time space sometime around 1952. She disappeared, but the ideas she sparked didn't. Ever since then there are timekeepers who have been carrying the torch that Lisavet Levy lit all those years ago. Trying to salvage what people like Moira Donnelly and that boss of hers, Jack

Dillinger, want to destroy. That's what they mean when they talk about rebels. It's just a blanket term they use for anyone who doesn't believe in their grand vision of what the past should be."

Based on the way that James was talking, Amelia wasn't sure she entirely believed his assertion that he wasn't involved.

"What happened to the book when she disappeared?"

"Odds are she hid it somewhere," James admitted. "Hid it good too. People have been looking for over a decade."

"And Lisavet Levy? What happened to her?"

"Nobody knows. At least nobody who will admit to it. It was covered up, you see. One day, everyone just stopped talking about her, your uncle included. I asked Ernest about her once, when we got a little bit more comfortable with each other and he acted like he had no idea who or what I was talking about. But somebody knows what happened. If I had to guess, I'd say that woman you came here with does."

"Moira?"

James nodded. "I only heard things through the grapevine at the time, so this is all speculation. Back then, even I knew that the person who would take over Jack Dillinger's director role if and when he moved out of it was supposed to be your uncle. Then Lisavet Levy started interfering with things, and circumstances changed real quick. I got the sense that Ernest was at risk of losing his job over it. Then, five years later, when Jack finally got promoted . . . Moira Donnelly got his old job. Before that, she was just a secretary. No college education, no previous experience. And all of a sudden, *she's* the director of the whole damn department."

"I thought that was because Uncle Ernest took a different job. In timekeeper relations."

James shrugged. "Maybe. Or maybe not. Either way, suddenly the son of the TRP's founder is in another department and a secretary with only five years' tenure is director of a major branch of the CIA. Stuff like that doesn't just happen. I'm not one to gamble, but I'd wager my shop, the mortgage, and all three of my children on the odds that Moira Donnelly played some kind of role in what really happened to Lisavet Levy. I'd bet it's what got her that job." He suddenly moved away from the window, coming closer. "I really have no idea what happened to your uncle. I wish I did. When he stopped by to see me last, he was just passing through the neighborhood on his way to New York. Said he needed to go there to pay a visit to someone about some things that had gone down at the department that he wasn't okay with."

"Things? What things?"

"I don't know. He wouldn't say. But the thing is . . . he was going to see *her*." James jerked his thumb in the direction of the window.

"He went to see . . ." Amelia broke off, the name sticking in her mouth.

James responded, but Amelia didn't need the confirmation to know he meant Moira. *Moira* was the last person to see her uncle alive. He had gone into the city to see her and had never come back. What if he hadn't died in the time space at all?

"I don't know what the hell they're thinking dragging you into all this. The conflicts brewing in the time space are serious. Not a place for a kid," James said heavily. "But what I can tell you is that I don't think the rebels have anything to do with it. It's just as likely that the department concocted that story themselves, so they'd have an excuse to get you involved."

"But why would they want me to be involved?"

"I don't pretend to understand their logic." He paused, glancing at the door as if expecting Moira to burst through it at any moment. "Look . . . If you ever need anything . . . help or a place to hide . . . look for the time-keepers with blue flowers. They're the ones you can trust."

"Blue flowers?" Amelia asked.

"Forget-me-nots for Lisavet Levy. Tell them that you're Ernest's niece, and they'll help you."

Forget-me-nots for Lisavet Levy. A symbol of the rebels? She thought of the book again. Blue leather with the five-petaled flower pressed on the front. Like a forget-me-not. Amelia's hands were shaking, and she shoved them into the pockets of her coat. Something cool and smooth to the touch met her fingers and she pulled it out, frowning down at it. It was silver and circular and fit easily into the palm of her hand. But she didn't recognize it.

"What is that?" James asked abruptly.

When Amelia looked at him, his face was dark.

"I don't know. I've never seen it before."

"Bullshit," he said. Instantly he was as he had been. Cold and aloof. All traces of sympathy or friendliness gone. "That's a transmitter. She's listening, isn't she?"

His eyes flew to the bedroom door where his children and wife were hiding. Fear shone on his face. Suddenly Amelia remembered Moira's comforting half embrace, a strange gesture, in retrospect. Moira had planted this.

"What have you done?" James murmured, as much to himself as to her.

"I didn't know. I swear, I didn't know."

Moira's voice sounded from the doorway. "It's all right, Amelia," she said, stepping into the apartment.

James crossed the room in seconds. "You set this up," he growled.

"Of course I did. And clearly I made the right decision. The rebels wear blue flowers, you said? That's interesting." She gestured to Amelia. "Come on, Amelia. It's time to go."

She turned toward the door and James suddenly slammed his hand against it, holding it shut. Amelia's throat constricted.

"Please . . ." he said desperately. "Don't do this."

Moira slid one hand into her coat. "Mr. Gravel, step aside."

"If you think I'm just going to let you . . ."

There was a click and a rattling noise and then Moira raised a silver revolver to the underside of James's chin. Like the badge, Amelia had not known she was carrying it.

"Excuse us," she said calmly, tapping two fingers against the door.

James hesitated, his eyes darting from Moira to the bedroom door and back again. At last, he dropped his arm and stepped aside. Amelia felt his eyes trained on the back of her head long after the door closed behind them. Her heart thudded as Moira unlocked the car and motioned for her to get in. Only when Moira had started the engine and shifted the gears into drive did she put the gun away.

MOIRA COULD feel Amelia's anger pulsing in the air. Building steam. She cursed Jack in her head. Damn him. If it hadn't been for his impatience, they wouldn't be in this situation. He had to have known this would happen. That James would say or do something to sow the seeds of doubt in Amelia's head and derail everything. She kept driving, pulling onto the highway. Her eyes gravitated to the cassette recorder in the back seat. Evidence that James Gravel was in fact affiliated with the growing movement of rebels. Rebels who could be identified by the forget-me-not insignia they carried on their person. All in the name of Lisavet Levy. She thought about the other things that James had said. There were things on that tape that Jack didn't know about. Things that might make him question her loyalty.

She veered off course, taking the exit south toward Providence.

"Where are we going?" Amelia asked at once.

"You'll see."

Ten minutes later, they reached an old wooden bridge over the river. Moira stopped the car right in the middle.

"Where are we?"

Moira didn't answer. She turned the car off and reached into the back seat. She removed the cassette from the tape deck and held it out to Amelia.

"Here."

Amelia stared at it. At her.

"Go ahead," Moira said, extending it farther. "Get rid of it. I'll tell Jack the mic malfunctioned. It's new technology anyway; he'll believe me."

"You mean . . . you won't . . . tell him?"

"We'll tell him that James was telling the truth. That he doesn't know what happened to Ernest."

Amelia hesitantly took the tape, holding it between two fingers. "What about everything else? About the flowers and . . ."

Moira reached into her coat and pulled out a cigarette and a lighter. "If we tell Jack about the flowers, he'll send people in after James. They'll kill him. His wife and children will lose a husband and a father. And then he'll start using the intel to hunt down every other rebel he can and do the same to them. Whether or not that happens . . . that's up to you." She nodded at the tape.

Amelia made a noise of confusion. "I don't understand. Why did you take me there? Why would you plant that mic if you're just going to let me destroy the tape?"

Moira lit the cigarette and took a long, deep breath, shutting her eyes so she could think. "It wasn't my idea."

"Was it Jack Dillinger's idea?"

Moira instantly disliked the way his name sounded coming out of Amelia's mouth.

"Yes. He wanted to see what James might tell you. He suspects that James might have been involved in Ernest's death. That maybe he's the one who's been allying himself with the Russians."

"But you don't think that?"

"I think we can both agree that he's far too disagreeable to be forging any kind of secret alliance with another country. As for the part about your uncle . . . no, I don't believe he was involved in that."

"What makes you so certain?" Amelia asked.

"Intuition."

"That's not a real reason."

"Maybe not. But it is my reason." Moira took another pull from the cigarette and let out a long, loud exhale. "Here's our predicament, Amelia. I *did* see your uncle the night he died. But Jack doesn't know that." She met Amelia's gaze and held it.

"H-he doesn't?"

"No. And it's best for everyone if he never finds out."

"But . . . why? Why were you meeting with him?"

"I can't tell you that. Which is why I called this a predicament."

"I don't understand."

"I know. I know. But I need you to trust me on this. Ask me anything else, and I'll answer. Just not about that. Okay?"

Amelia was quiet, scrutinizing her. Trying to decide whether or not to believe her. "What about the rest of the things James said about you? The disappearance of Lisavet Levy? Were you involved in that?"

Moira liked hearing *that* name come out of Amelia's mouth even less.

"If you consider the timing just for a moment, you'll have your answer. James said that Lisavet Levy disappeared from the time space in 1952. I didn't begin working for Jack until 1955. How could I have had anything to do with what happened to her?"

"But do you know what happened?"

Moira looked away, past Amelia and out the car window. "I don't. Those files have been sealed for years."

"Does Jack know?"

"He might. Probably."

"You don't like Jack that much, do you?"

Moira had to bite back a smile. "Not particularly, no."

"Then why do you work for him?"

Moira's first instinct was to give Amelia a small lecture about the world and a woman's role in it, but refrained, opting for a less pedantic, albeit uncomfortably personal version of things.

"What James said about the abnormal trajectory of my career is true. I was just a secretary before I got promoted, and before that I was nobody. Jack was the first person who saw something in me worth taking a chance on. Before him, the life laid out before me was a bleak one. So though I may not always like him . . . he is the reason I've gotten to where I am."

Moira could tell that Amelia was too young to fully understand the logic of this. The doubt in her eyes was tilting in both directions. She believed nothing and no one. Trusted no one. Not James, and most certainly not her.

"I understand why you might not want to believe me," Moira said at last. "But even if you don't, I need you to trust me. I need you to trust that I'm keeping the truth away from Jack for a reason. So do us both a favor, me and James Gravel, and get rid of that tape."

They stared at each other, listening to the sound of the river outside the car. After a time, Amelia got out, clutching the tape in one hand. Moira watched her cross to the side of the bridge and throw the tape over the railing. They were silent all the way home.

7

1948, Somewhere in the Time Space

IT TOOK FOUR MONTHS before Ernest admitted that he was falling in love with Lisavet Levy. In that time, he saw her at least once a week, meeting her between the shelves so she could sweep them away somewhere else. Lately, they met almost every day. Over time, he had become aware of the strange harmony of her world. The memories she visited most often. The eras in which she felt most at home.

His previous assumptions that she must be lonely were proven false. Hers was a life more full than any he'd seen before. Years of walking through time had cultivated her into a woman of endless knowledge and incalculable wisdom. She hadn't been to a proper school in a decade and yet she knew more than most of the academics who worked with Ernest in the department. She had learned the languages of half a dozen countries: English, French, Russian, Arabic. She had mastered history, of course, but she also knew math and science and could sense the interconnected strands of everyday things with remarkable intuition. She was, in Ernest's eyes, a wonder. A small piece of perfection. When he finally recognized that he had fallen for her, he wondered why it had taken him so long to notice.

He realized it as he watched her lean down to pick a single rose from a bush in the gardens of Versailles.

"Isn't it beautiful?" Lisavet's cheeks were flushed from the warmth of the sun, and her hair glowed in it like pale moonlight.

He reached out to touch the soft petals, knowing that the moment she let go, he'd no longer be able to. His hand brushed against hers as he did so, sending a bolt of lightning down the length of his spine. When she leaned forward to smell the rose again, he wanted to lean closer. To press their foreheads together, to trace her lips with his thumb the way hers touched the flower petal.

"Red roses are my favorite," she said with a smile. "What's yours?"

You, he wanted to say. But that made absolutely no sense. *Blue*, he considered. Like the dress she wore. Was there such a thing as a blue rose? He couldn't remember.

"White," he said at last, catching sight of some over her shoulder.

She turned to retrieve one and he tried to ignore the feeling welling in his chest. To love her was impossible. It was foolish, knowing who he was and the order he'd been given. He'd been postponing the inevitable, telling Jack that he'd lost track of her. That she'd caught on to the fact that he was following her and had gotten better at hiding. For now, it worked. Jack had other things on his mind, including dealing with the Russian timekeeper who had shot him.

It wouldn't last. Eventually, Jack would get suspicious. He would start demanding the book be taken from her, or perhaps he'd want *her* instead. To continue like this, to let himself get any closer to her, was self-destructive. But the idea of not seeing her was equally unbearable. For the first time since he'd enlisted as a soldier at the age of sixteen, Ernest began to question the legitimacy of the machine in which he was a vital cog. He began to consider what might happen if he chose to break rank.

He watched Lisavet bend down to pick one of the white roses, noticing the way she chose only those flowers that looked to be on the verge of wilting.

"Have you always been able to touch things in memories?" he asked as she held the white rose up to him.

"Not always. Just for the past four years or so."

"Did something change four years ago?"

"Not that I know of. Azrael doesn't understand why it happened either. For a while I worried that—" She broke off, shaking her head.

"Worried what?"

"I worried that maybe it meant that I was dead. Memories go to the time space when they die, but nobody knows what would happen to someone who dies inside of it. I thought maybe I had died and walked right out of my own body without even realizing it."

"But . . . you're not? You're certain?"

"I wasn't for a while. Not until I met you."

"Me? Why me?"

Lisavet reached for his hand and tucked her fingers around his palm. An echo of their first handshake. Ernest's pulse quickened.

"Memories can't touch people. If I were dead, I wouldn't be able to do this."

The idea struck an anxious chord in him. He vowed to find some way to touch her every time they met. Just in case.

That night when Ernest returned home, there was a letter at his front door with a German return address in the left-hand corner. He picked it up right away and stepped into his apartment, bolting the door shut behind him. It had been several weeks since he'd had the idea to write a letter to the old watch shop in Germany to see if he could figure out what had become of Lisavet's father and brother. Moreover, he wanted to know what the world said about the fate of Lisavet Levy herself. If she was remembered and by whom. The letter was disappointing in every regard.

Dear sir,

Apologies for the long delay. The man who you were seeking is not at this address. I have been the owner of this shop since the start of the war and do not know what happened to the family who lived here before me. Public record here in Germany suggests that the clockmaker you mentioned, Ezekiel Levy, was killed on Kristallnacht and the two children were taken to camps. There is record of a boy named Klaus Levy being killed at Auschwitz in 1943, but there is no record of what happened to the girl named Lisavet Levy. It is presumed that she died as well. I am sorry I am not writing to you with better news.

Ernest took the letter to his desk. That was it then. There was no trace of Lisavet Levy left in the real world. He sat down and let the letter fall to one side. It landed among the dozens of other discarded papers. Notes he'd been taking after each visit with Lisavet that noted where they went and any notable things she said. Sketches of her face, drawn haphazardly in the margins. Among the many pages were old letters that had been written to his father from a man who owned a watch shop in Nuremberg: Ezekiel Levy. He'd found them on his last visit to his mother's house, where he had gone on account of his sister. News that she was pregnant had sent his mother into a fit of rage, and Ernest had been trying in vain to convince her to go easy.

In between bouts of arguing, Ernest had hidden in his father's office. That was where he'd found the letters.

Not long before he died, Gregory had commissioned Ezekiel to make a set of five watches for the recently expanded Temporal Reconnaissance Program. The only people who had ever known how to make these kinds of watches resided in Germany and those who still had the skills even then were few and far between. The original school in Glashütte where they were made had been bombed by the Russians in the first war, and those that survived composed the entire Russian arsenal. The remaining watchmakers had been hunted down by Nazis in the decades that followed and forced to make more watches. When the war ended and the Nazis knew they had lost, the watchmakers were killed, their memories burned inside the time space.

Ezekiel had delivered the watches in the early months of 1938 and hadn't written again until August when he'd asked Gregory for help. He had been approached by the Nazis about his work and needed a way out for himself and his two children. Gregory had responded, offering him a job and an apartment in exchange for his services as a watchmaker for the TRP. Things were all set to receive them, but Ezekiel Levy decided to wait for the opportune moment. He waited too long. Now all that remained of him was a few fragments. Scraps of memories, like these letters, that existed only because Lisavet had managed to salvage them. But the rest, including the knowledge of how to make a watch that could bend the folds of Time, was gone.

In addition to the copious notes Ernest took on Lisavet herself, he had begun trying to piece together the mystery of her solidity inside of memories. It troubled him, and long before he'd asked her about it, he'd started theorizing, matching it to the science he'd been taught while training for the TRP. He already knew the foundational theory of the time space. His own father had been the one to connect the dots between its existence and Hermann Minkowski's theory on Time as the fourth dimension of the universe. The forward movement of Time, or the temporal continuum, had been identified as its own separate plane of reality, confirming what timekeepers had already known for centuries: Time was a real place. A spatial plane all its own. Gregory Duquesne had acknowledged this when he founded the TRP, but none of the time-keepers, at least not in Ernest's department, had gone much further than that, writing it off as an act of God.

To fill in the gaps in his knowledge, Ernest attended lectures at universities. He spent hours in the Library of Congress, pulling books on the newly emerging science. Quantum theory in particular caught his attention; the idea that things—particles and atoms and such—could affect each other even though they existed very far away from one another. They could become entangled. Connected despite the fact that they existed on separate planes, such as the time space and the observable plane of existence they knew as "reality." All of it made his head spin, and then he came across a paper which suggested that the conscious mind and the physical body were two entirely separate things. That acts of learning, remembering, processing, or imagining were all distinct acts of consciousness, untethered from physical actions. Here was the missing piece. The two theories together suggested that memory and body could live on two separate planes, one in the time space and one outside of it.

But when both converged on the same location . . . when Lisavet's physical body joined with her conscious thoughts, not just for a short time the way his did, but for years . . . it triggered some kind of anomaly that allowed her to move through memories like one who was really there. The physical and the mental combined into the fourth dimension known as Time.

It began to occur to him that what had happened to Lisavet, after so many years in the time space, was something entirely new. Something he referred to in his head as "temporal departure." A severance of Lisavet's physical form from the dimension of Time. A body and consciousness untethered from her own time and set adrift. What did this mean for the Lisavet of the present day who lived in the time space? And furthermore, what did it mean for her in the future? Was it even possible to remove her as Jack had insinuated they should? Or in doing so, would they be condemning her to a fate worse than death? A separation of body and mind so abrupt that both suffered as a result?

Ernest thought about this each time he submitted a false report to Jack about his progress in obtaining the book. How many more times could he report failure before Jack insisted on bringing her out? The department saw Lisavet Levy as a threat, and Ernest as a means of neutralizing it.

"How often do you see that boy now?"

Lisavet opened her eyes to find Azrael hanging over her while she rested on the floor of the time space. He wore a crease in his brow.

"Not that often," Lisavet lied.

"Lisavet," Azrael said sternly. "I'm dead. Not blind."

She sat up, sighing. "Then why did you ask me? I'm being careful. That's all that matters. You don't have to worry."

"I know you *think* you're being careful. That's why I worry so much. You don't know him very well."

"He won't hurt me," Lisavet said.

"My dear girl, have you learned nothing from your time in the past? Somebody always gets hurt in love."

Lisavet snorted derisively. "Good thing we're not in love then." She pushed herself to her feet and began walking down the row of shelves.

Azrael followed. "You know, in addition to my ability to see, I am also not an idiot."

"We're *not* in love."

"Well, of course *you're* not. You're in denial. It will pass. *He*, however, . . . well, he is entirely smitten with you."

Lisavet could feel herself blushing. "He is not. I'd be able to tell if he was. I've seen so many people in love by now. I know what it looks like."

"You think you do. In other people. But seeing it and experiencing it firsthand are two very different things. Believe me."

"Hmm." Lisavet turned away from him and shrugged. "Well. Sorry to ruin it for you. But Ernest Duquesne is not in love with me. I'm certain of it."

He looked so worried that if Lisavet could have kissed his cheek to reassure him, she would.

She and Ernest *had* been seeing quite a lot of each other. She couldn't help it. He was the first person she'd had contact with in years. The first person who knew her name. And he was kind to her. Curious about her life, before and after she'd entered the time space. She wanted to show it to him. All the parts of history she'd walked through, all the memories she'd seen so many times that they felt like her own. She showed him Paris in the '20s, Renaissance Italy, the mountains of China. She loved watching his face each time she took him someplace new. The way his eyes glowed with wonder, reaching out to touch something only to remember that he couldn't. That light in his eyes, the same one she'd seen in so many people in love, had never once been directed at her. It annoyed her that it bothered her, so she told herself it didn't.

"Have you ever thought about trying to leave?" Ernest asked her one day.

They were in Munich in 1860, where Lisavet and her brother would visit with their grandparents over half a century later. The year outside the time space had lurched onward into 1949, but Lisavet was scarcely aware of it.

"I used to," Lisavet said, leaning back to look up at the autumn leaves over their heads. "But when I first got stuck in the time space, I couldn't be sure which timekeepers were Nazis and which ones weren't."

"Well, there are no Nazis anymore," Ernest pointed out. "And you have me. I could help you leave."

Lisavet's stomach did a little flip at the thought of leaving the time space with Ernest Duquesne. She shook her head. "There's nothing out there for me. Both of my parents are gone. I wouldn't even know where to begin to look for my brother. And besides, if I leave, who will stop the timekeepers from changing the past?"

"They still *are* changing the past," Ernest reminded her. "Even with you trying to stop them."

"That doesn't mean I should stop trying," Lisavet said, a bit indignantly. She gestured to the book on the ground beside her. "If I leave, who is going to remember them? And who will be here to stop *my* memories from being erased one day? Or yours."

Ernest made that face he so often used whenever she said something that contradicted his own outlook on the world. As if he'd never considered that someone might try to erase *him* one day, as he had done to so many others.

Lisavet shook her head. "Besides, this is my home," she said, gesturing around them. "It's enough."

"Is it, though? I mean, as beautiful as all of this is . . . it isn't real. It's just a memory."

Lisavet frowned at him. "It *is* real. Just as real as anything else."

"But don't you want memories of your own? Ones that don't belong to someone else?"

Lisavet sat up, pulling her knees into her chest. His words bothered her. They reminded her of things that she hadn't thought about in years. Of living and what that really meant. If what she was doing even counted. She was silent for a while until she felt Ernest's hand on her arm.

"Hey," he said gently. "I didn't mean to upset you. I was just . . ."

"You didn't upset me."

"No, I did. I don't mean to say that this isn't real. I guess I just . . . to me a life like that feels unbearable. Like that poem by Robert Frost, 'Acquainted with the Night.' Like walking in the middle of a beautiful city but still being completely alone."

"Poem?" Lisavet asked.

Ernest nodded a bit sheepishly and began reciting the poem.

Lisavet watched him, the smile growing on her face. "I've never heard that before," she said. "Can you recite a lot of poems like that?"

"Unfortunately, yes," Ernest said, rubbing the back of his head and refusing to look at her. "It's one of my less masculine talents I'm afraid."

Lisavet giggled at him. "Tell me another one."

Ernest obliged, with a nod. "As you wish, milady."

The next poem he recited was a love poem. He took up an affected Scottish accent, singing about "A Red, Red Rose," emphasizing each word in an effort to make her laugh. Toward the end, he tilted his head back and began speaking to the sky and Lisavet found herself wishing he would look at *her* instead. That he would recite such words, about love and all that came along with it, to her. She realized then, watching him recite love poems to the sky, that Azrael was right. That she was in love with Ernest Duquesne.

The next time they met, Ernest brought her a book of poetry, handing it to her with uncharacteristic shyness.

"I thought you might like these," he said, looking at the green-covered book with particular fondness. "Some of them, they, uh, . . . well, they kind of remind me of you."

The thought made Lisavet's heart beat faster. She spent the next three days before she saw him again reading each and every one, scanning them for hidden clues. Her own feelings clouded her perception and she looked for herself in every love poem, wondering if it might be the one he meant. After a few weeks of agonizing, she made the decision to do something about it. She planned to take him to the most romantic memory she knew, the one of the couple in field, and see if it had the same effect on him as it had her.

On the day between their usual visits, she sifted through memories in search of a dress that nobody would miss. A dress that would clue him in that this was a special evening. She also needed to find something she could use to carry around both her book of memories and the poetry Ernest had given her. She found both in the memory of an old playwright and his wife from the 1920s on the night their home was burned to the ground by a group of angry men, upset by the content of the writer's latest play. The dress was a deep blue gown, like the night sky, hung with silver beads that glittered like stars. For the books, she opted for function over beauty, taking a brown leather messenger bag from the floor of the writer's study just as the flames began to build.

The next day, she changed her clothes inside another memory, borrowing the vanity of a ballerina backstage at a performance, feeling giddy. Ernest was meeting her in just under an hour. She returned to the time space, so distracted that she nearly walked right out in front of an oncoming timekeeper. At the last moment, she ducked into a different row out of sight. He was Russian, wearing a brown uniform and tossing a lighter up and down in the air in front of him. At the sight of the lighter, Lisavet hesitated. She looked down the row in the direction of where she was meant to meet Ernest. There was still time, she told herself, then set off after the Russian timekeeper. He had begun whistling to himself, so nonchalant about the destruction he was about to bring that it made Lisavet's stomach turn.

He chose his book quickly, almost without looking for it. She watched him light the pages, still whistling that infuriating tune. Before the flames had even fully caught, he dropped the book on the ground and moved away. Lisavet waited the requisite number of seconds for him to be far enough and then she moved in. Barely any of the book had burned by the time she reached it. She smiled to herself, basking in his foolishness.

The smile was still on her lips when suddenly somebody grabbed her by her hair.

She screamed, the sound stifled by a large hand covering her mouth. Her assailant jerked her backward and an arm latched around her middle. He slammed her into the ground so hard it knocked the wind out of her lungs. The Russian who had shot at her before loomed over her, eyes flashing with vengeful malice. Between terrified breaths, Lisavet realized that she had walked right into a trap.

"We've been looking for you," the man said in broken English. "Where is your American friend this time, German bitch?"

Lisavet tried to free herself, struggling against him. He struck her hard across the face, snapping her head to one side.

"Where is he? Who set you up to this? Who are you working for?"

"Nobody," Lisavet gasped. "Nobody, I'm not . . ."

He hit her again and this time she saw stars. "Do not lie! You are an American spy, eh?"

"No! I . . ."

"You think you can interfere with our work?" He clasped one hand around her throat, squeezing the air from her lungs. "Well, I will teach you how we do things in my country. Consider this a warning to the American. When we catch a rat, we kill it."

Lisavet grappled with his arm, fighting for air, but he was too strong. In a panicked attempt to free herself, she drove her knee up as hard as she could. She heard him grunt in pain, felt his grip loosen. Air rushed into her lungs. She drew an aching mouthful and struck again, this time driving her fist into his windpipe. He let out a howl of pain. Her other hand found the book on the floor, and she swung it hard, delivering a blow to his nose that sent blood spraying. Suddenly the full weight of the timekeeper's body fell into her. His grip on her neck released. Lisavet struggled to free herself from the weight of him. There was blood on his face and on her hands and he wasn't moving. She felt faint. What if she had killed him?

Panic made breathing even harder. But then she noticed the time-keeper's chest rising and falling. He made a small noise, already beginning to stir. She needed to move. She made it to her bag and dragged it around the corner before collapsing onto the floor in a shaking heap. Blood on her hands and on the night blue dress, tender bruises blooming on her cheek. At some point she heard the timekeeper begin to move. Heard him drag himself to his feet and stumble a few times, cursing and shouting in Russian. She held her breath until she heard his footsteps fade off in the opposite direction.

The minute Lisavet heard him go, she began sobbing uncontrollably. This was where Ernest found her ten minutes later.

"Lisavet?"

She didn't look up. She didn't want him to see her like this.

"Lisavet?" He came closer, kneeling in front of her. "Are you okay? Look at me." He put a hand on her head until she glanced up. His eyes widened at the sight of the bruises. "Oh my god. What happened to you? Who did this?"

Lisavet started to say something but ended up crying harder instead. Ernest lowered himself the rest of the way to the ground. He put his arms around her, pulling her into him.

"It was the Russian timekeeper who shot you," she said through shaky breaths. "He thinks I'm some kind of spy. That I'm working with you, I guess."

Ernest cursed under his breath and tightened his grip. She basked in the feeling of being held by him, in spite of the circumstances.

"I'm sorry," he said after a long bout of silence.

"It isn't your fault."

"No, it is. If I hadn't been following you in the first place, he never would have seen you the first time. I wouldn't have gotten shot. Things wouldn't have escalated between the American and Russian timekeepers, and he wouldn't have targeted you again."

Lisavet pulled away to look at him. "Things have escalated? What do you mean?"

"It's nothing, just . . . tensions are higher. Things were fine before, just a little awkward given everything going on in the real world. Then I got shot and things got hostile. My boss . . . well, it doesn't matter. It's just a mess. And it's my fault. I should have left you alone."

Lisavet immediately shook her head. "No, I . . . I'm glad you didn't.

I mean, I'm not glad you got shot, or that things are tense now, I just mean . . . well, I'm glad I know you."

Ernest held her gaze, his lips parting in mild surprise. She thought she saw a glimmer of emotion cross his face but then he shook his head. "You shouldn't be. I've done nothing but cause you trouble. Before me, nobody even knew you were here. You were safe, and now . . ." He reached up and ran his thumb over one of the bruises. Gently. As if he might break her. "I should have never come after you. If I could change it . . . well, selfishly, I don't even know if I would. For what it's worth, I'm glad I know you too."

Lisavet's heart skipped a beat. They held perfectly still, looking at each other, his hand on her cheek. The air between them seemed to pulse. He pulled away, clearing his throat. To give him something to do, he took a handkerchief from his pocket and handed it to her.

"For the blood," he said.

Lisavet took it gratefully. His initials were embroidered on the handkerchief, EGD.

"That's a pretty dress by the way," Ernest said. "Where did it come from?"

Lisavet looked down at the dress, stained with the timekeeper's blood. "Oh. I got it from a memory of a burning house. It was supposed to be for tonight."

"Tonight?"

"I was going to take you somewhere special."

"Oh." Ernest looked down at his own clothes, a cable-knit sweater and a pair of trousers. "Could have warned me. I would have dressed better."

"You look perfect. Besides, it doesn't matter anymore."

"What do you mean? We can still go."

"No. No, we can't. It's ruined now."

"Why would it be ruined?"

Lisavet let out a huff of frustration. "Because. I had a plan, and it didn't involve me crying on your shoulder for thirty minutes first."

"Then let me take you somewhere."

"What?"

"Yes. Actually, that's a wonderful idea." He stood up, pulling her to her feet after him.

"Let me take you someplace for once. A memory that I choose this time."

"Where?"

Ernest thought for a moment. He smiled and took both of her hands in his. "You'll see. I have an idea."

He stooped to pick up her messenger bag, sliding it over his shoulder, and began walking. They were in the American section before they stopped. Lisavet watched him as he picked over the volumes on the shelves, his brow creased. That crease meant something different for him than it did for Azrael. Over the months she had learned to recognize such nuances of Ernest's face. The delicate, almost feminine curve of his cheekbones. The way his jaw, strong and angular, ground together when he was contemplating something.

He pulled a book from the shelf and held it up to show her. Lisavet took his outstretched hand, placing her other palm on the volume. Ernest whispered as the air began to shift.

"This is one of *my* favorite memories."

The world around them was replaced with another. The first thing Lisavet noticed was the music, which burst from the stage, filling every ounce of space. Tables lined a dance floor, and a bartender was serving cocktails to glamorously dressed guests. The sound of a saxophone blared through the air as glittering couples spun past them.

Ernest navigated them carefully through the crowd and up a set of stairs where the tables were farther apart and mostly empty, but where they had a full view of the stage and the crowd below.

"Where are we?" Lisavet shouted over the music.

"This is New York City. Manhattan. I came here a few months ago to see the show. That's Billy Eckstine up on the stage. We're in the memory of that man over there," he said, pointing to someone seated at the table.

"What year are we in?"

"1949."

"*1949?*" Lisavet whirled around to look at him. She hadn't been this close to present day in . . . well, since she had been living it.

Ernest nodded, his eyes on the stage where a Black man wearing a green suit sang into a microphone. "Yup. Swing music has already lost some of its popularity but there are a few good places that still play."

Lisavet was speechless. *1949.* Her eyes scanned the room, noticing all the subtle changes. The length of the women's skirts. The cut of their dresses.

"Come on," Ernest said. He had set her bag down and was holding out his other hand. "Want to dance?"

"D-dance?"

"Sure. We've got plenty of space up here."

"Oh . . . I don't know." Lisavet had danced alone hundreds of times before. She knew how to do it, having watched all different styles over the years. But the moves the people were doing below were new and unfamiliar.

"What's the matter? It's not like anyone can see us."

He had a point. Lisavet took his hand and laughed in surprise as he swung her arm so fast that she nearly fell into him. It was immediately clear, as they started to move, that Ernest had absolutely no idea how to dance to this music, either. He guided her through a kind of mismatched samba, keeping her pressed tight against him so she wouldn't stumble. They tripped over each other a few times until they found the rhythm, adjusting to each other's movements like two birds learning to fly together. Eventually, Lisavet stopped worrying so much about where she was going to put her feet, trusting him to keep her from falling. She thrilled at the feeling of his arms around her. The closeness with which they danced. The music swelled and then ended with a final blaring note from the saxophone. Lisavet started to step back as applause sounded, but Ernest held on.

"Not yet," he said. "The next one is my favorite."

Lisavet's stomach fluttered at the look in his eyes. Glowing, the way she'd seen him look in other memories, this time directed at her. Like starlight. Like someone who might possibly be in love.

The next song was slower, punctuated by the high keys of a piano. The tune of the saxophone rang low and mournful, and Lisavet marveled at how such an instrument could make two such different sounds, until the man started singing and then all she could hear were the words. The song was called "Blue Moon," and it felt as though he were singing to them directly, and only to them. The rest of the memory was irrelevant. This time they danced slowly, fluidly, two birds soaring side by side. Ernest's gaze held steadily on her own. His hands on her waist were real and solid. The only real thing she had ever known.

The song was coming to a close and so was the memory. The world had already begun to blur at the edges. Lisavet didn't want it to end. She wanted to stay here in Ernest's arms, reliving this dance for the rest of her life. The final note rang out and Ernest stopped dancing but didn't let go. He moved closer, his head tilting toward hers. She had seen this happen before, the cautious descent before two lovers' lips met. Was he going to kiss her? Lisavet put one hand on his chest.

"Wait . . ."

For a moment, Ernest feared she was rejecting him. That he had mistaken the look in her eyes. The momentary feeling was so crushing that it took all he had not to crumple beneath it.

"Not here," she said. "Not at the end of a memory."

"Where?" he asked her.

She took him to a field in the middle of Spain, full of stars and the most beautiful moon Ernest had ever seen. Off in the distance, a laughing girl in a yellow dress ran through the dewy grass, pursued by a young man. Close enough that they could hear their laughter, but not so close as to disturb their own walk under the stars.

Ernest held tightly to Lisavet's hand as she guided them up the hill. In the moonlight, the bruises on her face were more obvious and he felt another pull of guilt. *Your fault. This is your fault*, the voices in his head scolded. But then she smiled at him, the moon making her blond hair glow white, and all other thoughts flew from his head. She turned toward him, letting go of his hand to twirl. The navy blue dress glinted like starlight, casting her in the same pallor as the sky.

"This is where I wanted to take you," Lisavet said breathlessly, gesturing to the endless stars above them. "Have you ever seen anything so beautiful?"

Ernest stepped toward her, smiling coyly. "Oh, I've seen better."

"Where?"

"I'm looking at it."

A blush rose in her cheeks. He caught her hand and pulled her closer, wanting to feel her against him once more. He held her the way he had in the dance, drunk on the feeling of being so close to her.

"But have you looked at the moon?" Lisavet asked, her voice soft, eyes wide.

"I don't need to," Ernest whispered, touching her cheek. "You *are* the moon."

Lisavet let out a single trembling breath. Ernest felt it against his wrist as he moved closer. This time, she didn't stop him. Her lips were warm and soft and anything but shy as they pressed against his own. She exhaled again and he breathed in the taste of it, wanting every part of her to become a part of him too. He kissed her over and over again, scarcely breathing himself, until they fell back into the grass. Until this memory, like the last, faded to a close. Lisavet moved them seamlessly into another, neither of them willing to let the new memory they were creating end so soon. Ernest barely registered that they were back in Switzerland in the hotel near her parents' memory before he was swept away in the moment again.

He had been wrong, he thought to himself as Lisavet's hands slid under his sweater, the first to give into their mutual desire for more. He had assumed that the way Lisavet lived her life, in stolen memories and moments long past, was somehow less real than his own. But *this* was real. Her lips, her hands, the warmth of her skin against his own as he removed her dress beneath the sheet she had taken from the bed to cover them. It was more real than anything he'd ever known outside the time space, made even more so by the shifting and fading of worlds as they fell in and out of the past. Only once did he stop in the midst of their dance, pausing to lay remorseful kisses along the bruises on her neck where the Russian had choked her. Proof that he had failed her, just like everyone else had. Never again.

Her long blond hair spilled over his arm as she lay beside him, and he ran his fingers through it, swearing a silent oath that he'd never let anyone hurt her again. Not the other timekeepers. Not Jack. And certainly not him. Even if it cost him his job. He fell into sleep with the taste of her still on his lips, the warmth of her nestled safely in his arms.

LISAVET PROPPED herself up on one elbow to watch Ernest's face as he slept. She herself hadn't slept in years, not even in memories. Her body had forgotten how to, it seemed. But to watch him sleep was fascinating. She marveled at the gentle rise and fall of his chest, and at the stirring within her own. She had spent years at a time walking through every age and era of history. Going everywhere yet belonging nowhere except for right here in his arms.

As time moved forward, she noticed a subtle stream of light hovering just over him, like luminous sand falling upward toward the ceiling. It reminded her of the sky inside the time space, the swirling tendrils of light that Azrael had said were living thoughts in motion. Those must be Ernest's recent memories, she realized. Visible since he was already in the time space, his consciousness moving along to join his other memories. She wondered what they would be like. Memories untainted by retrospect, pure and unadulterated. She reached out a hand, wondering if she could see them that way. If it worked anything like time walking. Her fingers brushed the glowing tendrils. Instead of falling into the memory as she normally did, images of the past played like a foggy movie in the air before her. She saw the memories as though through a frosted pane of glass, and to her surprise, they weren't of their time together that day at all, but something else entirely. A well-lit office. A man with blunt features seated behind a desk, tossing a ball up and down in the air.

You owe me an update on the German girl, Ernest, the man said, his voice crackling like a poorly rendered recording.

Lisavet drew back in surprise. She looked down at Ernest's sleeping face, wondering if she should stop. Maybe he wouldn't want her to know about this? But the pull of the memory was too strong. Something about it raised the hairs on the back of her neck. After a moment's hesitation, she reached out and watched the memory take shape.

WHEN ERNEST awoke, Lisavet was no longer beside him. It was still dark in the room. He wondered what had woken him until his pants flew through the air and hit him in the face. He let out a grunt of surprise and sat up, legs still tangled up in the sheet. Lisavet was standing in front of him, one foot on the blanket. She was fully dressed, coat and all. She had the book of memories clutched tightly over her chest, a look of betrayal in her eyes.

She stepped forward and thrust the book in his face. "Here," she said forcefully.

Ernest blinked. "Wh—"

"Take it," Lisavet said, dropping it on his lap. "It's what you want, isn't it? That's what your boss sent you here to get?"

Ernest's heart sank. "How . . ."

"I saw it in your memories," she said.

"You what?"

"I think you should leave," she said, tears filling her eyes. "Just take the book and go."

"No, Lisavet, I can explain . . ."

Before he could finish, she turned away from him and stormed out onto the balcony. The sheet passed right through him in her absence. He scrambled to put his pants on, ignoring the fact that he had no idea where his sweater was, and ran after her. Leaving the book on the floor.

"Lisavet . . ." he said, stepping out onto the balcony.

"What?" she snapped, turning to glare at him.

Ernest opened his mouth to speak but suddenly realized how utterly indefensible his actions were. The bruises on her face had deepened overnight and the sight of them made his stomach churn with fresh guilt.

"It doesn't matter. You have your book now. There's no reason for you to toy with me anymore. Just go away."

"No," Ernest said forcefully.

She spun back around. "No?"

"I'm not leaving."

"Fine, then I'll go."

"No." Ernest stood in her way, bracing his arms against the door.

"Move," she snapped.

"No. Not until you listen to me. You're right, okay? Initially, when I started following you, it was because Jack told me to. You were interfering with things. He thought you were dangerous."

Lisavet scoffed at him. "Oh yes, really dangerous. A girl who saves memories from being destroyed by men with guns and a false sense of authority. If you want to talk about which one of us is really dangerous, why don't we look at the one blindly following orders handed down by his superiors without stopping to think for himself?"

"You're right, you're right," Ernest said emphatically. "I know that now."

"Oh, do you? Then tell me, was it your boss's idea to make a fool out of me?"

He stepped toward her and caught her in his arms despite her efforts to dodge him.

"Lisavet, listen to me. Please . . ."

"No!" she shouted, straining away from him. "I trusted you. You were the first person I'd spoken to in years. I believed you cared about me."

"I *do* care about you. None of that . . . the dancing or our time together or last night . . . none of that was a lie."

"I don't believe you."

"*I love you*, Lisavet," Ernest said desperately, gripping tighter to her arms.

"You . . . what?" Lisavet asked, falling silent.

"I love you. I've been fighting with myself for months over it all. Agonizing over it. I didn't mean for any of this to happen. I told you yesterday, I regret ever meeting you because all I've done is get you hurt. People are targeting you now, including my boss. Because *I* told him about you. Because I was stupid enough to think nothing bad would come of it. I never meant to hurt you, you have to know that."

"I heard you talking to him. You were going to take the book."

"Yes. I was. But only because otherwise Jack was going to force me to drag you out of the time space so he could question you in person."

Lisavet drew back as much as she could. Ernest knew he should let go of her arms but couldn't force himself to do it, fearful she would vanish from his life and never return if he did.

"You would do that to me?" she asked, her voice small. "The time space is my home, Ernest. The only home I have left."

"No," Ernest said, knowing at once that he meant it. "I couldn't. Maybe once I could justify it as following orders. But not anymore. I love you. I would *never* do anything to hurt you."

"And the book?"

"I don't want it," he said instantly. "Hide it. I'll make up some excuse. I'll tell Jack I lost track of you. I'll resign. Whatever I have to do, as long as I don't lose you."

Even as he said it, Ernest could point out the many, many flaws in this plan. But right then, he didn't care. He was so sure of himself, so strong in his convictions to protect her, that he almost believed he could pull it off. Lisavet stared at him for a long time. The eyes that had become his moon, his sun, his entire world, were full of mistrust. He couldn't bear it. He retrieved the book from the room, pressing it forcefully into her hands.

"Take it. And hide it. We'll figure everything else out from there, just trust me."

Lisavet hesitated, her fingers curling around the cover of the book.

"Please," he said, his voice scarcely a whisper. "I can't lose you."

At last she took the book from him. She nodded.

"Can I see you tomorrow? Please?" he asked, knowing that he needed to ask. That she may not want to see him ever again.

She took a moment to answer, the seven most agonizing seconds of Ernest's life.

"Tomorrow," she said.

Ernest exhaled with relief. Unable to stop himself, he pulled her into his arms again and kissed her hard. The depth of their embrace allowed him to relax as they said goodbye. He watched her go, feeling the weight of everything settle over him, and then he returned to his apartment where he had been when he first wound the watch. It was daylight, early morning, and the sunlight stung his eyes. He had been gone for twelve hours. The night still clung to every inch of his body.

The calendar on his wall read April 4, 1949. Monday. He had a meeting with Jack that day. Another meeting where he was going to have to lie. He thought about Lisavet's bruised face. The Russian who had attacked her. The solution to his problems was right there, he realized. Staring him in the face. He showered in a daze and cooked himself breakfast. He dressed in a suit and tie and left for work in time to make it to the nine o'clock meeting with Jack where he would detail the Russian attack. Where he would inform him that Lisavet Levy was dead.

8

1949, Somewhere in the Time Space

SEVERAL MONTHS AFTER THEIR night in the Swiss hotel, Ernest brought Lisavet a little paper-wrapped package with a blue ribbon tied around the middle. At first, Lisavet had assumed it would be a book. Lately, they'd been spending almost every night together walking through the endless expanses of history before disappearing somewhere they could fall into each other, and nearly every week, Ernest brought her a new book of poetry. She memorized new stanzas the way she had spent the past eleven years remembering thousands of altered versions of history.

But the shy, nervous look Ernest gave her told her this was no volume of poetry.

"I've been looking for this for months," he told her. "Ever since you told me your name."

A strange buzzing feeling seemed to radiate from the box as she opened it. When she saw what it was, she cried out. Her father's pocket watch, old and bronze and patinated from age, passed down from father to son for over a century. Lisavet sank to the ground, holding it in both hands.

"How did you find this?" she asked.

"Lots of letters back and forth to German timekeepers. A little bit of arm twisting. A great deal of bribery. It's his, right?"

"Yes," Lisavet gasped, clutching the watch tighter. "Yes. It's his."

She was almost afraid to open the case, wondering if it was even pos-sible for it to still work. As if reading her mind, Ernest took the watch from her.

"I had it looked at by a friend of mine who works in our servicing department. It still runs." He spun the crown on the side of the case to demonstrate. The watch's hands sprang to life, ticking out an old familiar pattern.

Lisavet held her breath, waiting for a door of some kind to appear. When none did, she frowned. "Does it still . . . I mean, could I use it to . . ."

"To leave?" Ernest asked, giving her a tentative smile.

"Hypothetically, I mean," she said hurriedly. The idea still terrified her, especially in light of Ernest's theories, but the notion of having a choice set her pulse racing in an entirely different way.

"You could," Ernest confirmed.

He wound the watch backward a few times, the way all watches like this one worked, until the ticking of the gears grew louder. His thumb hovered over the crown before pressing it down with a click. A few feet ahead of them, a door of worn wood materialized, appearing like the specter of a distant memory. Lisavet stared at it, dumbstruck, as though it were more than just a door, but a portal to the past. Wondering where it might lead. Wondering if it would take her home again. But the ques-tions soon faded from her mind as she remembered that this watch had served ten long years in the service of Nazi soldiers since the last time she'd seen it. Who knew how many doors it had opened in that time? Who knew where this one might lead her?

Ernest pressed the watch back into her palm and kissed her knuckles without a word, seeming to understand implicitly what she was thinking. Together, they watched the door disappear, their hands holding either side of the watch.

That day he also gave her a gun. A silver revolver that fit easily into the pocket of her coat. The incident with the Russian was still burned into the back of her mind and she held the gun with trembling fingers. Ernest showed her how to use it, warned her to be careful, and then never spoke of it again.

From then on, Lisavet kept both the watch and the revolver on her at all times, measuring the hours from one visit to the next. Occasionally, as the months continued and the year became 1950, she daydreamed about leaving the time space, all the while knowing that she never would. Ernest had told her about his theories. The reason she could touch things when they time walked. The reason she could see his memories. He called it "temporal departure." A part of her marveled at the idea that Time was no longer a part of her. That it could not control her. Standing motionless in the time space, she could still feel its presence, could identify its subtle whispering the way she had when she was just a child. It still spoke to her, she realized, only now she understood what it was saying. Now, she could whisper back to it.

Ernest's theory gave her a new kind of freedom. She tested the limits of Time, becoming a master of it, so skilled in her ability that she no longer needed to use a book to time walk. She needed only to think. To conjure a place or a memory in her head before it appeared in front of her. She never did this around Ernest, not wanting to alarm him.

The first time she inserted herself into a memory, she did so entirely by accident. She was in Ancient Greece, a scene plucked from a book. In front of her, a group of shepherds herded sheep up the hillside, talking and laughing. Lisavet had come here for the sunshine and the ocean and to taste one of the apricots growing on this side of the island. She sat in the shade, the watch in one hand, a piece of fruit in another. Watching a tiny lamb walking away from the herd on uneasy hooves. It stumbled over the rocks and landed flat on its back. Lisavet laughed at the indignant bleating noises it made.

The animal's ears pricked at the sound. It looked at her. Sure she was imagining things, Lisavet took another piece of fruit from the tree and bit into it, entirely unconcerned. The lamb teetered closer to her. She held out a hand, more curious than anything, and was shocked when its smooth nose pressed into the palm of her hand. Its tongue lapped up the juice from the apricot, warm and wet and real. She made a noise and drew back in alarm. She'd never been able to touch a living thing in a memory before. Only objects.

Down the hill, one of the shepherd boys came running after his missing lamb. He suddenly stopped, staring right at her.

"I see you've met my lamb," he called out in Greek.

Lisavet froze. He was talking to *her*. Smiling at her. The apricot dropped from her hand. She shook herself loose from the memory instantly, grateful when she saw the safe, quiet shelves of the time space around her once more. The book she had used to enter the memory had changed. Some of the pages turned to dust beneath her hand. Gone.

It happened two more times before she became aware of the pattern. The soft hush of Time that seemed to wrap around her in the instant before the memory parted, allowing her into it. Both times, it was the same, a handful of pages destroyed. She swore to herself she wouldn't do it again, but on the third occasion, she heard it coming and leaned into it anyway, wanting to test her theory. That time, when she emerged from the memory, she saw the whole second half of the book disintegrate in her hands. She was changing Time, she realized with a shudder. And by changing it, she was destroying it.

Never again, she told herself. And this time, she meant it.

JACK HAD bought Ernest's lie without a hitch. It wasn't hard. A Russian timekeeper *had* attacked her. That was easy enough to prove. They caught the man a few weeks later, dragging him out of the time space and subjecting him to thorough questioning. He admitted readily to what he had done and claimed that Lisavet had knocked him unconscious. He didn't know what happened to her, but when Ernest suggested that he might have killed her, he didn't outright refute it. Ernest told them he'd found her body. Her neck bruised, her larynx crushed just enough to cause gradual asphyxiation after she'd escaped her attacker. He wrote a full-length report and submitted it to Jack, each word making him nauseous.

"It's a real shame, that," Jack said. "We could have used her."

Ernest said nothing, remembering the Russian timekeeper's screams as they pried information out of him.

He didn't tell Lisavet what he had done to buy their freedom. Both of them were too in love, so blinded by their feelings for each other that everything else felt insignificant. Deep down, however, Ernest knew that it wasn't freedom he had bought them with his lies: It was time. More of it, but never enough. Eventually, it would catch up to them.

His fear showed plainly on his face, even though he tried to hide it.

"Why do you always look so sad?" Lisavet asked him one day.

They were lying in a forest somewhere in Russia, watching the first snow of winter in 1745. Ernest had laid his coat over the ground for the two of them and they were close. So close that he could hear the ticking of the watch in her pocket. He had been watching the snow fall against the ink black sky, but she was watching him. Noticing the way his eyes seemed to darken and change until it was like he was looking through it all to somewhere far away.

"Do I?" he asked.

"Sometimes. Whenever things get quiet it's like you go someplace else."

Ernest grimaced. His mother used to say the same thing after he came back from war.

"That's just called thinking."

"Then what do you think about that makes you look that way?"

I was thinking about losing you. About all the lies I've told so that we can be here like this. I was thinking about what happens if they find out.

He decided to answer the question more broadly to avoid having to talk about his *current* thoughts.

"I was just thinking. Why haven't you ever visited memories closer to the present?"

It was something he'd always wondered. Aside from the single New York memory he'd taken her to, Lisavet had never been to any memories after the year 1938.

"I just haven't. I guess . . . I don't really want to know what happened to the world after I left it. The idea that everything I used to love might be gone or, worse, that it's been changed by memories I couldn't save from the timekeepers—" She broke off, staring up at the falling snow. "It's safer in the past. Everything is already over."

Ernest had to agree with her, despite the obvious flaws in her reasoning. Sometimes, when he woke up from nightmares in which he watched his friends die or walked through the concentration camps on Liberation Day all over again, he wished he had never gone to war at all. That he could take it all from his memory and forget it. And as for the other part . . . well, even he couldn't know what pieces of his world had been altered without his knowledge. He thought of Ezekiel Levy and how little remained of his memory. His whole identity taken and destroyed. If Lisavet didn't want to know all that had happened, who was he to tell her? Who was he to ruin what few precious memories she had of her life before the time space?

He had begun to wonder how much of his own life had been altered by timekeepers like him. Occasionally, Lisavet would mention something that he himself had forgotten. Historical figures erased. Details of an event altered, even those that had happened in his own lifetime. At first, he'd been horrified at the realization that she could remember the things that somebody else had erased. Wary even. The knee-jerk reaction of a soldier discovering a breach in the ranks.

Before long, that horror turned to frustration, until it morphed into something closely resembling shame. He, too, was beginning to see that what they were losing was not just memory, but truth. Sometimes, when they met in the time space, he brought pages from books he himself had been ordered to erase, asking her to keep them. He never said much when he did this, simply handed her the pages, grappling with guilt and a new sense of duty that was slowly replacing the old.

When he returned to his apartment after their visit to Russia, he noticed that the lights in the living room had been turned off. He passed a weary hand over his face, checking his watch. It was a little before midnight. He had been in the time space with Lisavet since dinner. He stumbled out into the kitchen in the dark. As he was fumbling around for the light switch, he heard the click of the lamp across the room.

Jack stood in the middle of his apartment. One hand on the lamp switch, the other holding a black notebook open to the center.

"Good evening, Ernest," Jack said in a dry, self-satisfied tone. "Nice of you to drop by."

"What are you doing in my apartment?" Ernest blurted out.

"I came to check in," Jack said, snapping the notebook shut with a loud clap. He set it down on the coffee table.

"Awfully late for a visit."

"We need to talk."

"And it couldn't wait?" Ernest asked, the initial shock balling itself into a hard lump in his stomach.

"Do you remember what the primary mission statement of the TRP is?" Jack asked in a deliberately condescending voice.

Of course he knew. His father was the one who wrote it.

Jack didn't give him a chance to respond. "To protect, preserve, and immortalize American interests within the collective memory of history.

To eradicate antidemocratic ideologies and defend *American* values inside the temporal realm . . . that's why we do what we do. To keep another Hitler from spreading his ideas. To prevent another war like the one we both fought in."

"What's your point, Jack?" Ernest snapped impatiently.

Jack reached into his jacket, pulling out a single sheet of paper. "Charles Lambert. Beverly Hawkins. Melvin Caldwell. Ralph Newton." He paused, holding the sheet up. "Any of those names sound familiar to you?"

Ernest's brow twitched. He didn't answer.

"They're all names of people whose memories you were supposed to eliminate. Only . . . you didn't. Did you?"

Suddenly, Ernest understood. He had been given those names to destroy months ago and, after reviewing the contents of their memories, had taken them to Lisavet to hide.

"They must have slipped through the cracks. I'll amend it in the morning," he said, trying to play it off.

Jack let out a lengthy sigh. "You've always been the most thorough of all the timekeepers on staff. If you were to tell me that one name escaped you, I might believe it. But it isn't just one. In fact, we've started to notice a pattern."

"We?" Ernest asked, feeling a twinge of foreboding.

Jack ignored the question and set the list down on the coffee table next to the notebook he had been reading, drawing Ernest's attention to it. He realized with horror that it was his own. The notebook he used to log all his visits to Lisavet from the very beginning. It had been on the desk in his bedroom. Which meant that Jack had seen everything atop it as well. The notes on Lisavet's predicament. The other letters from the shop in Nuremberg. Records he'd pulled on her family, her history, *her*.

Jack passed a tired hand over his face, looking like a teacher about to scold a disobedient pupil. "I asked Brady and Collins to keep an eye

on you the next time you went into the time space and . . . you'll never
believe who they saw you with."

Ernest's mouth went dry. "Jack . . ."

"You've been lying to me, Ernest," Jack interrupted. Anger had begun
seeping into his voice, the edge as sharp as a knife. "The German girl is
still alive. Lisavet Levy. That's her name, right?"

"Jack, I . . ."

"I read all about your little relationship in that diary of yours. Instead
of doing your duty, you decided to extend the honeymoon by telling us
all that she was dead."

"She isn't a threat! It's not her fault she got trapped there, I was just
trying to protect an innocent girl from getting hurt."

"Not a threat? She's been interfering with our mission. Saving memories we're trying to destroy, getting you to lie for her. A girl who can walk
through memories of the past and take things right out of history—
I read your notes on her 'condition.' If you believe a girl like that isn't a
threat, then you're a bigger fool than I thought."

"Jack, please," Ernest said shakily. "She is saving memories, but it isn't
what you think."

Jack scoffed. "I don't care why she's doing it, and neither should you.
She's the daughter of the last man alive who knew how to make a watch
that could access the time space. I'd bet money that that's what she's got
stored away in that book. And here you are, letting her walk free with
secrets that could change *everything*. That fact, paired with your theories
about her condition . . . she needs to be stopped."

Ernest's face paled. He knew where this was going. "Jack, no. If you read
my notes, then you know . . . if you take her out of there, she could die."

"After all the trouble that girl has caused, you're lucky I don't send
someone in to shoot her outright."

"This is my fault," Ernest said, clenching his fists. "She didn't do anything. It wasn't her idea."

"You're right, it is your fault. So you're going to fix it. It seems you've got *quite* the rapport with her if those notes you left are anything to go off of. None of the others have even seen her up close before, whereas you're over here going on dates with her every other night. So you get to be the one to bring her out."

Ernest stiffened his jaw. "Like hell I am."

"I figured you'd say that," Jack said smugly. "But here's the thing. If you don't, I'll do more than just end your career. I'll contact the head of the CIA myself and let him know that Gregory Duquesne's son, golden boy of the TRP, has been committing treason right under our noses."

For a moment, Ernest wanted to dare him. To spit in his face and hand in his resignation all at once, damn the consequences. But then he thought of his mother and what it would do to her. He thought of Lisavet, who would be dragged out of the time space even if he refused. He needed to play his cards right. To buy himself time. He said nothing, but Jack seemed to recognize the resignation in his eyes. He clapped him on the shoulder. Hard.

"Attaboy," he said with a vicious smile. "I'll give you one week to coax her out before I send someone after you both."

Never had Ernest wanted to punch him more than at that moment. Jack turned to pick up the black notebook and left the apartment.

Later, when Ernest returned to his bedroom, his desk had been cleared of his notes. Taken for evidence maybe. Something to hold over his head. Everything was gone. Every scrap of paper, every theory, leaving his desk empty and barren. As though she'd already been ripped from his life.

ERNEST CAME early the next evening. Lisavet was busy folding a new set of pages into the book of memories. When she saw him coming, she quickly shoved the book into her messenger bag, hoping he hadn't noticed. She'd return it to its hiding spot later, she told herself, smiling at him until she saw the look on his face.

"Ernest? What's . . ."

Her words were cut short as Ernest pushed her up against one of the shelves and kissed her with bruising intensity. She could almost taste the frenetic energy spilling off him.

"Ernest? Is something wrong?"

He pressed his forehead to hers, eyes shut. "I know we were going to Carnival in Brazil today, but can we go someplace quieter instead? I . . . need to talk to you."

Lisavet nodded and took his hand. He clung to her more tightly than usual, as if she might slip away. She took them straight to the hotel in Switzerland. Ernest didn't flinch when she took them there without using a book. Didn't even notice. He let go of her hand and began pacing back and forth in front of the fireplace.

"What's going on?" Lisavet asked.

"If I asked you to leave the time space with me, would you do it?"

Lisavet took a step back in surprise. "Leave the time space? And go where? Out into America with you?"

"No. God no. Not there. Somewhere else. Anywhere else. Anywhere you want to go."

"But . . . I thought you said I couldn't leave?"

"I don't know if you can or not. I've been trying to figure that out. I spent all day today looking into it. And I think it's possible. You were born outside of this place. You have memories outside of it as well as inside, so in theory, you should be able to readjust. Now, I'm not one hundred percent certain, and it might take some time for you to return to normal but . . ."

"Whoa, whoa. Slow down. Where is this coming from?"

Ernest's eyes were full of fear, something she'd never seen in him before. "Just tell me you'll consider it."

"But . . . why now? And why can't we go back to America? Where would we live?"

"Together," Ernest said at once. He came forward and took her hands, raising one to his lips. "We'd be together. We could start a life together. You and me. It's all I want, Lisavet. A life with you, always with you. God . . . I'm not doing this right, am I?"

"I don't understand."

Ernest shut his eyes. Drew a deep breath. "I'm asking you to marry me, Lisavet. To leave this place and marry me."

Her heart skipped a beat. But there was something he wasn't saying.

"Ernest . . . what about your job? What about your life?"

"Forget about that. We can't go back there."

"Did something happen?"

"No. No. Nothing happened. Everything's fine."

"Then why all this talk of leaving? Why do you suddenly want to run away?"

There was a long, aching pause.

"I can't tell you," Ernest said.

"Why not?"

"Because I screwed up. I thought I had this under control. I thought I'd taken care of the problem but . . . I was wrong."

"Are you in trouble?"

"Yes," he said in a tense exhale. "And so are you."

Lisavet withdrew her hands in alarm. "Me?"

"We both are. I'm sorry, Lisavet. I didn't mean for this to happen. But it isn't safe here anymore. You're not safe here."

"This is the safest place there is for me, Ernest. I can't leave."

"I know you're afraid," Ernest said, stepping closer. "Believe me, I do. But we can't stay here, and we can't go back to America, either. They'll come for you. For both of us. We have to go somewhere they won't think to look."

Lisavet studied his face, taking in the desperation in his eyes.

"Please, Lisavet," he whispered.

"How long do I have to think about it?"

Ernest didn't answer right away, and she understood it then. They didn't have time. He needed her answer tonight. Lisavet wished she could stop time, to give herself more of it so she could think. She realized bitterly that Ernest was probably right about her being able to leave. Time hadn't completely forgotten her. It still went by too quickly for her, same as everyone else. She swallowed the lump in her throat and nodded.

"Okay," she said, eyes stinging with tears. "Okay, I'll leave with you."

Ernest exhaled in relief, his shoulders slumping. "Thank god."

"But . . . not yet. Give me a few hours. Please."

Time to say goodbye. To the time space. To Azrael. To these memories of her parents she might never see again.

Ernest nodded. "Of course. Yes, of course."

He kissed her very softly and she pulled him closer, hand reaching for the buttons of his shirt. Now she was the one who was frantic. She was the one whose kisses were desperate. They folded into each other and Lisavet held on to him tightly, trying to find solace in the now familiar contours of his body. He held her close and buried his face in her neck, whispering over and over again.

"I'm sorry. I'm sorry. I'm sorry."

I love you, I love you, I love you, she chanted silently in response.

When he finally fell asleep, exhausted from two straight days with no sleep, Lisavet went onto the balcony. She gazed up at the moon, then down at the streets below, where her parents were dancing the night away together. If she left, she would lose this. She would lose all of it, possibly forever. There was no time walking in the real world. There was no past at all. Only the present and ceaseless forward march of Time.

Suddenly, Lisavet felt eleven years old again and realized that eleven was the last time she had ever been so frightened. How could she leave?

How could she walk away when there were still timekeepers who burned memories without remorse, erasing all the best parts of the past? How could she lose this to spend the rest of her life staring down the barrel of an unknown future? All of history was susceptible to the whims of time-keepers, every memory she held dear under duress, able to be altered at any moment. Panic began to creep in, and she suddenly wished she had never agreed to any of it.

In the next room, Ernest breathed fitfully, and she turned to see the outpouring of memories, traveling like stardust into the sky. She went over to him and reached for them, wanting to relive each moment they'd spent together this past year and a half. But instead, she saw something else. Other memories, not of her, but of Ernest's life outside of the time space. That was what he was remembering now. Not her and their future together, but his past without her. The life he was leaving behind. She saw his mother smiling with adoring eyes at her only son. She saw his wayward sister. His cousins. The colleagues he liked and those he didn't. She saw all the quiet moments she hadn't gotten to be a part of. Newspapers over breakfast with his sister. Autumn leaves on his walk to work. Flowers blooming in the back garden at his mother's house.

They were painful to see, not because they were sad, but because he was going to lose them. Those quiet, familiar moments wouldn't exist if he left with her. His mother. His sister. They would never know what happened to him. Lisavet pulled out of the memories. She realized she was crying and wiped the tears away. His life without her was so much fuller than hers was without him. And he was willing to lose all of that. For her. What would their future even be? Two fugitives, name-less, placeless, untethered, not just from time but from the whole world. Such an existence was fine for her. But she didn't want that for Ernest. Ernest who had a mother and sister and so much left to lose.

Suddenly she knew what she needed to do. She took out the most recent book of poetry he had given her from her bag. Wincing, she tore a set of pages from the back. Thick enough to cover one year and six months of time. She turned to look at Ernest, pausing to brush the copper curls back from his face. He stirred, eyes opening halfway.

"Lisavet?"

She shushed him, smiling in spite of the tears. "It's all right. Go back to sleep."

His tired eyes trailed across her face. "You really are the moon," he whispered.

She leaned forward and kissed his lips gently. *I love you, I love you, I love you.*

He fell into slumber once more. Lisavet forced herself to look away from him. To focus. She reached out again, one hand on the pages, doing what she had seen so many timekeepers do over the years. In his memories, she looked for all the ones that had her in them, pulling them out one by one and depositing them onto the pages. Their dance in New York. The kiss in the field. A red rose offered and then taken away. There were certain things she couldn't erase completely. He would still know how to time walk. But she would not be in any of the places he visited. She removed her face, her name, her very existence from his mind. They couldn't condemn him if he couldn't remember her. They couldn't tear them apart if she never existed at all.

When she was finished, she held the pages in both hands, amazed and heartbroken at how little space they occupied between her thumb and forefinger. A year and a half was nothing at all compared to a lifetime of memories, and yet it felt like she was holding her whole world. She tucked them safely in the book of memories, giving them a special place toward the beginning, close to the memories of her father where all this had first begun.

Ernest lay sleeping in the dark room, breathing more easily now that all his reasons for worrying had been erased from his mind. Lisavet stood over him for a moment longer, knowing she should leave before he woke up. Knowing she was nothing to him now. Not even a ghost. She took her bag off the floor and pulled herself out of the memory, back into the lonely silence of the time space.

When Ernest woke up the next day, he would assume he'd fallen asleep while time walking. He would be groggy and confused. He would get up. Maybe he'd spend another few moments inside the memory. Perhaps he'd watch the couple having coffee at the café across from the balcony. Eventually he would leave. He would go to work where he was sure to encounter a bit of trouble; Lisavet had seen the memory of his confrontation with his boss and had taken that too. There would be some awkwardness. Some anger perhaps. But if Jack Dillinger was smart, and Lisavet assumed he must be for Ernest to be so afraid of what he might do, eventually he would figure out that Ernest truly didn't remember. That a timekeeper, a man who dealt in the keeping and erasing of memories, had been sent to capture a girl who lived untethered from Time and had come out missing a few memories of his own. He would piece it together. He would stop asking questions that Ernest couldn't answer. They would move on. Ernest would move on, his life continuing as it always had. Without her.

And she would go on as she had, too, carrying the pages of their memories in secret. Remembering him far longer than she'd ever known him. Forever whispering to him whenever she saw him passing through the time space.

I love you, I love you, I love you.

9

1965, *Boston, Massachusetts*

AMELIA WENT BACK INTO the time space the day after her visit to James Gravel. It was evening. She and Moira had spent most of the day not talking. Amelia wanted to ask questions, but she didn't trust the answers Moira might give her. She wanted the truth firsthand. From her uncle's perspective. She was going to find his memories, even if that meant witnessing his death.

After she spun the crown of her watch, she stood on the threshold of her uncle's room, hand poised over the knob. In her other hand, she held a kitchen knife. Going into the time space without something to protect herself no longer felt like an option.

With a final gathering breath, she stepped through the door. The silence swallowed her instantly. She moved into the darkness, watching the light from underneath the door slip away until she was cast in shadows in all directions. Shifting the knife in her hand again, she took precise, careful steps.

"Back again?"

Amelia jumped in alarm, raising the knife on instinct. The strangely behaved memory from before had materialized just behind her, his bright shadow dragging through the air.

"Easy now. You'll frighten the dead acting like that," he said in a low voice that might have been harsh if it weren't for the laughter it hid beneath it. "Some of us died at the end of one of those, you know." He pointed to the knife.

"I'm sorry," Amelia said, tucking it out of sight.

"Still looking for that book?"

"Actually, I'm looking for my uncle's memories."

"Ahhhh, yes. Ernest Duquesne."

"Yes, him. Can you help me?"

He shook his head. "I'm afraid not."

Amelia let out a sigh of frustration. "Great. Thanks." She started to turn away, but the memory called after her.

"Aren't you supposed to be looking for the book?"

"Well, yes. But I don't suppose you want to help me with that either?"

He gave her a bemused look that would have made her want to hit him if it weren't for the fact that he was a ghost. "I'm sure you'll figure it out."

Amelia glared at him. "Who *are* you?" she asked.

"People call me Azrael."

"People?"

"Well, one person did." He tilted his head slightly, eyes narrowed. "Try listening for them."

"For what?"

"For the memories. Memories talk. So listen."

"What am I listening for?"

He shrugged unhelpfully and she scowled at him. He didn't want to help, that was fine. She'd figure it out on her own. She turned on her heel, this time scanning the shelves for any signs of blue while keeping an eye out for the specter of her uncle. Listening against her better judgment. For footsteps. For noises. For anything that might indicate she was going the right way.

Then suddenly, she heard it. A whispering. A distant hush. Like a thousand voices speaking under their breath all at once. She stopped walking, heart thudding. It came again to her left, a noise that almost sounded like her name. Was this what Azrael had meant? Should she follow it? She walked toward the sound. The farther she went, the louder the voices got. Louder and louder and yet seemingly no closer. She was certain that if she just kept moving, if she just kept following, eventually she would catch up to it.

When she rounded the corner, she immediately stopped in her tracks. A little ahead of her, crouched between two shelves, was a person. A young man made of flesh and blood, not the transparent shadows of memories. Amelia ducked around the corner to hide, the mysterious whispers still ringing in her ears. From where she stood, she could just make out the hollow features and wavy dark hair of Anton Stepanov, his head bent over a book. He was holding it with great care, wrapping it carefully in a piece of tattered moleskin. Before it disappeared, Amelia caught a glimpse of the cover: dark blue leather with a single flower stamped in the center.

She gasped. Anton's head snapped up and she drew back behind the shelf, heart thudding. There was a rustling, then footsteps. Amelia turned the corner in a panic, holding her breath until she heard him pass her by. Only when his footsteps had faded did she dare make a move, stepping into the aisle and making a beeline for the place he'd been kneeling. Her hands shook as she removed the moleskin-wrapped book from the lowest shelf, pulling back the fabric to stare at the stamped flower on the cover. Why would he have left it here? The book itself was worn and battered, but the pages were intact. A subtle whispering sound rustled from within, steady as a heartbeat. She was opening the pages when a voice spoke.

"I thought I heard somebody."

Amelia leapt to her feet, book in hand. Anton was standing at the end of the row watching her with a distinctly curious look on his face.

"I see you were not too scared to come back," he joked. He was smiling faintly, his posture relaxed and casual.

Amelia took a step back from him, a single word repeating in her head. *Murderer. Murderer. Murderer.*

He frowned. "Is something the matter?" he asked, eyes trailing to the book in one hand, and then to the knife in the other. "What are you doing?" he asked, taking a single step forward.

Amelia ran. Clutching the book tight against her chest, she sprinted down the row of shelves.

"Hey, wait!" Anton called after her. "Stop! Not that way!"

His footsteps came fast and hard. Amelia fumbled the knife in one hand as she reached for her watch. She ran down the rows as fast as she could, ignoring Anton's shouts. She didn't notice the shelves turning to dust around her, didn't noticed the gaping hole in the floor until one foot landed halfway over the edge. Her arms flailed, dropping both the book and the knife to the ground. She grabbed hold of a shelf, but it crumbled under her touch. She felt herself falling, and then a hand caught her wrist.

There was a wrenching feeling in her shoulder, nearly pulling her arm from its socket. A second hand grabbed her other arm, dragging her to safety. They toppled backward. Amelia landed on top of Anton's solid figure. She locked eyes with him and for a split second, she wished she had taken her chances with the cliff.

"Are you all right?" Anton panted, his hands gripping tight to both her arms.

Amelia jerked away from him, ignoring the searing pain in her right shoulder. She scrambled to her feet, dragging herself upright against the dust-covered shelves.

"I was trying to warn you," he said in his deeply accented voice, rising to his feet.

Amelia searched frantically for the knife and found it lying beside the book, a few feet from the edge of the . . . what was that? A chasm between two rows of shelves, so shrouded in shadows, the only way to notice it was by looking down. Around her, the shelves were filled with holes and dust, the books within them tattered beyond recognition. This was nothing like the rest of the time space. Something had happened here, was still happening here. From deep within the chasm came the whispering sound she'd been following.

Movement out of the corner of her eye brought her attention back to the Russian boy. He was moving toward the knife. Amelia lunged for it before he could and swung it at his head. He ducked at the last second and the knife struck the shelf above him. Dust and dirt shot out in all directions, coating them both. She swung again and this time he caught her wrist. He twisted her arm and knocked the handle of the knife from her grasp with the adeptness of someone trained in combat. It fell to the ground and slid over the edge of the abyss.

Amelia kicked him in the shin as hard as she could. His knees buckled but he didn't let go. He slammed her back against the shelves, knocking loose more dust.

"What are you doing?" he demanded. "Why are you attacking me?"

"Let me go!" Amelia shouted, struggling to loosen his grip on her.

"No. First you explain."

Amelia leveled a harrowing glare at him. "You're Anton Stepanov. You're Russian."

"And that is so threatening to you that you would try to kill me? After I helped you? Typical American."

Amelia's fear morphed into anger. "You killed my uncle!"

"What? Who are you talking about?"

"Have you really killed so many people that you have to ask? My uncle, Ernest Duquesne."

Anton leaned back to assess her more closely. His grip slackened.

"You are Amelia," he said quietly.

Amelia swore her pulse stopped. *He knew her name.*

She responded violently, bringing her knee to his stomach so hard that he doubled over in pain. She threw all her weight forward and shoved him back. He fell against the shelves, snapping them on impact. Amelia ran without looking back. Not stopping for the book, not daring to try with him so close by. She spun the crown of the watch and sprinted for the door, pulling it open almost the instant it appeared.

Her knees hit the ground on the other side just as the clock downstairs was chiming out midnight. She kicked the door shut behind her and collapsed to the floor. Desperate, retching sobs racked her body. She couldn't stop. It was as if the dam had burst and all the confusion and grief and pain she'd felt in these past two weeks came flooding out.

A light flipped on in the hallway, footsteps stopping at the door, but Amelia didn't look up.

"Oh dear . . ."

Moira's voice wormed its way through the dark room. Another round of gagging sobs ensued. Moira held still in the doorway, watching her. Amelia expected harshness. Scolding perhaps. But then she felt the warmth of Moira's presence as she knelt down beside her.

"I . . . I went back in," Amelia choked, her voice thick with tears. "P-please don't make me go in again. I can't."

Moira shushed her gently and reached out, laying one hand against her hair. Her face was a mix of emotions. She was in a set of purple satin pajamas. All the makeup had been washed away and for once, she looked human.

"Oh, Amelia," Moira said softly. As if her heart was truly aching for her.

Amelia stiffened as Moira's arms settled around her. She was unaccustomed to this kind of touch, especially coming from a woman. The only person who had ever attempted to comfort her like this was Uncle Ernest and it had been years since he had needed to do so. Before him, she supposed the last person had been her mother. Her body yearned for it even as her mind resisted, and soon she found herself leaning into Moira's embrace. The silky purple material of her night shirt felt cool and soft against her cheek. Her shoulder ached painfully.

"I saw him. Anton Stepanov. He was there. He . . . he has the book."

Moira's arms tightened around her. "Did he come after you?"

Amelia tried to answer but the words stuck in her throat. She cried harder, burying her face in Moira's shoulder.

"I'm sorry, Amelia," Moira said gently. It sounded genuine. "I'm so sorry. You have been braver than you ever should have needed to be." She pulled back and cupped Amelia's face in her hands. "I promise I will not let them hurt you."

Them, she said. Not just Anton. There was such heaviness in her voice that Amelia, for once, trusted her completely. There was no one left to trust but her.

MOIRA HELD Amelia as she sobbed. One hand continuously stroked her hair, half to comfort her, half to give Moira something to focus on while her mind ran a hundred miles a minute. Anton Stepanov had attacked her. There was dust in her hair and on her clothes, and something about the way she held her right shoulder told Moira that it was injured. Her worst fears about Jack's decision to send Amelia into the time space were already being realized. No part of her had expected Vasily Stepanov's son to be in the time space. But he was. Worse yet, he had found the book. And now he had attacked Amelia. But why? Could it be that he was out for some kind of vengeance for what had happened to his father?

As Amelia began to calm down, Moira sent her to her room to change out of her clothes and went downstairs. In the kitchen, she fixed a cup of tea, listening to the sound of the water running upstairs. She took two mugs upstairs with her, finding Amelia back in Ernest's bedroom, curled up under the blankets of his bed.

"I made tea," Moira said, handing one of the mugs to her.

Amelia sniffled. "I thought you hated tea."

Moira raised the second mug. "That's why mine is whiskey."

"Oh," Amelia said in surprise. She lifted the cup and took a delicate sip. "Thank you." She relaxed, slumping down into the pillows.

After a moment of considering and reconsidering, Moira sat down on the edge of the bed. "Is your shoulder all right?"

"Yes. Just a little sore." Amelia frowned down at her tea. "Did you know there's a chasm in the middle of the time space?"

Moira took a drink, letting the burning feeling of the whiskey distract her from other thoughts. "I did."

"Have you seen it?"

"No. I don't go into the time space myself anymore."

"Why not?"

"I'm the director of the Temporal Reconnaissance Program. I don't need to go in."

"Then how do you know about the chasm?"

Moira gave her a pointed look over her mug. "I'm the director of the Temporal Reconnaissance Program," she repeated. "I know things."

"Do you know what it is?"

"Our best theorists say it's most likely a hole in the space-time continuum."

Amelia made a face. "That doesn't sound real."

"And a chasm in the center of a library full of dead people does?"

Amelia's lips twitched slightly. "How did it get there?"

"No one is quite sure. They say it appeared around the time Lisavet Levy disappeared from the time space, but that's all just conjecture."

"But how . . ."

Moira shushed her. "Enough for now. Go to sleep, Amelia."

"But . . ."

"Hush. We'll talk more tomorrow."

Amelia let out a huff of annoyance and for once, Moira smiled at it. So she was feeling better then. She took the mug and Amelia slumped farther down under the blankets.

Moira didn't leave. She stayed beside her, listening to Amelia's breathing until it evened out. She looked around the room, suddenly remembering where she was. This was Ernest's bedroom. In here, like the rest of the house, there were books lining two of the walls, almost as if Ernest had been attempting to create a version of the time space in his own home. His clothes hung in the closet, a pair of his slippers sat by the door. A coat hung on one of the bedposts as if he'd placed it there with every intention of returning to it. Moira reached out a hand and let it hover over the coat, thinking of the man who had worn it. She touched the fabric, running her fingers along the soft wool.

When she was sure that the girl wouldn't wake up, she left the room and went downstairs to call Jack. They were done with this. She would not let him force Amelia to go back in. It was too much to risk. It took only fifteen minutes for Jack to reach the house from his hotel nearby. Moira heard his car pulling up, idling on the street for a moment to talk to Fred, who was always close by. Just in case.

"Miss me already?" Jack asked when she opened the door.

Moira ushered him inside. He sauntered through the house and into the living room as if he owned the place.

"Where's the girl?" he asked as he surveyed the shelves of books along the back wall.

"Amelia is asleep upstairs."

"Is she? Pity. I thought you were going to let me meet her."

"You have met her."

"Yeah, but that was years ago. She was only a kid then."

"She still is a kid," Moira said flatly. "That's actually the reason why I called you here. Amelia will not be going back into the time space."

"No?" Jack asked, smiling in amusement.

"No. I'm putting my foot down. It's too dangerous."

Jack let out a bemused sigh. "Okay. What happened?"

"Anton Stepanov confronted her. She saw him with the book, and he attacked her. I've already started considering other options for us, but the girl can't do it." Jack started to speak but Moira pressed on, giving him no room to protest. "I'm telling her tomorrow that she shouldn't go back in anymore. I just wanted to inform you."

He made a humming sound and began pacing up and down the length of the room. Taking his sweet time, as usual. "Fair enough. Last thing we want is for the kid to get killed in there. So then the only question is, what do we do with her now?"

"Nothing."

"Nothing? But she knows too much now. She's a liability."

"She's still cooperating. It's not an issue. I'll remain here to keep an eye on her like we planned. Nothing else needs to be done."

"That's not your decision to make. If you don't want to use her, then something needs to be done."

"No, Jack. She's a child. I'm not going to let you lock her up the way you did to me."

Silence passed between them. Jack was still smiling, even after the reminder of what he'd done when *she* wouldn't cooperate all those years ago.

"My, my," he said, letting out a chuckle. "What's this? Has that little girl gotten to you, Moira?"

Moira held his gaze, refusing to react.

Jack came toward her, still laughing. "Has someone finally managed to crack your cold, dead heart?"

"This isn't about me, Jack."

"No?"

"It's about being efficient. We've lost enough time as it is. If you just let me go in instead . . ."

Jack interrupted. "You're right. We have lost time. We've lost time, resources, momentum . . . and you lost that tape the other day."

Moira gave a callous shrug. "I told you, the device malfunctioned. It's new technology. It happens."

"Sure, sure," Jack said, only half convinced. "Fine. You can let the girl off the case. But . . . not just yet."

"What?"

"Anton Stepanov has the book, you said?"

"What does that have to do with Amelia?" Moira asked, dreading the look on his face. It was the same one he wore when he was getting ready to test her.

Jack's smile widened. "Call Fred in here for me, will you? Let's talk business."

"Jack . . ."

"Don't worry, Moira, you'll have your way. After tomorrow, the girl stays out of the time space. But we need her to go back in. One more time."

10

1950, Somewhere in the Time Space

LISAVET WAS TIRED. SHE wasn't accustomed to the feeling. Nor was she quite sure why, after twelve years of feeling nothing of the sort, she suddenly felt like her body had been drained of energy, like a marionette with its strings cut. Limbs so heavy that the simple act of walking was a trial. She wanted to do nothing but sleep, but no matter how hard she tried, either inside of memories or in the time space, she couldn't manage it.

"Perhaps I'm ill?" she suggested to Azrael.

He shook his head. "No, it isn't possible. Not in the time space." He paused, watching her weary face as she leaned against the shelves in a dark corner. "Though I suppose heartbreak is a kind of illness all its own."

Maybe that was it. Maybe it was heartbreak making her so tired. Now *she* was the one following Ernest in the time space whenever he made an appearance. Seeing him, even from a distance, was as much a relief as it was painful. He was alive and well and unharmed. No longer in danger.

She, however, still was. She could sense something had changed for her within the time space. Timekeepers were watching for her now. Not just the Americans and the Russians, but the British, the French, the Italians . . . they worked more quickly, lingering longer. Memories were burned before she could reach them, and it became harder and harder to stay hidden.

Twice now she had been forced to run away when a timekeeper pulled a gun on her. Three times she had found one following her the way Ernest had when they'd first met. Another Russian, this one with dark hair and hard, sullen eyes. He tracked her every movement from afar. Another hunter. Another threat. She kept the silver revolver close at hand, but she doubted she'd ever be able to bring herself to use it. Death was another kind of erasure, and she did not want to be the cause of it.

Every time her salvaging efforts were thwarted, she cursed Jack Dillinger in her head. She was certain that this was his fault. That he, realizing what she had done to Ernest, had put the word out about her, telling every timekeeper in existence that the girl who saved memories could also take them away completely. She was in more danger than she had ever been. Azrael remained particularly vigilant, staying by her side in ways he hadn't since she was small. The exhaustion settled deeper as time passed. No matter how much she rested. No matter how often she tried to sleep.

But then, four months after her last night with Ernest, she awoke to the feeling of something moving within her. She was on a ship sailing from England to India on calm, clear waters, tucked into the memory of a sailor standing watch up on deck. The rocking of the hull had helped lull her to sleep but now, all of a sudden, she found the movement unsettling. Her eyes searched the interior of the ship, looking for the cause when it happened again. She sprang from the bed, smacking her head on the low ceiling. With one hand on her forehead, she stumbled out of the memory and back into the time space, panting in fear. Azrael was beside her in an instant.

"Are you all right?" he asked.

"I don't know. I thought I felt something moving."

"Moving? Moving where?"

She pressed a hand against her abdomen. "Something inside of me. It . . ."

She broke off at the sight of Azrael's face. "What is it?"

"Come with me," he said gravely.

He took her through the shelves of the time space, his liquid form moving so quickly he was almost a blur. He stopped in between two rows and summoned the specter of a woman Lisavet had never seen before. She was dressed like Azrael in simple brown robes. They spoke in whispers, pausing every once in a while so the woman could assess her. When they finished speaking, the crease in Azrael's brow was deeper than Lisavet had ever seen it.

"Oh, Lisavet. Oh, my poor child."

"What's wrong?"

"It seems that . . . well, there's no other explanation. The exhaustion, now this . . . My dear, you are pregnant."

Lisavet's knees buckled. No, that wasn't possible. She couldn't get pregnant. It was something she had been so certain of. She had never even bled! *That's because you're in the time space*, a little voice in her head said, almost mockingly.

"H-how? It's been over three months since Ernest and I last . . ."

Azrael consulted the woman again. "She said that would put you somewhere between sixteen and twenty weeks along. Around the time the baby starts to move."

As if on cue, the thing inside of her shifted again. She put a hand on her stomach. Was it possible? Was she carrying a child, Ernest's child? A baby that belonged to a man who no longer remembered she existed? The tiny being kicked again and this time she felt it against the palm of her hand. She fainted cold onto the floor.

THE MONTHS moved quickly.

It was getting harder to stay hidden. Harder to run away whenever danger drew closer. Lisavet lingered inside of memories more than she stayed outside of them. In the hourly increments of sleep she managed to get, she began having nightmares of Jack Dillinger's voice ordering Ernest, who had forgotten that he loved her, to shoot her dead, her baby dragged from her arms the minute it was born. She was restless with worry, wondering how long she could outrun them. All the while, the baby inside of her grew as restless as she was. Its constant kicking kept her awake and she took to humming songs to it in an effort to get it to stop. Every song, save for one, seemed only to excite it. But whenever she sang "Blue Moon," the baby at last held still.

One evening, she sang the song until the baby stopped moving and leaned her head back against the shelves, still humming.

"My brother loves that song," a woman's voice said suddenly, jerking her out of her momentary peace.

Her eyes found the woman at once. Over the years, Lisavet had encountered hundreds, if not thousands of spectral memories, but never had she seen one she knew. Or . . . knew of, at least. There was no mistaking the copper hair and hereditary blue eyes of Ernest Duquesne's younger sister. Lisavet had seen her in his memories; the wayward girl who'd gotten pregnant out of wedlock and been disowned by her family. By everyone, that is, except her older brother. What was she doing here?

"Who?" she asked instead, feigning confusion.

"My older brother," said the memory of Elaina Duquesne. "He plays it all the time on his record player."

He still played their song.

"It's a beautiful song," Lisavet said. She didn't know how to talk to this person.

"It is." Elaina lingered beside her, just as uncertain as she was. "You're having a baby?"

Lisavet touched her stomach. "Yes. Not long now."

"I had a baby too," Elaina said.

I know, Lisavet wanted to say.

"She died just a few days after she was born. She was so little. And the doctors said she was ill."

"I'm sorry," Lisavet said. She hadn't known the baby had died. When she and Ernest parted ways, the baby was just a few weeks away from being born. "So . . . your brother never got to meet her? His niece?"

"No. He came to see me in the hospital a few hours too late. He was the only one. The rest of my family . . . they weren't happy with me. But Ernest, my brother, he was different. He offered to help me raise her. When she died, he even said I could come live with him, but I was too stubborn."

"How did you die?" Lisavet asked, knowing it was a touchy subject among the dead. Usually, she didn't dare ask.

Elaina dropped her eyes and looked away. "I did it to myself. I couldn't handle it. Losing the baby, I mean. So six months after, I . . ." she broke off and shook her head violently. "It was stupid. It was so stupid. If I could change it . . ."

Lisavet nodded in understanding. She had met many memories who had taken their own lives over the years. Every one of them regretted it.

"I'm sorry for bothering you," Elaina said after a moment. "I heard you singing, and I couldn't help it."

"It's all right. I don't mind company. I only wish I could help somehow."

"Could you?" Elaina asked hopefully. "I don't mean to be too forward, but I've seen the other timekeepers around here. Hardly any of them bother with random girls who offed themselves and I don't want Ernest to be the one to see all my memories. It would . . . it would break him."

Lisavet started to tell her that she wasn't a timekeeper. But she stopped short. Why shouldn't she help her? She had a watch. The book of poems was certainly big enough to hold the memories of this woman's short life. She was as much a timekeeper as anyone else. And besides, she knew what Elaina said about Ernest was true. She agreed, watching the relief spread across the young woman's face. Using the shelf to pull herself up, Lisavet took the poems from her bag. She did what she had seen the other timekeepers do, letting her fingers rest on the milky shadow of Ernest's younger sister.

The memories began to flow throw her. Moments that flew by in snippets. The memories of Elaina's earlier years were painfully short, but chock-full of the same quiet moments she'd seen in Ernest's mind. The flower garden at the grand house. The father and mother who loved and cared for them. The older brother she adored. Lisavet delighted in seeing the younger version of Ernest, with his copper hair and stubby legs, grow into a fiercely protective young man. She held her breath, as Elaina did, when he went off to war at sixteen, and held it again when he returned a different person. It was his sister, Lisavet learned, who had brought him out of the shadows after he came home. They were close. So close that when Elaina was cast out for the affair and resulting pregnancy, Ernest remained by her side, as steadfast in providing her a lifeline as she had been for him. Only unlike him, Elaina chose to pull away.

The other memories were short as well. It was too much, the baby, the separation from her family, the rejection of the man who had caused it. Lisavet watched it all unravel, and when Elaina stood alone on the bridge six months after her baby died, she didn't look away. When the memories faded, Elaina was gone. Lisavet stood alone with tears running down her cheeks. One hand pressed against her stomach, the other holding the book.

For the first time, she wondered what happened to an infant's memories when they died. Did they even have any memories to save? She had seen plenty of children over the years, had played with them when she herself was still a child, but none of them had been any younger than four or five. So what about the rest? She didn't have any memories of her own that reached back that far, so what happened to them?

She was still pondering this when she felt the familiar sensation of being watched creep down the length of her spine. When she looked up, she saw the Russian timekeeper standing at the end of a row of shelves. He made no moves toward her. Simply watched curiously, the way Ernest had in the beginning. She wanted to shout at him but didn't dare. She'd learned her lesson about talking to timekeepers.

His gaze trailed down to the swell of her stomach, and he frowned, raising his eyes back to hers, concern etched onto his sharp features. Lisavet hardened her expression and retreated to safety inside of a memory, leaving him and his prying eyes behind.

SPLITTING PAIN pulled Lisavet from the middle of a dream. She sat up in horror, gripping her stomach. It wasn't time yet. She wasn't ready. She had a blanket. A set of clothes. But she hadn't yet found the right place for the birth to happen. Somewhere with proper supplies for a newborn baby and medicine for her if she needed it.

Another rolling pain in her abdomen told her that, once again, Time didn't care if she was ready or not. The baby was coming, and it was coming now. She pulled herself out of the memory, fighting not to cry out in agony.

"Azrael!" she called desperately. "Azrael, help!"

He didn't come. Perhaps he was too far away to hear her, or maybe he was out time walking himself. Around her, other memories awakened at the sound of her voice, watery phantoms appearing around her. She heard them whispering among themselves. Desperately, she began sifting through the books on the shelves. She was in the Austrian section.

That was good. She could find a hospital close to modern day and watch what the doctors did, the way she'd watched the nurse stitch up a gun-shot wound. The next pain in her stomach was so strong she nearly vom-ited. When it subsided, she took another book from the shelf, thumbing through it so quickly she risked tearing the pages.

Lisavet pulled herself into a memory, immediately aware of the bus-tle of a hospital all around her. There would be no doing this herself, she realized after another jolt of pain, reaching into her bag for her father's watch. She needed help, history be damned. Right now, her baby was the most important thing. She waited several seconds for the shudder-ing feeling of Time parting to cease, allowing her to become a part of the memory. Eyes that previously passed over her suddenly paused on her figure. She ignored their looks and approached the nearest nurse.

"I need help," she said in her mother tongue. "Please. I'm having a baby."

The nurse didn't question where this strangely dressed young woman had come from, and instead called out for someone to bring her a wheel-chair.

It took seven hours. There was blood and pain. Worried looks on the doctors' faces.

"Complications," they said to her, offering no other explanation.

They gave her medicine that made her uncommonly dizzy, working quickly to extricate the child from inside of her. *Complications*, Lisavet murmured through her haze. That explained the suddenness of labor. The early birth. Her heart thudded out the beat of every passing second. Her mind oscillated between fear and once again wondering where a baby's thoughts went to when it died. She thought of Elaina's baby, the image of the cold dead thing lying still in its cradle seared into her head. It wouldn't happen to her, she told herself. It wouldn't.

When at last, the baby's cries pierced the air, the other doctors in the room applauded.

"Healthy lungs," the nurse told her as she lay the screaming bundle on Lisavet's chest.

"The baby will live?" Lisavet asked in between choked sobs of relief.

"She will be just fine," the nurse told her with a reassuring smile.

"She?"

"It's a girl."

A girl. Lisavet held the baby close as the nurse cleaned her up, refusing to let them take her. The doctors warned her that she had lost a lot of blood. She would need to stay in the hospital until she recovered. Was there anyone they could contact? Where was the baby's father?

Lisavet didn't answer them. She was tired, pain numbing her senses to anything else but the baby in her arms. A girl, a daughter. Ernest's daughter. She traced one hand over the infant's tiny head, haloed in a wreath of copper-colored hair. Ernest's hair. Deciding her lack of response was likely drug induced, the doctors eventually cleared out of the room, giving her orders to rest. The nurse stayed a bit longer, showing her how to get the baby to latch and feed.

They offered to take the baby to the nursery so that Lisavet could sleep, but she refused. She didn't dare let go of her, fearing what could happen if she did. This was still a memory after all. They couldn't stay. Who knew what sort of damage Lisavet had already caused by being here? She shook the fears away, holding her daughter more tightly in her arms. Complications, the doctor had said. If she hadn't come, neither one of them would have survived. History be damned. When the nurse finally departed, Lisavet kissed her baby's forehead, whispering softly to her as she slept.

"I'll take care of you. I won't let anything happen to you," she promised her. "I'll rewrite all of history if I have to."

As night fell outside the window, Lisavet left the room, carrying her baby down the hall. Her dress had been taken but she still had her coat. She exchanged her hospital gown for a nurse's uniform she found in a

supply closet. Her very bones felt as though they had been stretched and
remolded by a careless sculptor. She was weak from blood loss, but she
couldn't risk staying any longer.

When they returned to the time space, Lisavet found herself staring
at the heap of dust and broken wood before her. Not just one book, but
an entire row had fallen, dozens of lives altered.

"Lisavet . . . what happened?"

Azrael had come at last. There was no mistaking the horror in his
tone. The baby made a small sleepy noise, drawing his attention to her.
"But how did you . . . Lisavet, what did you do?"

"It doesn't matter," Lisavet said, pressing the baby closer. "It was for
her."

Azrael stared down at the pile of dust that had once been memories
and said nothing.

IT DIDN'T take long before Lisavet realized what was going to happen.
Not even twenty-four hours had passed, no time for healing, no time
for sleep, before the sound of the baby's cries drew the attention of the
timekeepers already lying in wait for her. Twice in one day, she had to
run from them, forcing her pain-stricken body into motion. She took
to keeping the gun closer at hand, counting out the number of bullets
she had in the chamber. The number of timekeepers she would kill to
protect her child, but only if she had to.

The timekeepers were not the only problem. In fact, they weren't
even the most pressing. What was more urgent was the fact that Lisavet
didn't know how to take care of her daughter. The baby had physical
needs as any other child would. She fed every two hours, a pace Lisavet
could not keep up with. After just two days, her body had begun failing to produce enough milk to satiate her. It was as if, with the child no
longer growing inside of her, her connection to the physical world, the

human world, had once again been severed, leaving her unable to produce milk the way most new mothers could.

The baby, however, was all human.

"I don't understand," Lisavet lamented. "She shouldn't need to eat in
here. Why is this happening?"

Azrael peered over her shoulder, his expression heavy. "An infant has
no memories of its own. Her mind, her thoughts, they haven't yet begun
to take proper shape. Perhaps when she is older, she will no longer need
food."

"And until then?" Lisavet asked. "I've tried to give her food from memories, it goes right through her. Just like Ernest."

The baby let out another heart-wrenching cry. Lisavet's eyes darted
between the shelves, searching for timekeepers. Convinced she heard
footsteps, she moved farther into the shadows. Azrael followed her.

"Lisavet," he said quietly. "You cannot continue like this."

"I don't have a choice. Like you said, it's only a matter of time. It will
get better."

"It will get *harder*," Azrael pressed in a grave voice she had never heard
before. "The child was born inside a memory. Inside the time space. She
may never cease to feel hunger, even once her own consciousness becomes stronger."

Lisavet shook her head adamantly. "I can handle it. I'll figure something out."

"I don't know if you can."

"I *have* to."

"Lisavet . . ."

"What else would you have me do, Azrael?" Lisavet asked, tears streaming down her face. "It's not as if I can just leave her somewhere for Ernest
to find. He wouldn't know she was his. Who knows what would happen?"

Azrael gave her a deep, sad look. "I'm trying to suggest that you leave,
Lisavet."

"L-leave?"

"Leave the time space. Take your child and go on your own terms. Before they can force you out."

"I can't do that. You know what Ernest said. I might die."

"If you don't, she *will* die."

Lisavet clutched her baby tighter, blinking back tears. "I'll figure something out. I *will*," she promised, more to her daughter than to Azrael.

"All right, Lisavet," Azrael said heavily. "I trust you'll do what's best."

He left her to think. Lisavet took herself into the memory of the hotel in Switzerland, a place she had not been since the night she'd removed herself from Ernest's life. There, she sobbed openly, stroking her daughter's face as she slept.

In her sleep, the baby whimpered, her mouth opening and closing in search of food where there was none. Azrael was right. Her baby couldn't stay here. Here, where there was nothing but memories. No food. No safety.

Lisavet began running through her options. She could stay and pray that her dwindling milk supply would last long enough for the baby to stop needing it. They could live inside of memories. Lisavet had a gun, she could keep them safe. But could they really outrun the timekeepers forever? Maybe if she gave up salvaging memories, they would decide she wasn't worth it and leave them alone. The very thought made her chest ache with guilt, but things had changed. What had mattered to her before now paled in comparison to the child in her arms.

Her second option was no better. She could leave like Azrael suggested and hope that Ernest's theory was wrong. But even if she left, their life would not be an easy one. She would be alone, no money, no connections. She had seen enough of the world through memories to know how unkind it could be to a mother and child alone.

Her tears subsided as the baby opened her wide blue eyes. Ernest's eyes. Their daughter was more like him than she was anything like her mother. Lisavet began to sing "Blue Moon" as the baby screwed up her face fitfully. The song worked to soothe her. Lisavet choked out the last words and walked out onto the balcony. Down below, her father and mother were walking hand in hand down the cobbled street.

"See those two people?" Lisavet asked quietly. "Those are your grandparents. I know they would have loved to meet you."

In response, the baby made a small cooing sound. Lisavet sniffled and wiped her eyes. She thought of her father and what he had done on the night the Nazis came for them, wondering what he might do now if he was in her position. Only, he *had* been in her position, in a way. When the world had proven to be unsafe for his daughter, he had taken her to the time space. Even though at least some small part of him must have known that by closing the door between them to go after his other child, he might never see her again, no matter how hard he fought to get back to her. He had chosen his children over all else that night. Even over his own life.

If only there was a place where she could be certain her daughter could be safe. A third kind of universe where they could hide. She shifted her daughter in her arms, feeling the tug of her bag against her shoulder. The book of memories in its faded leather cover was heavier than ever before. Lisavet took it out of the bag with one hand, propping it against the railing and flipped through to the memories she loved most.

"Perhaps we should just hide in here," she said lightly, tapping the pages of the memories. "I can bring us into the memories and it will be as if nothing ever changed."

She meant it as a joke. A simple fantasy. But then her spine stiffened. She looked back down at the child, a feeling of dread and knowing filling her simultaneously. There *was* another option. She could feel her heart splintering the way it had the last time she'd stood on this balcony. Like last time, to do what was right meant losing someone she loved, possibly forever.

Lisavet dried away the remaining tears with some effort. She held her baby tightly, savoring the warm, milky scent of her.

"Come on, little one," she whispered, forcing herself to smile. "Before we say goodbye, there are some things I want to show you."

She took her everywhere. Every memory that had ever meant something to her. Every moment in history, showing her daughter the pieces of time that had made up her whole world in hopes that somehow, some small part of her might remember them. That she might remember *her*. She took her to the field where she and Ernest had shared their first kiss. To forests in Russia where the snow fell in perfect flakes. To the gardens of Versailles, stooping down to brush her daughter's fingers over soft rose petals. She noticed that the baby had a particular fondness for the animals on the African savanna, her tiny eyes holding focus with the large looming beasts. As she made her way across the tapestry of memories, she continued singing her lullaby. She continued whispering, between each passing verse. *I love you, I love you, I love you.*

Azrael found her in the time space just as the baby fell asleep in her arms. Lisavet told him her plan, watching the contours of his face shift and change before settling into the same, accepting expression she wore herself.

"You know that if you do this, you can never take it back."

"I know."

"No one has ever done what you're doing. No one has ever altered the past so entirely. You might be untethering her from Time the same way you are. Are you sure that's wise?"

Lisavet didn't answer. In truth, she wasn't certain. It might be better if her daughter was untethered from the forces of Time. She would never be affected by the memory games played by men at war.

"And what about you?" Azrael asked. "You're staying here?"

Lisavet swallowed the growing lump in her throat, never taking her eyes off the sleeping child in her arms. "If I'm still in the time space, I can protect her from whatever might happen out there. I can change the past. Stop the bad things from happening."

"Bad things will always happen, Lisavet," Azrael said softly. "You can't protect her from all of them."

"But I can try," she said stubbornly. "I have to try."

Azrael didn't attempt to stop her as she reached into her bag to remove the two things she needed. The watch and the book containing Elaina Duquesne's memories.

For the second time, Lisavet found herself standing in a hospital. This time, she was in a quiet room, late at night. No nurses or doctors were around, only the sleeping young woman in the hospital bed in front of her. Somewhere in the nursery ward, Elaina's infant daughter, only two days old, had just drawn breath for the very last time. Lisavet removed her coat and set her bag on the floor. She was still wearing the nurse's attire she had taken from the Austrian hospital, almost as if her past self had known what was coming. She bit back her tears and listened. Time shuddered open, letting her in.

Elaina sat up in alarm at her sudden arrival. Her eyes were panic-stricken. The eyes of a mother who had been informed earlier that day that her baby may not make it through the night.

"What is it?" she asked frantically. "Who are you?"

"I'm the nurse on the night shift," Lisavet said, forcing her face into a gentle smile. The baby made a noise.

Elaina looked at the bundle fearfully. "Is she all right? They told me she was struggling to breathe."

"Yes, she's fine," Lisavet said with difficulty. "She's perfect. Just a cold it seems, but she's got strong, healthy lungs."

Elaina relaxed into the pillow, tears gathering in her eyes. "Thank goodness. I was worried. I had a nightmare that she . . ." The baby began crying in earnest and Elaina's brow creased with worry again. "Is she hungry?"

"Yes. We were going to feed her in the nursery but since she's feeling better . . ."

"No, I'll do it," Elaina said at once. "Please. I want to."

She reached for the baby and for a moment, Lisavet almost changed her mind. In three days, she had not set her daughter down once, not even for a moment. She forced herself to come forward. To deposit her child into Elaina's outstretched arms. To watch this other woman hold her baby to her breast and give her what Lisavet's own body had failed to provide.

"Thank you," Elaina said quietly. "For bringing her. I don't know what I would have done if . . ."

Lisavet swallowed, offering her as warm a smile as she could muster. "Have you decided what you're going to name her?"

"I hadn't yet. I didn't want to risk it in case . . . but I suppose she's better now."

"Much better," Lisavet said.

"I hadn't given much thought to girl names. I was so certain she would be a boy," Elaina admitted. "What would you name her? If she were yours."

It took everything Lisavet had left not to break down at those words. Instead, she told her the name she had picked out for her daughter the moment she was born.

"Amelia. I would name her Amelia."

"Amelia," Elaina repeated, savoring the name carefully. "It's perfect."

The baby stopped feeding and let out a satisfied gurgle.

"Should I take her back to the nursery for you?" Lisavet asked. "So you can rest?"

Elaina nodded reluctantly.

Lisavet left Elaina to sleep, pausing to pick up her things before sliding out of the room. Keeping her head high to avoid suspicion, she carried Amelia down to the nursery, waiting outside until she was certain nobody else was there. She located the cradle where Elaina Duquesne's real daughter lay, cold and unmoving. She forced herself to lay Amelia down in the empty cradle next to her and paused just long enough to write her new name on the plate affixed to the bed. She read the date on the bottom, committing it to memory.

With great care, Lisavet took Elaina's dead infant from its cradle and forced herself out of the memory. Leaving her child in the past where Ernest was sure to find her. Where he would not know she was his daughter, but where at least, he would be there to love her. Even if it meant Lisavet could not.

Before returning to the time space, she visited another memory to give Elaina's baby a proper burial. She sobbed over its tiny figure as if it were her own. The desperate, heartrending sobs of a mother who had lost a child.

She braced herself for the return, knowing that she would have caused damage. A dead child replaced. A mother whose suicide stemmed from grief over a lost child recalled to life. The course of both their stories altered forever. She knew there would be consequences, but nothing prepared her for the reality of what she had done.

As the time space came into focus before her, she gasped. She nearly lost her balance, arms flailing out to prevent herself from falling into the hole, the chasm, that had opened in the middle of the floor. It stretched wider than she was tall, creating a rift that swallowed the shelves around it. She dropped her messenger bag onto the floor, falling to her knees.

A loud whispering came from within. It was Time, fraught with the echoes of the memories she had destroyed, calling out to her.

She heard another sound and looked up. Through her tears, she saw the Russian timekeeper. He was close. Too close. She scrambled to her feet.

"Don't run away," he said in Russian. He caught the strap of her bag as she tried to pick it up. "I only want to help. What happened to—"

"Stay away from me," Lisavet said, wrenching the bag away with a violent tug that almost sent her sprawling.

She ran from him. But instead of following, he bent down to pick something up. Her heart skipped a beat. Her book. He had her book. It had fallen out of her bag when he'd tried to take it from her. She considered turning back for it, but he was already turning the crown of his watch, taking her book, and all her memories of Ernest with him.

TIME MOVED forward.

Though she knew she shouldn't, Lisavet visited her daughter through memories dozens of times over, entering them through the altered pages of Elaina's past. She watched Ernest meet her for the first time, watched Elaina try to care for her. As it turned out, her child's death hadn't been the only thing that forced Elaina over that bridge. Lisavet had brought a woman back from the dead, but it didn't mean she had saved her life. To compensate, Lisavet did what she could to make things better. She made more changes to the past, telling herself that it was worth the consequences. It was for her daughter. In the first two years of Amelia's life, Lisavet interfered no fewer than seven times, doing what she could to keep Elaina afloat. Sending money her way when the rent was due. Preventing her from getting fired. Stepping in to prevent an accident on Amelia's second birthday when Elaina left the stove on.

All the while, the chasm in the time space grew wider.

"Lisavet, you have to stop this," Azrael told her. "You cannot rewrite the past every time you don't like the outcome."

"I will, I promise. As soon as they get through this."

"No. Not when they get through it. You have to stop now."

"I can't. Amelia needs me."

"You're destroying the past, Lisavet. Can't you see it's gone too far? I can't keep watching you do this."

"Then look away!" Lisavet snapped, wheeling around to face him. "I'm not a little girl anymore, Azrael. I don't need your help."

Azrael looked at her sadly. He wasn't upset or even hurt by her words. He was too old for that. Too wise to be fooled by her anger. "That's where you're wrong, my girl. You need it now more than ever."

"Well, I don't want it. Just leave me alone." She didn't wait to hear his retort before storming into another memory.

Perhaps if she had known that would be the last time she saw him, she would have turned back. She would have left things in a better place. But it was as he always said; Time was not a friend. It did not care for parting words and final goodbyes.

They came for her that night in 1952.

As she walked the time space hours later, she saw a timekeeper standing very still in the middle of one of the rows. An American, with tightly cut brown hair. The way he held himself, with his head cocked to one side and his shoulders tense, seemed strange to her and she drew back into the shadows. He did not reach for a book and instead took several deliberate steps to the end of the shelves, craning his neck to see around the edge. Lisavet followed him, taking her leather gloves from her bag so that she would be ready when he finally chose his mark. He stopped in the middle of another row and raised one arm, bent at the elbow as though he were waving. She squinted at him in the darkness, so perplexed by his movements that she didn't notice the shadows shifting around her. Didn't hear the quiet footsteps. Only when his arm straightened, his finger pointing in her direction, did she realize what he was doing.

Someone grabbed her from behind. Violent hands gripped her arms so tightly they left entire handprints on her skin. Everything happened in a blur. The other timekeeper came to help, the two of them grappling to get her under control. Someone struck her when she fought too hard. She begged, but neither of them listened. One of them spun a watch, the other forced her through the door that appeared. As they drew close to it, she gave one final, adrenaline-fueled twist, managing to loosen her captor's grip enough so that he dropped her. She scrambled to her feet, tripping over hands that tried to grab her, and sprinted down the row of shelves. She almost got away, she almost escaped.

Until she rounded the corner and ran straight into Jack Dillinger's waiting arms. She recognized his voice, despite the fact that she'd never heard it outside of memories.

"Settle down now. No one is coming to save you."

He held her in a chokehold so tight that she couldn't breathe. The cold metal of a pistol pressed against her temple as he shoved her toward the waiting door.

In a final, desperate attempt, she called out Ernest's name. Even if he didn't remember her, maybe he'd still come. Maybe he would save her from this.

"Scream all you want, Miss Levy," Jack said cruelly. "He can't hear you."

She was forced through the door. On the other side, two more men in white coats were waiting. Jack held her still while one of them inserted a syringe into her neck. A sickly chill washed over her as her muscles gave way to the sedative.

The door to the time space closed behind her as she slipped into unconsciousness. It never opened again.

11

1965, Boston Massachusetts

WHEN AMELIA WENT DOWNSTAIRS to the kitchen the next morning, two men were seated at the table drinking coffee.

"There she is," one of them said, smiling at her. "Morning!"

Moira stepped into view, her expression oddly tense. "Amelia. You're awake."

"What's going on?" Amelia asked tentatively.

"Amelia, this is Jack Dillinger, my boss. And one of my colleagues. Fred Vance. They're here to help us with something."

Moira's voice was casual and calm, but Amelia could see in her eyes that something was off. She looked at the two men. Jack Dillinger looked just how she'd expected the head of the CIA to look; broad, blunt, and authoritative. Fred, by comparison, was stocky and bullish.

Jack waved her into the room. "Don't be shy, sweetheart, come have some breakfast. You've got a big day ahead of you."

Amelia's eyes flitted back to Moira. "What's he talking about?"

Moira put a plate of eggs into her hands. "They are here to help us catch Anton Stepanov."

"Catch him?"

"That's right!" Jack exclaimed. "We heard you saw him with the book we need, so we figured it was high time to bring the bastard to heel."

"So you're going in after him?"

Jack chuckled at her. "Oh, we're not. You are."

"Me?" Amelia turned to Moira, but she wouldn't look at her.

"Sit down," Moira said, squeezing her shoulder. "We'll explain while you eat."

Amelia did as she was told, sitting on the end of the table closest to Jack. She didn't eat, feeling sick.

"All right, here's the plan," Jack said between sips of coffee. "We talked it over and what we're going to do is send you into the time space with Fred here. He'll wait near the door to catch the Russian and drag him out when he gets close enough, but it's going to be up to you to lure him that way."

They were using her as bait. She looked at Moira. "Can't you go in with me instead?"

Jack answered before she could. "Hunting down a Russian criminal is a man's work. Besides, Moira doesn't go in the time space, do you, Donnelly?"

Moira ignored him. "We agreed that Fred is the better option. In case something goes wrong."

They continued talking but Amelia could barely hear them over the ringing in her ears. After she'd choked down a few bites of egg, Moira gestured for Amelia to follow her upstairs, grabbing her purse from the table in the foyer. Jack and Fred had begun pushing furniture around in the living room.

"What are they doing?" Amelia asked when they entered her bedroom.

"Oh, you know. Checking angles. Measuring the distance between doorways. Whatever else it is that men do before committing acts of violence."

Moira set her bag down on the desk and began examining the room, the purple quilt, the tiny painted stars on the ceiling that Uncle Ernest had made when Amelia first moved in. The woman was pretending that this was fine. That everything was normal. It was infuriating. Amelia watched her as she took the book she had been reading from her nightstand. *Aurora Leigh.*

"Did you read this?" Moira asked, holding it up.

Amelia nodded. Moira looked surprised as she flipped through the pages of the book.

"I really liked it," Amelia said, forcing the words out with great effort.

Moira smiled. "I had hoped you might. It helped me through some dark times when I was younger," she said, her voice softer than normal. Warm even.

"Oh?"

"I had a very lonely childhood," Moira continued. "And then there came a stretch of time when poetry was the only way I had of coping. Of touching something real."

"Something real?" Amelia asked with a frown.

Moira took a moment to answer. "We fill our homes with furniture and our minds with facts, but poetry is how we fill our souls. It's the poor man's medicine . . . the deepest expression of mankind. If you can read poetry, then you have already felt the shadows of humanity's most potent emotions."

"Is that from a poem?"

Moira lifted her eyes to the ceiling as if she couldn't quite remember and shook her head. "No. I don't believe so."

"Sounds like one," Amelia said. She hesitated before adding, "Maybe you should be a poet. You know, if the whole scary CIA agent thing doesn't work out."

Moira let out a small laugh. She put the book down and pulled out the desk chair, gesturing for Amelia to sit.

"Don't you have a mirror in here?" Moira asked as she picked up the hairbrush from the dresser and brought it over. "No wonder your hair's always such a mess."

Amelia tried to turn around to glare at her, but the tug of the brush against her scalp held her in place. "It's not a mess. There's just too much of it."

"I can cut it for you if you'd like. Shorter hair is in fashion these days."

"If you touch my hair, I'll shove *you* out a window."

Moira chuckled at her and set down the brush. Her fingers slid up into Amelia's hair. She began pulling the red strands into a neat French braid going straight down her back. Amelia froze under the unfamiliar touch.

"I want you to be careful in there today, all right?" Moira said quietly. "If things start to go wrong, I want you to come back out right away. Regardless of what Fred might say. You trust your own judgment first. Understood?"

Amelia nodded.

Moira paused and gripped her chin in her palm. "I mean it, Amelia. I want to hear you say it out loud."

"I'll be careful."

Satisfied, Moira let go and commenced braiding her hair again. Cool fingers brushed against the back of Amelia's neck, making her shiver. Jack called out for them. Moira finished braiding and faced her so they were at eye level. She looked as though she wanted to say something else. Instead, she leaned forward and kissed Amelia on the forehead.

"Time to go," Moira said.

Amelia stood up and followed her out of the room. Downstairs, Jack and Fred had moved all the living room furniture to the foyer, blocking off access to other rooms.

"That should about do it," Jack said, slightly breathless. "We've closed off all the doorways he could possibly go through if he manages to get loose." He turned to Amelia, surveying her carefully. "Should we give her a gun, do you think?"

Moira shook her head. "No. She's never learned how to use one."

She had removed her own silver revolver and was checking the chamber as she spoke. Where she had been keeping it, Amelia had no idea. Her white blouse and wool trousers left little room. But she had learned to stop questioning Moira.

"What if he's not there?" Amelia asked. "How long should I stay and wait for him?"

"You can stay as long as it takes," Jack reassured her. "We'll wait."

Amelia swallowed, palms sweating. "Are you sure I don't need a gun?"

Moira smiled faintly and nudged Amelia in the direction of her uncle's office. The only door they'd left unblocked. Amelia stepped toward it, feeling Fred following at her heels. She spun the crown of the watch.

"Good luck!" Jack's chipper voice said behind her. "Bring us that Russian."

Amelia took a breath and then opened the door. Silence enveloped them as they stepped into the time space, and Fred prodded her forward. He shut the door behind them and scanned up and down the row of shelves.

"I'll be right behind you," he said. His voice was deep and grating. "When you find him, get him to chase you and then open a door. I'll make sure he goes through it."

"And what if he catches me before you get there?"

"Best to make sure that doesn't happen."

That wasn't very reassuring. Amelia walked forward down the dark shelves. She hadn't had time to give much thought to how she might go about finding Anton Stepanov amid the labyrinth. Wandering aimlessly would do her no good. She decided that her best bet was to wait for him in the center of the rows, the place he had shown her where the painted ceiling was most visible. Using the swirling memories overhead to guide her, she weaved her way toward the center, keeping track of each and every turn. Right, then left. Then left again. She encountered nothing, alive or dead. No flecks of stardust, no watery shadows. The time space seemed chillingly empty, like it knew what sinister intentions awaited the day. She wondered if this was what Anton had experienced before he loaded his gun and fired it at Uncle Ernest. The silence and stillness as if the time space was standing in audience.

An hour passed with no sign of him. Then a second. She saw a figure moving at the top of hour three and turned abruptly. But it was just the liquid specter of one of the dead slipping between the shelves. Tired of waiting, Amelia took a few steps farther in the direction of the chasm. This was pointless. Timekeepers didn't just hang out in the time space all day, and he'd been there only the night before. What if it was days before he came back? She walked down the center of the rows, peering down each one. Another hour. Two. Three.

Six hours passed before she caught a glimpse of another person down one row of shelves. She ducked around the corner. A timekeeper stood with his back to her, watching the phantom memory of one of the dead fade away before him. His head tilted up to watch the stars travel inward. Dark hair. A lanky frame. It was him. This was her chance.

She stepped out from behind the shelf. Anton turned in her direction, their gazes locked in cold combat, each one waiting for the other to react first. For a moment, he almost turned around. Amelia could see the hesitance in his stance, the desire to walk away from whatever this was. But he didn't. He took a step toward her, slow and careful. Another step, then a few more. Amelia waited until he was following at a normal pace before turning around.

She quickened her steps, scanning to see if Fred was nearby. When she looked back over her shoulder, Anton was closer than she'd expected. The sight of him gaining on her drove her to run, choosing a shelf at random. She had a plan in leading him, but in following, he must have one too. His longer strides far outpaced hers. He was catching up. Terrified, Amelia reached for her watch and spun the crown. The door appeared but Fred did not. A pang of dread ran through her. Too late to stop now. She kept running toward the door, hoping maybe their momentum would carry them both out.

She was inches from it when Anton caught up to her.

The full force of his weight and hers slammed against the surface of the door. So hard she was sure they could hear it on the other side. She reached for the knob but Anton caught her, dragging her back. Their feet tangled together, toppling them both onto the ground. Amelia clawed at his neck and beat his chest. He fended off her blows and reached for one of the shelves, trapping her body with his legs and torso while he pulled a book down at random. Amelia panicked. What was he doing? With her free hand, she grabbed a handful of his hair and pulled as hard as she could. Then she froze.

Beneath his coat, pinned to the front pocket of his shirt, Anton wore a painted picture of a blue flower. A forget-me-not, with a bright yellow center. *Look for the timekeepers with blue flowers . . . they're the ones you can trust.*

Anton was breathing hard, still fumbling with the book. "Hold on tight, American," he said.

Amelia heard Fred call out to her from afar, heard the rush of his footsteps, followed by the sound of Anton cursing. She let out a scream as the ground dropped out from under them and the world around them became something new. They landed in a dark room with wooden floors, Anton still on top of her. Amelia swung out and hit him hard in the jaw. He cried out and she struck again, catching him across the face. He slammed both her wrists into the ground.

"Would you stop it!" he spat.

He pushed himself up off the ground and away from her, pinching his nose to stop the blood from trickling down his face. She sat up, pressing one hand to her head. Her ears were ringing. The sleeve of her shirt was torn above her left wrist. She stood up and looked around the strange room. They were in an attic of some kind. The air was musty and cold. Moonlight streamed in through a set of curtains.

"What have you done? Where are we?" Amelia gasped. "Have you brought me to Russia?"

"Russia? No, don't be stupid. I would not bring an American girl to my country. They would shoot you."

"Where are we? What is this? Take me back," she demanded.

"No. Not yet."

Amelia drew her arm back to take another swing.

He caught her wrist and gave her a stern look. "If you hit me again, I will leave you here." He pulled her over to the window roughly. "Look there. See? Not Russia."

Below them, a cobblestone street cut through a town full of squat wooden buildings. There were no streetlamps, rendering the little town dark save for the moonlight, nor was there anything to indicate that this wasn't Russia. She spun around to confront Anton. He had his back to her, still nursing his injured face.

"Okay. Not Russia. But where *are* we?"

Anton turned around. "What do you mean? This is America. This is your America."

"No, it isn't. I've never seen this place before."

Anton muttered something else and returned to the window. "See there?" He pointed up at a flag affixed to the top of a building. It was, in fact, an American flag, missing about a dozen of its stars. "We are in Philadelphia. Eighteen forty-three."

"Eighteen . . . wait. Hang on." Amelia grabbed his arm. "What did you do?"

"I brought you to the past so you can explain to me why you decided to attack me. Not just once but a second time. What did I do to you?"

Amelia's face darkened. She didn't know which was worse. The fact that he killed Uncle Ernest, or that he seemed genuinely confused about it. Like he had forgotten. "You murdered my uncle."

"Why do you keep saying that? I did not murder Ernest Duquesne."

Amelia glared at him. "Don't play dumb. It's insulting."

Anton made a series of sputtering sounds. "I do not play dumb!"

"Then why do you know my name? And why were you chasing me back there?"

"You clearly wanted me to."

"But you didn't have to follow. Who told you about me?"

A pause. A heartbeat. "I don't think I can trust you with such information. First you were friendly when we met and next you bring a knife and try to stab me. Then you try to lure me back into your country. What do you want from me?"

"I attacked you because I thought you murdered my uncle."

Anton shook his head. "I didn't murder anyone. I did not even know Ernest Duquesne was dead until you said it."

Amelia stared at him, beyond comprehending. "You didn't?"

"No. I would not hurt Ernest Duquesne. He is a friend of mine. It was he who taught me how to do the time walking."

"The what?"

Anton gestured to the room around them. "Time walking. We travel back in time. Like in a book."

"He taught you how to do this?"

"Yes. So, see? We were friends."

None of this made sense, but at least he didn't seem keen on hurting her. Amelia rubbed her knuckles, which were throbbing from the multiple collisions with Anton's face. Anton stepped back. A temporary truce. He winced, pinching the bridge of his nose.

"I think you broke something," he said.

"If it were broken, there would be more blood."

"Why do you know that?" Anton asked incredulously. "Is bloodshed a subject Americans learn in school?"

Amelia glared at him. "No. It isn't. Why do you speak English?"

Anton returned her glare. "Because I learned it. Why don't you speak Russian?"

"Why would I?"

"Oh, right, I forgot. Heaven forbid you learn languages other than your own. It would upset the Western agenda to acknowledge other people's culture."

Amelia sighed in frustration. "This is pointless. I don't want to keep arguing with you. Take me back."

"You think I want to keep arguing with you? It is like talking to a cat. I do nothing at all and scratch, scratch, scratch."

Amelia resisted the childish urge to hiss at him. "Well, you're the one who brought me here. I told you why I attacked you. What more do you want?"

"I want to know who is telling lies about me. I want to know who told you that I killed Ernest Duquesne, and I want to know whether you're going to keep attacking me every time we see each other."

"I haven't decided about that last part yet," Amelia grumbled, rubbing her sore fist again. She studied his bloodied face and hollowed cheeks. His eyes were half sunken and sharper than knives, making him look dangerous . . . but he was wearing a blue flower . . . and he had stopped her from falling into the chasm before.

"Moira is the one who told me you killed him."

"Moira?" Anton repeated. "Who is this Moira?"

"She's an American federal agent who worked with my uncle. She knew you'd been following him before he died. She said the Russians wanted my uncle dead. Plus, you had the book," she added.

"Book?"

"Lisavet Levy's book. The one my uncle was looking for with the memories the rebels stole. Moira said they were after him, too, to try and keep him from finding it."

Anton folded his arms and leaned back against the dusty alcove by the window. "Okay, I understand why you attack me now if you believe all these things. But you should know something that might change your opinion."

"And what's that?"

"Ernest was not an enemy of the rebellion. In fact, it was the opposite." Anton straightened up and took a square of white fabric from his pocket, holding it out to her. "This was his."

Amelia looked down at the piece of fabric and took it cautiously. It was a handkerchief, one of the many her uncle kept on hand that had his initials embroidered on one edge. EGD. His mother had sent a set of them as a gift every Christmas until she died. But this one was different. In one corner, opposite to where his initials were, was a periwinkle blue flower with a bright yellow center. A forget-me-not, the size of a thumbprint. Amelia stared at it in disbelief.

"Do you know what that is?" Anton asked.

"Flowers for Lisavet Levy," Amelia said quietly. "You have one too. On your shirt."

"Ahhh, yes. Only mine is not so pretty," Anton said, pulling his coat aside to reveal the painted flower pinned there. "So you see? We were on the same side."

"The side of the rebellion."

Anton scrunched up his face. "Ehhhh, it is not so much a rebellion. More like a movement. To change how things are."

"Moira told me that the rebellion was dangerous. She said that it was destroying the order of Time. But you're saying my uncle was a part of this?"

"He wasn't just a part of it. He was the leader. He recruited other timekeepers who shared the beliefs that memories should be saved, not burned. Together, we do what we can to stop the big changes from happening. He showed us what to do. He taught us how to time walk so we could hide. And he helped keep other timekeepers hidden from those who work for the state."

Amelia stared at him. She wanted to hit him again and tell him that he was wrong. That he was lying. But she was holding the indisputable proof of it in her hand.

"Then . . . how did he die?"

Anton walked toward her again and came to a stop in front of her, inches away. "Why don't you ask this Moira? Since she is so certain that it was me. Show her that handkerchief"—he pressed two fingers to Amelia's temple, lowering his voice—"and see how long it takes for them to put a bullet in your head. Like they want to do to me . . . like they probably did to Ernest Duquesne."

Amelia jerked away from him, slapping his hand out of the air.

He smirked at her, unbothered by the violence this time. "It is the weak man who follows the orders of others without questioning. Obedience may make for good soldiers, but it makes for even greater tragedies."

Around him, the room started to fade out. The darkness of the time space was closing in around them again.

"What's happening?" Amelia asked.

"The memory is ending," Anton said with a shrug. "We go back to the time space now."

"But I . . ."

Anton wagged a finger at her. "No more talking. You go back through your door, and you tell your American friends that I was too smart for you. And the next time you attack me, I will not be so understanding. I only do this now because Ernest Duquesne was my friend. I hope you and I might also be. But until then, we will be like our countries. You hit me, I hit back harder."

Seconds later, the world had faded completely. Anton was gone before her eyes even had time to adjust to the darkness, leaving her with the incriminating handkerchief in her hand.

WHEN FRED emerged from the time space alone, Moira's heart sank clear down to her stomach. She paced as Jack berated Fred for information.

"What do you mean they disappeared? He took her through his door?" Jack was asking.

"No, not a door. They were just gone. Out of thin air."

Moira's heart clenched. "Time walking," she said quietly.

Jack looked at her. "A little louder, please, Donnelly."

Moira swallowed, instantly wishing she hadn't said it. "They're time walking. He took her back into a memory."

"Why would he do that?" Fred asked.

"I don't know," Moira said, trying to look calm. But inside, she was screaming. Anything could happen inside of a memory, and they would never know.

"How would he know how to do that?" Jack said skeptically. "I thought the only people who knew were Ernest and—"

"I don't know," Moira said before he could finish.

There was a tense moment of silence and then Jack took a few steps in her direction. "Someone taught him."

"Apparently," Moira said with a half-hearted shrug.

"Ernest taught him," Jack said, voice full of suspicion.

Moira met his eye. In an instant, she knew what he was thinking. And she needed to stop that train before it got too far away from her.

"We don't know that."

"Don't we?" Jack asked flatly. "Maybe those lies we orchestrated about Ernest being a communist were true."

"If that were true, then why would Anton Stepanov have attacked Amelia? He could have learned on his own."

"Oh, I doubt that. I've been involved with the TRP for years and never knew a man who figured it out. Not without help. And now all of a sudden we get a Russian boy, a kid who was seen trailing after Ernest for weeks before he disappeared, and you're telling me it's a coincidence?"

Moira stood up again, her own anger beginning to surface. "Jack. Please. Let's focus on the situation at hand. Amelia is inside the time space with a Russian aggressor. I told you this was a bad idea."

"Calm down . . ."

"Don't tell me to calm down. Do something."

"What do you want me to do, Moira? Go in after her? If she's in some kind of memory, there's no reaching her."

"Then I'll go," Moira said, starting for the door.

Jack caught her arm roughly. "You don't honestly think I'm going to allow that, do you?"

"Amelia is in trouble."

"No, she's not," Jack said harshly. "At this point, she's either dead or she's compromised."

Moira stared at him, mouth agape. "Compromised? After one conversation? He's a communist, not a carrier of viral plague."

"Doesn't matter. If this kid knows how to time walk, who knows what else he's privy to. He could be telling her all manner of things. About the rebellion. About Ernest's history." There was a momentary pause in which Jack glanced warily at Fred. "About Lisavet Levy."

Moira's stomach flipped. If Anton Stepanov had told Amelia about any of that, there would be no talking Jack down from whatever he decided to do. She opened her mouth to argue but the sound of something moving on the other side of the door stopped her short. Jack's head snapped toward it. The knob began to turn. Fred shifted forward. Jack raised his gun.

The door opened and Amelia came into view. Moira let out a sigh of relief, doing a quick assessment of her condition. Torn sleeve, bruised knuckles, hair coming loose from the braid. But she was alive.

The girl's wide, terrified eyes saw the gun first thing. Jack didn't lower it.

"What happened?" he practically growled.

Be smart, Amelia, Moira willed her.

Amelia stepped backward toward the time space, one hand reaching for the door.

"I don't think so," Jack snapped.

Amelia let out a squeal as he grabbed her arm and dragged her into the room. He kicked the door shut, throwing her down hard. He raised his gun again. Ready to shoot. At the sight of it, something inside of Moira snapped completely. She raised her own weapon and held it level with Jack's skull.

"Get away from her, Jack," she ordered.

Jack turned his head, eyes widening in disbelief. "Moira? What the hell are you doing? Don't point that thing at me."

"I said put the gun away."

After a moment of tension, Jack returned his gun to its holster. "Fred, take the watch from her," he said, jerking his head at Amelia.

Moira moved to stop him, but Jack turned on her, eyes flashing.

"Who the hell do you think you are, pointing your gun at me?" he said, getting in her face. "You work for me. If I want to shoot the kid, I will."

"Not as long as I'm here," Moira said through gritted teeth.

Fred cried out, distracting them both. His face was bleeding, bright red fingernail marks streaked across one cheek. Jack grunted in frustration and grabbed hold of Amelia's wrist, finishing the job of removing the watch quickly and efficiently. He tossed it in Moira's direction. When Amelia lunged at Jack, he turned around and struck her across the face so hard that her whole head snapped back. The sound made Moira's stomach turn.

Jack knelt down, elbows on his knees. "Finished?"

Amelia glared at him defiantly, one hand clutching the side of her face.

"Listen here, sweetheart. We can make this as easy or as difficult as you want it to be. It's up to you. What did that boy say to you that's got you all riled up?"

"I wasn't riled up until you pointed a gun at my head," Amelia spat.

Jack raised his hands, admitting fault. "All right, all right. Fair enough. Then what did happen? Can you tell me that?"

"He caught up to me before I could get to the door."

"Sure, sure. And then what? Where did he take you?"

"Somewhere in the past. He used one of the books." Amelia looked at Moira over Jack's shoulder. Just for a moment. "He was wearing a blue flower," she said quietly.

Moira stiffened.

"A blue flower?" Jack repeated with a snort. Not understanding the significance. "Sounds adorable. What did he say to you?"

"That he didn't kill my uncle. That it was just as likely that one of you killed him."

"And you believe that?"

Amelia said nothing, staring him down.

Jack sighed, pushing onto his feet. He waltzed over to where Moira was standing and plucked the watch from her hand. A sharp, warning look passed between them.

"Let me tell you a few things about your uncle. I worked with Ernest for a long time. I knew him before you were even born. Everyone paints him out to be some kind of saint, but the fact of the matter is he wasn't always that way. He was a decent man, don't get me wrong. But what he possessed in manners and good breeding, he lacked in other areas. Truth is, he was difficult. He was self-righteous, arrogant, and self-destructive. And it got him into trouble. Now, I'm starting to see far too much of him in the way you're acting right now, and let me tell you, I don't like it one bit."

Moira willed Amelia to stay silent. She knew what it was that Jack saw in her at that moment. It was the same thing Moira herself had seen so many times already. And it had nothing to do with Ernest. Thankfully, Jack hadn't realized that just yet.

"Is that why you had him killed?" Amelia demanded.

"Amelia . . ." Moira tried to cut in.

The girl glared at her. "It was you, wasn't it? You're the one who killed him. Is that what happened the night he came to visit you?"

Silence hit the room like a cold wet blanket. If Moira had been standing any closer to Amelia, she might have slapped her.

"What did she say?" Jack asked in a low voice.

"Amelia, go upstairs," Moira said. Then to Jack and Fred. "We should discuss this in private. Give Amelia a chance to cool down."

"I'm not going until you give my watch back," Amelia piped up, glaring at Moira right along with the rest of them.

Moira turned a cold eye on her. "Fred, take her up."

Amelia sprang to her feet before Fred could get within ten feet of her. She stormed up the stairs, every bit the bratty teenager.

Nobody spoke for a full minute after she was gone. Moira was watching Jack, Jack was watching her, and Fred was watching them both, perhaps discerning the tension between them. But then again, perhaps not. Fred wasn't exactly that bright. Finally, Jack spoke.

"Would you care to explain, Donnelly? Or shall I begin pulling teeth?"

Moira folded her arms. "I don't know what she's talking about, Jack. Anton Stepanov is trying to cause trouble. He's planting ideas in her head on purpose to try and save his own skin."

"Or something else is going on," Jack said pointedly.

"Jack, I don't know what you're trying to insinuate here but—"

"Did Ernest come to see you before he died?"

"If he did, don't you think I would have told you?"

"I don't know. Would you?"

"Are you calling me a liar?"

"Oh, don't pull that crap, Moira. You and I both know you haven't always been honest with me." He came closer, shoving the watch against her shoulder roughly. "In fact, I'm starting to wonder if you know a lot more about what's really going on here than you're letting on."

Moira stiffened her expression and remained quiet.

Jack sneered at her. "Fine. You want to play games? Let's play a game. Fred, go get the kid and bring her back down here."

"Fred, don't go anywhere," Moira snapped.

Fred froze halfway to the staircase, torn between two bosses.

Jack spoke again, his voice loud and demanding. "Go and get her, Fred. That's an order."

Moira's heart thudded with every step Fred took up the stairs. "I'm not going to let you interrogate her," she said sharply.

"Oh, I'm not going to interrogate her," Jack said with a dark laugh. "You're going to clean this up for me."

Clean it up. It was an order Moira knew too well. But this time, especially this time, she was particularly loath to comply.

"No."

"If you won't let me question the girl my way, then you're going to get the information out yourself. After all, she's only Ernest's niece. What do you care what happens to her?" He broke off and tilted his head. "Unless of course . . . there's some reason why you want to protect her?"

A tense silence passed between them.

"Hey, boss?" Fred said from the stairs.

"What?" Jack snapped, wheeling around to face him.

"She's not up there."

"Excuse me?"

"The kid. She's not upstairs. She's gone."

12

1952, Washington, DC

No one was coming.

Lisavet didn't know how long she was alone in that room. She drifted in and out of this world and the one she knew better, her consciousness suspended somewhere between. Every now and then, she was aware of someone in the room with her. Of hands checking her pulse and administering more medicine. In the far reaches of her mind, she knew she was alive, but it was almost as if her body had forgotten that fact.

But then one day, she awoke with a gasp and sat upright, feeling a rush of blood through her veins. Her eyes opened on a stark white room, the lights dim so as not to overwhelm her. Her vision was blurry and strained. Her skin was clammy, and she was desperately thirsty. Everything seemed to hum, from the walls to the floor to the very air inflating and collapsing her lungs. Across the room there was a metal table with a tray of food covered in plastic next to a glass of water. She was no longer wearing her own clothes, dressed instead in a set of plain gray pajamas. Her feet were bare. Her coat, watch, and everything else she'd been carrying with her were gone.

Her legs shook as she moved to the side of the bed and braced herself into a standing position. Every part of her body screamed in protest.

She forced herself forward, anyway, intent on that glass of water. She took several steps, struggling to keep her balance. When she reached the table, she grasped the cup and gulped it down quickly, sloshing half of it down the front of her shirt. She lost her balance and she let go of the cup to catch herself on the table. It hit the floor with a loud crack.

There was a shuffling sound outside the door. Lisavet was still dragging herself upright when it opened and a man in a navy blue uniform appeared. She glowered at him with as much ferocity as she could muster. He called for a nurse, who approached Lisavet as if she were a feral animal.

"You shouldn't be trying to walk," she said.

Lisavet jerked her arms away, stumbling against the table. With the help of the guard, the nurse returned her to the bed. Someone administered another injection in her neck, which made her limbs feel leaden, her brain foggy. They forced water down her throat but it all came back up. She drifted around in the haze of drugs, aware of two people standing on the other side of the room but unable to raise her head to look at them.

"Her system is in shock," the nurse said. "She can't even keep water down."

"I told you, you need to be careful. She hasn't eaten anything real in a very long time."

Jack Dillinger. He was here. And he was talking about her as if she wasn't.

"She doesn't look malnourished," the nurse said suspiciously.

"Treat her like she is, anyway," Jack said. "It's refeeding syndrome. Like what happened at Belsen. She can't digest food normally, so give her IV fluids."

This became her routine. For weeks, she fought to stay awake in the white painted room. The nurse came in twice a day to administer fluids straight into her arm. When she was alone, Lisavet sat perfectly still on

the bed, staring at the wall or, occasionally, out the window. Beyond the
bars there was very little to look at. A tree missing its leaves that indicated it was winter. A brick wall across the way. A tiny, almost imper-
ceptible square of sky that she could see only when she craned her head
as far as it would go. Three times a day someone escorted her down a
hallway so she could use the bathroom and wash. The only thing that
kept her mind from going mad was the familiar whisper of Time ticking
in the back of her head. It had not abandoned her.

They kept her there for three months with no explanations. Long
enough for the seasons to change outside the window, barren branches
blooming into decadent white flowers. Three months of wordless hands
delivering food and then taking it away. And then Jack Dillinger came
to see her. She was sitting on the bed with her head down when he
came. Legs pulled up to her chest. She heard the creaking of the door,
but assumed it was her dinner.

"Hello, Miss Levy."

Her head snapped up at the sound of his voice. Jack was standing in
the doorway, dressed in a neat gray suit. On his left wrist, a watch ticked
with tantalizing consistency.

When she didn't respond, he came a little farther into the room and
shut the door.

He was watching her more intently than she'd ever seen another
person look at anyone before. When he reached the end of the bed, he
pulled the chair from the table around and sat backward to face her,
arms propped up on the back of it. Close enough in the tiny room that
she could have reached out and touched him.

"Do you know who I am?"

Lisavet nodded. This pleased him. She could see it in his face.

"Good. You can call me Jack."

He held out a hand for her to shake. Lisavet refused to take it. He
was here. He was real. He wanted something from her.

"No need to be afraid, Miss Levy. I'm just here to ask you a few questions. Would that be all right?"

She didn't answer. Jack sighed and reached into his pocket. He took out a lighter and a pack of cigarettes and held the carton out to her.

"Want one? I find that smoking makes awkward situations easier. Something to do with your mouth while you're thinking of what to say next."

This time he didn't give up when she didn't accept his gesture right away. She took a cigarette from the carton with two fingers.

"Let me get that for you," he said.

Lisavet froze as he leaned forward and held the lighter up to the cigarette between her lips. Up close he had aggressive features, intensely masculine and lacking any kind of nuance whatsoever. Nothing like Ernest, who was all nuance, all subtlety. She took hold of the lit cigarette between her first two fingers and inhaled, refusing to cough as the hot smoke hit the back of her throat.

"Attagirl," Jack said.

He sat back and lit his own cigarette, taking his time. Lisavet cleared her throat a few times discreetly. She wasn't certain if she liked smoking, but it was something to do. And it did seem to make the unfamiliar ache in her stomach less painful.

"Right," Jack said at last. "Now. I'm gonna need to hear some words out of you, little miss. How about we start with something easy? What year were you born?"

Lisavet didn't want to answer him. She never wanted to speak to anyone ever again. But there was a certain look about this Jack. A malevolence that told her that, eventually, she wasn't going to have a choice in the matter.

"Nineteen twenty-seven," she said quietly.

"Nineteen twenty-seven," Jack repeated. "So that makes you ... about twenty-five, twenty-six?"

Lisavet had no idea how old she was. She had stopped measuring the year outside the time space after Ernest. If she was almost twenty-six, that meant the year was 1953. It was winter so it must be January. Amelia would be three years old soon. That seemed right.

"I guess so."

Jack didn't say anything for a moment, pausing to take a pull from his cigarette. Lisavet did the same, mirroring him.

"You were stuck inside that place for a long time," Jack said at last. "Thirteen years. Almost fourteen."

"It didn't seem that long."

"I was hoping we could talk about Ernest."

"I don't want to talk about him."

"That was some little memory game you played on him. He doesn't remember a single thing about you. After nearly two years together. Not a thing." Jack paused, eyeing her with greater interest. "How'd you do it?"

"What makes you so certain it was me?"

Jack peered at her down the length of his cigarette. "You know, Miss Levy. This will go much better for you if we agree to be honest with each other."

Lisavet could hear the subtle threat in his voice. In her memory, she felt the harsh grip of his hands on her arms. She looked away, down at the cigarette between her fingers.

"It's hard to explain."

"Try."

"When he was sleeping, I could see his memories."

"See them? But not when he was awake?"

"No. Only while he slept."

"And you were able to get rid of them? Erase them?"

Lisavet nodded.

"Do you know why? Why you could see them, I mean."

"No."

"Ernest had a theory about you. Wrote about it in his notes. Did he ever mention it to you?"

"Once or twice."

"So you know about this whole 'temporal departure' thing? That you were somehow disconnected from the physical world and therefore able to pass through the dimensions of time."

"Yes, I'm familiar."

"Would you say that it's an accurate theory?"

Lisavet met his gaze, saying nothing. Jack gleaned all he needed from her silence. He leaned forward, blowing a long stream of smoke into the air.

"So . . . besides erasing memories, what else can you do?"

"What else?"

"Well, I assume that isn't the only thing. Am I right?"

Lisavet hesitated.

Jack made a clicking noise with his tongue. "You know, Miss Levy. If you answer all my questions in a satisfactory manner, maybe we can start talking about getting you out of here."

Lisavet looked up at him, unable to keep the hope from showing on her face. He smiled at her, a smug, manipulative sort of smile.

"I can take things from the past. Touch things when I'm time walking. Ernest was never able to do that."

"Time walking? What's that?"

"Visiting memories from the books."

He seemed to find this particularly interesting because he paused for a moment before continuing. "And?" Jack prompted. "What else?"

"I can insert myself into memories."

"Insert yourself?"

"Make myself a part of them. As if I'm actually there. I can change things that happened. Alter the outcome."

Again, this caught Jack's interest. He leaned forward. "What sort of things?"

"Anything. Everything. But it comes at a cost."

"The chasm."

Lisavet nodded.

"So that was you?"

"Yes, it was me."

Jack actually laughed. "I lost a man to that thing. Fell right in and we never saw him again."

"Oh. I'm sorry."

Jack shrugged it off. His cigarette had burned its way down to a stub. He gestured for hers and she handed it to him apprehensively. He stubbed them both out on the table and then opened his briefcase.

"I'm sure you're wondering why I had my men targeting you."

"Not really."

"No?"

"Ernest told me it was because I was interfering. You wanted me to stop."

"And do you know why I wanted him to stop you?"

"Because you and your fellow timekeepers fancy playing God."

Jack laughed again. Lisavet decided she didn't much care for the sound.

"Funny you should phrase it that way," he said. "You're Jewish, right?"

"I was."

"Not anymore?"

"When you spend enough time in what others might call the afterlife, you stop believing in things like that."

"I see. Your father was Jewish."

"Yes, he was."

"Do you know what happened to him?"

"He . . . he died. He was killed by the Nazis."

"And do you know why?"

Lisavet could sense this conversation taking a turn she wasn't sure she was ready for. "Because they wanted his watch."

"Sure, sure. That was part of it." He stopped digging around in his briefcase, returning to his chair with a thick folio in one hand. "Ernest tells me you never visited memories after 1938."

Lisavet tried not to show her surprise at how much Ernest had told him about her. "No, not really. I only know what I saw in the memories I saved."

"So then you don't know."

Lisavet frowned. "I know there was a war. I know that the Nazis lost and now the Americans are fighting with the Russians."

Without a word, Jack extended the folio in her direction.

"What's that?"

"Something I had put together for you. Newspaper clippings. Headlines. Photos of the past fourteen years. All of the things you missed."

Lisavet eyed the folio as though it had teeth. There were pictures of war in there. The war that had brought the shadows into Ernest's eyes. She wasn't sure she wanted to see that.

"No, thank you," she said.

Jack held it out farther. "It's either this or I strap you to a chair and play it back on tape. Your choice."

There it was again. The glint in his eyes that promised pain if she failed to cooperate. She took it from him, letting it fall open on the bed in front of her. It began with 1938, the night she'd entered the time space for the first time. They had named that night now: Kristallnacht. Broken shop windows, hundreds killed in riots across Germany, including in Nuremberg. From there it got worse. Headlines spoke of a war building and building before it finally broke. She read articles about two halves of the same war. One in Europe, one in Japan.

"Did you fight in this war?" she asked. Hoping she could distract him with questions to avoid seeing any more of it.

"I fought in Japan," he said with a nod. "Keep going."

What came next was worse. Victory in Europe, followed by something called Liberation Day. Her hands trembled as she looked over the images. Skeletal faces, more dead than alive. Piles of bodies. Mass open graves. Headlines that had phrases like "gas chambers" and numbers of the dead that reached into the millions.

"What is this?" she asked, struggling to breathe.

"Death camps," Jack said matter-of-factly. "A little something the Nazis called the Final Solution."

"W-what?"

"This is what happened to the Jewish people while you were trapped inside the time space. This is what your father saved you from when he locked you in there."

"Did my father ever . . ."

"End up in one of these? No. He was killed long before he made it to one. But your brother did." He gestured to the folio.

Lisavet thought she might be sick. She turned the page to find a written record with her brother's name at the top. Klaus Levy. Her eyes skimmed the page, noting the details of his death. The brief, merciless account of his short, half-lived life. She shoved it away.

"I don't want to see any more."

"That's too bad," Jack said, pushing the folio back in her direction. "You need to see this, just like the rest of us did. You need to know."

"But why?"

"So you understand," Jack said, his voice taking a more forceful tone. "So you know what it was that me and the American timekeepers were up against. What we're still up against. So you understand what you were doing by interfering. All that work you did to stop the Nazis and preserve the past . . . in the end it didn't make one lick of difference out here in the real world. Bad things still happened. They keep happening. Time is just too big a thing for one person to tackle."

"Then why was I considered such a threat?"

"You weren't a threat, you were a nuisance. But then Ernest got shot saving your neck and the Russians started believing we were spying on them. They weren't the only ones. Other timekeepers believed you were one of our spies, and the way you and Ernest started carrying on certainly didn't help things. Churchill said that history is written by the victors. But it's deeper than that. History isn't written by victors, but by the ones holding the pen. And you, Miss Levy, upset the Russians and got blood in the inkwell. That's why you're here."

Lisavet let out a shuddering gasp. "Why are you telling me this?"

"So you understand that what you've been doing . . . the interfering, the saving memories . . ." He paused, gesturing to the folio again. "It never made any difference."

His words felt like a punch in the gut. "But I thought . . ."

Jack gave her a half smile that was almost kind. Almost, but not quite. "I know what you thought. But you were wrong."

A single tear fell on her cheek. Jack took another cigarette from his coat and lit it.

"What's going to happen to me now?" she asked quietly, pulling her knees in close to her chest.

"We'll have to discuss it," Jack said.

"Will I get to leave here?"

"Maybe. We'll see. It will have to be under my terms."

Lisavet didn't like the sound of that. Her fate rested entirely on the whims of this man. "Why your terms?"

"Because, Miss Levy, you are a criminal. A refugee with a history of working against the US government. There is no Lisavet Levy out here in the real world. She doesn't exist. You have no home. No papers. No one even knows you're here. You have no place in this world except for the one I choose to give you."

Lisavet squeezed her eyes shut, wishing she could shut him out too. She wished she was back in the time space. Where everything made sense, and nothing could hurt her. There she'd had a place to go. There she belonged.

"I just have one more question," Jack said abruptly. "What happened to the baby?"

Lisavet opened her eyes. Surely he didn't mean . . .

"Baby?"

"One of my agents saw you with a baby once."

Lisavet swallowed, wiping her eyes with the backs of her hands. "She died."

"She?"

"It was a girl."

"That's too bad. I suppose the time space wasn't habitable for a child."

That wasn't entirely true, Lisavet wanted to say. It had been habitable for a child once. It was her home, even though it couldn't be her daughter's.

"It was Ernest's. Wasn't it?"

Lisavet didn't answer. She didn't need to.

He stood up to go. Lisavet looked at his large, violent hands as he held one out for her to shake. As if they'd just finished a business meeting. This time, she took his hand, already playing his game.

"Until next time, Miss Levy," he said. He started for the door.

"Wait," Lisavet called after him.

He paused, arching one eyebrow as he looked back at her.

"Do you think . . . would it be possible for me to have something to do? Like a book or some paper and pencils or something. Anything. I just . . . I feel like I'm going crazy in here."

Jack tilted his head to the side, studying her. "I'll see what I can do."

THE NEXT time Jack came, exactly one week after the first visit, he brought her three books. Lisavet thanked him enthusiastically. The books were gloriously long ones. All in English, naturally, but she didn't mind that. *The Three Musketeers*, which she enjoyed. *Gone with the Wind*, which she found melodramatic. And *Aurora Leigh*, a long-form narrative poem that she adored. That was the one she read the most. Over and over again until the cover became worn. Noting her preference, Jack brought her more poetry next time he came. She might have been touched by his gesture if it weren't for the fact that he was so condescending about it.

"Ernest likes poetry, you know," he told her. "Recites it like some kind of pretentious academic."

Jack began each visit the way he began the first—by offering her a cigarette, leaning in close so he could light it for her. He didn't trust her to handle the lighter. *Smart man*, she thought, surveying the fabric of his suit from up close. It looked flammable. She came to rely on their little ritual, needing the smoke to keep her nerves at bay. At first, he asked a lot of questions, covering every detail of her life in the time space with special emphasis on the book of memories. When she'd told him that it had been taken by a Russian, he had her describe him, then recall each and every memory contained in the book. As the months dragged on, the questions became less urgent. Jack, it seemed, had gathered all the information he needed.

Lisavet's nerves ramped up to an all-time high. A silent question hung in the air at the end of every visit. Then Jack came in one day carrying a coat and a cardboard box.

"Did you know it's been one whole year since we took you out of the time space?" he asked after lighting her cigarette and taking his usual seat by the window.

"Has it?"

"Mm-hmm. A little longer, actually."

That meant that the year was 1954. Amelia was four years old. It also meant that, when they'd first brought her out, she was unconscious for over two months. Her body and mind had taken *two months* to catch up to each other again, and even longer to return fully to normal. Just as Ernest had predicted.

"How would you like to get out of this room for a bit?" Jack asked suddenly, interrupting her thoughts.

She looked up in surprise. "R-really?"

"If you'd like. I'd say it's been long enough for us to assume you aren't going to suffer another mental disconnect, don't you think?"

Lisavet's mouth was dry with nerves. "I suppose."

Before they left, he gave her the coat and a pair of gray slippers.

"Don't be nervous," Jack said as he held the door open to let her out. "I'll be with you the whole time."

Sure enough, she hadn't taken more than a few steps before he took hold of her arm. They passed through a set of locked doors that had to be opened by a guard and entered a part of the building Lisavet had never seen before. Her eyes scanned the hallway as they walked, and she realized that this wasn't a prison at all. They were on the lowest floor of some kind of medical facility. Patients dressed in the same gray garb she wore could be seen through the windows they passed, their eyes cloudy, expressions vacant. Many of them were moving in erratic patterns, jerking as though their limbs were being pulled by an invisible string.

Lisavet looked up at Jack. Standing beside him, rather than sitting as she usually did, she realized that he was quite tall. Taller than she'd expected.

"Is this . . ."

"A psychiatric hospital. Yes. Finest one in the DC area," he said without batting an eye. "Oh, come on, don't look at me like that," he said, his hand shifting from her arm to the back of her neck. "We needed doctors who knew how to help someone suffering a disconnect from reality. It was the best option."

Jack took her past the front desk. The main entry was devoid of people. Jack opened the door and she stepped into the courtyard.

It was raining. Cold water droplets hit her cheeks. The courtyard was walled off on three sides, leaving a small space for a wrought-iron gate that opened onto the street. Dead leaves crunched underfoot, deafeningly loud. Cars breezed past the gate just twenty feet away. The sound of rain. The smell of the wind. The rustle of trees. Lisavet's heartbeat raced. She swayed, overwhelmed by the rush of sounds and sensations. Jack slid his hand around her arm again, this time to keep her steady. He said something to her. She didn't answer. A car honked its horn. Rain hit the top of her head. It was too much after so long with so little. Too much light. Too much sound. On the verge of hyperventilating, she squeezed her eyes shut and heard the familiar hush of Time ticking in the back of her head. Calling out to her with its soothing embrace. As her mind turned toward it, everything around her stopped. No more noises. No more rain. She let out a gasp of relief.

Beside her, Jack gasped as well.

"What the hell?" he murmured.

Lisavet opened her eyes to see that the world around them had stopped. It was frozen, suspended in time, unmoving.

"What did you do?" Jack asked, his voice hushed in either awe or horror.

"I . . . I don't know."

Lisavet's pulse slowed and calmed as she looked around. At the raindrops hovering in the air. The cars and their occupants outside the gate, frozen midmotion. The tree branches bent midbreeze. Her doing.

Jack let out a rough, strained laugh. "You stopped Time," he said, more curious than alarmed. "Have you ever done this before?"

"No. Never."

She had never known this was something she could try. Time was still within her, even though she had returned to the physical world. It had not forgotten her. That single fact brought her more comfort than any poem ever had.

Beside her, Jack reached out to touch one of the suspended raindrops, letting his thumb and forefinger flatten it completely. "My god. You are a wonder," he said. He started to let go of her arm.

"Wait," Lisavet said. She latched on to his wrist, keeping him beside her. "Don't let go of me."

He gave her a strange look. "Why not?"

"Whenever I was time walking, Ernest could only touch things when I was holding them."

"And?"

"And if you let go of me, I'm worried that you might freeze too. Like them."

As she said it out loud, she wondered why she cared. If he was frozen, she could leave. He would never know where she went. But the thought of running off and disappearing into the world alone was unsettling at best. A familiar cage was less frightening than an endless void, even if there was a tiger inside.

"Alrighty then," Jack said. He gave her arm a reassuring squeeze that made her want to punch him. "Okay. I think that's enough. Undo it."

"I don't know how."

"What do you mean?"

"I don't even know how this happened. I'm not sure if I can."

"Try," he said impatiently.

Lisavet shut her eyes. She could hear the seconds passing anyway. Then the almost maternal whisper of Time. The harder she listened, the louder it got. Time spun closer, parting like a set of warm black curtains to beckon her in. All at once, the rushing sounds of movement resumed. Rain hit her cheek. The roll of car engines droned on. Lisavet opened her eyes to find everything as it had been. Moving forward once more.

"Attagirl," Jack said.

When Lisavet looked up at him again, he was looking at her with the glint of a man striking gold. As if she were something very valuable and he, the owner of it.

After their first outing, Jack took her outside every time he came to visit. First their walks were confined to the courtyard, and then, eventually, other places. He took her on brief excursions to the park nearby, taking her there in his car. Then to more and more populous locations. He slowly reintroduced her to the world through quiet cafés and shops. For these outings, she was given normal clothing to wear. Her long hair was braided by one of the nurses and the shoes they gave her were the kind that buckled, rather than the flimsy slippers from before. For a brief two hours every Saturday, she remembered what it was like to be human. She spoke to real people, although Jack usually did the talking for them. She ate food that didn't come from a plastic tray. She heard music playing on the radio, saw real, living people. As much as she hated Jack, she began looking forward to his visits, anticipating where they might go next. She felt as she had when she was a child and Azrael had first taught her how to time walk.

Returning from each excursion became more and more difficult. She dreaded the moment when Jack would tell her it was time to go, knowing that she had another full week ahead of her until she could go out again.

One night in June, Jack came on a Wednesday.

"Good. You're up," he announced. "I want you to come with me. There's something I want to try."

He hadn't brought her a change of clothes this time. Only shoes. Lisavet put them on, stealing a glance at his watch to check the time. Eleven thirty.

"Where are we going?"

"You'll see," he said.

Outside it was dark and dewy. They drove past monuments and large government buildings and pulled up to an office building not far from the center of it all.

"What's going on?" she asked, her voice trembling. "What is this?"

He slid an arm around her shoulders and walked her forcefully up the stairs. "Nothing to worry about. This is where I work."

He took her through the doors and down a series of long hallways. They encountered no other people until they reached the lowest level, where two men wearing watches and dark suits eyed her with curiosity.

"Is this her?" one of them asked, looking her up and down.

"Yes, this is her. Lisavet, do you remember Patrick Brady and George Collins?"

Lisavet suddenly recognized them as the timekeepers who had helped drag her out of the time space almost two years ago. She recoiled as Jack ushered her into a room where a man lay asleep on a thinly padded bench. His hands were bound and there was nothing else in the room. No table. No chair. Not even a window.

"What are we doing here?" she asked the moment Jack closed the door, leaving Brady and Collins on the other side of it. "Who is this?"

"This poor lad is named Harry," Jack said, placing both hands on her shoulders. "He accidentally got himself caught up with one of my timekeepers. Saw some things he wasn't supposed to. So we brought him in."

Lisavet studied the man's unconscious face. He looked young.

"I was hoping you could help me clean it up," Jack continued.

"Clean it up?"

"His memory."

Lisavet's eyes grew wide. "You want me to . . ."

"Erase the memories, yes. Like you did to Ernest." From his pocket, he took out a black notebook. Pages for storing the memories.

She shook her head, pulling away from him. "No, I can't do that."

"Can't or won't?"

"Can't. I could only do that in the time space."

"Have you tried?"

"Well . . . no."

"Then try."

"I can't."

"Lisavet." Jack's voice hardened.

She looked back at the sleeping man. Only a boy really. Time ticked in the back of her head. Even from several feet away she could sense it. His memories swirling up and away from him. Not visible in the real world but still there. She *could* do it. If she wanted to. But what would that mean for him? Which pieces of his life would she be erasing?

"If you don't do this, it will only be worse for him," Jack said over her shoulder. "You realize that, right? Worse for him . . . worse for you."

Lisavet's eyes snapped to him. He meant isolation. He meant death. For Harry . . . but also for her if she didn't comply. Jack would keep them both locked up like this until she did what he asked or perhaps he would kill him. And really what were a few lost memories worth when the alternative was perpetual imprisonment? What value was the truth in comparison to death?

She took the notebook from his hands. As she stepped closer to the sleeping man and cleared the memories from his mind as instructed, she felt Jack's eyes on her. A smile curling the edges of his lips, he was pleased with the outcome he had wrought.

When she was finished he led her back to the car, where they drove in silence. Lisavet seethed in the passenger seat before Jack spoke.

"Something the matter?" he asked, even though he knew perfectly well what was wrong.

"How do you live with yourself?" she asked bitterly. "Knowing how many people's lives you've erased."

Jack looked taken aback at her accusation. "By thinking of all the lives I've saved. We're preventing a war, remember? A few memories are nothing in comparison to keeping the world from another disaster."

"And what gives you the right to choose what's worth saving?" Lisavet asked. She'd asked Ernest the same question, years ago, but Jack's reaction to it was far from what Ernest's had been.

"If it isn't me, it's someone else. You think if I quit, it'll all just stop? Think again. It's bigger than that, and the way I see it, it's better to be the one erasing than the one getting erased. This way I at least have a shot at protecting what matters most."

"What matters to you, you mean."

Jack gave her a vacant look as he braked for a red light, one corner of his mouth raised in a wry smile. "Isn't that what you did? Altered the past. Changed memories to save the people you cared about."

Lisavet frowned at him. "What I did was different."

"Is it, though? I've seen that chasm. Whatever you changed, it must have been something big. Nothing I've done has ever had an impact like that."

The light changed and he began driving again, turning his eyes back on the road. For a moment, Lisavet assumed they were done talking, but then Jack spoke again, his voice low.

"I've been asking myself about that chasm a lot, you know. Wondering what it could have been. What could have made the girl who fought so hard to save meaningless scraps of history alter the past so drastically like that? Something to do with Ernest maybe or . . . something to do with your daughter?"

Lisavet froze, every inch of her body going cold.

"You know, Brady thinks she's still alive," he continued in an offhand manner. "His theory is that she's out there somewhere. That you altered the past to save her and hid her in one of the memories that you kept in that book of yours. But of course, that's all just speculation."

Jack didn't so much as look at her, nor did he say another word about it. He didn't have to. Lisavet knew him well enough by now to understand that behind his statement was an unspoken threat. One that would ensure that, the next time he asked her to erase someone's memories, she would comply without a fuss.

Two DAYS later, Jack came at his usual Saturday time. He pulled up his chair and offered her a cigarette, which Lisavet took eagerly, as dependent on them now as she was on him. At first he said nothing at all, but then he spoke in a remarkably casual sort of way, examining the tip of his cigarette.

"I talked to your doctors today," he said.

Lisavet often wondered what they talked about when they discussed her case. Not the time space, certainly. Lisavet herself had never even spoken to any of these doctors. What kind of illness had they given her? How had Jack explained away her condition?

"You did?" she asked hesitantly.

"Yup. They said it's about high time we get you out of here."

Lisavet blinked several times, not fully comprehending.

"You've shown remarkable signs of improvement these past few months. On our little outings you behave almost normally. You're eating better, though still not enough. Sleeping more. You've almost completely reacclimatized to life outside of the time space. And they think the best way to move forward is to let you rejoin society."

Lisavet scarcely dared to hope. "And . . . what do you think?"

Jack took an agonizingly long pull on his cigarette, prolonging his response. "I think they're right."

She struggled to swallow. To maintain normalcy. "R-really?"

"Uh-huh. So I've started putting together a plan for you. I was hoping I could run it by you before our outing today."

"Okay. What is it?"

"I want you to come work for me."

"Work for you? As in, for the TRP?"

"I want to bring you on as my secretary. It's a low-level job, but the pay is good. Perfect for someone like you. You're a little inexperienced, but I'm sure that won't matter given your other talents. You'd work normal hours, Monday through Friday. There's an open room at a ladies' boardinghouse not far from the office. Normally you need a guardian to sign a waiver, but I could put it in my name." He paused, watching her closely to gauge her reaction. "You'd be doing me a favor, too, Lisavet. I could use someone like you."

Someone like her. Someone who could stop Time. Someone who could, when prevailed upon by him, alter Time and erase living memories at will. He could use someone like her indeed.

"Would that even be approved?" she managed to ask.

"Already has been." Jack took a stack of folded papers from the inner pocket of his coat. "The pardon for your past actions made it through the necessary levels of approval about six months ago. I've had a buddy of mine in the INS department working on securing your identity papers."

"Identity papers?"

"Birth certificates. Passports. You can't very well come work for the TRP as Lisavet Levy, now, can you?"

"I guess not."

Jack set the papers down in front of her. "I've filled out the application for you. If anyone asks, you're a second-generation immigrant of Irish descent who grew up in Brooklyn. Your parents worked in a factory. Both died before the age of fifty. Lung disease. A real tragedy. You're an only child and all your other relatives are still in Ireland. Last name, Donnelly."

"What's my first name?" Lisavet asked, noticing that section was blank.

"I thought maybe you'd like to decide that for yourself."

"Really?"

"Sure. Why not? But, I should add, you won't be permitted to discuss your former life. In the office or otherwise. You would assume your new identity in every aspect of life. Lisavet Levy would cease to exist entirely."

"But . . . I would get to leave?" Lisavet asked tentatively.

Jack smiled at her. "Yes, Miss Levy, you would get to leave."

"And . . . what about . . ."

His smile widened in a darkly bemused fashion. "Ernest? What about him?"

"He also works for the TRP. Right?"

"Yes."

"And that won't . . . it wouldn't be . . ."

"A problem? Why would it be? It's not like he remembers you."

Lisavet looked down at her hands. Sure, it wouldn't be a problem for him. But what about her? Could she work that close to Ernest all the time, knowing what had passed between them? Could she listen to him talk about Amelia and not have it break her into a thousand pieces?

"What do you say, sweetheart? Want to come work for me?" Jack asked, breaking through her cloud of thoughts.

He was leaning forward, elbows on his knees, watching her think this over with an infuriating smirk fixed to his face. He knew exactly what this arrangement would do to her. But what other options did she have?

"When would I start?"

"Next week. We just need you to pick a first name."

Lisavet looked down at the papers, thinking.

"Moira," she said after a few moments.

Jack made a face. "You sure? You can take a second to think if you want."

Lisavet could tell he didn't like it and that pleased her.

"Moira was my mother's name," she said. The only name she could bear to be called that wasn't her own.

"Well, then Moira Donnelly, I'll get that taken care of for you." He wrote it down and stood up. "You ready?"

"For what?"

"We've got one more outing to go on before we bust you out of here," he said, holding out a conspiratorial hand. As if he wasn't the one keeping her here in the first place.

He took her two blocks south of the hospital to a tailor shop where a woman with a beehive hairdo took her measurements for a new wardrobe. She talked in a rapid-fire Boston accent as she did, asking all kinds of questions about where she was from and what her family was like. It was a test. Lisavet could sense Jack watching her as he smoked a cigarette on the sofa nearby, waiting to see if she would slip up. She delivered her lines with ease, fixing the woman with a confident smile that seemed to come from someone else. The woman tittered enthusiastically at her responses, claiming that she had a sister who married an Irish Catholic. As the woman went into the back of the shop to retrieve a bolt of fabric, Lisavet looked to Jack for his approval. In response, he raised his cigarette in her direction.

When they were finished, he took her down the street to a salon to get a haircut. Her pale, waist-length hair was one of the things Ernest had always loved most about her; she didn't want to cut it. But Jack insisted it was necessary. He stepped out to "take care of something" a few blocks away. Lisavet's heart was in her throat as the stylist took her to the back, conscious that this was yet another test. To see what she might do when left alone.

"So what are we doing today, dear?" the stylist asked.

Lisavet bit her lip, studying her face in the mirror. It looked different than she remembered it. Her hair hung limp, her cheekbones seemed sharper, her cheeks hollower. But it was her eyes that looked the most changed. Haunted, like Ernest's had been. The person staring back at her in the mirror was not the girl who had danced with Ernest in 1949 and kissed him under a sky full of stars. This person was someone she didn't recognize. A stranger wearing her hair like a wig.

"Cut it off," she said at last.

The stylist's eyes widened. "What? All of it?"

"All of it."

Recognizing the determined look in her eyes, the woman leaned closer and pulled her hair back away from her face. "Have you ever considered a darker color?"

When Jack returned, Lisavet emerged from the shop with her hair cut just below her chin, dyed a shade of dark midnight brown. His eyes widened when he saw her, his mouth dropping open in surprise.

"Damn," he said with a chuckle.

"Do you like it?" Lisavet asked.

He took one of the strands between his thumb and forefinger, examining it. A smile broke out over his face, still smug but a little more genuine than normal.

"I do. It suits you. Sharp and dark. Just like you are."

As they went to the car, Lisavet rolled the words over in her head. *Sharp and dark* he had said. That's what he saw when he looked at her.

She was the moon no longer.

13

1965, Boston, Massachusetts

THE FIRST THING AMELIA noticed when she parked the car on James Gravel's street was that the windows of the pawnshop had been broken. The lights were off, but the sign on the door was flipped to open. Opaque plastic sheeting had been hung where the windows should have been. Shards of glass lay on the ground. She turned off the engine and set aside the map she'd found in the glove compartment, placing it alongside the little black notebook with James's address, which she'd taken from Moira's handbag. The same two gentlemen from before were perched on the stairs.

"He doesn't need your trouble, girl," one of the older men said as she approached. "Why don't you turn around and go back home? Last thing we need in this neighborhood is a white girl bringing her problems."

"What happened to the shop?" Amelia asked.

The man narrowed his eyes at her. "Couple of feds carrying a warrant showed up just after you left. Terrorized the Gravels, had his kids crying. They smashed in the windows of the shop and tore through just about everything they owned. James is lucky that's all they did. Edith took the kids to her folks' place outside the city."

Amelia's mouth was dry. "And James?"

There was a long, suspicious pause. "He's in the shop trying to clean things up."

Amelia felt their eyes on her as she climbed the steps of the shop, careful to avoid the remaining glass. The bell above the door jangled loudly, making her jump. The shop was dark, some of the lights smashed to pieces. The place was in disarray. She let out a shaky breath as a voice behind the counter spoke.

"Selling or buying?"

James Gravel had his back to her, marking something in the shop ledger. His shoulders were rolled forward in defeat, but his voice was unshaken.

Amelia opened her mouth to respond but nothing came out.

"Sorry for the mess. I'm afraid we . . ." His words died on his lips as he turned to face her.

"Mr. Gravel. I came to . . ."

"Get out," James said darkly.

"But I . . ."

"Go on. Get out of here." He came around the counter, a menacing expression on his face.

Amelia stepped back. "I need to talk to you."

James ignored her. He pulled aside the plastic sheeting and scanned the streets, letting the cold air trickle in. There was a bruise on the underside of his jaw. Another on the back of his hand. The crystal of his watch was cracked.

"Where's your handler?" he asked in a mocking voice. "She waiting around the corner?"

"No, she isn't with me."

"What about those trigger-happy gentlemen who came after you?"

Amelia swallowed nervously. "I'm sorry. But I *need* to talk to you. I didn't know who else to go to."

"Well, I can't help you. Now if you're really sorry, you'll get the hell out of here and take your trouble with you."

Amelia's eyes passed over the broken windows behind him. The damaged shelving. Her shoulders slumped and she turned to go. James caught her wrist as she reached for the door. He was staring at the bruises on her knuckles. At the angry mark on her face from Jack.

"One of them do that?" he asked.

Amelia nodded. There was a long pause. James let go of her wrist. He turned to the door and flipped the Open sign to Closed.

"Come on to the back," he said gruffly.

Amelia followed him behind the counter and through to the back of the store. He didn't look at her and instead began unlocking a wooden chest of drawers.

"What happened to your watch?"

"They took it."

He scoffed. "You shouldn't have let them do that."

"I didn't exactly have a choice in the matter."

"Right," James said with a sigh. "Have a seat." He gestured to a clutter-filled table.

Amelia didn't sit. She watched as he lifted the bottom of the wardrobe and reached deep inside. "The Russian boy had a blue flower," she told him.

James's hands stilled in their search. "What's his name?"

"Anton Stepanov."

"Oh. Yeah. He's one of ours."

Amelia swallowed shakily. "H-he said my uncle was too. That he was the leader."

"Uh-huh."

"You didn't tell me that before."

"I didn't trust you. With good reason, it seems." He turned back around. In his hands was a wooden box with a heavy padlock.

"What's that?" Amelia asked.

"Sit down."

This time she did, sliding into the seat. "Were you lying about not knowing what happened to my uncle too?"

"Unfortunately, no. That part was honest. But he did come to see me. Brought me these."

James undid the padlock on the box and opened it. Inside there were watches. Seven of them, all ticking to the same tune. Amelia leaned forward to get a closer look.

"Are those . . ."

"Watches he stole from the department. Yup."

"*He* stole them?" Amelia asked incredulously. "Does the department know that?"

"I imagine they're starting to figure it out," James said with a small chuckle. "Just as they're probably starting to realize that it wasn't Anton Stepanov who killed him."

"So it's true then? Anton isn't a murderer?"

"No. Quite the opposite, actually. He's a target."

Amelia didn't know why but she felt relieved.

"A target of who?"

"The department. The Russians. Everyone really."

"Why? What did he do?"

"Aside from being a rather ardent participant of the resistance? He stole the Russians' watches too. All of them. That was the plan, you see. We were working on organizing the mass removal of watches from government-run timekeeping organizations. America, Russia, Great Britain . . . any nation that has one. We weren't planning to act just yet, but something happened that made Ernest change his course at the last minute."

"What happened?"

"He found Lisavet Levy's book. The one she used to store the memories she saved."

Amelia frowned at that. "Anton Stepanov has the book now," she said, thinking aloud. "Do you think my uncle gave it to him?"

James shrugged. "Couldn't tell you. He was in a hurry when he came to see me and only mentioned the book in passing. He brought me the watches before he went off to have a little talk with Moira Donnelly."

"How is she connected to all of this?"

"Ernest didn't say. Just that he needed to talk to her about the book. I tried to tell him that going to her was a bad idea. But he insisted. Said it was important."

Amelia felt as though her head was spinning. What on earth was in this book that would make her uncle risk everything?

Shouts outside made James leap to his feet. He tore through the shop to look out the window, pulling aside the plastic.

"Shit," he hissed. "They're here."

Amelia's stomach plummeted.

James raced past her and began securing the box's padlock, his frantic hands making the whole thing rattle.

"What do we do?" Amelia asked.

James stashed the box back inside the wardrobe and returned the false bottom. He shut and locked the whole thing and turned back to her.

"Come with me."

He pulled her into the main shop and began spinning the crown of his watch. The entryway to the back of the shop transformed into a door.

"You first," he said, the dark expanse of the time space stretching before them. "Wait inside, I just need to . . ."

The shop door burst open. A shot rang out. Amelia screamed as James's grip on her arm went slack. He fell backward onto the counter and hit the floor, head cracking against the wood.

"Don't move or the next one's for you!"

Fear gripped Amelia's whole body as she saw Jack standing in the doorway. Behind him, Fred and Moira entered with guns raised. Moira's silver revolver was the one that made Amelia's heart pulse with rage. Even after everything else, it still felt like a betrayal.

Jack came forward, keeping his gun trained on her. "You have one chance, sweetheart. One chance to come quietly or I'll shoot you right here. Understand?"

At her feet, James let out a groan. Jack swung his gun at him, ready to shoot, but Amelia lunged for his arm, knocking it off course.

The gun went off two inches from her head, the bullet ricocheting down into the floor. Jack threw her off violently, landing her just beside James. She scrambled sideways, positioning herself in front of him.

"Leave him alone!" she shouted.

"I've had just about enough of you." Jack raised his gun toward her this time. Amelia braced herself, squeezing her eyes shut.

There was a bang. A shot, but no impact. No pain. Instead, everything held still. Everything fell silent. The room had stopped. Jack was still in front of her. He still had his gun pointed at her head. James was still on the ground. But they were all still. Completely frozen. Suspended in Time.

Amelia's breath came hard and fast. The only other person unaffected was Moira. She had her gun raised, like Jack, only instead of pointing at Amelia, she had it aimed at Fred.

"Are you all right?" Moira asked, lowering her weapon.

"Are . . . how . . . are you doing this?" Amelia stuttered.

"I'm not," Moira said with a grimace. "You are."

That's when Amelia noticed the bullet suspended in midair, halfway between Moira's revolver and the center of Fred's skull.

"Me? That's not possible. I don't even know what this is."

"Neither did I the first time it happened," Moira said in a vaguely mournful voice. "It's called temporal departure. It's what happens when someone's mind and body exist on separate planes of time. Like you." She came to offer her a hand. "Stand up."

Amelia scrambled onto her feet, eyes darting around the scene. "You shot Fred."

"Yes. I'm going to shoot Jack, too, in just a moment so you might want to look away." She took the gun from Jack's hands and slid it into her belt.

Amelia stared at her in shock. Moira eyed Jack distastefully, her finger poised on the trigger.

"I don't understand."

Moira turned toward her. "I can't explain it all now. I need you to go inside the time space and wait there until I come and get you." She gestured to the door James had opened.

Amelia's eyes widened in horror. "What? No."

"You said that Anton had a blue flower, right?"

"Yes."

"Good. Go and find him. He can help you."

"But I thought . . . *you* killed my uncle!"

Moira winced. "Go find the book like I told you to. Then you'll understand. And as soon as I fix things out here, I will come back for you."

Amelia shook her head frantically. "No. No, I can't. I-I-I don't have a watch. I'll be stuck."

"Yes, I know. It won't be for long. I promise." Moira reached out and ran a hand over Amelia's hair, tucking one of the strands behind her ear. "I'm sorry, Amelia," she said in a hushed voice.

With one hand, Moira shoved her backward through the door to the time space. Amelia stumbled and fell. Before she could recover, Moira had pulled the door shut, trapping her inside.

THE DOOR closed. Amelia was safe. Safe from Jack and far away from what Moira was about to do. Keeping the gun pointed at Jack, she willed Time to move again. She didn't need to touch the watch to do it. Time

was within her. Fred's body hit the ground in an instant. A direct shot
to the head.

Jack's eyes flickered in that hazy way. The way people always looked
when emerging from an altered past. He wouldn't know what had happened. Wouldn't know why she had her gun pointed at his head. A part
of her regretted that. She wanted him to know why she was doing this.
She wanted him to understand why she was about to kill him. As he
turned to look at her, eyes going wide, she settled for the fact that, even
if he didn't know what exactly had brought them to this moment right
here, he knew damn well everything he'd done to her up until then.

"Moira," he said in a hushed voice. He looked around and noticed
Fred lying on the floor. He checked behind her where Amelia had been
standing before. His hand went to his holster, finding it empty.

He smiled. Still a prick even when staring death in the face. "Where's
the girl?"

"Safe."

Jack narrowed his eyes at her. "You trapped her there, didn't you?"

Moira said nothing.

"And so it all comes full circle. How charming." He shifted and Moira
matched his movements, keeping him right where she wanted him.

Recognition registered on his face, all the pieces coming together.
Pieces that had been right in front of him the whole time, so close to
the surface that Moira had been terrified he might see them too soon. It
wasn't her cleverness or his stupidity that kept him from realizing it. Jack
Dillinger was many things. Crass. Violent. Chauvinistic. But he wasn't
stupid. It was arrogance that kept him from seeing the truth. The sincere
belief that he still had her, that he had all of them, under his thumb the
whole time.

"So this little rebellion . . ." Jack said, swirling his finger through the
air. "How long have you been a part of it?"

"Does it matter?" Moira said.

"I should have known. Ernest isn't even dead, is he?"

"I guess you're about to find out."

"And the girl . . . that's her, isn't it? The child born outside of Time. The baby girl you told me was dead."

"How long have you known?" Moira asked. She hated herself for giving into his taunting, but she had to know.

"I didn't. Not for sure. But I've suspected ever since that day Ernest brought her to the office. You're a good liar, Moira, but I know you too well."

Moira cocked the gun and pressed it against his temple, tired of his games. "Not well enough to save yourself, I guess."

For a moment, his well-constructed mask slipped. A phenomenon she'd witnessed only once before, years ago. "Just do me one favor. For old times' sake," he said, some of the smugness leaving his voice for this final request. "Don't burn my memories."

A slight tremor ran through Moira's hand at his words. "I won't," she promised.

He raised his chin defiantly, refusing to give her the satisfaction of seeing him scared. "Well played, Miss Levy."

Without hesitating, she pulled the trigger twice.

14

1955, Washington, DC

MOIRA, HER NAME WAS Moira.

Lisavet said this to herself dozens of times in the week before she started her job, trying to get it to stick. She practiced saying it out loud as she paced in her new bedroom, unable to sleep as always. Her apartment was hardly bigger than her room in the psych ward had been, but to her it was heaven. A bed of her own with soft white sheets and a quilt. A dresser to put clothes in. A vanity with an actual mirror. The room had two windows and was in close proximity to the bathroom she shared with three other girls. In the boardinghouse, nearly everything was communal, but she was one of just a few residents who did not have a roommate. Something Jack had arranged for her, apparently.

"Moira, my name is Moira," she repeated as she got ready for work that first morning in early 1955.

She dressed in a knee-length black skirt and a collared shirt in pale green that had been made for her by the seamstress. Jack had ordered her an entire closet's worth of clothing; five shirts, six dresses, a number of skirts, and three pairs of heeled shoes.

"The director's secretary needs to look sharp," he told her when he saw the look of surprise on her face. "I know you're just a poor girl from Brooklyn, but I can't have you dressing like one."

The boardinghouse matron called up the stairs to tell her that the car was here for her. Lisavet . . . no Moira, her name was Moira . . . took one last look in the mirror and went downstairs, locking the bedroom door behind her. On the front steps, she stopped short when she saw who had come to pick her up.

"Look alive, Donnelly," Patrick Brady said, waving for her to hurry up.

She started to get into the back seat, and he shook his head.

"I'm not your chauffeur. Sit up front." He tapped the passenger seat with one hand, smirking at her as she got in. "What's with the face?"

"Nothing. I just assumed that Jack would be the one taking me. That's all."

Brady shot her a look. "Now, now. You're his secretary, not his girlfriend. You have to call him Mr. Dillinger."

"Oh. Right."

There were so many things to remember.

"Besides, he's the director. He doesn't have time to be checking in on you all day, so he asked me and Collins to give him a hand. We'll be around if you need any help."

Moira studied him out of the corner of her eye. Be around or be watching her?

Brady took her into the office and introduced her to one of the other secretaries. A bright-eyed blonde named Shelley Watts.

"What happened to Suzanne?" Shelley asked.

"Gone," Brady said with a shrug. "Do me a favor and show Miss Donnelly what's what." He left them alone.

She turned to her and smiled. "Well, then. Welcome, I guess. That's your desk over there."

Shelley pointed to the desk closest to the corner office. She went over to it and dropped a nameplate that read Suzanne Tomlinson into the garbage.

"Were you and Suzanne . . . close?" Moira asked tentatively.

"Oh, no. Not at all. She was only here for a few months. Most of Mr. Dillinger's secretaries don't last long." Shelley grimaced at her own words and gave her an apologetic look. "He has high standards. But I'm sure you'll do great."

Shelley gave her a tour of the office and helped her obtain an ID badge with her name and photograph on it, warning her that she should keep it on her at all times.

"You'll need it to get in the building," she explained. "And if you're ever working late, they'll ask for it on your way out too."

"Do you stay late often?" Moira asked her.

"Only on occasion. Some of us do more than others. Amanda and Pauline are both general secretaries, so they stay late fairly frequently."

"General secretaries?"

"Yeah, as in they work for the whole office. I work for the senior staff members like Mr. Collins and Mr. Brady. Mr. Dillinger is the only one important enough to have a secretary of his own. Well, I guess Mr. Duquesne technically could have one but he's never hired anyone."

At the first mention of Ernest, Moira felt her face go numb. In all her worry about getting here and figuring things out, she'd almost forgotten she might be running into him today.

By the time Shelley finished the tour, more people had arrived. Three men in brown suits, all on the younger side, were loitering near Shelley's desk. One of them, a bulky young man with dark hair looked Moira up and down as they approached.

"Can I help you gentlemen with something?" Shelley asked.

"Morning, Miss Watts," the young man responded, eyes on Moira still. "Who's your friend?"

"This is the new secretary, Moira Donnelly."

"Well, well, new secretary," he said, sidling up to and giving her a flirtatious smile. "Don't you look sweet."

"Leave her alone, Fred," Shelley warned, taking her seat. "She's not here for you, she's Mr. Dillinger's new secretary."

"Is she? Jack always did have taste," Fred said, winking at her.

Moira looked away uncomfortably and moved over to her own desk. Fred and the two other boys snickered.

"You're supposed to smile," Shelley said when they were gone.

"Huh?"

"When they flirt with you like that. You're supposed to smile."

"But I don't want to."

"Doesn't matter. Didn't you learn that in secretary school?"

"I didn't go to secretary school," Moira said. She immediately regretted it when she saw the look on Shelley's face. Was she supposed to say she had gone? Jack hadn't mentioned anything about secretary school.

By the time Jack showed up, Moira had already worked herself up into a proper panic. So much so that she stood up as soon as she saw him walking in, the way she had been taught to stand for teachers at school in Germany. He pretended not to notice, pausing to say hello to the other girls before addressing her.

"Morning, Miss Donnelly," he said with a covert smile. "How are you settling in?"

"Good," Moira squeaked.

"Why are you standing?"

"Oh, I . . ." She sat back down, aware of Shelley and the other girls watching her. "Just stretching my legs."

"Right." He reached into his leather briefcase and pulled out a sheet of paper. "Here. First assignment for you. This is the week's calendar. I wrote it all down on Friday and I can't read my own handwriting. Would you type it up for me?"

Moira's eyes slid to the typewriter at the top of the desk. It was electric.

Not manual. She had never used an electric typewriter before. Actually, she had barely ever used a manual one. They were common enough in Germany when she was a child, but she'd been too young to learn, and her father had always done everything by hand anyway.

"Problem?" Jack asked, noting her long pause.

Moira lowered her voice. "I don't know how to use this thing."

Jack frowned. "Ahhh. I see."

Behind him, Amanda and Pauline started whispering tensely. Jack's eyes slid in their direction. He clapped his hands together once and came around the other side of the desk.

"Well, let's fix that," he said.

He showed her how to load the paper and then gave an uncharacteristically patient demonstration of how to do other things like change the ribbon and correct mistakes. All the while, Moira could feel the other secretaries watching her. Of course they were confused. In their eyes, Jack had just fired a perfectly qualified girl and replaced her with a technologically stunted imbecile. An imbecile he was now wasting his own precious time to train on the most basic of secretarial functions. Eventually, however, all three of them got called away to take notes or write up reports of their own, leaving them alone.

"Tough crowd, those girls," Jack said under his breath in their absence.

"They know I'm not qualified for this," Moira told him. No point in trying to deny it.

"Who gives a shit about them? They're just secretaries."

"So am I."

"Yes, but you're not like them."

"I'm worse than a secretary?"

Jack snickered and set his left hand on the desk beside her, gesturing to the watch on his wrist. "I'm saying you're the only secretary who knows what this department really is."

"What do you mean?"

"I mean . . ." Jack leaned in closer and set his other hand on her shoulder. "Here at the TRP we don't tell our secretaries the truth about what really goes on."

"You don't?"

"Nope. They think we're just another intelligence agency, trying to track patterns across history to get ahead of future wars. Not even my last girl knew the truth. Which meant she couldn't take notes for me in department-wide meetings or handle any of the more sensitive paperwork I get as the director. Kind of defeats the whole point of a secretary, don't you think?"

"I guess."

"But you, my dear . . . well, you're something special. That's why I hired you. All that other bullshit you can learn." He straightened up, adjusting his suit jacket. "By the way, you can stop watching the door like that. He's not here today."

Moira felt some of the tension in her shoulders loosen. "He's not?"

"He's out for the next two weeks. Some family situation. He's working out of the Boston office."

"His sister?" Moira asked, feeling anxiety bundle in her stomach.

Jack gave her a strange look. "No. Something about his mother being sick." He tapped two fingers on the sheet of paper he'd given her. "Type that up for me, will you? It'll be good practice." He left to go to his office, calling back over his shoulder. "If you need anything, just knock."

The door closed. Shelley gave Moira a confused look. "Are you dating him or something?"

"N-no. Why?"

"I've never seen him be that nice to one of his secretaries before. Especially not one who doesn't know how to use a typewriter. No offense."

Moira didn't say anything. Things got easier as the days went on. The other girls didn't hold her inexperience against her as she expected they might. They even seemed worried about her, exchanging glances when they learned she would be joining Jack for his meetings. Something his previous secretaries hadn't done before. Shelley showed her how to use the dictation machine and Amanda and Pauline gave her typing exercises they'd learned in secretary school to help her improve. She got used to the strangeness of her role.

Jack at work was a different Jack from the one she'd known before, but she could sense his other self, his real self, looming just under the surface. Always watching to make sure she stayed in line. He remained lenient as she adjusted, but the more days that went by, the more stringent his expectations became. She got used to sitting at his side to take notes during meetings, bringing him coffee, sorting his mail, keeping his calendar. One thing that she wasn't getting used to, however, was that the timekeepers who followed her in the time space for years had no idea who she was, thrown off by her hair and her new clothes. A part of her almost wished they did recognize her. Maybe they wouldn't flirt so brazenly if they knew who she was.

Fred Vance in particular was becoming a problem for Moira. He, along with two others, made up a new team of timekeepers who were still in training. She staunchly refused to "smile and accept it" the way Shelley recommended she should, and Fred appeared to consider this as some kind of a challenge. She did her best to ignore them.

Until one day, in her third week, Fred Vance sought her out before a big meeting when the office was relatively quiet. Most of the timekeepers had already gone into the boardroom, and Moira was in the break room waiting for Jack. It was to be her first time in an important meeting like this and she was already wound up. So when Fred came along with his lackeys and his catcalling, her patience was already worn thin. When he trapped her against the counter and put his hand up her skirt, however, she snapped. She punched him hard across the face. Fred stumbled backward, grabbing his bleeding nose and howling with pain.

"What the hell is going on in here?"

Fred immediately stopped shouting. He and the other two time-keepers in the room straightened up.

Moira turned to see Ernest standing in the door of the break room. He was dressed in a suit and tie, hair combed and styled. He was giving her a scolding, accusatory look she had never seen before. When had he come back from leave? She swallowed at the feeling of his eyes on her, suddenly unable to think of anything but the way his lips felt pressed against her skin.

"Well?" he prompted.

Moira blinked. "I'm sorry. What did you say?"

Behind her, the trainees were snickering. A single stern look from Ernest silenced them.

"I asked who you are."

"I'm J-... Mr. Dillinger's new secretary."

"Well, Mr. Dillinger's new secretary, do you have a name?"

"M-Moira Donnelly."

"Got it. Now do you want to explain to me why you punched one of *my* trainees?"

"I didn't realize he was yours."

"And if you had, you wouldn't have hit him?"

Moira folded her arms. She didn't like being scolded by him. "No, I still would have."

"Do you make a habit of punching your superiors?"

"Only if that superior is being a disrespectful prick."

The sound of snickering picked up again.

Ernest snapped at them. "Why are you all standing around? I know you've got better things to be doing so I suggest you do them. Now."

The three young men lit from the room like a pack of dogs with their tails between their legs.

Ernest turned his harsh gaze back to Moira.

"Miss Donnelly, was it?" he asked, scrutinizing her. "I don't know what Jack told you about how we conduct ourselves around here, but violence will not be tolerated. I would have expected better from the director's secretary."

"So because I'm Mr. Dillinger's secretary, that means I get reprimanded while your direct reports can run around harassing young women without consequences?"

This struck a nerve. She could tell by the way he ground his jaw. She was not behaving the way a normal secretary would. The way he and the other men were used to. Anyone else might fire her on the spot. But she knew Ernest too well.

"What did he do?"

"He put his hand up my skirt."

Ernest's ears turned pink. "I see. I'll . . . talk to him."

"Don't bother," Moira said, rubbing her sore knuckles. "I think he got the message."

Ernest let out a single chuckle before remembering himself. "Right. Well, consider this a warning, Miss Donnelly. I won't tolerate violence, even if you are Jack's secretary. If they give you trouble again, come talk to me."

"I'll be sure to do that, Mr. . . ."

He held a hand out to her. "Oh, right. Duquesne. Ernest Duquesne."

Moira smiled, amazed at how easily she could still turn him around. "Nice to meet you, Mr. Duquesne."

Jack entered the break room just as their hands met, holding a stack of files. He took one look at them and stopped dead in his tracks.

Ernest let go of her hand. "There you are, Jack."

"Is there a problem here?" Jack asked, narrowing his eyes at them.

"No problem. Just getting acquainted with your new secretary."

"Were you now?"

Moira swallowed, feeling her heart pulse in her throat. She could hear the skepticism in Jack's voice already. Ernest had been back for less than a day and here she was getting caught in a room alone with him.

On his way out of the room, Ernest paused to pat Jack on the shoulder. "Careful, Jack. You might have hired the only woman in the world who can give you a run for your money." He actually sounded vaguely impressed.

Jack's eyes followed Ernest all the way down the hall before turning back.

"I punched one of the new timekeepers in the face," Moira said at once, wanting to dispel any doubts right away.

Jack cocked an eyebrow. "Oh?"

"I might have broken his nose. It won't happen again."

"Which one did you punch?"

"Fred Vance."

Jack cracked a bemused smile. "Good choice."

She followed him into the boardroom. The timekeepers exchanged glances as Jack began the meeting without bothering to address Moira's presence in the room.

"Uh, Jack . . ." Ernest said, cutting him off. "Shouldn't she . . ."

"She's got clearance," Jack said dismissively.

"How?" Ernest asked with a frown.

"Ernest, I suggest you focus on keeping your new hires in line and stop concerning yourself with my employees."

The silence in the room was tense. At the other end of the table, Brady and Collins traded amused looks.

Jack made it clear in that first meeting that when it came to Moira, he wasn't going to accept criticism. She was, in a way, protected by him and this protection served a dual purpose of keeping him from having to deal with his subordinates' skepticism, and keeping her from having to answer any prying questions about her personal life. She became known throughout the TRP as one of two things: the secretary who broke Fred

Vance's nose or simply as "Jack's girl." Both deterred the timekeepers from flirting with her.

AFTER ONE year on the job, in 1956, Jack finally asked Moira to do what he'd really hired her for.

"I need you to clean something up for me," he said, when he called her into his office that night.

This time, the victim was someone she knew. Pauline, one of the general secretaries, had walked in on a conversation she wasn't supposed to hear. She was being held in an unconscious state on the lower floors until they could find a solution. Moira fingered the black notebook Jack had given her to store the memories, studying Pauline's face. At the first sign of hesitation, Jack was quick to remind her of his previous threats.

"Try not to think about it too much," he said softly, one hand on her shoulder. "In the past, a slipup like this could cost a girl like Pauline her life. It's happened to more than one of my secretaries. Surely keeping her alive is worth a couple of fleeting memories?" He paused, leaning in a little closer so that he was speaking directly into her ear. "But if you still aren't compelled . . . maybe I ought to have Brady do some more digging about that theory of his. You remember? The one about your daughter?"

Moira stepped away from him, removing her arm from his reach. As much as his threats scared her, they also made her furious. After all, it wasn't like he could read *her* memories to learn the truth. Even so, it wasn't worth the risk. He had her cornered and he knew it. So Moira did as he asked.

"Attagirl," he said when she was finished.

As she turned to go, he caught her wrist.

"Did you need something else?" she asked, her tone void of emotion.

The smug look on his face had shifted. He was eyeing her with something almost akin to concern. "Did you know it's been over a year since you started working here?" he asked.

"The longest you've ever had a secretary, or so I've heard," Moira said dryly.

"Hey now, that's not nice," Jack said. But he was smiling.

"I didn't make your reputation, Jack. I'm just letting you know what gets said around here."

"And what gets said about you and me?" He still hadn't let go of her wrist.

Moira shifted uncomfortably. "Nothing. Just that you've never kept a secretary this long. Everyone assumes we're sleeping together."

"Sleeping together?" His thumb stroked the inner part of her forearm. "Isn't that something?"

Moira pulled her arm away. She didn't like the way he was looking at her all of a sudden. The dark, heavy expression that looked nothing like the way Ernest used to look at her but every bit the way Fred Vance did.

He stepped closer to her and tucked a hand under her chin. "You know, I heard they call you my girl."

She stared him down. Unsure of where this was going, but very certain she didn't like it.

Jack made a humming noise, moving his hand from her chin to the curve of her hip as if it had any business being there. "Has a nice ring to it, don't you think?"

Moira returned upstairs to her desk fifteen minutes later, her skin crawling.

He called on her to help him alter memories regularly in the months that followed, each set of living memories joining the first in the pages of the notebook. This new book, like her old one, never left her side, and the sheer rate at which its pages filled left her with a gnawing sense of unease. As the world around her was molded and remolded under the whims of the TRP, she alone knew that it was burning.

ERNEST HAD assumed that Moira Donnelly wouldn't last. He had ab-
stained from joining the betting pool the other timekeepers had going,
but his money would have been on a particularly expedited departure.
After all, she was untrained, uneducated, and, given her proclivity for
violence, entirely unfit for the role of secretary. But somehow, she stayed
the course. Not only that, but she was allowed in meetings that no other
secretary had ever attended, privy to the inner workings of the CIA's
most clandestine department. Furthermore, she had the protection of
Jack, who swiftly told off any employee for questioning her presence,
Ernest included. No one had ever seen Jack go to bat for any employee,
let alone a secretary. It made Ernest wary of her, but also curious. Perhaps a little too curious.

He found himself staring at her from the open door of his office. In
meetings, too, eyes fixed to the spot where she sat at Jack's shoulder, head
lowered over her notes, her quick, steady hands transcribing every word
that was said. At least twice each meeting, she would look up and catch him
in the act, a sharp zap traveling down his spine every time their eyes met.

It was the eyes that made him keep looking. A sense of *knowing* that
unnerved him.

Unfortunately, his curiosity did not go unnoticed by his colleagues.

"Close your mouth, Duquesne," Brady said to him as he shut the door
to his office one afternoon. Blocking his line of sight to Moira's desk.
"You're drooling."

Ernest glared at him. Normally, he wouldn't let another timekeeper
get away with that, but Brady was one of Jack's direct reports. He passed
a hand over his face and leaned back in his chair.

"Sorry. Tired. Must have zoned out."

Brady chuckled at him. "Hey, you don't have to explain it to me. She's
a looker, that's for sure."

"With a wicked right hook," Ernest added in a mumble. There was no point denying it to Brady. He had been in the FBI for five years before joining the TRP and so he knew how to read people.

Brady sat down in the chair across from him.

"True, true. Just . . . watch yourself with her, all right?"

"Why?" Ernest asked.

Brady gave him a stern look. "You heard what Jack said. She's got *clearance*, Ernest. More than you or I have if I had to guess. You know they don't give that out to just anybody. Odds are, she's some kind of Soviet ex-spy or German turncoat the head office recruited. Besides, she's Jack's girl. Even if you and him got along, stealing the boss's girlfriend wouldn't exactly be the fastest way to promotion."

Ernest frowned at that. "So it's true then? She and Jack are . . ."

Brady shrugged. "Who knows? But she must be doing *something* right to make it this long, if you know what I mean." He dropped a thick file onto the desk with a smack. "Enough about her. Temporal adjustments from Jack. Small stuff mostly. He wants you to give them out to your new guys as practice."

Ernest's heart sank. He lifted the file up and leafed through it. Names and histories, plucked from the past, waiting to be erased. "I'll get on it," he said, tossing the file to one side.

After Brady left, Ernest let out a long sigh, eyes straying habitually to Moira's desk again. This time, Jack was standing next to her, one arm propped against the desk, the two of them looking down at the page lodged in her typewriter. She said something that made Jack smile, and then he looked up, locking eyes with Ernest through the doorway. Ernest gave him a nod and looked away. Resolving not to look back at her until the day was over.

A few months ago, his attraction to Moira wouldn't have been such an issue. That's not to say he would have pursued her as he might have when he was younger, but he might have at least been able to behave a bit more normally around her. Might have even flirted with her. But lately, things had changed.

About two years ago, Ernest had stopped burning memories. Not completely, of course. His position required him to continue in some capacity. But less. *Much* less. He didn't know exactly when it had started. The hesitation. He supposed it began sometime around the time he'd figured out how to time walk. A discovery he had more or less stumbled upon. Something about being able to walk through memories made them feel all the more precious to him. He felt so strong an attachment to those first memories that the idea of destroying them seemed unbearable. Before he knew it, he had started stepping out of line. Disobeying Jack's directives.

That night, Ernest took the file with him, rather than giving the contents to his direct reports. He slipped into the cool quiet of the time space as the clock struck midnight and set off in search of the memories. Each time he found one of the books he was looking for, he flipped through the pages with care to find the ones that Jack and those up on Capitol Hill had deemed worth destroying a person over. Those specific memories he burned, knowing that if he didn't, Jack would catch on. The sound of each burned memory echoed in his ears like the dying breath of another human. The rest of the book he would hide, burying it somewhere amid a more distant stack. Leaving the remainder of the memories intact.

It was nearly morning before Ernest made it to the last one, a slim volume containing the memories of a boy barely twenty years old. This one he held with great care, noting what precious little there was. He had only just identified the part he was going to erase when a voice spoke behind him.

"I don't mean to be a bother . . ."

Ernest nearly jumped out of his skin, dropping the book in surprise. He wheeled around, one hand reaching for his pistol, and found himself confronted by a specter. A man dressed like a monk, hovering a few feet behind him.

"God, you nearly gave me a heart attack," he said, bending down to pick up the book. "You should announce your presence or something."

"I thought I was," the memory said pointedly, eyeing him in amusement. "My apologies. I had a question for you."

"Sorry. I'm not here to store memories today," he said.

"That wasn't my question."

Ernest blinked. The specters did not normally talk to timekeepers unless they wanted their memories stored. "Oh. Okay. What is your question?"

"Why are you doing that?"

"Doing what?"

The monk gestured to the book. "Sparing the memories. Forgive me, it's not like your kind to do that."

Ernest didn't answer right away, shifting the book from one hand to another. "It just . . . no longer feels right," he said as forcefully as he could. "To burn them."

There was a pause and for a moment Ernest thought the memory might simply accept his answer and leave. His ghostly eyes studied him closely.

"You should be careful," he said at last. "I knew a girl who used to do that very same thing. It only brought her trouble in the end."

"A girl?" Ernest asked, frowning. "What girl?"

The man gave him a vacant, searching look and then nodded at the book. "There are others, you know."

"Others?"

"Others who hesitate to do what is asked of them. Others who no longer wish to burn . . ."

"There are?"

"Of course. There is no thought that has only been had by just one man. Some ideas are inevitable." The man paused and smiled in a wry, ironic sort of way. "No matter how many men try to get rid of them."

Ernest hesitated. He was curious. "Is it another American? Like me?"

"I'm afraid not." There was another pause and then he said, "I could . . . introduce you, if you'd like. You'll never meet him without help. Not unless you feel like getting shot at."

Ernest eyed him with suspicion. "What do you mean?"

"His name is Vasily Stepanov."

Ernest drew back on instinct. "A Russian?"

"See what I mean? Not exactly someone you can waltz up to without some kind of mediator. But if you'd like . . . I could facilitate something."

Ernest's frown deepened. "Why would you do that?"

"Same reason *he* stopped burning memories," the man said, his expression deepening into a kind of mourning. "For her."

Ernest considered the offer, wondering what could possibly come out of such a meeting between him and a Russian timekeeper. Surely nothing good. He wanted to say no to the monk, but the words slipped out before he could stop them.

"Next Friday," he said. "Midnight. Tell him to come."

15

1965, Somewhere in the Time Space

No one was coming.

Amelia had been wandering the time space for hours. She was exhausted by the time she found herself sitting in front of the chasm, dusty shelves arching high up overhead. Head cradled in her hands, knees pulled up to her chest. She was in the middle of her third round of hyperventilating when she heard footsteps approaching.

Anton stood in front of her with his arms crossed. A scowl fixed to his face.

"Back already?" he asked. "Where is your watch?"

Amelia lifted her head from her hands to look at him. "They took it."

Anton knelt down in front of her. He reached out and touched her cheek where it was bruised, having no regard for personal space.

"I see you started asking questions," he said softly.

"You were wrong. She didn't kill him," Amelia said faintly. Still trying to wrap her head around it.

Anton sighed. "Are you all right?"

"I'm exhausted. I need to sleep."

"People don't *need* to sleep in the time space."

"Apparently some people do," Amelia said, shutting her eyes in annoyance.

He looked at her for a moment longer and then held out his hand. "Come with me, *koshka*. We will find you someplace better to sleep."

JAMES GRAVEL was slow to regain consciousness. Moira sat at the kitchen table, nursing a cup of coffee while she waited. She kept one nervous eye on the window. More than once she imagined she heard sirens outside but brushed it off. No one was coming. Why would they? Nobody knew.

James stirred. His eyes opened, glassy and distant as he looked down at the bandages Moira had used to dress his wound. He tried to sit up, gasping in pain.

"Don't do that," Moira said. "I only just managed to stop the bleeding."

"You," James said in a deep, raspy voice. He began struggling to right himself. "What the hell are you doing here?"

"Saving your life, apparently. Now hold still. You'll ruin the stitches."

"Stitches . . ." James stopped moving and assessed his bandages again. "You did this?"

Moira took her empty coffee cup to the sink. On the counter there was a bottle of pain medication she had bribed one of the porch dwellers into picking up from the pharmacy. She took two from the bottle and filled a glass with water before bringing them both over to James.

"What's this?"

"Something for the pain."

He eventually took the medicine from her hand. She watched as he swallowed them down. He glanced at the spattered blood on her white blouse. Some of it was his. Some of it wasn't.

"I need to know where you're hiding the watches," she announced abruptly.

James took another gulp of water to avoid answering. "What watches?"

"The ones Ernest stole from the department."

He narrowed his eyes at her. "Don't know what you mean."

"I know he brought them to you. He told me. Where are they?"

James scoffed at her in disbelief.

Moira let out a huff. "There are two dead bodies in your shop right now. One of them is the head of the CIA. Now you can tell me where the watches are, and I'll make sure those bodies get taken care of. Otherwise, I'll be very annoyed that I wasted all that time and effort saving your life only to have you sentenced on two counts of second-degree murder."

James glared at her. "*Two* bodies?"

Moira rolled her eyes impatiently. "The girl is fine."

"Where is she?"

"Safe."

"Safe?"

"Yes. But she won't be for long if you don't tell me where those watches are."

James didn't reply.

"Well?"

"You didn't kill Ernest."

"No."

"Damn. I thought I had you pegged."

"Mr. Gravel. Don't make me shoot you again."

James's lips curled in a combination of hatred and amusement. "The wardrobe in the back of the shop upstairs has a false wooden bottom. There's a box inside. The keys were in my pocket but I'm going to assume you already have those."

"Thank you," Moira said. "In a few days you should go see a doctor to get the wound checked. There's more pain medication on the counter. I'll clean things up upstairs, but you might want to join your family out of town for a while." She turned to go.

"I don't get it," James called after her. "You've been on my case for over a year now. Harassing me. Terrorizing my family. And you expect me to believe that all that time you've been some kind of double agent? That you were on our side?"

"I wasn't on your side," Moira said tensely. "And I'm not a double agent."

"So you decided to shoot your boss for what? The thrill of it?"

Moira shot him a wry smile and opened the door. "Goodbye, Mr. Gravel. If all goes well, you won't be seeing me again."

"Thank god for that," he said as she shut the door behind her.

The bodies upstairs were already locked in the trunk of her car. It had been the first thing she'd done while waiting for James to wake up. She returned to the shop to get the watches and locked the door behind her before dropping the keys in the mailbox. Neither of the two men on the porch said a word as she got in her car and drove away. They'd seen her with the bodies, but she wasn't worried about them. They weren't about to willingly call more law enforcement into their neighborhood.

Between the shop and her first destination, she smoked three cigarettes, hoping they would help clear her head. When they didn't, she threw the third out the window, only half spent. She reached the bridge where Amelia had discarded the tape as the sun was going down. The wind had picked up. It was going to rain.

There was no one around to see her as she dragged the heavy bodies from the trunk and laid them side by side on the riverbank beneath the bridge.

"Sorry, Fred," she muttered as she laid his pistol in his open palm to make it look like he was the one who'd done this.

By the time she finished, she was sweating and dirty and still covered in blood. She returned to her car just as the sky opened up. Good. Rain meant fewer people on the road. It took Moira seven hours to reach DC from Boston. She pulled the car up to the gates of Jack's office at half past one in the morning. All the lights were off. As the security guard approached, she quickly slid into her coat to hide the bloodstains on her blouse and rolled down the window.

"Name?" he asked, looking down at a clipboard as rain pelted his umbrella.

Moira cocked an eyebrow and waited. He looked up and immediately began apologizing.

"Oh, Director Donnelly. So sorry, I didn't realize it was you."

"I need to get into Jack's office," Moira said curtly. "He's currently detained in Boston but he needed something."

He didn't question her story, immediately opening the gates for her. "If you give me a moment, I can come and escort you in."

"No need," Moira said. "I'm in a bit of a hurry."

There were two other cars in the parking lot when she parked. One belonged to the security guard, but the other . . . She studied the plates, tapping one finger on the steering wheel. Who was still here this late? Cleaning staff perhaps? Just in case, she reloaded her revolver and tucked it into her coat.

Rain pelted her as she got out of the car and climbed the staircase, heels clicking against the concrete. It had been five years since Moira had relocated the TRP to the New York offices. It had been framed to the others as a strategic choice, allowing for their work to stay as protected as possible as CIA operations in the capital expanded. But really, it was a way for Moira to get away from Jack. He still worked in DC, and so she knew exactly where he kept things. Most importantly, she knew exactly where he kept the things he didn't want her to know he still had. Inside, the building was warm and quiet. The hum of the radiator was the only sound. Maybe no one else was here. She didn't turn on any lights as she made her way down the hall and up the elevator. On the third floor, she stopped to listen, hearing nothing, and then stepped out of the elevator.

She stood by the desk of Jack's new secretary, staring down at the seat that used to be hers. The name on the desk was different than the

last time she'd been here. Poor thing didn't know yet that she was out
of a job. Moira took out her wallet and laid two fifty-dollar bills on the
desk, knowing that, in the chaos that was about to ensue, it might be
a while before Jack's new secretary received her last paycheck. Moira
hoped, though she doubted it, that this one would at least be getting out
before he manipulated her into sleeping with him. As he had done with
every single one of his secretaries. As an afterthought, Moira laid down
another twenty.

She let herself into Jack's office using the keys she had taken from his
coat. The air smelled like copy paper and cologne. His desk was as neat
as his appearance, not a stray pen or paper clip out of place. The safe she
was looking for was underneath the desk. Heavy and metal and tucked
inside a cabinet. She knelt in front of it and began fiddling with the
combination lock, hoping to God he hadn't gotten wise and changed the
code. It opened with a satisfying click.

Inside was exactly what she had been hoping to find. Her coat, her
father's coat, was folded neatly atop a box labeled with her initials. Her
real initials. Her fingers curled around the door to steady herself while
she reached out with her other hand. She touched the soft brown wool,
suddenly feeling as though her hands belonged to someone else. Beneath
the coat, the box was filled with notes that Jack had taken from Ernest
over fifteen years ago. Among them were the drawings Ernest had done
of her face, the notebook where he'd chronicled every encounter they
had, along with all his theories. The files closest to the top were slightly
different. Reports from Brady and Collins. And of course, notes from
Jack himself. Taken during the two years he had kept her locked away in
the psychiatric ward.

The final file, kept on the very top of the pile for easier access, was
labeled *Amelia Duquesne*. The file itself was already alarmingly thick.
The bastard, Moira cursed under her breath, her hands shaking as
she retrieved it. Deep down, she had known that he suspected there

was something different about Amelia. Moira had seen the look in his eyes the first time he'd met her nearly a decade ago. But she hadn't known about this. Moira set the files aside. Those weren't what she was here for.

There was a final box in the safe. This one needed a second key, the smallest one on Jack's key ring. Her hands shook as she opened the box, already imagining that she could hear it. Her father's watch had stopped ticking years ago from lack of use. Moira ran one hand over the crystal, the patinated brass. The hush of Time gathered in the back of her head, and she tapped one fingernail against the pocket watch. It began ticking once more, springing to life like a child coming home. She smiled to herself as she lifted it from the box.

A light in the hallway flipped on. She frantically returned the files and slid her father's watch into her pocket, closing the safe. She slung the coat over one arm and straightened up just as the door opened.

"Patrick," she said, fixing a passive expression on her face.

Patrick Brady stood in the doorway, looking at her strangely.

"Hello, Donnelly," he said. "I thought you were in Boston."

"I was. Jack needed something."

Brady took a step into the room, looking down at the coat. Moira shifted slightly, adjusting her lapels to cover more of the bloodstains.

"Must have been pretty urgent to send you all the way here in the middle of the night."

"It was," Moira said with a curt smile. She was the director of the Temporal Reconnaissance Program. She didn't need to explain herself to him. Even if he did work for Jack and not her. "If you'll excuse me, I should get back."

She tried to step around him but Brady blocked her way.

"Aren't you supposed to be looking after Ernest's kid?"

"It's none of your business what I'm supposed to be doing, Brady," she said, glaring at him. "By the way, what are *you* doing here so late?"

"Oh, you know. Waiting for a call."

Something cold settled in the back of Moira's throat. "A call?"

"From Jack. He rang late last night and said some things were about to go down in Boston between Ernest's kid and that Russian boy. Said he was going to call me tonight at some point once everything was all said and done. Said I should wait around until he did. To make sure nothing went wrong." Brady paused, eyes flickering down to her shirt, the bloodstains just visible. "You see . . . he had some concerns."

Moira reached behind her. She seized the lamp from the desk and swung hard at Brady's head. He ducked and the lamp shattered against the wall. She ran from the room, feeling the pull of Time stirring in her chest. She thought about Amelia in the time space and resisted the urge to stop Time, knowing that the chasm only grew each time she did. She shut the door to Jack's office behind her and slammed the keys into the lock before Brady could recover his balance. He began banging on the door, cursing her by name, her real name, as she fled.

She made it to her car and pulled out of the parking lot, following the signs for Manhattan.

AMELIA WOKE to the sound of birdsong.

Sunlight streamed in through the crack in the floral curtains, filling the little room with warm golden light. The room itself was tiny, with sloped ceilings and a window at knee height. She was lying on a ragged old rug beside a bed. Her brain felt fuzzy, and it took several moments for everything to click into place. She was in a memory. Amelia forced herself into a seated position, her neck sore from sleeping at an awkward angle. Anton was nowhere to be found. She listened closely for any signs of what era they might be in. Anton hadn't told her last night, and she had been too exhausted to ask. Out the window was a golden meadow dotted with wildflowers. It was summer. Somewhere provincial. She could hear muffled voices below, the creak of old hinges, and then the sound of children laughing.

Amelia descended the ladder to the floor below. The house was much smaller than she expected. Three rooms in total, including the loft where she had been sleeping. A little kitchen with a stove but no sink. She still didn't see Anton. The children's laughter grew louder outside so she followed the sound. Soft summer sun nestled against her face as she stepped out.

Ahead of her, just beyond a little gate, four young children—three girls and a boy all younger than ten years old—danced around a tall man who must be their father as he carried two empty buckets. He called out to the youngest in Russian, a little girl who was lagging behind. Her brown curls bounced as she ran on infant legs to catch up to them. Amelia's eyes fell on a figure sitting beneath a sprawling oak, arms resting on his knees. Anton. Amelia cut across the grassy meadow toward him. He didn't look at her until she was right in front of him, his eyes on the children.

She sat down in the grass beside him. Birds flew in and out of the branches of the oak over their heads, twittering their morning songs. This place was peaceful but beside her, Anton seemed on edge.

"Where are we?" she asked.

For a minute, Anton remained quiet. "Russia," he said at last, trilling his r with a bit more emphasis than usual. "Nineteen fifty-five."

Amelia followed his glassy gaze to the children running up the hill after their father. Her eyes fell on the boy of about six or seven with sharp dark eyes and clumsy long limbs.

"Oh, so this is—" She broke off as Anton's shoulders tensed. There was another pause. "Is this your . . ."

"Yes," Anton said before she could finish. He pointed. "That man over there is my father. The girls are my sisters."

"Where's your mother?"

"She died in childbirth two years before this day."

Amelia looked back at the littlest girl, struggling to keep up with her siblings. "I'm sorry," she said faintly. *I lost my mother too*, she wanted to say.

Anton frowned. "There is no reason for you to be sorry. You do not know me. I am a stranger to you."

"Where are your sisters now?" Amelia asked.

Anton's face darkened. "Dead."

"All of them?"

"My father was a timekeeper before he was killed by the Americans. Our life was better then. Normal. My father was saving up money to send me to America on a school exchange program. I used to be very good at math. But . . . well, then he died, and it was all over for me. I was forced into the timekeeper program in his place. The government put me through their three-year training regimen in Moscow. By the time I was allowed to contact my sisters again, they were gone. Nobody could tell me what happened to them. Later, I learned they had died of starvation in an orphanage."

"Starvation?" Amelia asked.

Anton shrugged. "It is common in places like this."

Amelia looked at the three tiny girls, tripping over themselves with laughter. "Why did you decide to come here?" she asked. Clearly this was difficult for him. Such a vulnerable thing to share with a total stranger.

"I wanted to see it again. I always wish that I could experience these moments a second time. I dream about it always. Back then, I didn't know any of this was worth cherishing."

There was such pain in his voice. The joyful shouts of the youngest girl rang out again, followed by the father's laughter.

"*Remorse is memory awake*," Amelia murmured quietly. Too quiet for him to hear, or so she thought.

"What did you say?" Anton asked.

"Oh. Nothing."

"No, what was it? Something about a memory?"

"It's a poem. By Emily Dickinson," Amelia said sheepishly. "'Remorse is memory awake / Her companies astir / A presence of departed acts / At window and at door / its past set down before the soul / and lighted with a match'—" She broke off, blushing at the strange look he was giving her.

"Is pretty," Anton said, considering it. "How do you know it?"

"I memorized it when I was younger. This . . . time walking . . . it made me think of it."

"This is what you think about when you are on the run from the US government?" Anton asked, sounding amused. "Poems?"

"Sure, don't you?" she asked sarcastically.

Anton chuckled. "I am Russian. We destroyed all our poets with the rise of communism and the ones that are left tell only of the glory of the state. None of these remorseful memories of windows and doors."

"I'm sure it seems stupid to you," Amelia said, looking away. "But it's how I handle difficult things."

"No, not stupid," Anton said. "You were lucky to learn of such things when you were so young."

There was a glint in his eyes but it wasn't mockery. It was jealousy.

"Tell it to me again?" he asked, his tone softer. Shy even. As though asking to hear a poem was a sign of weakness.

Amelia repeated the poem through to the end and saw the shadows under Anton's eyes deepen. There was a long, weighty silence in which Anton stared over the flaxen hillside, watching his family disappear over the crest.

"Is pretty," he remarked a second time. "You have a nice voice."

"Thanks," Amelia mumbled.

There was another long pause. "So . . ." Anton said, leaning back on his hands. "What happens now?"

"What do you mean?"

"Well. You are stuck. You do not have a watch."

"But you do."

"Sure, but unless you want to get shot at by the Russian government instead of the American one, I would not recommend using mine."

"You mean . . . you've been stuck in here?"

"Yes. For about a month now. I am a target of the KGB so I couldn't leave even though I still have my watch. That's why your uncle was helping me. I thought you knew that."

"I guess I just didn't realize you were trapped."

"Well. Now you do. Turns out we are both criminals, eh?" he said, bumping her shoulder with his own.

Amelia smiled at him and looked away quickly. "Any chance you remember where you left that book?" she asked. She hadn't seen it on him since that day. "The blue one with the flower on it?"

He gave her a vaguely suspicious look. "You mean Lisavet Levy's book? What do you want with it?"

"Moira said I should look for it. She said it would help explain."

"And you don't think it could be a trap?"

Amelia bit her lip. "I don't think she's trying to trick me. She shot her own boss to save my life."

"Sure," Anton conceded. "But she *did* try to have *me* killed."

Amelia winced. "That was sort of my fault. She thought you had attacked me, and I didn't correct her and so . . ." She trailed off, giving him an apologetic look.

Anton narrowed his eyes at her, scrutinizing her closely. "You are a lot of trouble, you know that, *koshka*?"

"What does that mean?" Amelia asked.

"What does what mean?"

"*Koshka*. You've said it twice now."

A mischievous look appeared on Anton's face. "Kitty cat. Because of the scratching."

Amelia rolled her eyes at him. "So will you show me where it is?"

Anton took his sweet time responding, tilting his head back and forth as he contemplated. "Okay. I will show you."

He hopped to his feet and offered her his hand, along with another vexatious smile. "So what do you say? Are we done being enemies now? We can be friends?"

Amelia wanted to say something snarky, but for once, couldn't think of a single retort. Instead, she accepted his offer of friendship along with his hand and let him lead her out of the memory, back into the time space.

ANTON HAD hidden the book up high.

"I move it every day," he said as he boosted himself up on the lower shelves to reach it. "So that way no one will find it."

"Why don't you just carry it with you?" Amelia asked. "That way you'd know if someone was trying to take it."

Anton took small steps along the shelf as he responded. "It is safer this way. Me, I am easy to find. But a book in a place full of millions of books? Not so much." As if to make a point, he climbed down from the shelf and moved to another spot a little farther down to keep looking.

"So, how did you end up with the book anyway?" Amelia asked. "James told me that it was missing."

"It *was* missing. A lot of timekeepers were looking for it. Including me. But we were all looking in the wrong place." Anton jumped off the shelf with a thump, holding the moleskin-wrapped book in one hand. "It turns out that it had already been found."

"By who?"

"My father," Anton said with a proud grin. "He'd had it for years. Kept it hidden beneath the floorboards of his living quarters. They put me in his room when I was recruited, but I didn't find it until about a month ago, completely by accident."

He delicately removed the fabric covering from the book and held it out to her. Amelia took it, tracing one hand over the worn blue cover. She listened closely for the whispers she'd heard before, hearing the subtle sound coming from within the pages, begging to be opened. Still, she hesitated.

"Have you seen what's in it?" she asked.

Anton shook his head. "Once I figured out what it was, I took it to Ernest. He decided to look at the memories, but I had to go back. Next time I saw him he was . . . different. He told me that it was time to act on our plan to steal the watches from our departments. He told me to hide the book somewhere and then we split up." Anton broke off, staring wistfully down at the book. "When I finished my part, I waited for him to come back but . . . he never did. I assumed he had been caught. I didn't know he was dead until . . ."

"Until I showed up," Amelia said, swallowing the lump in her throat. "Where are the watches now?" she asked, not wanting to dwell on it.

Anton's face lit with mischief. "In the chasm."

"The chasm?"

"It is a good hiding place, no?"

Amelia laughed at him. "I suppose. So all this time and you still haven't looked to see what's in the book?"

Anton shrugged. "I guess I didn't want to see."

Amelia couldn't blame him. Now she wasn't even sure if *she* wanted to look. She swallowed and ran her thumb down the spine of the book again. "Would you look with me?" she asked.

Anton raised an eyebrow.

"I want to see the memories, but I don't know how to time walk," Amelia explained hastily. "And besides, I . . . I don't want to go alone."

Anton studied her apprehensively, as if she was asking him to do something very painful. Maybe he feared seeing his father in these pages, the same way she feared seeing Uncle Ernest. She held her breath, waiting for him to respond. At last he nodded and reached for her hand.

Anton placed his palm on the book and the next thing Amelia knew, the dark and shadows of the time space faded out around her, transforming into someplace else. A bedroom, filled with the warm glow from the fireplace, a single bed in one corner where a little girl with golden hair sat waiting. Out the window, the streets had long since gone dark and chill with November winds.

From the doorway, a man with a voice that crackled like flames in a hearth spoke.

Time for bed, Lisavet. You've had enough stories for tonight . . .

16

1957, Washington, DC

IN THE SPRING OF 1957, Moira learned through the other secretaries that Elaina Duquesne had succumbed to her depression, leaving Ernest to take Amelia in on his own. During her two years working at the TRP, Moira had mostly refrained from asking about Amelia, not wanting to rouse suspicion. But this was particularly difficult to ignore.

Ernest spent the entirety of the summer in Boston so he could be with Amelia. There was talk of him transferring out there permanently, and Moira struggled to hide her interest as the fate of Ernest Duquesne and his new ward was discussed in planning meetings. Then suddenly, one day in September he returned. He came back subdued and quiet. No longer half as vocal as he had been. He started working later hours, staying long after everyone else had left.

"Poor man," Shelley said one rainy afternoon. She was watching Ernest through the interior window of his office.

"What's wrong with him?" Moira asked, feigning disinterest.

"His mother died last week. Just a few months after his sister and everything. The last of his family, apparently."

"Doesn't he have a niece?"

"Well, sure, but I don't think she lives with him. She goes to a boarding school in Boston. He's all alone in the lonely little apartment."

Shelley was looking at him wistfully in a way that made Moira unspeakably irritated. Who was she to look at Ernest, her Ernest, like that? *He's not yours anymore*, she reminded herself. And neither was Amelia.

A week later, Jack left early to catch a flight out to Denver for a two-week trip. His first prolonged business trip since Moira had come to work for him. Before he departed, he called her into his office.

"While I'm gone, you'll temporarily be assisting Ernest."

Moira did a double take. "I . . . what?"

"Well, he is the deputy director. If I assigned you to anyone else, it would look suspicious."

"But I . . ."

He chuckled at her as he put on his coat. "Just do what he asks and don't let him sweet-talk you into anything I wouldn't like. Got it?" He patted her on the cheek, dragging his thumb across her cheekbone. "Remember, you're still *my* girl."

As it turned out, she needn't have worried. It was clear after the first day of Jack's absence that Ernest had absolutely no intention of exercising his rights as her temporary boss. The most he did was ask her to type up the memos Jack had left behind, leaving her to her own devices for the rest of the day. As if he was avoiding her. It was she who finally took the initiative. On Tuesday he was working late as usual and she, as his temporary secretary, hadn't left yet, either. He looked tired, running his hands through his hair as he struggled to type up notes from his meetings that day. As if he'd written them in another language and forgotten how to translate. Moira sighed at him and got up from her desk.

"I've got this," she said, taking the notes from his hands and holding them hostage. "You go home. You look like the walking dead."

"Miss Donnelly, you don't have to . . ."

"I'm doing this for both of us. I'm a much faster typist than you and I can't leave until you do."

"Oh. I didn't realize you were waiting on me."

"You think I hang out here just for fun?"

Ernest gave her a weary half smile. The first she'd seen from him in weeks. "You can go home. I don't want to make you do my work." He reached for the papers and Moira slapped his hand with them.

"Ow! Take it easy there, Sugar Ray Robinson," he said, shaking out his fingers.

Moira frowned. "Who?"

"Really? Legendary boxer? Hero in our time?"

"Can't say I've heard of him."

Ernest squinted at her. "You should pick up a newspaper every now and then."

"With all that free time I have for reading?"

"Right, I forgot. Jack's a real slave driver, isn't he?"

She scoffed at him. "Go home, Mr. Duquesne. You can work yourself to death when Jack gets back, but until then I'll handle your reports."

Realizing he had lost, Ernest relented at last. He stood up to get his coat and hat.

"So it's 'Jack,' is it?" he asked, giving her a scrutinizing look.

Moira's lips parted in surprise, realizing her error. And now he was looking at her as if she had just confirmed what everyone else already assumed about her and Jack's relationship.

"Well, calling him Mr. Dillinger feels a little too respectful for someone as crass as he is, don't you think?"

He blinked in surprise. A look of mutual understanding passed between them, and he finally allowed himself to smile at her. A real smile this time. "Have a good night, Miss Donnelly. Thanks for doing this."

For the next two weeks, Moira made it her job to make Ernest's life as easy as possible. She arrived before him every morning, removing all files and reports that should be done by a secretary from his office before he even had a chance to see them. She had his calls routed to her phone first and took the liberty of hanging up on the more unsavory bureaucrats. When she got the sense that he was working through lunch, she had food brought to his office and held back thirty minutes a day on his calendar so he could eat it. She took care of him. Not in the way she wanted to, but in the only way she could.

"How long have you been working here?" he asked on the Friday of their second and final week together.

He had come in late that morning and in consequence they were both staying later than usual, even though he told her repeatedly to go. She staunchly refused and busied herself with organizing the files in Ernest's office while he finished. It was time-consuming work. Ernest was surprisingly quite disorganized.

"Um. I'm not sure."

"At least two years, right?"

"A little longer I think."

Two years, eight months, and seventeen days to be exact. Not that she was counting.

"Interesting," Ernest said, more to himself than to her.

Moira frowned as she shuffled files into a stack. "Are you implying I should have been fired by now?"

His eyes widened. "Oh, no, I wasn't . . ."

"I'm kidding."

Ernest cracked a smile. "I'm just saying, Jack's picky. That's all. You must have impressed him."

Moira smiled to herself, changing the subject to stop the blushing. "So why don't *you* have a secretary, Mr. Duquesne?"

"Oh, I don't know. Never could find one who suited me."

"Now who's the picky one?" she teased. "It would save you a lot of late hours here in the office."

Ernest smiled a second time and leaned back in his chair. "Well, you just tell Jack he better be nice to you. Or else I might steal you for myself."

Moira's heart skipped a beat. Was he . . . flirting with her?

"I, uh, . . . I heard about what happened," she said, glancing at Brady's office to see if he might overhear. "With your mother and sister. I'm sorry."

Ernest dropped his eyes to the table. "My sister was . . . troubled. She and I hadn't spoken much in about seven years. And my mother was sick for a long time. It was time."

"That doesn't make it any easier."

"No, I suppose not. I was supposed to go home and take care of the house, but I already used up all my time off dealing with my sister's death. I've had to make all the arrangements to sell it over the phone."

Moira thought of the house he'd told her about back then. The old-fashioned architecture. The garden out back. He and Elaina both had so clearly loved that old house.

"You're selling it?" she asked, attempting to hide her concern.

"I wanted to keep it," he admitted, more to himself than to her. "But I'd never be able to take care of a place that big. I bought a smaller place nearby so I could at least keep some of the furniture without hauling it all out here, but . . . it isn't the same."

"Is that why you were late today?"

"Oh, no. Trouble with my niece."

"Trouble?"

Ernest didn't clarify right away, and she wondered if maybe she was overstepping. He blew out a long, tense breath. "It's nothing really. Just . . . she started going to a boarding school in Boston this year. Really nice place. But she's racked up about five demerits since the school year started and it's not even half term. Last night they caught her sneaking a bucket-ful of frogs from the pond into the dormitory. The dean is threatening to expel her."

"Frogs?" Moira asked, trying not to smile.

"Yes. Apparently she had big plans for them."

"Oh, I bet."

Ernest sighed. "She's a good kid, I know she is. She's just had such a rough time. Amelia was the one who found her mother."

"That must have been hard on her. I can't even imagine."

"She didn't talk for months when she first came to live with me. It took weeks to get her to say anything at all. And then all she wanted to talk about was guillotines."

"Guillotines?"

Ernest waved a hand. "Long story. I'm sorry. I shouldn't be dumping all this on you."

"No, no. It's okay. I don't mind. You're raising her all by yourself?"

"Well, me and the illustrious Pembroke Academy. But yeah, just me. Unfortunately for her."

"Oh, don't say that."

"It's true. I don't know how to raise a kid. Maybe if she were a boy."

"What does her being a girl have to do with anything?"

"Well, I was a boy once. I went to an all boys' boarding school. I was in the army. I know boys. But girls . . . girls need their mothers."

Moira felt an odd pull in her chest and had to look away. "'Among their burning terms of love, none so devotional as that of 'Mother,'" she said absently.

Ernest frowned at her. "Edgar Allan Poe?"

"Oh. Um. Yes."

"You read poetry?"

"Sometimes."

"Thought you didn't have time for reading," Ernest said in a teasing voice.

"Well, not anymore. But I used to." There was a pause. "You should try the zoo."

"The zoo?"

"For your niece." She herself had loved the zoo as a child.

"I mean, I know she's misbehaving but that feels a bit extreme, don't you think?"

Moira laughed at him. "I meant you should take her there. It might get her to open up."

"You think?"

"Well, you said she likes animals, right?"

"I did?"

"The frogs?"

"Ahhh. Well. Okay. I guess it's worth a shot."

She thought nothing more of it, assuming he would disregard it.

On Monday morning Moira came into the office early. Jack was meant to be getting back that day and she wanted to make sure everything was in order. When she arrived, Ernest was already there. She caught him in the act of laying something on her desk.

"Mr. Duquesne?" she asked as she removed her coat.

He jumped back in surprise. He clutched the paper-wrapped package in his hands, looking remarkably guilty.

"M-Moira," he said. "I mean . . . Miss Donnelly."

"Did you need something?"

"Yes. Or, uh, . . . no. I just came to give you this." He held out the package to her. "As a thank-you for everything you did for me the past two weeks."

"I was just doing my job," Moira said, feeling herself blush.

"I know, but it meant something to me."

Meant something to him. Moira took the package from him, heart in her throat. She opened it carefully to find a slim volume of poems by Edgar Allan Poe bound in red, pages edged with gold foil.

"In case you ever find time to read again," Ernest said sheepishly.

"Thank you," Moira said softly. She couldn't look at him. If she looked at him, she might start crying and that was unacceptable.

"I took your advice by the way. I went up to Boston over the weekend and took Amelia to the zoo. It worked like a charm. She finally started speaking to me. And we're talking full sentences."

Moira smiled, brimming with warmth. "That's wonderful. And did she tell you her plans for the frogs?"

Ernest laughed, the sound of it sending shivers down Moira's spine. "Apparently there's this girl, Rebecca, who's been giving her a real hard time. The frogs were inbound to Rebecca's bed when the house mother intercepted them."

Moira laughed with him, but in her head all she could think about was her daughter's craftiness. How very like her she was after all. Ernest would certainly have never come up with such an elaborate revenge plot, diplomat that he was. As the laughter died between them, Ernest held her gaze, looking as though he wanted to say something else.

"Well, anyway. I just came to say thank you. For the suggestion."

"Anytime," Moira said.

He turned to go. Stopped halfway. Started walking again. Finally turned back. "I was wondering. Would you . . ." He paused, eyes drifting up as if reconsidering.

Moira waited expectantly. "Yes?"

"Would you maybe . . . want to get dinner sometime?"

"As in a date?" she asked, her voice a much higher pitch than usual.

"Well . . . yes."

"A date with you?"

His lips tilted upward. "Preferably. But I suppose that's negotiable."

Moira hesitated. A date with Ernest. Jack would be furious. She should decline. But something stopped her. It had been more than two years. She'd been an exemplary employee thus far. And it wasn't like Ernest remembered her. What was the harm?

"Okay," she said at last. "I'd like that. When?"

"This Friday night maybe?"

"Friday is good."

"Good." Ernest smiled to himself. "I'll pick you up at seven. You're at that boardinghouse off Fifth, right?"

Moira made a noise.

"I'm not stalking you," he said at once. "I just . . . Collins mentioned it once and I . . . have a good memory I guess."

Moira's stomach flipped again. He had talked about her with other timekeepers.

"Oh, right, I'm sure that's it," she said, hardly recognizing the flirtatious nature of her own voice.

He blushed. "Right, well. I'll see you Friday night. Not that I won't see you around the office this week, but especially on Friday, I . . . I'll see you." He turned to go and then stopped yet again. "Hey, um, . . . would you mind not saying anything to Jack? It's not that I think he'd mind or anything, I just . . . well, he's bound to be insufferable about it."

Moira smiled at him. "Not a problem at all."

When he left, she hid the book of poems in her desk drawer so Jack wouldn't see them. She started typing his schedule for the day as usual, smiling at him when he finally came into the office.

"Anything noteworthy happen while I was away?" he asked as he undid his scarf.

Moira kept her eyes on her work. "Nope. Nothing at all. Things were rather quiet without you actually."

"Quiet?" Jack repeated.

"Yes. In fact, the rest of us finally managed to get some work done."

Jack gave an incredulous laugh. "Watch it, Donnelly. I'm not about to take that kind of talk from the likes of you."

His tone was lighthearted. Completely unaware that she had just succeeded in lying to him for the very first time without him noticing. She smiled to herself as he went into his office and shut the door. After almost four years since she'd left the time space, she was finally figuring out how to play his game.

ON THE night of his date with Moira Donnelly, Ernest was in the time space, pacing.

"You look nervous."

The voice came from several feet away, emerging from the darkness.

"Do I?" he asked, running a hand through his hair distractedly.

Vasily Stepanov stepped out from behind the shelves. "I have not seen you look this nervous since the day we met," he teased.

"I wasn't nervous the day we met," Ernest muttered begrudgingly.

Vasily's lips curled at the edges. A hint of a smile, as though his mouth had forgotten how long ago but still wanted to try. Vasily was a tall man, but not overly large for a member of the KGB. Broad shouldered but thin, with dark hair and a pair of thick, serious eyebrows that accented the cavernous depth of his eyes. Eyes that carried a spark of intrigue in them as he removed his gun from his belt and laid it on the shelf next to where Ernest had placed his upon arrival. Their standard greeting. A way of establishing trust.

"So what is it today? Is it a woman?"

Ernest grimaced. "What makes you think that?" he asked, trying to seem casual but failing.

Vasily leaned forward in a conspiratorial manner, dropping his voice into a whisper. "It is always a woman. What else can turn hardened soldiers like us into spineless ninnies?"

Ernest chuckled softly at his phrasing. Spineless ninny was right. In the days leading up to his date, Ernest thought about canceling on four separate occasions. It was to be his first date in years, and he could think of a dozen reasons not to go through with it. But despite his rationalizing, he couldn't bring himself to cancel.

"So, are you going to tell me?" Vasily prompted again.

"I have a date tonight," Ernest admitted at last.

"Ahhhhh," Vasily said, smiling a little more freely. "That is wonderful for you. What is she like? Is she very beautiful?"

Ernest smiled in spite of himself. "Well, yes, she is. She . . . she's luminous."

"Luminous," Vasily repeated, measuring the word. Anyone else would mock him for his overtly poetic language but not Vasily. The Russian man had an admiration for beautiful words.

Ernest had been meeting with Vasily Stepanov at least once a month. After Azrael, as the memory of the monk called himself, had introduced them, they'd begun a wary but cooperative relationship of sorts, exchanging notes on what was to be burned, working together to salvage what they could without risking their own lives in the process. They'd developed a system for communicating where to meet by marking the spot with a drawing of a flower in chalk. Easy to erase with a single swipe of the hand once seen.

"Forget-me-nots for Lisavet Levy," Vasily had said, drawing one on the floor of the time space to demonstrate. The drawings had been his idea.

Forget-me-nots: a flower whose name held the same meaning in English, Russian, and German.

Ernest had tried to ask about the girl called Lisavet Levy, but Vasily had never given him the full story, claiming that it was too dangerous. That knowing too much might lead Ernest down the path of destruction they were both so desperately trying to avoid. Whoever she was . . . whatever had happened to her . . . Vasily seemed to feel personally responsible. At first it made Ernest suspicious, as did everything the Russian man said or did those first months. He wasn't alone in it.

Vasily was just as wary of him, both of them watching the other's every move.

Over time, however, their suspicions toward each other had grown into a begrudging respect, then a cautious friendship. Ernest learned more about his former Russian adversary. About his children, a son and three daughters. About his late wife. In turn, Ernest had told him about the death of his mother and sister as they'd happened, leaning on him in his time of grief. He'd told him about Amelia, getting advice on how to handle a wayward little girl from a man who already had three of his own. They had a lot in common, Ernest and his former adversary.

"So this woman you are seeing . . ." Vasily asked when they'd finished exchanging their notes for the evening. "Is she a good match for you?"

Ernest's stomach flipped a little. "I guess we'll find out tonight."

"You do not know already?"

"Tonight's our first date."

At that, Vasily gave him a knowing look and patted him on the shoulder. "Well, I wish you luck then, my American friend. We meet again soon?"

Ernest nodded, reaching to take his pistol from the shelf and return it to its holster. "Three weeks from tonight. Same time."

Vasily gave him a sharp nod and a salute before taking back his own gun and leaving the time space.

By the time Ernest had returned to his apartment, he had less than thirty minutes before he needed to leave. He showered hastily and styled his hair as fast as he could. His mind continued to fret as he tied and retied his tie with nervous, unsatisfied fingers. He couldn't get the damn thing to cooperate. He let out a puff of breath as he stood at the mirror, thinking yet again that he should have canceled. A part of him couldn't help but be suspicious. As if Jack was sending Moira in to try and find out what secrets he was keeping from the TRP. Which wouldn't matter if he didn't have anything to hide . . . except he did. And yet here he was, about to go on a date with her anyway. For the first time in his life, Ernest understood what had attracted the men of Greek mythology to the sirens of certain death. Unable to stop themselves from willingly stepping out to sea.

The sound of the clock in the hall told him it was time to leave. He let out a grunt of frustration and finally cast off his tie altogether, letting it drop to the floor of his bedroom. He was being foolish, he told himself. Moira Donnelly was not a mythological creature of doom, nor was she some conniving, ill-meaning double agent who would sell him out to Jack. What she was was a woman. A kind, lovely woman who had made disparaging jokes at Jack's expense and could recite poetry by heart. That was the woman he was going on a date with. His embattled feelings about her were just that. Feelings. Based on nothing but paranoia and his own guilty conscience.

Moira was waiting for him on the steps of the boardinghouse, dressed in a pale blue dress he'd never seen her wear to the office, short hair pinned back away from her face. She smiled and raised her hand in greeting as he parked the car, and for a moment, Ernest forgot everything he'd been worrying about up until now. She lifted the handle just as he was opening his own door and slid into the seat beside him. Ernest faltered, one foot poised on the pavement.

"Oh," he said, letting the door fall shut again. "Well, all right then."

Moira looked at him, a frown furrowing her brow. "Is something wrong?"

"No, nothing. I was just going to get the door for you."

"Oh!" Moira's cheeks flushed pink. "I'm sorry, I didn't realize."

"That's all right."

"If you want, I can get back out so you can ..."

"No, no, it's okay."

"I'm sorry," she said again, looking genuinely distressed. "It's just I've never ... I mean, I haven't ..."

Ernest smiled at her stammering. "It's been a while for me too," he admitted quietly.

Moira let out a breath and smiled back at him. "I guess we're both out of practice."

"I guess so."

They looked at each other for a long moment and then Ernest cleared his throat, turning to start the car again. Moira shifted in her seat as the engine turned over and Ernest was suddenly made aware of the scent of her perfume permeating the leather-scented interior of his car. It smelled of lilacs and some other, subtle yet impossibly familiar scent that made it rather difficult for him to focus on driving. He swallowed a few times as he turned down the street, trying to come up with something to say. Normally he was decent at small talk. Or at least he had been the last time he'd gone on a date. But now he couldn't seem to separate his tongue from the roof of his mouth long enough to string two words together.

"So . . . where are we going?" Moira asked, breaking the silence. She was twisting her hands in her lap.

"I made reservations at Salle Du Bois," he said. "They play music there on Fridays. I thought it might be nice."

"Salle Du Bois?" she repeated, sounding skeptical. "Isn't that . . . you know . . . a little upscale?"

"Well . . . yeah, a bit." Moira frowned down at her dress and Ernest suddenly understood her concern. "Don't worry, you look . . . I mean, that dress is . . . you'll be fine."

She bit her lip sheepishly. "It's not that, it's just . . ." Her cheeks were even redder than before.

"What is it?"

"Shouldn't you be wearing a tie?" she asked. "I mean, won't they not let you in?"

Ernest's heart sank a little. She was right. He thought of the tie he'd dropped in frustration onto his bedroom floor.

"I didn't think of that," he said, embarrassed. "I'm sorry. I normally wear one, I was just struggling with it because I was . . ." He paused and cleared his throat. "I was in a hurry."

Moira smiled faintly. "It's okay," she said, shaking her head.

"No, it's not, I promised you dinner."

"We can still have dinner."

"Where? It's too late to try and get in anywhere decent," he lamented, truly kicking himself now.

Moira was quiet for a moment. She turned her attention out the window and suddenly sat up a little straighter. "Turn here," she said, pointing.

Ernest, not knowing what else to do, obliged her, cranking the wheel sharply to make the turn. They drove for another few minutes before she had him pull over in front of a row of dusty-looking shops. Outside one of them, a bakery of sorts, an elderly man was sweeping the front steps. The sign on the door read Closed.

Ernest frowned. "It doesn't look open."

"It isn't."

She got out of the car before he could stop her and called out. Ernest followed, fumbling his keys as he locked the car behind him. By the time he caught up to her, she was in the midst of an animated conversation with the old man. His wrinkled, stern face lit up at the sight of her and the two of them were chattering away in . . . was she speaking German? Ernest stayed fixed to the curb, watching her exchange play out. The way her eyes seemed to sparkle. The way the old man smiled at her with a special fondness of two people who crossed paths regularly. After a few minutes, the man set a hand on her shoulder and stepped away into his shop, leaving his broom propped against one wall. Something pulled at the center of Ernest's chest as Moira turned to look at him, beaming.

"He's getting us bagels," she said, coming back to him.

"Bagels?" Ernest asked, eyeing the shop again.

"Is that okay?"

"Yeah, it's . . ." He blinked, looking back at her. "Where did you learn to speak German?"

For reasons he couldn't possibly fathom, her face suddenly fell. "Oh, I . . . my neighbors growing up were German. My parents were factory workers. They had to work late hours, so I spent a lot of time at their apartment."

"You speak Russian, too, right? I've seen you translating some of it for Jack a few times."

"Y-yes," she stammered.

"Another neighbor?" Ernest teased. He meant it to be a joke but could tell by the way her eyes darted around nervously that she didn't take it as one.

"It was an immigrant neighborhood," she said in a hushed, almost embarrassed voice.

"Huh," Ernest said, thinking this over. Soviet ex-spy, Brady had said. German turncoat. She was neither of those things. Just a poor girl from the other side of the tracks. Not like him, who might as well have grown up in a gilded bubble for all the worldly experience his childhood had given him. He felt guilty for ever assuming the worst of her.

"Well, I guess that explains why Jack was so eager to hire you," he said, trying to alleviate her shame.

"I guess so," she said, biting her lip.

Ernest wanted to ask her more, but then the old man returned holding two brown paper bags. He handed them to Moira with that same fond smile on his face and waved away the money that Ernest tried to hand him.

"He seems sweet," Ernest said, folding the bills back into his wallet.

"He is," Moira said, smiling at the shop windows. "I met him during my first months here. He reminds me a little of my father."

Ernest eyed her in amusement. "A German bagel maker reminds you of your father?"

She shrugged. "A bit."

"Aren't you Irish Catholic?"

"Yes," she said, offering no further explanation. She gestured down the well-lit street. "Should we walk?"

"Walk?"

"Sure. It's nice out. Not too cold."

Ernest tucked his keys back into his pocket, along with his wallet.

"Free bagels and a walk downtown. How's that for a first date?" He laughed, head shaking. "You're not hard to please, are you, Moira Donnelly?"

For the second time that evening, her cheeks were dusted with a blush as she dropped her eyes to the sidewalk. "It's the company I care about more," she said softly.

Ernest fought to swallow the lump that arose at her words. She met his gaze and once again he felt the tug of something inevitable drawing him further and further in. As if an invisible thread existed between them, had always existed between them, pulling them into each other like the moon pulling the tide to shore.

That night, they walked the streets of DC twice over, venturing up and down the sidewalks, eating bagels from paper bags. They didn't talk about work, not even for a second, and Ernest was glad for it, not wanting any mention of Jack or the office or the TRP to ruin the evening. Overhead, the moon shone down on them as if it was smiling and Ernest caught her looking up at it from time to time, her pale face illuminated in its glow. As they wound their way slowly back to his car, she reached for his hand, entwining her fingers in his as if that was where they'd always belonged. He didn't let go until they were standing at the gates of the boardinghouse hours later, the night drawing to a close around them.

She turned to him with a shy smile and Ernest, unable to help

himself, leaned forward to kiss her cheek good night. When he pulled
back, he studied her face in the lamplight, noting the way the very stars
seemed to shine in her eyes. With one hand, he brushed a stray hair off
her forehead.

"You are . . ." he began, hardly knowing what he meant to say, ". . . like
the moon, only brighter."

Her eyes widened at his words. His eyes darted down to her lips and
then back, and the next thing he knew, she stepped toward him, pulling
him close by the collar of his shirt. Ernest gasped as their lips met, and
then he sighed as she deepened the kiss. He pulled her closer, clasping
one arm around her waist, his other hand cupping her cheek. The lilac
scent of her perfume had faded, leaving behind that other, subtler scent
that seemed so familiar. Like a memory. Like nostalgia. Like home. The
sheer act of kissing her sent up a flare to his entire body, setting every
nerve alight.

Alarmed by the sudden, overwhelming crash of emotions, he moved
closer, pressing her back against the gate, one hand gripping the metal
bar just over her head. He should stop, he knew he should stop, and yet
he couldn't bring himself to pull away. Until she made a noise, and he became aware of a certain stirring where his lower body was flush against
hers. Instantly, he drew back in horror. Her eyes were just as wide as his,
and his heart sank in an instant, knowing he'd crossed a line.

"I . . . sorry," he said breathlessly. "I didn't mean to . . ."

He tensed, expecting her to slap him, but she didn't. Instead, the
shock of her expression gave way to amusement.

"Been a while, has it?"

Ernest began stammering at once. He ran an anxious hand through
his hair, ruining the gel he'd so carefully put in place. "I-I-I'm sorry, I
didn't realize that I was . . . I shouldn't have . . . I swear, I would never
try to . . ."

"Ernest," she said, taking his hand to cut off his babbling. "It's fine."

"No, it isn't. I . . ."

Moira started laughing, which almost mortified him further until she said, "Don't worry about it. But if you want to make it up to me . . . do you think we could do this again sometime?"

"Do . . . *that* again?" Ernest asked, swallowing hard.

"I meant the date. But that, too, I suppose."

Ernest took in the flirtatious look on her face, the stirring feeling inside of him surging with renewed intensity. He looked away and cleared his throat loudly.

"Yes, I . . . I would like that. The date, I mean," he added for good measure.

She laughed at him and leaned forward to kiss his cheek. "How about next week?"

He relaxed at the simple, uncomplicated gesture, returning her smile. "Next week sounds perfect."

As he watched her walk away, the world seemed to move in slow motion. The blue of her dress as it swayed in the night air. The bright light of the moon blazing in her eyes. The graceful, fluid movements of her body as she turned to smile back at him. All of it left him breathless. A strange feeling crept up on him. Nostalgia for a moment that had not yet passed. A trick of the memory that made him feel as if he had stood here before in this very spot, watching this woman walk away from him under the light of a full moon, the phantom feeling of her lips still lingering on his.

As Moira Donnelly slipped through the door to the boardinghouse and out of sight, Ernest let go of the remainder of his doubts and allowed himself to be swept away. A tide pulled inexorably to shore by the ceaseless draw of the moon.

17

1965, New York City, New York

THE CLUB WAS ALREADY full of life when Moira arrived. Music poured from the windows, getting louder or softer as the doors swung open and shut for the patrons. Moira took her things from the passenger seat and got out of the car.

"Park it someplace far away," she said to the valet as she tossed him the keys. "I won't be needing it."

She walked straight past the club's entrance and around to the back alley. It had stopped raining, but everything was still slick. Climbing up the fire escape in heels wasn't easy but she managed, wanting to avoid being spotted by another tenant in case someone came looking for her. At the top, she jimmied the window lock on the third floor open and let herself inside, closing it behind her.

It was nearly two in the morning now, and the tiny apartment was completely dark. There wasn't much to it. The walls were thin, so thin that you could hear the music two floors down loud and clear, but she didn't mind it. It was the club where she and Ernest had danced in 1949. Sometimes they still played Billy Eckstine's songs. There was a card table next to the window and a small galley kitchen with a single burner, no oven. The room just down the hall was practically a closet, and the bathroom actually had been a closet at one point or another. But it was hers. The first place she'd ever had that didn't have Jack listed as cosigner on the lease. The only place no one at the TRP would ever think to look for her.

Moira set her things down on the counter. She removed her coat and slung it over the back of the folding chair beside the table. The radiator didn't work consistently and the air in the apartment was bitingly cold. She moved over to fiddle with the knobs on the radiator when the bedroom door creaked open.

"Don't move," a man's voice said. She heard the click of a gun.

"Relax," she said, turning around.

"Oh," said her would-be assailant, lowering his gun. "It's you."

"At ease, soldier," Moira said, rolling her eyes at him.

"I didn't know you were coming."

"I should have called."

"Why are you here? I thought you were with Amelia." His expression tensed. "Did something happen? Is Amelia . . ."

"She's fine."

"Fine?"

"Safe. She's in the time space."

"In the . . ." His eyes trailed downward, taking in her appearance. The blood on her shirt. "What did you do?"

Moira hesitated. "I killed Jack."

He blinked. "You . . ."

"Fred too."

"That wasn't a part of the plan."

"I had to. He was going to kill Amelia."

The tense look returned. "But she's okay?"

Moira set one hand on her hip. "Yes. She's safe. She's with Vasily Stepanov's son. You know. The Russian boy you failed to tell me about. Which, by the way, almost ended up being a *very* fatal omission."

"Right. I guess I forgot to mention him." He stepped farther into the room, running a hand through his red hair. The same red hair that he shared with Amelia.

"You look tired," Moira told him. "When did you last sleep?"

His eyes slid upward, thinking. "I slept a few hours yesterday."

"I meant a full night."

"I can't sleep. There's still work to be done."

"There's always work to be done. And you can't do it in your state."

"But I . . ."

"Ernest . . ." Moira said warningly. "You need sleep."

There was a pause. Ernest's shoulders slumped in defeat. "All right, all right. But first, tell me what you mean by 'fatal' omission."

"Anton and Amelia had a run-in in the time space while she was looking for the book. I didn't know that he was working with you and after everything that happened with the department and his father, I assumed he was a threat. I wasn't thinking clearly. As soon as Amelia told me he had the book I should have known that he—"

"Wait, hang on. What was Amelia doing in the time space? I thought you were supposed to go in."

"Things didn't exactly go to plan," Moira said, rubbing her eyes with one hand and coming away with a black streak of her own eye makeup. Annoyed, she pulled a handkerchief from her pocket and wet it under the sink to begin wiping it off.

"Well, what happened?"

"Jack happened," she said, tossing aside the handkerchief a bit more violently than intended.

Sensing her frustration, Ernest came toward her and pressed a kiss against her temple, one arm sliding around her waist. Moira leaned into him, savoring the familiar feeling of being in his arms. Like the soft murmur of waves finally returning to shore.

"Is that what I think it is?" He was looking at the box of watches. He stepped around her to look closer, frowning. "Did something happen to James?"

Moira sighed. She could tell by his expression that neither of them was going to get any sleep until she explained herself.

"Sit down," she said, gesturing to the card table. "At least let me make some coffee before you interrogate me."

She watched him cross the room and lower himself into the chair. Watched him run both hands through his hair in distress the way he had ever since she'd met him. He really did look exhausted. Exhausted and worried and perhaps still a bit angry with her. But at least he was alive.

As she and Anton walked through the memories one by one, Amelia felt a slow tension building in her chest. They witnessed the memories of the man called Ezekiel Levy, watching the remnants of his life one at a time, including the final memories he had of his daughter. They walked through fragments of lives otherwise destroyed by timekeepers. Quiet moments of love, life, pain, and grief, each one little more than a glimpse into a soul that had long been forgotten. Amelia began to wonder why Moira had wanted her to see this, until at last they came upon a set of memories that stole the air right out of her lungs.

"Uncle Ernest," she said, watching his glassy image come into focus.

They were in the time space, tucked between shelves. Ernest was watching something, but Amelia was too distracted to notice what it was. She took a step closer, feeling her heart beating out of her chest at the sight of him. He was not quite the uncle she had always known. He was younger. His features less firm, his eyes brighter, as though the world had not yet finished forming him. But beneath the youth and naivete, it was still him. His mannerisms were still familiar to her.

Beside her, Anton frowned, pointing to a second figure a little ahead of them. "I think that is her," he said.

Amelia tore her eyes away from Uncle Ernest to see what he meant and was confronted by the sight of a girl in a periwinkle dress kneeling on the ground beside a burning book. Her sheath of blond hair covered her face as she carefully extricated a set of pages away from the fire. Lisavet Levy.

Amelia studied her, head shaking. "This must be my uncle's memory, but I—" She broke off as a sound met her ears. A hushed whisper emanating from the girl on the ground. She frowned and listened closer, when suddenly, Lisavet looked up from what she was doing.

"Hello there," Ernest said. He had stepped out of the shadows and was holding the cover of a book in his hand. Blue with a flower stamped onto the front.

Lisavet Levy stared at him as one would a hunter on the prowl.

Amelia and Anton watched as they met for the first time. Watched as Ernest tricked the girl and stole the pages, leaving the cover behind for her.

They continued onward. They were flung forward into a tumult of her uncle's memories, watching as he fell in love with Lisavet Levy. Watching as they danced in the memory of a club in New York. As they walked through time together, their love flourishing in the annals of history. Watching as he lied to Jack and was eventually caught. And then watching the scene shift back into a place that was a fixture in all their memories, the hotel in the Swiss Alps where a terrified Ernest begged Lisavet to leave with him.

Amelia held her breath as the memory ended, waiting to see what the outcome of this decision would be. But the next image to fade into view was not one of her uncle's memories, but someone else's entirely.

"Wait. That can't be all of it," Anton said abruptly, making Amelia jump. She'd been so engrossed in what was happening that she had almost forgotten he was there.

"Maybe there's more later?" Amelia asked. "Or maybe it's . . ."

She fell silent, the blood draining from her face.

"*Koshka?*" Anton asked, reaching out to touch her arm. "What is the matter?"

Amelia raised a hand and pointed to a person within the memory they'd just entered. A young woman with hair as red as her own, sobbing on a hospital bed, head buried in her hands.

"T-that's my mother," she said in a barely audible voice. The mother who had neglected her. The mother who had abandoned her. She took a frantic step back, as though to distance herself from the memory. "I can't watch this," she said.

She knew what would be here in these memories. But then she saw the baby in the cradle by the bed. The nurses lingering by the door with their mournful expressions. Amelia's lips trembled as she came forward to get a better look at the baby. Its face and lips were blue. Its body limp and motionless. Void of life.

"W-what?" she stammered. She took a horrified step back. "That isn't possible. I don't understand."

She heard Anton say her name, his voice hazy and distant. Her knees started to shake, and she felt Anton grab hold of her arm before all of a sudden the world around them screeched to a halt. Everything froze as the memory stood still. Anton let out a shout of surprise. Amelia drew in a gasp and the memory around them shifted again before jolting back into motion. Only things had changed. There was no more baby beside the bed, and the woman was asleep. The nurses had gone, and everything was quiet.

"What just happened?" Anton asked, still holding on to her arm.

The door behind them opened and they turned in unison to see someone walking into the room. Lisavet Levy, dressed in a nurse's uniform, holding a baby in her arms.

Amelia let out a gasp as she drew closer, allowing them a better look at her face. "Oh my god," she murmured.

"What is it?" Anton asked, his voice a whisper.

"I think that's . . ." She broke off and looked closer, wanting to be certain that the person she was looking at was in fact who she thought it was. Lisavet Levy, the girl who had sparked the rebellion, looked an awful lot like Moira Donnelly.

"I see you've figured it out," a voice said.

They turned a second time to see the spectral form of Azrael standing with them in the memory.

"Who are you?" Anton asked sharply.

Amelia ignored him. "Figured what out?"

"You're moving yourself through two versions of the same memory. One that was altered from what it once was into something different."

Anton made a sputtering sound. "Wait . . . you know him?" he asked, looking at Amelia.

"Well . . . sort of. He just kind of keeps showing up."

Azrael smiled wryly. "The memories of the dead only hold half of the story. If you want to know everything, you're going to have to walk through the memories of the living."

Anton scoffed at him. "Memories of the living? That is impossible."

"For you maybe," Azrael said calmly. "But not for her."

"I can't do that," Amelia said, shaking her head.

"Just as you can't travel along your own timeline?" he said pointedly. "Just as you can't stop Time in its tracks?"

Amelia's pulse quickened.

"It's called temporal displacement. Leaping from one memory to the next. Traveling through the folds of Time as if they are no obstacle to you."

"Temporal displacement . . . Moira said that to me once before," Amelia said, remembering.

"Ahhh, yes. Lisavet was always clever like that."

Anton looked between them, his eyes wide with confusion. "What is he talking about?"

"The child born outside of Time does not face the same constraints as the rest of us," Azrael continued.

"Born outside of Time?" Amelia repeated.

Azrael gestured to the child Lisavet carried in her arms. "Perhaps it's best if you see it firsthand. Through memories."

Amelia stared at his hand, contemplating. "Whose memories?" she asked.

Azrael smiled. "Hers," he said, nodding at Lisavet. "There are living memories in the time space, too, if you recall. Most cannot reach them. But you can, if you try."

Almost at once, the whispering sound Amelia had heard before started up again, coming from Lisavet herself. She frowned, looking back at Azrael.

"But . . . how do I . . ."

"Just listen and Time will do the rest," he said reassuringly.

Amelia cast an imploring look at Anton, to which he only nodded, offering her his hand once again. The whispers became louder. She shut her eyes, letting the sound travel down the length of her spine until the memories began to take shape.

And then it all unfolded before them.

18

1958, Washington, DC

MOIRA SAT FIDGETING AT her desk, watching the door to Jack's office. Ernest had been in there for over an hour. Surely that wasn't a good sign. She tried to busy herself with typing up memos, but the sound of Jack's laughter on the other side of the door spiked her blood pressure. Was laughter a good thing?

She and Ernest had been seeing each other for six months and last night, Moira had spent the night in his apartment for the first time, putting to an end the long torturous waltz they'd been doing on their way to the bedroom. Ernest was much shyer about sleeping with her than he had been in the time space. Seven years and two significant familial losses had made him more guarded. Until last night.

That was why he was in Jack's office. Moira had woken up to find him already awake beside her, fretting over what he was going to say to Jack. He was determined to tell him, convinced that their charade was sure to be found out now. Moira felt a sharp pain in her chest at the very thought and tried to dissuade him. But Ernest was firm. And what could she say to stop him?

Moira's foot tapped ceaselessly on the floor while she waited. So loud that Shelley shot her several annoyed glances. She was in the middle of imagining the worst-case scenario when the door opened, and Ernest stepped out. He shut the door behind him, head bent, chewing on his lower lip as he approached her desk.

"Well? How did it go?" she asked breathlessly.

Ernest raised his head to look at her, one corner of his mouth lifted into a half smile. "He wants to talk to you."

"H-he does?"

"Uh-huh. But don't worry. He didn't seem angry. I think we're in the clear."

Oh, Ernest, Moira thought to herself. If only he knew that they would never be in the clear. With a final encouraging grin, he returned to his office and she went in to see Jack, feeling like one of the damned on the road to hell.

Jack was closing the door to his safe, holding a velvet drawstring bag in one hand.

"Shut the door," he said, returning to his chair. He opened his desk drawer and took out a pack of cigarettes. Without speaking, he held the carton out to her. She took one warily, recognizing their time-honored tradition. He lit the cigarette for her and did the same to his own. She didn't smoke it, holding it awkwardly between her fingers. Ernest didn't like her smoking, always reading off the health warnings whenever she picked up a cigarette. She was trying to kick the habit.

When Jack finally looked at her, he had a tense sort of smile on his face.

"Six months," he said. "Six months it took you to tell me. Or excuse me, for *him* to tell me. I expected better from you."

Moira blinked. "You . . . you knew?"

"Of course I knew. What, do you think I'm an idiot? I saw the way he started giving you those puppy-dog eyes almost as soon as I got back from Denver. You, my girl, are very subtle, but he reads like an open book. I caught on around the time you two had your fourth or fifth date and sent someone to tail you. Just to confirm things."

"Brady?" Moira asked.

"Fred Vance," Jack said with a conniving grin. "I'll tell you, he's not the brightest bulb in the box but he's sneakier than we give him credit for."

"I don't understand. You knew and you never said anything?"

"I wanted to see how it would play out. And I wanted to see how long it would take you to crack. You never did. You kept your cool the whole time. It was quite impressive. I underestimated you, Moira."

Moira wasn't reassured by his words. Here she'd thought, yet again, that she was fooling him when in reality all she had done was teach him what she really looked like when she was lying. Maybe that was his whole point.

"So . . . you're not angry?"

He looked down at her untouched cigarette. "No, I'm not angry. But I am disappointed. Letting yourself get caught up again with the man who got you pregnant and made you vulnerable. He betrayed you back then, you know. Told me everything there was to know about you with the same mouth he used to tell you that he loved you. He's the reason that you're here. And now you're falling for his doe-eyed, good soldier act all over again."

"What happened then was different," Moira said.

"If you say so. All I'm trying to say is you could do better. There are plenty of other men out there. A pretty girl like you has options."

Options, he said. She didn't have any options and he knew it. He'd made himself such a domineering presence in her life that any other man would never dare look twice.

"Did you tell Ernest that he could continue seeing me?" That was all that mattered, after all.

"For now. Who knows? I might even be able to use it to my advantage one of these days." Jack stubbed out his cigarette in the little glass ashtray. "Speaking of advantages . . . I hope you and Ernest don't have any plans for this evening. Or else I'm going to need you to cancel them." He took a file from the stack beside him and slid it over to her. "Because you and I have a date with a Russian tonight."

Moira opened the file to find the profile of a Russian timekeeper, a hollow-eyed man in his thirties. She recognized him at once. The Russian who had followed her in the time space. The one who had taken her book.

"Vasily Stepanov," she said, reading off the name.

"Do you recognize him?"

"I saw him a few times, but we never spoke. He's the one who took the book."

"Interesting. He's been interfering with our timekeepers lately. Saving memories the way you used to." He slid the velvet bag he'd taken from the safe over to her. "Here. You're going to need this too."

Moira opened it hesitantly. Inside was a familiar silver revolver. The one Ernest had given her seven years ago, still loaded with six bullets in the chamber.

"What's this for?"

"Just in case," Jack said, giving her a kind of smile that made her skin crawl. "It seems that this one knows a thing or two about Lisavet Levy."

A foreboding feeling settled in Moira's stomach. This was another test of her loyalty. Timed so perfectly after the confession that she wondered how long he'd been planning it.

THEY STOOD on the other side of the door, waiting for the timekeepers to emerge. Jack remained by Moira's side, one hand on her shoulder. He had placed it there when Patrick Brady and Fred Vance had opened the door to the time space, noticing the way she'd stepped toward it, drawn like a moth to flame.

"How long does it usually take?" she asked, shifting on her feet in a way that made her conscious of the gun hidden in a holster beneath her skirt.

George Collins was the one who answered, turning the syringe containing the tranquilizer over in his hand to keep it from settling. "Took us about four hours to track you down. But you weren't exactly coming and going. I'd say we're looking at about six hours give or take."

They waited for seven. There were no clocks or windows in the tiny room on the lowest floor of the TRP building, so Moira measured the time through the scrape of seconds dragging by in the back of her head. A thudding sound came from behind the door, and Jack relinquished his grip on her to raise his gun.

"Stay behind me," he warned.

The door opened. Brady and Vance emerged, dragging a third person between them. Vasily Stepanov was fighting hard, a struggle that ceased only when Jack struck him across the face with the butt of his gun, dazing him. Moira looked away, her stomach queasy. The door to the time space slammed shut. Collins came forward with the syringe, but Jack raised a hand.

"Not yet," he said. "I want him to talk first."

Brady shoved his pistol against Vasily's head and jerked him onto his knees. Vasily spit on the ground at Jack's feet and said something particularly vulgar in Russian.

"No need to get cross with me, Vasily," Jack said in a calmly sadistic voice that Moira knew too well. "We just want to ask you a few questions."

"Why do you know my name?" Vasily asked as he tried to catch his breath. His eyes scanned the room in a frantic search for a way out. He locked eyes with Moira more than once, but it was clear that he didn't recognize her.

"You think I wouldn't know the name of the man who's been giving my boys such a hard time in the time space?" Jack said. "Collins and Brady said they've seen you interfering with our work. Saving memories we've chosen to eliminate. All in the name of Lisavet Levy."

"Are you going to get rid of me?" Vasily snarled at Jack. "Make me disappear like you did to that girl."

Moira flinched for more reasons than one as Jack struck him again.

"How about I ask the questions, okay? What do you know about Lisavet Levy?"

"Enough," Vasily said. Jack raised a hand in warning. "Before she disappeared, I was the one my country sent to find out about her. They wanted me to interrogate her and learn who she was working for . . . but I changed my mind."

Jack snorted. "Changed your mind?"

It took another blow from Jack to get him to explain. "She was with child," he said through a bleeding lip. "I was going to help her. I could have at least saved the child if she had let me. But she always ran."

"How noble," Jack said, squinting at him. "Rumor has it the child died."

Vasily Stepanov smiled in turn. "Oh, I wouldn't be so certain. A child born out of Time would not fall victim to it so easily."

Moira felt Brady's eyes on her and wished that the man would stop talking.

Jack laughed at him. Openly and cruelly. "So what is it you're hoping to gain by interfering? You failed to save her or the child, so what's your end game?"

"I am not the only one who knows what you did to her. There are others like me who see what you people do. We know that it's wrong. She was just the start of it. We are here to fight for her. To keep people like you who murder innocent girls from rewriting history."

"And what about the book?"

"Book?"

"The book of memories she carried around with her. Rumor has it you're the one who took it from her. What happened to it?"

The muscles in Vasily's jaw rippled. "Why do you want it?"

"Don't play coy with me. You know why. For the memories it contains."

Vasily's face twisted into an ironic smile. "Ahhh. Which memories are you afraid of my superiors seeing?"

Jack gave Vasily a dark smile of his own. "Does it matter? Where is it?"

Vasily laughed in Jack's face. "For that, Mr. Dillinger, you will have to kill me."

Jack let out a sigh and stepped back. "I could do that. But fortunately for both of us, we have other methods of getting what we want." He beckoned for Moira to come forward. "Clean this up for me. I want to see those memories before you get rid of them."

Moira didn't move. The man was staring at her with fierce hatred in his eyes. This man who said he fought for Lisavet Levy. Why had he mentioned Amelia? Did he know what Lisavet had done?

"Donnelly," Jack said. "Don't make me ask again."

Moira moved toward him, taking the black notebook in hand. Collins came forward to administer the tranquilizer.

Without warning, Vasily Stepanov broke free from the hands that were holding him. He took the gun from Brady with frightening dexterity and lunged forward, grabbing hold of the closest person. Moira screamed as he jerked her sideways. Her back slammed against his chest, the notebook flying from her hands. She felt the cold end of the pistol press against her temple. Vasily dragged her backward, one arm locked tight around her neck.

"Move away from the door or I will shoot the woman!"

Everyone in the room froze, guns raised. Moira looked at Jack, dread pooling in her stomach. Would he comply? Or was she expendable after all?

"Move. Now!" Vasily barked again, desperation leaking through the cracks in his voice. The pistol shook in his grip.

Moira squeezed her eyes shut. She reached for Time, feeling it shudder within her, and pulled it to a stop. The world froze for everyone but Vasily. She reached for his gun, twisting it from his grasp, her other hand gripping his jacket. Their eyes met as she cocked the gun back before he could retaliate.

"On your knees," she ordered in a voice that scarcely belonged to her. "Now!"

He dropped to the ground, disoriented and panicked, one hand twisting in her skirt. He could disarm her if he wanted, he was strong enough. But that was the benefit of bending Time the way she could. It put the fear of God into even the strongest of mortal men.

"You mentioned Lisavet Levy's child," she said sharply. "Tell me what you know."

He hesitated.

"Tell me!" she said louder, pressing the gun to his forehead.

"I saw Lisavet Levy take her into a memory. Time walking, they call it. The baby was alive when she went in but when Lisavet came back . . . she came alone. I saw the ground give way. We have been looking for the child. Searching all the memories the Americans try to destroy."

"Who else is looking?"

"Nobody. Just me. Nobody else."

Moira pressed the gun more firmly against his head. "You said 'we.'"

"I misspoke. It is my English. I meant me only."

He was lying. If she wanted to, she could unfreeze Time and let Collins knock him unconscious. She could find out the truth. But if she did that, then Jack would know too. She cocked the gun.

Vasily started begging. "Please. Please, I have children. A son. Three little girls. Their mother is already gone. They need their father. Please, think of the children."

"I'm sorry," she said. She meant it. Four orphaned children were a heavy price to pay to keep her own child from being discovered. "I have a daughter to protect, too."

In the last seconds before she pulled the trigger, she thought she saw a glimmer of recognition in his eyes. His body slumped to the floor, his hand falling onto her shoe. Moira let out a loud gasp. She allowed herself five seconds to compose herself before reaching for the hands of Time once more.

Behind her, the four timekeepers fell back into motion. She heard the sound of their breath catching in unison. The haze of memory slowing their ability to perceive what was in front of them. A dead body. Moira with Brady's pistol in her hand, blood on the front of her dress.

"Moira?" Jack asked, hesitant for the first time.

Sliding Vasily's hand from her foot, she bent down and removed the watch from his wrist. She tossed it and the pistol to Brady.

"Send that back to the Russians," she told him. "That ought to keep them from trying to interfere again."

At least she hoped it would. If this Russian knew that Lisavet Levy's child was still alive, how many others had he told? His superiors, certainly. But what about the others?

Jack caught her arm as she tried to pass him. "What did you do?"

"What I had to. I couldn't be sure if any of you were going to save me."

Jack stared at her. Something flickered in his eyes. A reminder that there were still things she could do that were beyond his control. Terrifying, unattainable things. He let go of her arm.

When Moira finally left the TRP building that night, Ernest was waiting for her out by his car. She froze in the doorway. Jack put a hand around the back of her neck as he passed on his way out.

"Not a word," he murmured in her ear, giving Ernest a wave.

Moira approached Ernest nervously. The night air was thick, the sky above hung with humid stars that lit the foggy parking lot with an eerie, night-blue glow.

"You didn't have to wait for me," she said with a smile.

Ernest didn't smile back. He was staring at the bloodstains on her dress. "Why are you covered in blood?"

She swallowed. "Please, it's . . . it's better if you don't ask."

Ernest's eyes slid to Jack's car behind her where he sat watching this play out while he smoked a cigarette in the driver's seat. After a moment, Ernest took a handkerchief from his pocket and used it to clean the spots of blood on her neck she had missed.

"Did Jack have you dictating notes for an interrogation or something?" he asked.

"Something like that."

"You okay? I know those can be rough sometimes."

Moira took the handkerchief from him. "Yeah, I'm okay. Can we maybe go get something to eat? I'm exhausted."

Ernest leaned forward and pressed a kiss against her forehead. Simple and familiar. "Sure. Let's get out of here."

She breathed a sigh of relief as he opened the car door for her and got into the driver's seat without another word. Ernest put one hand over hers as they drove, his jaw grinding the way it always did when something was really bothering him. Moira looked down at the handkerchief still in her hand. She ran her fingers over the newly embroidered blue flowers over and over again, the sound of Vasily Stepanov's pleading voice ringing in her ears.

MOIRA WAS distant for weeks after that night and Ernest, try as he might, didn't know how to reach her. He did his best to get her to talk about it, but she wouldn't give him more than a few sentences. Each time he mentioned it, he would watch as her expression tightened, her eyes filling with panic.

"Please, Ernest. It was nothing," she told him. "I'm fine. Really."

But then one night, he grew impatient and snapped. "It's not nothing, Moira. I'm not an idiot. Something happened."

"I don't want to talk about it," she insisted, turning away from him.

"Don't want to, or can't?" Ernest asked, catching her arm. "Did Jack tell you to keep it from me?"

"Ernest . . . I *can't*."

"Why did he have you involved, anyway? Secretaries aren't supposed to know about any of this and he's got you attending interrogations. Making you privy to more of what's going on than I am. What does he have on you? Or what do you have on him?"

"Nothing. Nothing."

"I'm not blind, Moira. I can see that there's something going on between you two." He didn't mean it. But the words slipped out anyway, a product of the endless heckling he got from the other timekeepers who had long believed that Ernest's girlfriend was sleeping with their boss.

Her eyes widened. "Ernest, you don't think I'm . . . you know I'm not . . ."

"Well, if it isn't that, what is it?"

She didn't answer, a look of hurt filling every feature of her face. Tears welled in her eyes, and he instantly wanted to take it back. Without a word she pulled her arm from his grip and left his apartment, leaving him to deal with his own regret. He tried to call the boardinghouse that evening but she wouldn't take his call and again the following day.

He didn't know to fear the worst. Until he saw the boy.

Ernest encountered him inside the time space two days after his fight with Moira, huddled and gasping on the floor. He was curled into a ball, tears streaming down his cheeks. Ernest could tell his nationality by his uniform, but approached him anyway, kneeling down to touch his shoulder. The boy reeled backward at his touch, scrambling away from him and raising one arm to shield himself.

"Hey, hey. It's okay," Ernest reassured him.

The boy began sputtering in unintelligible Russian. Ernest took one look at his tear-stained face and those wild, hollow eyes and knew immediately that this was Vasily's son. The watch on his wrist only confirmed it.

"Do not hurt me," the boy was saying in terrible, broken English. "Please, American. I do not want to die."

Ernest's eyes widened. "What's your name?" he asked in Russian, even though he already knew.

The boy blinked, taken aback. "Y-you speak Russian?"

"Only a little," Ernest said. Only what Vasily had taught him. He held out a hand to the boy. "My name is Ernest," he said in English this time.

The boy wiped his nose on his sleeve, eyeing Ernest's hand as though it had teeth. He was so young. Barely older than Amelia.

"Anton," the boy said at last. But he wouldn't take his hand. "Please, don't take me. I do not want to go."

"Take you? Take you where?"

"Out into America," Anton explained, his voice cracking. "They said that's what the Americans do to us. It's what they did to my father. Dragged him out and killed him."

Ernest's face went slack with shock. Vasily was . . . dead? His first instinct was to demand further explanation, but Anton was still trembling. Now was not the time.

"You can relax," Ernest said softly. "I won't hurt you."

"Y-you won't?"

"Nah. I'm off duty today," he teased.

Anton blinked several times and sniffled, slow to accept the joke.

"Are you lost?" Ernest asked, remembering how long it had taken him to navigate things in here when he first started.

"I . . . I do not know how to get back out," Anton said, hiccuping between his tears.

"They didn't teach you?" Ernest asked with a frown.

"They did, but I wasn't listening. They were going to send me in, and I was—" He broke off, either not knowing the word he was looking for in English, or not wanting to admit to his fear.

Ernest sat back on his heels. In their broken, half-baked second languages, they talked. Ernest asked him about his life in Russia and told him about his own. Little snippets of information that could do nobody any harm. Eventually, Anton took the hand that was offered. He let Ernest show him the way to navigate the time space using the stars overhead. Ernest gave him a handkerchief so he could wipe his eyes and taught him how to use his watch to get back out of the time space. But he didn't say anything more. Nothing about the Americans. Nothing about Vasily or the fact that they'd been friends. Not right now. The last thing Anton Stepanov needed was to be told of his father's past by one of the very same set who might have killed him.

When they finally parted ways, the door to Anton's world closing behind him, Ernest wandered the time space in a daze. He didn't know what to make of this. Had he caused this? Said something he shouldn't have without realizing it and jeopardized another man's life? It was possible that the Russians had lied about what happened to Vasily. An indoctrination tactic to get Anton to cooperate. Then Ernest thought of that night a few weeks ago. The blood on Moira's blouse. The terrified look in her eyes. Ernest grappled with his own grief as well, knowing that, whichever version of things was the true one, in both of them, Vasily Stepanov was dead.

When he finally encountered Azrael amid the shelves, the words tumbled out without greeting or preamble.

"Why didn't you tell me about Vasily?"

Azrael's ghostly eyebrows raised. "The truth has its own way of coming out. It's not my place to meddle."

"That's bullshit. You've done plenty of meddling already, haven't you? Introducing me to Vasily in the first place. Getting us involved. But now that someone has died you all of a sudden 'don't meddle'?"

Ernest knew he was being harsh but didn't care.

Azrael looked down at the floor. "In truth, I assumed you already knew. I didn't realize they had kept it from you."

So it had been the Americans. Ernest turned away, shaking with anger. "I have to do something about this," he said, reaching for his watch.

In an instant, Azrael was in front of him, head shaking. "Don't do anything rash, Ernest. It will only bring trouble."

"Well, maybe a little trouble is what the TRP needs."

"Maybe. But at least think it through."

"I have thought it through."

"Have you? Have you thought about how you'll explain your connection to Vasily? How you came to know about his death? Last time I checked, speaking with Russian timekeepers was not something the Americans did."

Ernest had already begun spinning the crown of his watch. "Doesn't matter. I'll make something up."

"You'll get yourself killed. Or arrested and tortured for information as they've done to others before you. You think your anger won't harm anyone else?"

Ernest's fingers paused as Azrael's words caught up to him. Arrested. Tortured. Killed. All those options felt like wild impossibilities, but were they? He shook it off and pressed down on the crown of his watch, seeing the door materialize before him. He started toward it, reaching for the knob.

"You think your actions won't affect Amelia?" Azrael asked in a hushed voice.

Ernest froze and looked back at the man, faltering a second time. "What does she have to do with this?"

Azrael gave him a sad look. "The most difficult part about dying is the people you leave behind. I imagine it's the same for getting thrown in prison for the rest of your life."

Ernest's hand dropped from the doorknob. A pang ran through him as he thought of Amelia, who'd already lost her mother, alone in the world. Abandoned by his recklessness. He couldn't do that to her. He thought of the other person he'd be leaving behind: Moira, who had been dragged into all this. Moira, who well might have been forced to watch the interrogation of Vasily Stepanov. If Ernest stepped out of line and revealed himself, would Jack force her to be a part of *his* interrogation too?

Ernest stepped away from the door and turned back to Azrael in defeat. "Help me keep an eye on the boy?" he asked weakly. "I know there's nothing I can do for him right now but maybe someday. If he turns out to be anything like his father."

Azrael said nothing, bowing his head in affirmation. A silent promise.

That night, Ernest went to the boardinghouse where Moira stayed and knocked on the door. He asked to see her, ignoring the house chaperone's reprimands about the lateness of the hour. He insisted that it was urgent. At last, the woman called Moira downstairs. She arrived in her robe and slippers, her eyes wide with concern, and joined him out on the porch.

"Is everything all right?" she asked.

He didn't answer. Instead, he pulled her closer and kissed her hard, pressing a hand to the back of her head. She made a noise of surprise, melting into him.

"Ernest, what are you . . ."

"I love you," he said quietly. Barely more than a whisper.

She inhaled sharply. He kept his eyes shut and pressed his lips against her temple.

"Is everything . . . are you okay?" she asked.

She sounded afraid.

He opened his eyes to take in her expression, reaching up to brush the hair away from her cheek. "I just came to tell you that I love you. And I'm sorry for the other night. I didn't mean it. I was . . ."

"I love you too," she said, cutting him off.

There were tears in her eyes and she looked terribly, painfully sad. He wanted to take her away from all this. From the TRP, from the boardinghouse, from Jack. He couldn't protect Anton Stepanov from what was happening to him, nor could he extricate himself from what he had started, but he could protect *her*. He could keep her safe from all of it, if she'd let him.

"I want you to meet Amelia when she comes to DC this summer," he said, still whispering.

Moira drew another trembling breath. "R-really?"

"I know it's still a few months away, but I . . . I think it's time. Don't you?"

She nodded, her eyes as wide and fearful as Anton's had been. Ernest kissed her again, knowing in that moment, and with absolute certainty, that he wanted her in his life forever. Knowing that soon, when summer came, he was going to ask her to marry him.

19

1959, Washington, DC

IT COULDN'T LAST. MOIRA knew this, and yet she took her months of happiness with Ernest for granted. For a time, everything seemed perfect. They were together. They were in love. He wanted to introduce her to Amelia. And yet all the while, Moira could feel something lurking just out of sight. A storm waiting to break.

After Vasily Stepanov, Moira was tapped more often to deal with the timekeepers Jack brought in for questioning. There was a kind of movement brewing. A sudden influx of timekeepers the world over who made it their business to interfere, all in the name of Lisavet Levy. Fighting for someone they had never even met, not realizing that she herself had stopped fighting that battle long ago. Not recognizing her when she ripped their conviction away by erasing their memories of it altogether. In the past, the idea of rebellion might have thrilled her. But now she had her own version of the past to protect. Her own secrets.

Ernest didn't know about any of that. The department kept it from him, not wanting him anywhere near talk of Lisavet Levy. It wasn't easy. He came close to the truth so often it was as though he were drawn to it by some invisible force. So things continued. The months passed, and Moira was beginning to hope, cautiously, that maybe this time she would get to keep him. Ernest had begun talking about the upcoming summer. They had made plans for her to meet Amelia the Tuesday after school let out. To spend a week with her, the three of them together.

But then things inevitably changed.

"Did you hear that another timekeeper went missing?" Ernest asked one morning.

She was sitting at the breakfast table, drinking coffee. Ernest was cooking them eggs, the windows flung open to let in the warm spring air.

"Which one?" she asked.

"A man from France this time. I saw him not too long ago and then all of a sudden he was gone."

Jacques Blanchard, Moira knew. She had been there when they brought him in. Had rifled through his memories herself, carefully searching for anything the man might know about Lisavet Levy's still living daughter before handing the rest over to Jack.

"Did you ask Jack about it?" she said, evading his question.

"I'm asking you."

"Why would I know?"

"Oh, I don't know. Because you're 'Jack's girl' and he tells you everything." He laid a kiss on her cheek to let her know he was kidding and set a plate of eggs down in front of her.

"He doesn't tell me *everything*," Moira said, shifting uncomfortably.

"Well, no. But you do keep his calendar. Has he had any strange appointments lately?"

"Strange appointments like what?"

"You know. 'Interrogate Frenchman. Nine o'clock.' Something like that."

"Is there a reason you're asking this?"

Ernest shrugged. "I'm worried, that's all. It's been happening more and more lately."

"If you're so worried, just ask Jack. You're his second-in-command, he can't keep you in the dark if you ask him outright."

Ernest snorted at that. "Does Jack know I'm his second-in-command? 'Cause I'm pretty sure he's forgotten."

"Then remind him," Moira said, kissing his knuckles.

It was the wrong thing to say. She had hoped Ernest would just inquire and move on. She knew that Jack would never tell him what was really happening. It would jeopardize everything and put them at risk of Ernest uncovering the truth about her. Her name, their history, her past. The man who had once been willing to throw away his entire life for her, who had almost turned his back on the department and committed the equivalent of treason, could not know what she had once been to him. Or what she had become.

She had hoped it would blow over, but instead it blew up in her face.

She heard the shouting as soon as she came into the office on Monday. Ernest and Jack were in Jack's office, having it out loud and clear. Shelley pulled her aside the second she saw her.

"Trust me, you do *not* want them to know you're here right now."

"What? Why?"

There was more shouting coming from the office. This time Moira was quite certain she heard her own name enter the mix.

"What are they arguing about?" she asked.

"Well. At first they were talking about something normal, but I couldn't tell what they were saying until they started screaming about you. Well, about Mr. Dillinger's promotion technically. But you came up."

"What promotion?"

Shelley gave her a surprised look. "Haven't you heard? Mr. Dillinger has been promoted. Head of the entire CIA. It's quite something really."

Moira frowned. "And . . . what does that have to do with me?"

Shelley looked as if she didn't want to say. "Because. There's a satellite office opening in New York and apparently he plans on transferring you there."

Moira felt herself go pale. To New York? Could he even do that?

"I assumed you already knew," Shelley said, giving her an apologetic look.

"No . . . I hadn't heard."

A loud crack sounded from the office. Jack punching either a wall or the desk.

"Somebody should stop them before it gets violent," Moira said.

"Do you think it will get violent?" Shelley asked, looking like a bystander watching a spectator sport.

Moira gave her an incredulous look just as the door to Jack's office opened. Ernest exited, still fuming, raking his hands through his hair. He froze when he saw her standing there. Moira gave Shelley a shove and the girl slunk away to spectate from afar.

"Moira," Ernest said, coming up to her.

"Is everything all right?"

"I need to talk to you," Ernest said, eyes shining in a half-angry, half-frantic way. "Can we . . ."

"Donnelly." Jack's voice punctuated the air. He was standing in the doorway to his office, his fists clenched at his sides.

Ernest glared at Jack over his shoulder. "Just a second, Jack."

"I wasn't talking to you, Duquesne," Jack growled.

"I'll be right there," Moira said.

"Donnelly. Now, or you're fired." He said it with such frightening gravity that Moira almost believed him.

She extricated her hand from Ernest's grasp. "We can talk later," she said.

"Moira . . ."

"Tonight," she said more firmly. "I'll come by tonight. Okay? Just go cool off."

Ernest reluctantly stepped back, shooting one final harrowing glare at Jack. He stormed off down the hall and into the elevator, leaving his coat and briefcase behind.

Moira followed Jack into his office and shut the door. He began pacing as she took in the state of the room. A stack of papers had been swept onto the floor. Several pens had been flung across the room, and sure enough there was a hole the size of Jack's fist about a foot to the right of the safe. His knuckles were still bleeding. She watched him carefully, weighing her next move.

"Is everything . . ."

She let out a squeal of alarm as Jack suddenly turned and gripped her head in both hands. She froze, wide eyes meeting his furious ones.

"*You* . . ." he said in a low, growling voice. He tilted her face back and forth, examining it as if it were a block of wood he was preparing to carve. "What is it about you that brings out the worst in him? He's always so quick to defend you. Always willing to throw away his whole career . . . for you."

"J-Jack," Moira stammered.

He thrust her away from him, scoffing. "You must be one hell of a lay," he said in disgust. "Tell me, what *do* you do to him to make him act so—" He broke off, kicking the pile of papers.

Moira said nothing. Keeping her distance as one would a feral tiger.

"I need you to clean this up for me," he said.

Moira swallowed. She knelt down to begin picking up the papers.

"Not those," Jack snarled. "*Him.*"

"H-him?"

"Yes. Him. I've been allowing you to see him for over a year now, and now I need you to use it to our advantage."

Their advantage? How was it any advantage to her at all?

As if reading her thoughts, Jack jerked her up by her arm, his eyes flashing. "He's asking questions about Lisavet Levy," he said in a low voice.

Moira's mouth went dry. "Jack, I didn't tell him anything. I promise, I..."

"I know you didn't. Do you really think you'd still be here if I thought you had?" He let go of her and stepped away, beginning to pace once again. "He doesn't know much. Just that she was a girl trapped in the time space who disappeared one day. Allegedly because of us. But that's enough to make him curious, which means it's too much. I need you to remove it. And take the memory of this morning out of his head, too, while you're at it."

She swallowed shakily. A sickening sense of déjà vu knotted in her stomach. Ernest, once again putting himself at risk because of her, only this time it wasn't just him who would suffer. How could he be so reckless when he had Amelia to think about? She resigned herself to what she had to do.

"Is that all you fought about?" she asked.

Jack scoffed at her. "No, that wasn't even half of it."

"It was ... about your promotion?"

Jack leaned back against his desk, folding his arms. "Who told you?"

"Shelley did."

He relaxed slightly, some of his anger giving way to smugness. "Yes, that was a good portion of it. Lots of shouting about not wanting to inherit my mess. Arrogant bastard already assumes my job is his once I'm gone."

Moira bit her lip, hesitating. "Jack, I ... I don't want to go to New York."

He looked up at her sharply. "That's too damn bad. You're *my* girl, remember? I need you there to be my eyes and ears in the new office."

Moira wanted to argue, but didn't, not wanting to anger him again when it seemed he was finally calming down.

"Clean up this mess when you go over to Ernest's apartment tonight, all right? And let him know about New York while you're at it."

It was all Moira could do not to shed tears of frustration. She refused to give Jack the satisfaction of seeing her run off to the ladies' room to cry, so she forced herself to stay at her desk and work the whole day through. Ernest did not return.

Moira took his coat and briefcase with her when she left, making her way to Ernest's apartment by bus. When he opened the door to see her standing there, he looked surprised.

"Moira? What are you doing here?"

"I told you I would come by," she reminded him.

Ernest's expression tightened. "Right. Right, I remember that now. It's just . . ."

The sound of a child laughing came from inside the apartment.

"Amelia's here," Moira said breathlessly. She forced herself to keep her eyes fixed on Ernest even though she desperately wanted to look over his shoulder. To catch a glimpse of the child she hadn't seen in years.

"Yes," Ernest said, shifting uncomfortably. "I went to pick her up from school over the weekend. I'm sorry, I thought I told you."

"No, you did; I guess I just forgot. I'm sorry, I can come back later. I just wanted to bring you these." She held up the coat and briefcase. "You left without them this morning."

Ernest bit his lip, looking a little ashamed for reasons she couldn't fathom. "You know what, actually, why don't you come in?"

Moira's heartbeat quickened. "Are you sure?"

"Sure. You were going to meet her tomorrow anyway. Maybe this is better."

Right. Tomorrow. Tomorrow he was supposed to bring Amelia into the office to introduce them before he took her out for the day. She was supposed to meet up with them for dinner and then to see a movie. Just the three of them.

Moira knew it was a bad idea. She wasn't prepared for this. To see her child, their child, with such little time to steel herself against the myriad emotions she was already feeling. Ernest opened the door to let her in. She had to remind herself to breathe as she stepped inside.

Amelia was seated on the sofa in the living room. Moira could only see the back of her head. The bright copper waves that matched Ernest's exactly. But then she turned around. The first thing Moira noticed was that she had her nose. Her pale ivory skin. Other than that, she was all him, right down to the freckles that only revealed themselves in the summertime.

"Amelia, this is Moira," Ernest said. "She's, uh, . . . a friend of mine."

"Is she your girlfriend?" Amelia asked, scrutinizing Moira through sharp, analytical eyes. The blue in them belonged to Ernest but the look . . . well, that look was all her mother. Moira wondered how Ernest didn't see it.

Ernest laughed nervously. "What makes you think that?"

"She's too pretty to be just your friend."

Moira cracked a smile.

"But not too pretty to be my girlfriend?" Ernest asked.

Amelia narrowed her eyes at Moira again. "Are *you* a spy too?"

Ernest made a noise. "Amelia, how many times do I have to tell you? I'm not a spy. And neither is she."

Amelia shrugged and turned back around to face the television. "That's exactly what a spy would say."

Ernest crept up behind her. "Well, in that case you better mind your manners, young lady. You know what they say about spies, don't you?"

Amelia's body tensed in anticipation. "What?"

He leaned closer, hissing in her ear. "That they're deadly." Ernest grabbed her around the middle and lifted her over the back of the sofa.

She squealed in delight as he swung her through the air. Moira thought her heart might burst out of her chest. Ernest set Amelia back down on her feet.

"All right, kiddo. Off to bed."

"But it's only eight!" Amelia protested.

"And you're only nine," Ernest said, tapping her on the nose. "Which means you have to listen to me."

Amelia made an indignant face at him and folded her arms.

"Sorry, kid, I don't make the rules," Ernest said apologetically. He kissed her forehead and propelled her down the hall. "Off you go."

Amelia shot Moira a scathing look as she passed, seeming to decide that her presence was the reason she was being sent to bed early. The door to her bedroom slammed shut and Ernest sighed.

"You didn't have to do that," Moira said.

"I did if I want you to have a good opinion about my parenting skills," Ernest said, coming over to slide his arm around her waist. "Amelia can be . . . a handful. Especially around company."

"You seem like you're doing fine," Moira said, reveling in the feeling of his arm around her. The brief glimpse of happiness soon faded, though, leaving her with the harsh reality of what came next.

Ernest stepped away to the kitchen to make coffee. As he did, Moira listened to the sounds coming from Amelia's room. The loud opening and closing of drawers in protest as she donned her pajamas.

"So . . ." Moira began, joining Ernest in the kitchen. "That was some argument earlier."

Ernest ran a hand through his hair. "Yeah."

"What happened?"

"I asked him about the Frenchman. He gave some evasive response. I pushed him." He paused in the middle of scooping coffee into the coffeemaker to look up at her. "Reminded him that I was supposed to be in the know about everything happening at the TRP. Especially in light of . . ."

"His promotion?" Moira finished for him.

"Yeah. If I'm going to be taking over for him, I need to know what's going on."

"So you've been offered the director position?"

"Not yet. Jack's still got a few weeks before his own role is finalized. Background checks and the like."

Moira busied herself retrieving mugs from the cabinet to avoid looking at him.

"Did he talk to you yet?" Ernest asked. "About New York?"

"He mentioned it."

"And?"

"And what?"

"Are you going to go?"

There was a pause. Ernest reached for her hand, turning her toward him. He studied her expression, blinking a few times.

"You are," he said, his eyes filling with distress.

"I don't have any other options," Moira said.

"What do you mean? Of course you do."

Moira tried to keep it lighthearted, forcing a laugh. "Yeah? What are they then? Because I sure don't know."

Ernest swallowed, dropping his eyes. "You could stay."

"Stay. And do what? Jack will fire me if I don't go. I'd be out of a job."

"Well, I've been thinking . . ." Ernest blew out a long breath. Wherever this conversation was about to go, he seemed to decide against it and abruptly changed the subject. "Have you ever thought about leaving?" he asked, turning back to the stove.

"Leaving?"

"Leaving the TRP. Going somewhere else."

She had thought about leaving. All the time she dreamed of what it would be like to be in control of her own life. But Jack would never allow it. She was as trapped here as she had been in the time space. By Jack, but also by her own desires to protect the people she loved.

"You're not thinking of leaving, are you?" she asked hesitantly.

"I don't know what I'm thinking anymore."

"Is this about your fight with Jack?"

"Yes and no. I don't know. I just . . . Lately I'm not sure if what we're doing at the TRP is right. I used to believe it was. I thought we were building something. Keeping dangerous ideas from dominating history, but now I'm not so sure."

So that's what they'd fought about that had made Jack so angry. His second-in-command veering off course.

"Jack always says what we're doing helps stop the spread of communism. That we're preventing wars like the last one. It's what's necessary."

Ernest was looking at her strangely. "Do you really believe that?"

"I have to."

"Have to? Because you're a part of it too?" He said this slowly as if he already knew the answer. "Because you've been helping him?"

"Ernest . . ."

"Moira, be honest with me. Those timekeepers who have gone missing . . . you know where they went, don't you?"

She didn't say anything. He understood.

"So when I asked you the other day if you knew anything, you lied?"

"I couldn't tell you."

"Why not?"

"Because of Jack."

"Right. Jack. So instead, you told me I should ask him and let me risk my career with that argument when you could have just told me the truth."

"I didn't think there would be an argument."

Just then, the kettle started to boil over on the stove. Ernest cursed under his breath and took it off the burner. This wasn't going the way it was supposed to.

Ernest sighed as he poured coffee into their cups. "I don't want to fight with you too. I just have one more question and then I'll drop it."

"Okay. What is it?"

"Has Jack ever spoken to you about someone named Lisavet Levy?"

The name was the final nail in the coffin. Moira knew then that Jack was right. She needed to fix this before Ernest's questions became something more. She gave him a vague answer, just convincing enough. She could have told him anything and he wouldn't remember it after tonight. Eventually he calmed down. They drank their coffee, and he began talking through the ideas he had for the TRP once Jack was gone. Ernest wanted to expand their relationship with other timekeepers and put an end to all the hostility. Always the diplomat.

Moira accepted his offer to spend the night, late as it was. She kissed him as he fell asleep, feeling the warmth of his arms around her, the realest thing she had ever known. For a moment, his eyes opened just a little, one hand reaching up to caress her cheek.

"Moira . . ." he said sleepily. "You—"

She shushed him before he could speak. Whatever he was going to say, she knew that hearing it would only make this harder. She waited for him to drift off again. When his breathing evened out and the hum of his dreams began, she did what needed to be done. Erased his argument with Jack. Removed the name Lisavet Levy once again, hopefully for the last time. She got rid of the entirety of that evening as well, knowing it would only lead to more questions if she left it there. When she was finished, she slid out of bed and dressed silently. She was on her way to Amelia's room to clear her visit from her mind as well when a little voice stopped her in her tracks.

"What are you doing?"

Amelia stood at the end of the hall, rubbing her sleepy eyes with one hand. Moira pressed a finger to her lips.

"Just going home," she whispered as softly as she could. "Your father is sleeping."

Amelia frowned at her. "He's not my dad. He's my uncle."

"Right. Go back to sleep."

"Will you make me some tea first?"

"What?"

"To sleep. Uncle Ernest always makes me tea."

Moira hesitated.

"I can wake him up if you don't want to."

"No, no," Moira said at once. "I'll do it. Why don't you go back to bed? I'll bring it to you."

"Two cups."

"Huh?"

"Make two. He always drinks one with me."

"Oh. Okay."

Amelia returned to her room and Moira went to the kitchen. Her hands shook as she prepared two cups of tea with milk and honey as quietly as possible. She took them to Amelia's room, pausing in the doorway to collect herself. The girl was sitting up in bed, propped against her pillows waiting. Her room in Ernest's DC apartment doubled as a guest room and looked far too formal for a little girl. Amelia's schoolbooks sat on top of the wardrobe, along with several volumes of poetry Moira recognized as the same ones Ernest had brought her in the time space. Something tugged at the center of her chest as she thought of her daughter reading those poems, turning the same pages she had once held dear. She handed Amelia the mug of tea. Amelia sipped at it, eyeing her over the brim of the cup.

"Is it okay?" Moira asked.

Amelia nodded. "You make it like he does."

Moira took a sip of her own tea, feeling the tug in her chest intensify.

"You don't like it?" Amelia asked, noticing her expression and assuming it had something to do with the tea.

"I think I added too much sugar," Moira said. She had never particularly cared for tea. It reminded her too much of her mother. But now, whenever she drank it, she knew she would be reminded of this night too. The realization left a bitter taste in her mouth.

"Are you sure you're not a spy?" Amelia asked, frowning slightly.

Moira suppressed a smile. "Why do you think I'm a spy?"

"You look like one. And my uncle said you work with him."

"And you think your uncle is a spy?"

"No. I know he is," Amelia insisted. "He said he works for the State Department but is never very specific."

Moira smiled at that. She was surprisingly perceptive for a nine-year-old. "Go to sleep, Amelia."

The girl let out a huff and finished her tea. She nestled down into the blankets, giving Moira one final suspicious stare. She dropped off to sleep quickly as children often do. Moira held very still, listening to the soft sounds of her breathing. She studied her sleeping face, every inch of it reminding her of either Ernest or herself. Just when she could stand it no longer, the subtle whisper of passing dreams picked up. Moira reached out and touched Amelia's face, gently pulling loose the memories of her visit. In a moment of weakness, she bent down to kiss Amelia on the forehead before leaving the room. She diligently washed the empty teacups in the kitchen, along with the mugs from their coffee. Leaving no trace that she'd ever been there at all.

THE NEXT day, Jack called her into his office first thing.

"Did you do what I asked?"

"Yes," she said, keeping her voice flat.

"Good. Good. And did you tell him about New York?"

Moira paused for a beat. "I did but . . ."

"But . . . ?"

"He and I got into a bit of an argument. I ended up erasing the whole evening from his memory."

"An argument?"

"Yes," Moira said, barreling past his question in hopes that he wouldn't pry into the substance of their argument.

"Okay," Jack said slowly. "Tell him again soon, all right? Today, maybe. He's only coming in for one meeting before he takes the kid to the museum or something."

Moira nodded and said nothing.

Ernest came in with Amelia at half past eight. He was smiling and alert. He waved at Jack as if nothing had happened between them. Shelley stared at him in confusion as he dropped his things off in his office. He lifted Amelia up and placed her in his desk chair, ruffling her hair, and then called out to Moira.

"Moira," he said, waving her over. "Come in here for a second. I want you to meet Amelia."

Moira stood, composing her face into the cheerful grin she had practiced. This time, she was more prepared.

"Amelia," Ernest said. "This is Miss Donnelly. We work together. She . . ."

"I thought her name was Moira," Amelia said.

Moira could have sworn her pulse stopped.

"What?" Ernest asked.

"I already know her," Amelia said impatiently. "You said her name was Moira."

"How do you already know her, Amelia?" Ernest asked.

Amelia let out a little huff of annoyance. "From last night?"

Moira felt her chest tighten. She had removed the memories. She was certain she had. Her eyes flitted to Jack's office. He had moved around his desk and was now sitting on the edge of it, listening intently.

Ernest frowned. "Last night?"

"Yeah. She's your girlfriend. Or at least *I* think she is, even if you won't admit it."

Moira let out a nervous laugh. "You must be thinking of someone else. Your uncle's *other* girlfriend, maybe."

Amelia made an indignant face at her. "Nuh-uh, it was you. You made me tea."

Ernest turned to look at her. "Tea?"

"Ernest," Jack said, cutting in. He came to stand at Moira's elbow, tapping his fingers against the doorframe. "You've got that meeting, don't forget."

"I know, just give me one . . ."

"Now," Jack said.

Ernest glared at him in annoyance. He cast one more doubtful look at Moira and then told Amelia he'd be back in an hour. In his absence, Jack sauntered into the office, his eyes fixed intently on the little girl. Moira felt panic brewing in her chest.

"Hey, sweetheart," Jack said, kneeling with both hands on the arms of the chair Amelia sat in, effectively boxing her into it. "Did you say you met her last night?"

"Yes," Amelia said. "She was at our apartment."

"Ahhh, okay. Well, I need you to do me a favor and don't tell your uncle she was there, all right?"

"But he saw her there."

"I know, but we can't talk about it, okay?"

"Why not?"

"Because . . ." Jack paused to think.

Amelia made an effort to squirm away from him, but he kept both hands locked on the chair. Moira desperately wanted to pull him away from her. To pick Amelia up and take her far, far away from him. Why had Ernest brought her here? Didn't he know that their boss was not someone their daughter should ever, ever be around?

"Because she was there to set up a surprise for your uncle," Jack said at last.

"For his birthday?"

"Exactly, for his birthday. That's soon, right? Moira, it's soon?"

"In July," she and Amelia said simultaneously.

Jack nodded. "That's right. We're throwing him a surprise party in a couple weeks and Moira here had to come in and see what sort of cake he likes. But to keep him from figuring it out, she had to give him a special potion to make him forget."

"A potion?" Amelia asked, raising an eyebrow. She was too old to believe in such things. Too much the realist.

"Like the kind that spies use," Moira chimed in.

"A spy potion?" Amelia repeated. "Like a secret serum?" That she was slightly more prone to believing.

"Yes, a spy serum," Jack said. "So he doesn't remember anything, and you can't tell him, or it will ruin the surprise, okay?"

Amelia chewed her lip, contemplating this. Her wide, skeptical eyes surveyed first Moira and then Jack.

"Okay," she said at last.

"Attagirl," Jack said, chucking her under the chin.

Amelia slapped his hand away.

Jack chuckled at her and stood up, beckoning Moira back into his office.

"Little brat," he muttered as he shut the door. "Why didn't you take care of that while you were there?"

"I did," Moira said without thinking.

"Then why does she still remember?"

"I'm not sure."

"Well, you must have made a mistake."

"No, I don't think so. I was certain that I . . ." Moira stopped talking. She hadn't made a mistake, she knew she hadn't. Something else was going on. What if Amelia was as untethered as she was? Azrael's words were in her head. *No one has ever done what you're doing . . . You might be untethering her from Time the same way you are.* Immune to the constraints of the temporal world. Immune to her mother's ability to alter and bend Time. Perhaps even able to do the same.

Jack had begun looking at her strangely in her silence. "Moira . . ." he said slowly. "Tell me why the girl remembers."

Moira stoically fixed her features, trying to conceal her internal panic. But even before she started talking, she knew he knew she was lying.

"You know what, it's my mistake," she said, shaking her head. "I forgot she saw me when I first came in last night, and only erased our conversation as I was leaving. That's my fault."

Jack pursed his lips. He looked at her and she at him. He didn't buy it. She could tell he didn't but she held her breath, hoping that he might decide to.

"All right," he said after a long, tense pause. "Well, crisis averted for now. Don't slip up like that again."

Moira promised she wouldn't and returned to her desk, struggling to remember how a normal person should sit. But whenever she glanced up at Jack through his office window, her pulse raced with terror. He was watching Amelia in Ernest's office with a kind of intensity she had only ever seen once before, on the day he had first come to see her in the psychiatric ward.

By the time Ernest's meeting was over, she knew what she needed to do. She should have done it a long time ago, before things had gotten to this point. She should have never agreed to go out with him at all, should have known it would only put him and Amelia in danger.

"Ernest, I need to talk to you," she said, standing the second he came out of the meeting room.

"Now?" he asked, eyebrows raised.

"It's about Jack's promotion," Moira said.

His expression faltered slightly. "Oh. Okay. Shall we . . ." He extended a hand to the hallway.

Moira followed him that way, feeling Jack's eyes on them as they passed. She took several deep breaths, adopting a cold, resolute expression. When they got out of earshot, Ernest turned to face her.

"Everything okay?"

"Yes. Well. No, not really. I'm sure you've heard by now that Jack was offered the new CIA director role."

"Yes, I heard," Ernest said warily. "I actually . . ."

Moira cut him off, barreling on with it before he said something that might change her mind. "He's asked me to transfer to the New York office for a while. And I said yes."

Ernest blinked several times. "You . . . you did?"

"Yes. We won't be able to keep seeing each other. I'm sorry." She started to turn away.

"Wait." Ernest caught her arm, letting out a laugh of nervous confusion. "Can we talk about this?"

"The decision has already been made," Moira said, her voice trembling despite her efforts to keep it steady. She couldn't look at him.

Ernest held very still. "I don't understand."

"There's nothing to understand. I'm leaving and you're staying. It would never work. It . . . it's better if we end things now."

"Moira, I . . ."

She shut her eyes. "I'm sorry, Ernest. I have to."

"But why? Why do you *have* to?"

Moira clenched her jaw. "There's no reason for me not to go."

"What if there was? What if . . ." He paused, reaching into his pocket. "I, uh, . . ." He cleared his throat and held something out to her. "I was going to give you this tonight. After dinner. I had it all planned."

She looked down at the ring box, unable to stop herself. "Ernest . . ." she said helplessly.

"Please, Moira. I don't want to lose you. I know we've not been together that long but I . . . I feel like I've known you my whole life somehow."

"Ernest, I can't. I already told him."

"Then tell him you changed your mind."

"It's not that simple."

"Why not?"

"Because . . ."

"Because why? I thought you and I had a good thing going here. I
thought you felt the way I did about where things were going. I thought . . .
I thought I meant something to you."

"You do. Of course you do."

"Then why are you doing this? I need a real reason because none of
this makes any sense from where I'm standing."

She shut her eyes. She couldn't breathe. Couldn't listen to this. It
was right there in front of her. Everything she'd ever wanted. A life married to Ernest. With him and Amelia, the three of them a family after
all they'd been through. It took everything she had not to reach out and
take it. But she couldn't do that. She opened her eyes and said the only
thing she knew would put an end to this for good.

"I'm sleeping with him."

Ernest's face fell. He let go of her arm. "You what?"

"For a few months now. It just happened. I'm sorry."

There was silence. Ernest was giving her a look so full of hurt that
she swore her heart was cracking into pieces.

She shook her head, forcing back the tears. "I'm sorry, Ernest. I am.
But . . . I can't. Please try to understand." She walked away from him and
returned to her desk.

Ernest stayed where he was in the hall, watching her as she began
typing up a memo. After what felt like ages he called out for Amelia to
come with him. The two of them left the office.

"Whoa . . ." Shelley said when he was gone. "Did he just propose?"

"Shut up, Shelley," Moira snapped.

Shelley closed her mouth.

Moira managed to hold it together for the rest of the day, forcing herself to focus on whatever task was at hand. Filing memos. Typing up notes. Listening to Brady and Collins drone on and on in a meeting.

Azrael was wrong, she thought to herself. Living was not the most dangerous thing after all. Loving was.

She made it until everyone else had gone home for the night, leaving her with just Jack and Shelley to contend with. When Jack came out of his office, leaning beside her desk with his coat and hat in hand, Moira didn't look at him, eyes focused on what she was doing.

"You okay?" he asked softly.

"I'm fine," Moira said. Her voice cracked, betraying her.

Jack put his hat on his head and sighed. "Come on, Donnelly. Let's go get you good and drunk."

"What?"

"Best cure for a broken heart is a *lot* of whiskey."

Moira considered him warily. Did he want something from her? She searched his face but found nothing but sympathy. Eventually, she gave in. She let him pull her to her feet and help her put on her coat. She let him slide his arm around her shoulders in a proprietary manner, calling out to Shelley to tell her to lock up for the night. She let him open the car door and help her inside, not stopping to ask where he was taking her. Not caring.

He took her to his own apartment. An opulent, utilitarian-looking place, void of any semblance of personality but filled with plenty of money. Jack was the kind of person who bought the most expensive furniture available as a way of making up for his lack of taste.

"Have a seat," he said, gesturing to the sofa in the living room.

As he took her coat from her, Moira noticed the way he let his eyes linger. She wondered if she had made a mistake coming here. He removed

his own coat as well, rolling his sleeves up to his elbows as he began preparing drinks at the bar cart.

"You did the right thing," he said.

"Did I?" Moira said distantly.

"I told you all along that you're too good for him. The man can't
think for himself. Always cowering in his father's shadow, playing off his
indecision by calling it 'morality.' As if he's so superior to the rest of us."

Moira accepted the glass of whiskey Jack put into her hand.

"Ever had whiskey before?" he asked, sitting down on the sofa beside
her. Too close for comfort.

"Never cared to try it," she said.

Jack smiled at her. "This will be fun then," he said, clinking his glass
against hers.

She took a drink, wincing at the burning feeling. She liked the distraction it gave her from other forms of pain and drained the whole
thing in a few gulps.

"Do you have more?" she asked.

Jack raised his eyebrows in surprise and handed her his own glass.
She polished that one off, too, coughing on the last of it.

"Damn, easy there, tiger," he said with a laugh.

Moira leaned her head back on the sofa, drawing a deep breath. "I'm
a fool," she said.

"Oh, come on now, none of that. You're not a fool. You're human. You
were just trying to do what everyone does at some point in their life."

"And what's that?" Moira asked glumly.

"You were trying to have it all. To relive the great love of your early
days without realizing that love like that doesn't exist once you grow up.
People are too complicated. Life is too complicated."

"Have you ever been in love?" Moira asked, smirking at the very
thought of Jack Dillinger swooning after some girl in a poodle skirt. The
alcohol was already hitting her.

Jack returned the smirk, reaching out to toy with a strand of her hair. "Love is for suckers," he said. "You know, we're a lot alike, you and me."

Moira laughed bitterly until she realized he was serious. "How?"

"We both carry a burden. Only we know how truly fragile it all is. We're the only two people in the world who see the whole picture. It all could vanish in a heartbeat, everything we've ever held dear slipping right through our fingers. It makes you want to hold everything as tight as you can, but at the same time . . . it's impossible to want to hold on to anything at all. So you push it all away. And before long you find yourself standing alone, watching the illusion that we call reality change with every passing day."

Moira looked at him in surprise. He wore an expression the likes of which she'd never seen before. A heavy, almost mournful look, the arrogant mask cracking to reveal the weight of all that he carried beneath it. A lifetime's worth of knowing too much, compounded by the isolation he'd foisted upon himself out of fear of it all being taken away. But then he blinked, meeting her gaze, and the shadows lifted. As if they'd never been there at all.

Jack took the glass from her hands and set it on the coffee table beside the other.

"I've been looking into apartments in New York. I was thinking we could get you your own place this time. No more boardinghouse."

"Really?" She didn't want to think about New York.

"Sure. You've been working for me for, what, four years?"

"Something like that." Moira shifted positions. Her shoulder brushed against Jack's chest. When had he gotten so close?

"I figure that's enough time to fully acclimate to the way things work out in the world. Plus, if you're in an apartment, you'll have a lot more privacy."

"Right. Privacy." Because that was what she needed after a lifetime of isolation.

Jack let out a sigh. "Look, I know this is hard right now. But you're gonna be all right. You have other options."

Moira scoffed at him, emboldened by the alcohol. "Like who? You?" she asked sarcastically.

There was a pause. He set one hand on her knee. "Well . . . you are my girl."

There was a look in his eyes that burned just like the whiskey. She cleared her throat. Tried to move away.

"I should probably . . ."

"Not yet," he said, cutting her off.

"But I . . ."

"Lisavet . . ." he murmured.

She froze at the sound of her name and then all of a sudden Jack's lips were on hers. They were hot and wet and tasted like whiskey and nothing else. She pushed him away in alarm.

"Jack. What are you . . ."

He shushed her and kissed her again, harder this time to compensate for her struggle to pull away.

"Jack, no. This isn't . . ."

"This isn't what?" Jack asked, his voice purring seductively.

"We can't do this," Moira said. "I don't want . . ."

He caught her arm, jerking her against him. "It's okay. You're not with Ernest anymore. This is allowed."

"That's not what I . . ."

Her words were cut short by the invasive presence of his mouth on hers once more. One of his hands roamed over her, inching farther and farther up her leg. She was truly trapped, her body wedged between him and the arm of the sofa. This wasn't about her anyway. It was about Jack and his need to feel powerful. It was about Ernest. Jack's desire to take something that was considered his.

"You've got no idea how long I've wanted you," he moaned as she finally relented and kissed him back.

How long? she wanted to ask. Was it when he'd cornered her into working for him? Or maybe when he'd first met her, scared and shaking, locked away for weeks under his orders? Had it been sometime like that? She heard a clicking sound as he unbuckled his belt.

"Wait," she said, turning her head away. "Not here."

"Huh?" Jack said impatiently.

"I think I deserve the bedroom at the very least."

The bedroom, where it was quiet and dark and where she could pretend this wasn't happening. That he was somebody else.

Jack chuckled at her and lifted her up off the sofa. A brief second of reprieve before his lips crashed against hers again. He pulled her dress up over her head as he walked her steadily backward and shut the door behind them.

JACK WAS a heavy sleeper.

As the sun rose through the blinds in the morning, it took several minutes for him to wake up. Moira stood beside the window, looking down at the streets below. She had taken a cigarette from his nightstand and flicked the lighter as loudly as she could, hoping it would wake him. He began to stir slowly just as she took her first breath of smoke.

"You're up early," he said with a small groan.

"I don't sleep much."

He sat up, taking in the sight of her standing in the window. She was wearing his shirt from the night before, the cuffs rolled up. She could tell he liked the sight of her in it. That it did something for him. She smirked at his predictability and took another drag. She kept her eyes focused on the window as Jack got out of bed and pulled on a pair of pants. He came up behind her, turning her face with one hand so he could kiss her on the lips. As if they were really lovers. The subtle taste of whiskey was still there, faded now.

"Last night was something special."

"Do you use that line on all your secretaries?"

"Now, now. You know you're not like those other girls."

Of course she wasn't, Moira thought bitterly. *They* had been caught off guard, surprised by the sudden, sinister turn of his demeanor, whereas she had known all along what kind of man he was. And yet the end result was the same. He pushed and they folded, knowing they had no choice in the matter.

"Get dressed. I'll drop you by the boardinghouse so you can change before work," he said, already headed for the kitchen. "You want coffee?"

Moira hummed a response, waiting until he was at the door before speaking again. "So. Who else knows about what you did in Okinawa?"

He stopped walking. "What?"

"Okinawa. Those girls. I saw it in your memory while you were sleeping."

He turned to face her, his movements heavy. "You read my mind?"

"Don't look so surprised, Jack. You know I can do that."

Of course he knew. He'd just been arrogant enough to assume she'd never use it on him.

"Moira. I don't know what you think you saw . . ."

"Did you know that that kind of behavior is a war crime, Jack?" Moira examined her cigarette lazily as he drew closer to where she stood. "You know. I wonder what your superiors would say if they knew. I'm pretty sure they wouldn't like it. It might even make them reconsider your promotion."

Jack's hand closed around her throat so fast she didn't have time to react. Her skull cracked against the wall, and she dropped the cigarette, her hands flying to his wrist.

"Listen here, you little bitch. I don't know what you're trying to do but you can't prove anything."

Moira laughed at him as best she could, struggling for air. "Does treating women like this make you feel powerful?"

His grip tightened.

"What are you going to do, Jack? Kill me? Shelley knows I went home with you last night."

She wasn't certain this would be enough to prevent him from snapping her neck. But apparently he wasn't completely above self-preservation because he stopped.

"What do you want?" he snapped. "You want something, don't you? That's why you brought this up?"

"Your job."

He blinked. "What?"

"I want your position. After your promotion is final."

"You want to be the director of the Temporal Reconnaissance Program?" Jack asked in disbelief.

"Yes. And I want to move the TRP to the New York office." Away from him. Away from Ernest. Someplace she could actually have a life.

Jack let go in surprise. She slumped against the wall, using the windowsill to drag herself upright.

"You're a secretary," he said, sounding disgusted.

"Now, now, Jack. I'm not like those other girls, remember? I know the time space better than anyone. Better than you ever will."

"Do you know what people will say if I give you that job? What they'll think?"

"They'll assume I'm sleeping with you. Which is what they've always thought. And now I have. But if I were you, I'd be more worried about what they'll say if they hear what I know about you."

"No one will believe you."

"Maybe. Maybe not. Should we find out?"

Jack stepped away. He studied her from head to foot, still pulsing with anger.

"This is blackmail."

"Yes, it is. But I'd say it's fair, don't you think? You give me a promotion and in exchange, I'll make sure you don't lose yours."

Another long pause. "You sure you want to do this? That's Ernest's position. You'd take it from him?"

"Find him something else."

"Something else?"

"Something better. In a different department."

"There are no other positions open."

"Then make one."

"It's not that easy."

"You'll be the head of the CIA, Jack. Create a new department for timekeeper relations or something. Call it the Office of Temporal Diplomacy. I don't care." She paused before adding, "Relocate him to the Boston office." Close to Amelia, but far from Jack. Far from her.

Jack shook his head in disbelief, the anger still there but waning.

"Fine. You can have the job. Ernest will go to Boston and head up this new department. But I'm not transferring the TRP to New York."

She shrugged and turned back toward the window. "Then no deal."

"Moira . . ."

"I'm not staying in DC," she said sharply. Staying here wasn't an option. There was nothing left for her here. "You wanted eyes and ears in the office, anyway, right?"

"Right, but I didn't plan on transferring the whole department out there." Jack reached out and toyed with the hem of the shirt she wore, some of last night's hunger surfacing. "Besides, now I'm not sure I want you to go at all."

Moira pulled away. "New York. Or you can kiss your promotion goodbye."

His expression hardened again. A reckoning with the fact that, in one single night, their entire dynamic had shifted. No longer would he be able to exercise such control over her life as he had before. It was too late to fix things with Ernest, but she might still be able to salvage a life for herself with what little remained. She would go to New York. Ernest would go to Boston. And Jack would stay in DC. She hoped that, with the three of them apart, no longer looking over one another's shoulders, Ernest and Amelia would be safe.

"Is that all?" he asked sarcastically.

"One more thing," Moira said, smiling smugly. "If I'm going to be the director, I'll need a watch."

"Absolutely not," he snapped. "You can't honestly think that I would—"

"If I don't have one, people will ask questions," she pointed out. "It will make them suspicious. And we don't want that."

"Fine," he said through gritted teeth. "But you will not enter the time space, is that understood?"

She faltered slightly. That would defeat the whole point. "Jack—"

"Those are my terms," he spat back. "If you take so much as one step into the time space without my approval, I'll find a reason to have Ernest killed. I'll have you arrested, and I'll deploy every last man I've got to hunt down that child of yours. Is that understood?"

Moira refused to let him see her shaken. She'd gained too much to let him win now. So she fixed a conniving smile to her face and extended a hand to him. "Then we have a deal?"

He ground his jaw, his large hand encompassing hers in a firm, be-grudging handshake. "Well played, Miss Levy."

He let go of her hand and stormed out of the room, slamming the door shut behind him. Moira took another cigarette from the carton and lit it, savoring the taste of smoke and victory.

20

1965, New York City, New York

MOIRA HAD NOT SEEN Ernest Duquesne for five years when he showed up on her doorstep in the middle of a rainstorm. She returned from work late that night, fighting to keep her umbrella open in the pouring rain and wind. It had been a long day, filled with multiple phone calls from Jack. Even after five years as the head of the CIA, he still hadn't been able to relinquish total control of the TRP to her. The rebellion picked up steam, despite her best efforts, becoming harder and harder to eradicate. Every month, there were new reports from other agencies across the world of suspected rebels lurking in their ranks. Rebels who continued to ask about Lisavet Levy, who searched for her book and occasionally asked questions about the child she had once been seen with.

So Moira doubled down. She erased the name Lisavet Levy from the minds of anyone who came across it and didn't stop to ask questions. She couldn't afford to think about morality with the rebel movement constantly threatening to expose the truth, putting both her and Amelia at risk. So she stayed in line and ran the TRP with an iron grip. She did what Jack asked her to do. And she did what needed to be done to keep herself and her daughter safe. For years, life moved forward. Until that night in 1965, when it came to a screeching halt.

He was standing on the stoop, waiting for her. Judging by his wet clothes in spite of his umbrella, he had been standing there for quite some time.

"Ernest," she said, freezing.

He didn't speak, staring at her with those blue eyes that never changed no matter how much time had passed.

"What are you doing here?" she asked.

"I need to talk to you."

"Is everything all right?" She and Ernest still spoke from time to time when their work demanded it, but always on the phone. Never in person. After he'd been informed that she would be taking the job as director, he had made a point never to deal with her face-to-face.

He laughed breathlessly. "Oh yes, everything is fine. That's why I'm standing outside your apartment at nine o'clock at night."

Moira looked at him. Ernest was more than angry, he was furious. She straightened. "Can I know what this is about?"

"It's about Lisavet Levy."

Moira tried to keep her face blank. Not this again. She had tried so hard to remove that name from his head. Why did it keep coming back to haunt her?

"Well, let's not have it out here in the street. Come inside."

In the elevator, Ernest stood beside her in silence, dripping water from his coat onto the floor. Moira stole a glance at him, noting the tension in his jaw, the unkempt look of his hair that indicated he had been running his hands through it obsessively. He was pushing forty now, but his hair still shone as bright and thick as it always had. Not a trace of gray or thinning. He caught her looking at him and stiffened his jaw even more.

They reached the top floor. Moira unlocked the door to her apartment and let him inside, shutting and bolting it behind her. She hung her own umbrella and coat on the rack and told him to do the same.

"Coffee?" she asked, setting her handbag down on the table by the sofa. Still playing cordial host until she knew what he wanted.

"No thanks," Ernest said tensely. He was looking around at the apartment.

This was Moira's third apartment in New York and was by far the nicest she'd had. She had made it her own, decorating with modern furniture in dark woods and heavy upholstery. The south-facing windows overlooked the city and there was a second room she used as a library in addition to the bedroom. For a moment, there was only silence, punctuated by the roaring of the wind and rain outside beating against the windows.

"Nice place," Ernest said bitterly. "Did Jack help you pick it out?"

Moira gave him a look and went into the kitchen. "Do you want tea instead?"

"No."

"Then how about a drink? You like gin, right?"

"Moira. I don't want anything."

He set his briefcase down on the coffee table by the record player and opened it. The latches clicked like the sound of knuckles cracking. She watched him uneasily as he turned his back to her and removed something from the case. In an effort to have something, anything to do, she reached into the drawer for a cigarette. As she was raising the lighter to the tip, she heard the soft scratch of a record starting to play and froze.

A song she knew too well poured from the horn. The trumpeting intro to "Blue Moon," sung by Billy Eckstine, filled the apartment. Moira's blood ran cold. Her eyes flew to Ernest, finding him standing in the center of the room, fists clenched.

"Sound familiar?" he asked.

"Ernest, I don't see how this is—"

"I asked you if it sounded familiar."

Moira swallowed. "Yes."

"Yes," he repeated softly. He turned to look back at the record player as the song continued to ring out. "I always loved this song. From the very first time I heard it, I thought it was one of the most beautiful songs I'd ever heard. I used to play it all the time when I was alone. Especially back when we were together. I was drawn to it because it reminded me of you, even though it wasn't a song we'd ever listened to together . . . or at least, I thought we hadn't."

He fixed his eyes back on her and she held her breath, waiting for whatever was coming next. After a long pause, he took another step in her direction. "I found Lisavet Levy's book. Or I guess I should say . . . I found *your* book." His words shook violently at the end.

"How much did you see?" she asked in a half whisper.

"Everything," he growled in a tone she had never heard him use before. "All of it. I saw every memory you *took* from me. I know who you are. I *remember* now." Ernest's voice cracked, some of the anger giving way to grieving pain.

"Ernest . . ."

"No," he said sharply. "You took my memories from me. Our memories. You made me forget you."

"I did it to protect you."

"Did you tell me you were having an affair with Jack to 'protect me' too?" he spat.

Moira looked away. "It was always to protect you. You have to understand. Jack was going to . . ."

Ernest suddenly reached out and took hold of her chin, forcing her to look at him. Moira resisted the urge to shrink back from him. She'd never seen him like this. He wasn't being rough with her. Not like Jack. But there was so much fire in his eyes. Anger and heartache.

"You made me lose you twice. And it's not fair, Moira. It's not fair. Neither time did I know how much I was really losing. The realest thing I ever had was you. You took that from me. You lied to me."

"To keep you safe."

"I get to decide what is and isn't safe for me. I loved you. Both times, I loved you. You're still the only person I've ever loved." His hand slid to the side of her face, and he looked as though he didn't know whether to kiss her or wring her neck. "We could have had something. A life together. Didn't you want that?"

"Of course. It's all I wanted. You have no idea how badly I do."

Ernest stared at her intently for a long, aching moment and then let go.

"Ernest . . . you didn't . . . you didn't show it to anyone else, did you?" she asked. Wondering how many people knew the truth about her now.

"No," he said.

"How did you even come across it? It was stolen from me when I was still in the time space."

"Doesn't matter," he said, waving a hand. "Now I know the truth. That Lisavet Levy, the cause behind the entire movement, is the same person trying to dismantle it." He sounded disgusted. Rightfully so.

"You don't understand. I've only been doing it to . . ."

"To protect me?" He scoffed loudly. "Moira, you don't need to protect me from the movement. I *am* the movement. Me. I'm the one who's behind all this. The one you've been working against for five years."

Moira's face went pale. "What?"

"You didn't know?" he asked, looking skeptical. "You, the reader of minds?"

"I don't do that anymore," Moira said quietly.

Not unless someone had memories of Lisavet Levy that needed erasing. When that happened once or twice every year or so, she was never looking for memories of Ernest. Hadn't known to look.

Ernest stared at her, struggling to process this. "How could you ever have done it at all? You, the girl who used to believe that memories were a sacred thing?"

She glared at him. "Don't look so shocked, Ernest. Even you've been guilty of burning memories."

"Until I met you. Until you showed me why it was so wrong. You used to save memories, not steal them. What happened?"

"I grew up," she snapped. "I realized it never made a difference anyway. That time is too big for just one person. None of my efforts ever changed anything."

"That's not true. You did change things. You changed me. Even though you took my memories, the ideas you gave me were already rooted deep. And an idea is an impossible thing to kill once it starts to spread. I spent the last ten years of my life following that idea and now there are a dozen others doing the exact same thing. Don't tell me it didn't matter, Lisavet."

Hearing him say her name like that after all this time made her dizzy with panic. His words stirred something deep within her. The old familiar grip of conviction. The pull of that idea she had so fiercely fought for came calling back to her like the echoes of Time. She shoved it down.

"No. No. I can't do this. I can't. I didn't ask you to fight for me. I didn't want this. Do you know what would happen if anyone else finds out you're the one behind all this? You'd be killed." She tried to walk past him. He stepped in front of her, grabbing her by both arms.

"Then kill me," Ernest growled. "They're already going to anyway. So go ahead."

Moira shrank back from him. "What do you mean?"

"I stole the watches from the TRP office before I came to see you."

"You did what?"

"I stole them. It was part of a bigger plan. I'm just a little ahead of schedule. I sent the word out and before long every government entity across the globe is going to find themselves in a similar situation."

Moira stared at him in shock. Who was this person? Ernest, the diplomat. Ernest, the peacemaker, orchestrating a movement and stealing from the very department his father had founded. Dismantling the whole system bit by bit. No longer a soldier, but a rebel. All because of *her*. Jack had been wrong.

"Yours is the last one," he said, nodding at her wrist. "So you see? I'm already a dead man walking."

"So is that why you really came here?" she asked quietly.

Ernest swallowed, some of the anger giving way. "No. I came because I . . . because I had to see you."

No, he needed to run, Moira thought. Once the others found out the watches were gone, they'd sound the alarm. They'd notice when Ernest didn't come into work the next day, and they would assume. He would be hunted down and killed for treason. The very thought made Moira's ears ring with terror. He knew his time was running out and yet he'd still come to see her, knowing she might very well turn him in herself. She could see it in his eyes, the hesitation as both of them wondered what the other was going to do next. She acted first. She took the watch from her wrist and held it out to him.

"Here. Take it. And get the hell out of here."

He looked down at the watch, hesitating.

She thrust it against his chest. "What are you waiting for? Take it. If you go now, you might have time to get away. You can hide in the time space. If you stole the watches, no one would find you there. You and your rebels can figure something out."

He reached for it, his hand trapping hers. "What are you doing?"

"What I've always done. I'm trying to protect you."

"Why? You should already have a gun to my head."

"I'm not going to be the reason you get killed."

"Why not?"

Moira let out a gasp of frustration. "Do you really still have to ask?"

A tense silence passed, the air between them wound like wire and coiled tight. He looked at her with a kind of yearning on his face, one that he was furious at himself for, but a yearning all the same.

"Ernest, please," she said.

The wire snapped. He latched one arm around her waist. She inhaled sharply as he pulled her close and kissed her. His kiss was passionate and firm, but still soft underneath it all. He lifted her up in his arms, sweeping aside everything on the countertop, setting her on the edge of it. He murmured her name in her ear as his hands reached for the buttons of her shirt.

"Lisavet," he said in that old familiar tone. The voice she heard every night as she lay awake, haunted by memories.

She could feel the anger just underneath the surface of his embrace, but it only added fuel to the fire sparking between them. An aching flame that she had carried with her for fifteen years. Her mind raced with possibility. All this time he had been fighting for her, and she for him and neither of them had known it.

Lisavet Levy had never been a nuisance but a real and tangible threat. Not because she saved memories the others chose to burn, but because she had become an idea. And ideas were much harder to kill, so Jack had gone after her instead. Her spirit, her conviction, her belief in her own cause. She had fallen for it, letting him plant his own ideas in her head instead.

Moira pulled Ernest as close as humanly possible, cursing all the years she'd spent working against him when they could have been doing this together. They folded into each other as the storm outside the window intensified. Hours later, they lay side by side in bed. Ernest had his arms around her, laying searing kisses on her shoulder. Stealing a few more moments of their reunion before the inevitable.

"What happens now?" she asked. "To you, I mean."

Ernest's arms tensed. "I, uh, . . . I'm not sure. This wasn't how this was supposed to go. We had it planned. I was supposed to have plane tickets booked for me and Amelia to get away. Somewhere to South America. It was supposed to happen in the summer so I could make it look like I was just taking my normal vacation. But then I saw the memories in the book, and I had to come see you. I figured you would turn me in, anyway, so I just—" He broke off, running one hand through his hair. "My god, this is a mess. We haven't even found a solution to part two of the plan."

"Part two?"

"Eliminate all access to the time space. Even ours. So nobody can ever interfere with it again."

"That seems rather extreme."

"It's the only way to make sure we keep control out of the wrong hands. Without that, there's no point. They'll just figure out a way back in. I was working on a plan before all this happened."

Moira reached out to run her own hand through his hair. "Then let me help."

"How?"

"We have until morning before anyone realizes the watches are gone."

"Lisavet . . ."

"I'm in this with you now, Ernest. Let me help. We can come up with something."

He leaned down to kiss her softly. "Okay. But you have to promise me something."

"What?"

"No more secrets. From now on, we have to be honest with each other. Promise?"

There was a long, weighty pause. Moira bunched the edges of the sheets in her hands. She sat up.

"What's wrong?" Ernest asked, taking in the look on her face.

"There's . . . one more thing I need to tell you. About Amelia."

WHEN ERNEST left Moira's apartment that morning, he did not do what they had discussed. Not right away.

He was supposed to disappear. That was the plan he and Moira had concocted. That he would go to the secret second apartment Moira kept downtown. He would stay there, hidden. At the same time, Moira would tell Jack that Ernest had been killed, assassinated by another timekeeper. Ernest had given Moira his watch so she could pretend that the Russians had sent it to her as proof of his murder the way the Americans had always done to them. As much as it pained him to give it up, he knew he couldn't risk being seen in the time space by members of opposing governments once word got out. Moira would go to Boston. She would watch over Amelia, protect her from Jack and the others, and eventually, she would explain to Amelia the secrets she and Ernest had both been keeping. Meanwhile, Ernest would work through part two of the plan, and when it was time, they would run. The three of them together.

In his absence, the department would do what they always did when someone was killed inside the time space and a body couldn't be recovered; they would stage a funeral anyway, closed casket, of course, to keep grieving family members from asking too many questions. To give them closure.

It was the thought of his funeral, and the idea of Amelia attending it alone, that drove Ernest to go, not downtown like they'd discussed, but to Boston. To Pembroke Academy where Amelia was just starting another semester. He didn't care that he was supposed to be gone already. He had to see her. When he arrived, he parked his car and stood outside of the dining hall until he saw Amelia emerge. She looked grumpy as she usually did when forced to wake up early and he smiled at the sight of her sleepy scowl. He could see it now that he knew. The nose, the high forehead, the pale, moonlit skin. Traits he'd always assumed had come from Elaina's Irish Catholic ex-lover, but that he now knew came from Lisavet. At fifteen, Amelia was beginning to look more like her mother in spite of the red hair and blue eyes that were his.

His daughter. She was his daughter. To him, that changed everything. He had always loved her as though she were his, that wasn't it. Rather, it was his own actions that he now viewed in a different light. He should have tried harder when she was small. Pushed to be a more constant presence in her life even when Elaina shoved him away. He should have done more to keep her safe from the perils of her young life. He had refrained then, assuming that he had no business inserting himself in the life of someone else's daughter. But he was her father. His anger at Moira, at Lisavet, resurfaced again. He didn't know how he'd ever forgive her for Amelia. For keeping him in the dark all these years. He watched Amelia cross the quad to her first class, wishing he could go to her. But he was supposed to be dead.

Half of him feared that trusting Moira was a mistake, while the other half knew that Lisavet would not do anything that might endanger him or their daughter. Either way, he didn't have a choice. There was nobody left to trust but her.

21

1965, Somewhere in the Time Space

AMELIA, ANTON, AND AZRAEL emerged from the last of Lisavet Levy's living memories, returning to the quiet darkness of the time space. All of them were deathly silent. Azrael had brought them to the edge of the chasm. Amelia could still hear the whispers calling out from the depths of it. Only now did she understand why.

"So this . . ." She swallowed, her voice shaking. "This exists because of me."

"In a way," Azrael said. "But . . . you were an infant. I hardly think you can blame yourself."

Amelia did blame herself though. This chasm was here because of her. Moira Donnelly . . . no, Lisavet Levy . . . no, *her mother* had done it to protect her. Over and over again, she'd rewritten the past for her. Over and over she had lied, interrogated, killed, and denied herself the only happiness she had ever known . . . for her. As if sensing her thoughts, Azrael gave Amelia a sad smile.

"Never underestimate what a mother will do to protect her child," he said.

Amelia shook her head, unable to reconcile this with the version of Moira she had met. The one who had thrown her out of windows, pushed her into an open grave, and sent her into the time space against her will. Was that all to protect her too?

Beside her, Anton had turned away from them. He was staring down at the chasm, still holding the book in his hands. Eyes heavy and full of shadows. Azrael bowed his head at her and removed himself from the scene, fading against the backdrop of dust-covered shelves. Amelia took a few tentative steps toward the chasm.

"Anton?" she said gently.

He was turning the book over in his hands. "He fought for her," he said in a quiet voice that shook with each word. "Not just at the beginning. His whole life he fought for her. And she killed him."

Amelia said nothing. What was there to say when *she* was the reason his father had been killed? How could she comfort him when the charmed childhood he envied, full of poetry and safety and love, had been bought at the expense of his own?

She swallowed back tears, reaching for his arm. "Anton, I—"

He flinched. "I need a moment," he said.

"Wait," Amelia said. "Please . . ."

"No, just . . . just give me a moment to . . . to . . . how do you say it? Process. I will come back," he said, eyes shut. "I promise, I just . . . I need to be alone for a moment."

Amelia nodded. Swallowed. "I understand," she said.

Anton didn't look at her as he turned on his heel and walked away, leaving her alone. She sank down onto the ground beside the chasm, pulling her knees up to her chest in the exact same position she had been in when he found her there the first time.

MOIRA AWOKE to the sound of Ernest shutting the window in the next room. It had begun to rain again, the wind tossing water droplets onto the edge of the table where he worked. She pushed herself up onto one arm, watching him. Before him were pages upon pages of notes. Books on quantum physics and space-time theory he was using to find a solution to their problem. To find a way to cut off access to the time space for good. A single lamp illuminated his face, casting shadows over the weary lines on his forehead that were now a permanent feature.

It was late. Ernest had put off coming to bed for hours, as he had every night since she arrived. He always waited until she had fallen asleep before doing the same. Always woke at least an hour before her. As if he didn't trust her to be awake while he slept. Moira sat up, letting the blankets fall away, and left the bedroom. He didn't notice her until she was right beside him.

"Ernest," she said.

He jumped. "Lisavet," he said, closing the pages of his notebook at once.

Moira's heart clenched at the familiar name. He called her that now, as if attempting to remind them both who she really was.

"It's three in the morning," she said gently.

He sighed heavily. "I know. Just a few more minutes."

"Any luck?" Moira asked, pulling out the chair across from him to sit.

He didn't answer right away, one finger tapping the notebook. "Nothing concrete. A few threads that always lead to nowhere."

"Tell me. Maybe I can help."

Ernest shook his head slowly. "No. You're right, it's late. I should get some sleep." He pushed back from the table, taking the notebook with him but leaving the books behind. "You coming?" he asked.

Moira could hear the tension in his voice. If she came, he wouldn't sleep until she did. And she wasn't tired. She shook her head.

"No. You go ahead. I'm going to stay up for a while." She pulled one of the books toward her and opened to the table of contents.

He held still, hesitating.

"You can lock the door if it will make you feel more comfortable," she said without looking up.

"Oh, I . . . that's not what I was . . ."

She looked up at him, forcing a benign smile. "Ernest. It's fine."

He stood there awkwardly for a moment, looking at her. "Good night," he said quietly.

He took the notebook into the bedroom with him and shut the door. Moira tried to focus on the book in front of her, tried not to listen to the sounds of movement in the next room as he undressed for bed and brushed his teeth in the bathroom. And when the lock on the bedroom door clicked into place, she tried not to let it wound her.

Ernest didn't like it when she smoked, so she took her cigarettes out on the fire escape once it stopped raining. The night was cold, the wind cutting straight through the shirt she wore. It was one of Ernest's and smelled like him, that musky peppermint scent that was so familiar, yet still made her heart skip a beat. She blew smoke up into the air and shut her eyes, listening to the jazz band playing downstairs as she replayed her earlier conversation with Ernest. They had argued during dinner, not for the first time since she'd arrived. The ease that had once existed between them had been eroded by time, leaving both of them tense, their trust in each other frayed. Especially his.

There existed three versions of her in Ernest's mind, each of them tainted by the other two. First there was Lisavet Levy, the girl he had fallen in love with. The mother of the child he didn't know he had. Then there was the second version. Jack's secretary. The woman he had bought a ring for. The woman who had broken his heart. And then there was her. The ruthless woman who had taken the job that was rightfully his and worked against the rebellion he'd led for five years. That woman, he hated, as much as he tried not to show it. That woman was what had made him keep her at arm's length.

Out on the fire escape, Moira stared down at the smoldering end of her cigarette, unable to bring herself to finish it. He hadn't forgiven her, and it was killing her. He still loved her, but it was different from before. He kissed her good morning and good night, but she could feel the wall between them. That was somehow more painful than any of the other times she had lost him. She flicked the cigarette over the railing in frustration. This wasn't productive, being here with him. She was a distraction, keeping him from finding a solution.

She didn't quite know how she felt about this plan of his. To seal off the time space for good. She wasn't sure if it was even possible, and if it was, what did that mean for their future? Or for the past for that matter? The time space was the only safe place she'd ever known. Would they be destined to live as fugitives? It seemed as though her choices always came back to that, her happiness in exchange for a solution to her problems. She had always chosen the option that would result in the least destruction for those she loved.

The sound of the window opening made her look up. Ernest was climbing out to join her on the fire escape, looking like a horse with too many limbs as he contorted himself through the frame. He cleared his throat as he sat down on the stoop beside her.

"Cold out here," he said, his voice gruff.

"I thought you went to bed."

"Couldn't sleep."

She looked away, wishing she hadn't thrown her cigarette away. "Me either."

He let out a long, steady breath. "I'm sorry."

"For what?"

"For acting so . . . wounded."

"You're right to be angry with me. It's okay."

"No. It isn't okay. I'm just . . ." He huffed again. "I don't know how I'm supposed to feel about you anymore. When I came to you that night, it was all so fresh. But here . . . I don't know."

She bit her lip and looked away. Then she said, "I shouldn't have come."

"Of course you should have come."

"I'm only making this harder on you."

"The alternative would have been worse. You would have been arrested for killing Jack. If you were killed when you could have been safe here with me, I never would have forgiven you."

"What's the difference?"

He looked at her helplessly. "I want to forgive you. Half of me already has. But it's just . . ."

"Amelia," she finished for him. "I understand. What was I supposed to do? I had already erased myself from your life when I found out I was pregnant. I did what I could . . . what I had to. For her."

Ernest was slow to respond. "I get that. Deep down, I understand. You were alone. I shouldn't fault you for the things you thought you had to do. But that doesn't mean I don't wish it was different. There is so much I regret. I feel so much guilt over everything that's happened, believing that I could have done something more. I could have saved you and Amelia from all this."

"If I had left with you when you asked the first time, you mean? It wouldn't have worked, Ernest. All your theories were right. When I first came out of the time space, I was in and out of consciousness for a long time. At least a month, although they kept me sedated. I had to be given fluids through an IV, I could barely walk. We would have been caught . . . you would have been killed. And then where would that have left us?"

Neither of them spoke but Moira could sense the wheels turning in his head as he grappled to reconcile his anger with the reality of the situation. After several minutes, he reached out and took her hand, entwining his fingers in hers.

"I would have taken care of you," he said.

She gripped his hand tighter, hoping it meant forgiveness. "Have you considered walking away from this? Leaving through the time space like you planned and abandoning the rest of it?"

Ernest sighed. "I have. I want nothing more than to take you and Amelia and run somewhere far, far away. Let the others figure this out. But I started this. I have to finish it."

Moira understood there would be no talking him out of this. This was a mess they had made together. They couldn't walk away now. They sat still, leaning against each other as the wind blew around them.

"Did you know that Elaina's memories aren't in the time space?" Ernest said abruptly.

"They aren't?"

"I looked for them for a long time. But they aren't there. I never understood why until you told me what you did, and now . . ." He began toying with the watch on her wrist absentmindedly. "Maybe it's part of the solution."

"What do you mean?"

"Have you ever heard the saying that time is a construct?"

"Yes, of course."

"Well, what if it isn't just a construct? What if we constructed it?"

"Meaning . . ."

Ernest took a moment's pause, sifting through the ever-shifting sands of his thoughts, trying to grasp the pearls hidden there.

"Meaning what if . . . there is no true past beyond the one we've constructed? No true history. If body and consciousness are separate things, why do we all accept this idea that we experience the same version of the world? Scientifically speaking, this idea of shared human experience . . . of collective consciousness . . . it doesn't add up."

He began speaking in terms of quantum physics and equations. Things Moira did not and had never been able to grasp.

"You're losing me here, Ernest," Moira said, cutting him off.

He paused. Regrouped. Began again.

"When we first met, you told me that everyone remembers things differently. That each memory, tainted by nostalgia and circumstance, presents a different view of the world. Who's to say that the same can't be said for all of history? What if the only reason all of us have this collective version of the past . . . of reality . . . is because we've been systematically constructing it ourselves for thousands of years?"

"But how?"

"Through processes of assimilation. By keeping the memories in books, by forcing memory to conform to a specific version of things, we're affecting the entire ecosystem of time and consciousness."

"Right . . ." Moira said cautiously.

Ernest barely heard her say it. "The theory of conservation of energy states that energy cannot be created or destroyed. Which means that consciousness cannot be created or destroyed. And so . . . all the consciousness that has ever existed or will ever exist has always done so. It transfers from a person, into the time space, and back, and when we die, it is trapped inside of books by timekeepers. Stored for all eternity—not dead, but imprisoned. When the memories are burned, the energy from the fire transfers that energy elsewhere through heat and flame, but a part of those memories remains. In the timekeepers who stored and destroyed them. In you . . ." He reached out, laying one hand on her cheek, his eyes bright with possibility. "The woman untethered from Time. But it isn't destroyed. Not truly. Because memories are energy and energy cannot be destroyed. So they must go somewhere. Right?"

"But where?"

There was another pause, this one longer than the first.

"I've been thinking a lot about the chasm," Ernest said slowly. "You said it appeared after you changed the past to put Amelia in it, right?"

She nodded. "Yes."

"Maybe it isn't a chasm at all. Maybe it's a passage."

"Passage?"

"To a different time. Like the Einstein-Rosen bridge. Maybe it leads to the alternative past you created. A different time altogether. Maybe that's where Elaina's memories are. And all the other memories we can no longer touch because we've eliminated them from our version of the timeline."

"I suppose . . . that's one theory at least."

He narrowed his eyes. "You don't like it?"

"I don't know. It's all just speculative."

"Maybe I'm wrong. But if I'm not . . . just imagine what the world might look like. Imagine all the different versions of history that might have existed. That might still exist. Somewhere."

"So what? You want to open a chasm that would swallow the whole time space?" Ernest didn't answer. "You do," Moira said, her eyes going wide. "Ernest, that's insane."

"Maybe. But maybe not."

"No. It is. That's just a theory anyway. What if you're wrong? Who knows what kind of damage you'd be doing."

"But what if I'm right? I was right about you, wasn't I?" He put his hand over her mouth playfully as she tried to protest again. "Say I was right in this case. How would you do it?"

She eyed him suspiciously before deciding to humor him. "I suppose . . . I suppose it would require another change to the past. A big one this time. But that's dangerous. You never know what the consequences will be. You can't control it."

It was the same way with the present. You never knew the future you were creating with your actions. As Azrael had always said, living was the most dangerous thing.

"But if you could?"

Moira looked at him intently. "Ernest, what are you planning?"

His eyes slid to the left evasively. "Nothing."

"Ernest . . ."

"Nothing yet. I'm still working it out." He stood up, still holding on to her hand, and pulled her to her feet after him. "Are you hungry? I can make something."

She wanted to press him but didn't want to argue. This was progress. She relented, nodding at him. He stepped toward her and kissed her softly on the lips. A real, lingering kiss. Neither heated nor distant, as all his others had been. She kissed him back, quieting her apprehensions, and followed him inside.

Ernest used the last of the bread to toast sandwiches on the stove. They were running out of time, but neither was ready to acknowledge it yet. Eventually, as Moira had known it would, talk turned again to Amelia.

"Why was Jack so insistent on getting Amelia involved?" Ernest asked.

Moira tensed, not wanting another argument.

"He had theories about her," she said. "He always suspected that I wasn't telling the truth when I told him she had died. Insinuated that he knew I'd put her in a memory. There was no way he could have known which one, so I thought as long as I did as he asked, he wouldn't go look-ing for her. But then Amelia remembered something I had attempted to erase, years ago when you brought her to the office, and I realized it too late. Jack saw your 'death' as an opportunity to test me and decided to get her involved. Threatened to have her locked away like he did to me when I first got out of the time space. So we sent her in to find the book. The TRP has been looking for it and I hoped that if she found it, it would help explain things."

"But how did Amelia remember what you'd tried to erase?" Ernest asked as he handed her a plate. "I don't understand that."

"The theory is that Amelia is untethered from Time even more than I am. I merely lived inside the time space, but she was born there. She can remember things I've erased. Can move along her own temporal plane. I saw her do it the first time she wound your watch. She is exempt from the ordinary forward limits of Time, almost like she exists separately from it altogether."

He pondered this for some time. Moira could sense him mulling it over, even as talk turned to other things. They finished eating and he left to go take a shower, kissing her in that lingering gentle way he had before. In his absence, Moira stood up to fiddle with the radiator, which had shut off yet again. Her eyes fell on the notes Ernest had strewn across the table. The black notebook he kept with him even when sleeping. Curious as to what he'd been doing, she glanced at the bedroom door, listening to make sure he was in the shower before opening the book.

SHE WAS waiting for him when he finished. She stood in the middle of the bedroom, her arms folded over the black notebook, chewing her lip anxiously. He stepped out of the bathroom with the towel still wrapped around his waist. He jumped when he saw her.

"Do you enjoy scaring the daylights out of me?" he asked, laughing until he noticed the book. "Why do you have that?"

"Don't do it," Moira said firmly.

"What?"

"What you're planning. Don't do it."

His eyes flickered down to the book in her hands, then back up to her face. He looked mildly impressed that she'd been able to piece together his chicken scratch notes, but mostly he looked guilty.

"You were going to do it without telling me, weren't you?" she said sharply. "That's why you were asking about Amelia."

He bit his lip. "I had to be certain she would be okay," he admitted.

She stared at him in horror. "You still intend to do it."

He gave her a long, heavy look. "It's the only option, Lisavet."

"No, it isn't. It can't be."

"I've been searching for months, even before I came here. It's the only thing that makes sense. The only thing that guarantees no one will take control of the time space again."

Moira stepped toward him urgently. "Ernest, if you do this, you'll be trapped. Not just for some number of years but forever."

"I know," he said, clenching his jaw.

"But Amelia . . ."

"She wouldn't be affected. You told me she's untethered from Time, which means she'll continue existing even if we change the rest. If I do this, nothing will happen to her."

Moira's stomach twisted at his certainty. "I don't mean that, Ernest. I mean she would be alone. If you're gone, who is going to take care of her?"

"She would have you."

Moira shook her head. "No, she wouldn't. You know what would happen to me." She thought about her brother. The cruel death he'd faced. With no time space for her father to hide in, would she suffer the same fate?

"It wouldn't," Ernest said firmly. "You and she are the same. Temporal departure, remember? You exist outside of the confines of Time."

Moira bit her lip. Even if that was true, even if they didn't change, everything else around them would. The world as they knew it, and all the people they'd loved, would become something else. Including Ernest. She reached for him, wanting to touch him, and then drew back, unsure. Instead, he stepped forward and caught her face in his hands. His skin was still warm from the shower, his eyes frighteningly sure of himself.

"Ernest, there has to be another way . . . I don't want to risk losing you."

"You won't lose me," he said, his voice barely a whisper. "We're linked, you and me. No matter where we end up, be it a country, an era, or an alternative version of the past, we'll always find each other."

She shook her head. "But what if you're wrong?"

He stepped closer, his thumb stroking across her cheek. "If my theories are right, then there could be hundreds of versions of the way things are. Thousands of paths that a single consciousness could create for itself. Surely in one of them we're happy."

She shook her head again, more vehemently. "But you don't know, Ernest. You can't possibly know if you're right. If this is your solution, then let me be the one to . . ."

His hands tensed. "No. Absolutely not."

"Ernest, it would be better that way. You could be destroying yourself completely. But like you said, I'm untethered. I might survive."

"I can't let you do that," Ernest said firmly. "On the off chance that I'm wrong about all of this . . . I'm not going to be left behind again. I'm not going to lose you when I actually have a choice this time."

Moira gave him a sad smile. "You wouldn't be losing me. It's impossible to lose what you don't remember."

"No," he said harshly, hands sliding down to her shoulders. "You don't know. It's never happened to you. When you made me forget you, it still hurt me, I just didn't know why. I knew something was missing. Some vital piece of my life was gone, and I couldn't figure out what it was. I thought it was just the latent effects of being a soldier. Some kind of long-term grief. But it wasn't. It was you. You have no idea what that's like. To lose a part of yourself and not understand why."

"If you do this, you'll be doing that to me. Is that what you want?"

Ernest faltered slightly. "No," he said quietly. Barely a whisper.

"Then find another way," she said. She pressed the notebook against his chest, eyes pleading. "Please, Ernest. There has to be another solution."

He let go of her to take the book, conflict still brewing on his face. "Okay," he said, pulling her to him with one arm. "Okay."

"Promise me. Tell me you won't do it. Promise me."

He kissed her forehead very gently, reaching up to wipe away the tear she hadn't realized she'd shed. He kissed the bridge of her nose. Both of her eyelids. He held her close and finally kissed her lips. But he didn't answer. He didn't promise. They slept together that night for the first time since she'd arrived. She could feel an urgency in his movements that set her on edge. It was familiar. A kind of desperation she'd seen in him once before on the night she had agreed to leave the time space with him.

It was after midnight when she awoke to the sound of a door closing. The bed beside her was still warm, but Ernest was not in it. She got up, assuming he was in the other room. When she opened the door, he wasn't there. Had he gone out? She began pulling on her clothes, paranoia creeping in. The chain was still on the front door.

Her eyes flew to the watches on the countertop. The box was open. One was missing. She cursed out loud, reaching for her coat. She grabbed her father's old one by mistake, feeling the shift of his watch in the pocket. As an afterthought, she took her revolver. She spun the crown of her own watch and marched through the bedroom door.

AMELIA HEARD footsteps. She looked up, assuming it was Anton. Instead, she saw her uncle standing at the end of the row, frozen in shock.

"No," she breathed, uncurling her legs. What was he doing here? Was he a memory? She struggled to her feet and began walking toward him, heart thudding.

"Amelia . . ." he said in a shaking voice.

She walked faster. "Don't be dead," she murmured. "Please, don't be dead."

She threw her arms around him, half expecting to pass right through. He caught her, his body as strong and solid as it had ever been. Amelia began to sob. She buried her face in his neck, feeling her feet leave the ground as he lifted her up. They stayed there, standing in the center aisle of the time space, tall shelves surrounding them, the chasm just beyond it all. He smoothed her hair back away from her face and she saw that he was crying too. She'd only ever seen him cry once before. At his sister's funeral.

"Why are you here?" she asked when she could finally breathe.

"I came to get you out," he said.

"Is it over?"

"Not yet. Almost."

"Where's . . ." Amelia paused. She didn't know what to call her anymore. Lisavet? Moira? Something else?

"She's outside still. I wanted to come and see you first."

First? Amelia sniffled. "I met Azrael," she said. "He . . . he showed me everything."

"Everything?" Uncle Ernest's arms tensed ever so slightly.

She pulled back to look at him. She'd always thought she looked like him but now she could really see it. "Everything," she said, choking on it. And then she was crying again. She buried her face against his shoulder. "Don't leave me again. Please. Don't leave me."

He kissed her forehead and held her closer. One of his hands rubbed circles against her back. After a long time, he asked, "Amelia. Where is Anton?"

22

1965, Somewhere in the Time Space

LISAVET LEVY HAD NOT been inside the time space for thirteen years. It greeted her like an old friend, the whispers of Time coming to meet her as they had the first time she had entered. She felt the familiarity of this place settling into her very bones. The silence and stillness were as they had always been. The shelves she had called home, unchanged. The mesmerizing stars overhead swirled like a beacon, stopping her in her tracks. She had to brace herself against a shelf as memories swept in and out like a violent tide. Her breath shook. And then she heard him.

"Welcome back, child," Azrael's voice said. She turned to find him standing where the door had once been. "You've been gone so very long."

She let out a gasp. "Azrael."

"Hello, Lisavet. I've missed you."

Tears came, even though she tried to stop them. If Azrael was here, then she still had time.

"Is Amelia . . ."

"She's fine," Azrael reassured her. "I've been looking after her for you. But so has that Russian boy. He seems quite fond of her, in fact."

"And . . . is she . . ." She hesitated, not knowing what it was she was trying to ask.

"Angry with you?" Azrael said, putting words to what she couldn't. "I don't believe so. Though that might have changed since I left her. I took the liberty of showing her what's going on."

Lisavet felt herself go pale. "So . . . she knows?"

"Everything. Yes. Now . . . can I ask what it is you've come to do?"

Lisavet suddenly found it difficult to breathe. "We . . . we're here to fix it. To seal off the time space from interference."

"Ahhh," Azrael said with a grim smile. "So that is what finally brought you home."

Lisavet's lip trembled like a child's would. He understood. And he didn't hold anything she'd done up until now against her.

"Do you know where Ernest is?" she asked.

"I believe he's found Amelia. Perhaps we ought to give them a minute?"

She nodded. Time is what Ernest needed. Maybe seeing their daughter would even change his mind. Everything else could wait.

"You should hide until then," she said to Azrael. "Just . . . stay close to me."

He smiled at her. "I always have," he said before fading into blackness.

Lisavet took a deep breath. She was still holding her revolver, her palms sliding against the metal. She had time. She walked slowly, drinking it all in. Her father's old coat enveloped her, making her feel every age she'd ever been all at once. Suddenly she was eleven, nineteen, twenty-six, and thirty-eight. She wasn't paying attention to anything in front of her, only staring up at the ceiling full of stars.

That was how he managed to get the gun out of her hand.

She felt a hand close on her wrist. Before she could turn around, he kicked the back of her knees, twisting the gun away as she went down. The metal pressed into her temple. In the past five years she'd made a point of learning how to get out of such situations quite easily. But then she saw who it was.

Anton Stepanov glared down at her, looking for all the world as desperate, angry, and terrified as his father had been.

"Do not move," he said fiercely.

She raised her hands, staying on her knees. Anton shifted. Now that he had her there, he seemed unsure of what to do.

"Do you know who I am?" he asked.

"Of course I do," she said in a calm voice. Trying not to let him see her shaking. She had been wrong when she assumed he would target Amelia to seek revenge for his father. But that didn't apply to her.

"You do not look afraid," he said.

"You are not the first Russian to hold me at gunpoint," Lisavet replied with perfect coolness.

This only made him angry. "You will not fight back?" he asked, pressing the gun harder against her skull. His whole hand was trembling.

She shook her head slowly. "No. I'm not going to fight you. You have every right to kill me if that's what you want."

The gun wavered slightly. She could take it now if she wanted to. But she waited.

"You murdered my father," he said.

"I did. I'm sorry. I didn't have a choice. He would have killed me. It was me or him."

"No. I do not believe that. My father was a good man. He would not have done that."

"Even good people make desperate decisions when trying to do what's best," Lisavet said. "He was thinking of you. You and your sisters. He would have done anything to get back to you alive, even if it meant killing me. I forgave him for that a long time ago. But he knew things about *my* daughter that put her at risk." She saw a flicker in his eyes and knew that he knew. "I didn't want to kill him. I was only thinking of her."

"Why should I believe that?"

Lisavet moved quickly, disarming him and taking back her gun in two practiced moves. She rose to her feet, raising it level with his head instead. "Because I haven't killed you yet," she said, then flipped the handle of the gun around, handing it back to him. He took it, looking skeptical.

"Listen to me," she said. "Ernest is here. He's here, and he's about to do something stupid. I need you to help me."

Anton rolled his jaw, mulling it over. "We all fought for you. My father fought for you. I do not want to fight for you anymore. You are not who we all thought you were."

Lisavet studied him. He was still so young. He'd become a Russian agent at just about the same age she had been trapped in here, forced into it, trained to obey orders. That was on her head too.

"Then don't. Help me put an end to all this." She gestured to the revolver. "Or shoot me now. I won't hold it against you."

For a moment, she thought he might do it. She was a beacon he'd fought for, costing him his friends, his family, his entire life as he'd known it. And she didn't measure up. Didn't deserve it. Anton handed the gun back to her.

"I am not a killer like you," he said tensely. "I will help. But not for you. For her. For Ernest."

She let out a breath of relief. "Thank you."

"So what is it we are doing?"

She hesitated, knowing he might change his mind. She removed the watch from her wrist and lifted the crown. She spun it three times but didn't push it back down to trigger the door. Instead, she offered it to him.

"What is this for?" he asked, eyeing it skeptically.

"Take it," she said. "I'll explain the rest on the way."

AMELIA FELT Uncle Ernest slide something into her palm. His watch. She looked down at it, frowning.

"Amelia . . ." he began carefully. "I need you to take this and leave the time space. Go find Anton and take him with you, okay?"

"Aren't you coming?"

He bit his lip. "No. I'm going to stay here. There's something I need to take care of."

"But . . . won't you be trapped?"

"Yes."

Amelia began to protest but he cut her short.

"I know. I know," Uncle Ernest said. "But listen to me. Lisavet . . . your mother . . . she's waiting for you on the other side of the door."

"I don't understand, what will happen to you?"

"She'll explain it when you get there. But I need to stay here, okay. And I need to know you and Anton are safe."

Amelia shook her head. "No. I'm not leaving you here."

"Amelia, listen to me . . ."

"No, Amelia. Don't listen to him."

Both of them turned their heads. Amelia's breath caught in her throat. Moira or Lisavet, or whatever she was supposed to call her, was standing alone down the center aisle. The shirt she had on was Uncle Ernest's, and she was wearing a worn brown man's coat that Amelia recognized from the memories. She was staring at Ernest, an expression of betrayal etched across her face.

"Lisavet," Ernest said. To Amelia's surprise, he took her by the arm and moved her behind him.

"Ernest, you can't do this," Lisavet was saying.

"Do what?" Amelia asked.

"Nothing. I . . ."

"He's going to sacrifice himself to seal off the time space," Lisavet said, her eyes brimming with anger.

"W-what?" Amelia asked, looking at her uncle.

"Lisavet, what are you doing here?"

"I thought we agreed you weren't going to do this," Lisavet snapped. The tone of her voice was one Amelia recognized. More like Moira than the girl from the memories. "You said we would find another way."

"There is no other way!"

"Uncle Ernest . . ." Amelia said hesitantly.

He turned to look at her, putting both hands on her shoulders. "Amelia. Please try to understand this. I'm trying to protect you."

"By leaving me behind?"

"No, I . . ."

"Amelia," Lisavet said, cutting him off again. When they looked back at her, she was holding the silver gun, pointing it directly at Uncle Ernest's head. "Get away from him."

"Lisavet . . ." he said, his voice trembling in disbelief.

"No!" Amelia shouted. "What are you doing!"

"Amelia," she snapped, still watching Ernest. "Please. Move away."

A tense silence passed between Lisavet and Ernest. Amelia felt his hand between her shoulder blades, pushing her down the aisle back in the direction of the chasm. Shielded between two shelves. She tried desperately to grab his arm, but he pushed her away.

"Stay there," he said. He tried to move out of sight, but she shifted, keeping both him and her mother in her line of sight.

"Do you really want to do this?" Ernest asked, taking a step toward Lisavet. "Are you really going to resort to shooting me?"

"No, of course not. I just needed Amelia out of the way for this next part." She lowered the gun. "Anton!"

Amelia only had a moment to be confused before Anton stepped out from in between the nearby shelves. He barreled toward her uncle and seized him from behind, twisting both of his arms behind him. One of his hands pressed down on the crown of a slim, white-gold watch. Moira's watch. Ernest attempted to free himself, but Anton held fast and began dragging him back through the door that appeared before them.

"Anton, stop!" Amelia said, rushing forward.

Lisavet caught her by the arm and held her back. The door slammed shut behind them, disappearing in an instant. Amelia wheeled around, jerking her arm free. She backed away, tears brimming in her eyes.

"Stay away from me!"

"Amelia, I'm sorry," Lisavet said.

"You lied to me!" Amelia snapped as tears began falling for a second time. "This whole time, you lied to me!"

"I had to. I was trying to protect you."

"Protect me?" Amelia let out a desperate laugh. "You weren't protecting me. You shoved me out a window! You let Jack use me! You let them shoot James!"

"Amelia, I . . ."

"No!" Amelia stopped walking, aware of the chasm behind her. "No. I don't want to hear what you have to say. How could you lie to me like that? How could you do all those awful, awful things to Anton's father and all those other people? How could you do that to Uncle Ernest? Don't say it was for me. Don't you dare say that. I didn't want . . . I wouldn't have—" She stopped abruptly, gasping for air.

Lisavet gave her a sad look. Watching as Amelia wiped the tears from her eyes. "Finished?" she asked, some of her familiar self returning.

Amelia glared at her. "It was wrong. It was so, so wrong."

"I know."

"You shouldn't have done it."

"I know that too." Lisavet took a step closer. "But I don't regret it. I would do it all again if I thought it would keep you safe. I would rewrite all of history for you."

Amelia scoffed at her, ignoring the other feelings that were trying to surface. "Why didn't you tell me? All this time I thought you hated me. I didn't know you were my . . . my . . ." She couldn't bring herself to say it.

Lisavet softened. She took another step forward. "How could I have possibly explained it?"

Amelia sniffled begrudgingly. "I guess you couldn't have." She looked down at the chasm behind her, folding her arms.

"Amelia. We don't have much time. I don't know how long Anton can keep your father out of here."

Her father. Amelia felt her stomach twist again.

Lisavet came closer, nodding at Ernest's watch in Amelia's hand. "I need you to go out there with them, okay? Help Anton."

Amelia looked up at her. "What about you?"

Lisavet shut her eyes for a brief moment. "I'm staying."

"Staying?"

There was a long pause. Suddenly Amelia understood.

"No," she said. "You can't."

"Ernest is right. It's the only option. And the only way to keep him from doing it is if I do it first."

Amelia's lower lip trembled. "But . . . but you can't go. I only just found out. I don't want to lose you so soon."

Lisavet blinked back tears of her own. "You won't. You'll still remember me. You'll remember all of this. I promise."

Amelia shook her head. "No. That's not it. I didn't even get a chance to know you. I didn't get a chance not to be angry with you."

Lisavet smiled at that. She took off her coat and slid it around Amelia's shoulders, bending down so they were at eye level. "This is something I need to do," she said softly. "This is my fault. And I need to be the one to fix it. Okay?"

"I'm not going," Amelia said stubbornly. "I won't let you do this."

Lisavet shushed her, pulling her into an embrace. "I'm sorry, Amelia," she said tearfully.

Amelia felt something drop into the pocket of the coat. She heard a ticking sound and pulled away. She reached into the pocket, her fingers barely closing around the brass pocket watch, before Lisavet spoke again.

"I'm so, so sorry."

Amelia looked up. In the split second before she knew what was happening, Amelia felt her mother's hand in the center of her chest. She felt herself slipping over the edge, falling into the darkness of the chasm below.

LISAVET STOOD still for several moments after Amelia was gone, letting tears fall down her face. A chasm was a passage, too, as Ernest had so diligently pointed out. Which meant that, with the watch in her pocket, it would be a passage out, same as any door. Amelia was safe. They were both safe. There was only one thing left to do now.

As if on cue, Azrael rematerialized beside her. "Do you know what to do?"

Lisavet nodded, wiping her eyes. "Yes. But that isn't going to be any easier."

To fix all this, she only needed to change one memory. His. He had been the very first. The reason why the time space was discovered in the first place. If she could alter that moment, removing the discovery completely . . . that would be enough. She looked at Azrael. He was content. His brow uncreased, unconcerned, even though he knew what was about to happen. That saving the world meant erasing him from it.

"And you brought a book?" Azrael asked.

She nodded, withdrawing the little black book of forgotten names from her trouser pocket. When she opened the book to the center, their eyes passed over the lines of names that the TRP had erased, that *she* had had a hand in erasing. Like a father watching the repeated, youthful mistakes of a child yet never ceasing to love them, Azrael did not accuse her or express even an ounce of the disappointment she was certain he felt.

"Are you sure you know what you're doing?" he asked. But he wasn't trying to dissuade her.

"Many things might change," Lisavet replied, her heart aching. "People who were erased will be remembered. Events that were tampered with will be altered. But if Ernest is right . . ." Her words trailed off.

He had to be right. They didn't know for sure what would happen. How could they? Not knowing the outcome was one of the many dangers of living.

"You could be unraveling the entire course of history," Azrael said.

"Then we'll only be making it right," she said. "As it should have been."

"And what about you?"

Lisavet shut her eyes. The chasm would open, taking her and everything else in the time space along with it. She couldn't know what that meant . . . if her mind would go on existing or not. The two of them stood still in the silence. She opened her eyes.

"Is it as empty as they all say it is? Death?"

Azrael smiled at her. "No, my child. There's no emptiness in death. You simply move on. Your consciousness continues, creating and recreating your happiest moments. And some new ones too."

Lisavet gave him a weak smile in return. "Like time walking."

"Yes. Like time walking. Shall we go on this one together?"

She heard the whispers of Time calling out to her as she reached for him, settling her hand along the side of his ghostly face. His eyes locked onto hers, reassured in his demise, as if he had known it was coming from the moment he met her. Perhaps he had known. Azrael had always been wiser than she was. As Lisavet pulled at the delicate threads of what remained of Azrael's memory and placed them in the book, she could already feel the time space beginning to shift around them. That gentle whisper that had been her constant companion wrapped around and through them. She tried to think about what Ernest had said. That somewhere, sometime, in some version of history, there was the possibility of a life where she was happy. Clinging to that promise, she stepped into the memories Azrael had left behind and parted the hands of Time, inserting herself into it.

Two thousand years in the past, Azrael stood on the precipice of a cliff, real, and solid, and alive, still dressed in the plain gray robes of either a monk or a pauper. He was watching the approaching Roman ships draw nearer on the choppy sea below him, helpless to the coming invasion that would decimate his people. Lisavet let out a shuddering breath, drawing his attention to her. He turned his head, eyes widening, words she did not understand falling from lips that had not yet learned to speak any language but his own. Lisavet almost expected to see a spark of recognition in his eyes, but there was only confusion. He did not know her and never would.

She stepped toward him, eyes shining with deadly intent. But he didn't run. Didn't lift a finger to stop her as she drew nearer. This man, a mortal being of forty years without the wisdom he'd accumulated in death, was so assured in his own existence, so certain that Time could not touch him, that he didn't see what was there so plainly in her eyes. He did not suppose that death was coming for him either way. She knew the fate that awaited him, even if she did not choose this one. When the Roman ships made landfall, he, along with his people, had but a handful of days remaining. They would rip his secrets from him, force him to teach them the ways of the time space before killing him and erasing the rest of him from history.

How fragile Time is, she thought to herself as she approached the cliff where he stood. The entirety of history hanging on one moment. One man, standing on the edge of a precipice with a single idea in his head.

"Please forgive me," she said in the language of her father and shoved him hard over the edge of the cliff and into the sea below. She watched with tear-stung eyes as he went under amid the crashing waves. Into the depths of the sea where the Romans would never find him, nor the secrets he kept.

Lisavet pulled herself from the memory and back into the time space just as Time began to splinter. Already the shelves were falling, crashing into one another and turning to dust, which filled the air and became a new atmosphere. She looked down as the book of lost names, which held the remnants of Azrael's memories along with all her regrets, disintegrated in her palms.

As the widening chasm began to crack the ground beneath her feet, Lisavet Levy turned her eyes to the stars.

23

1965, Boston, Massachusetts

AMELIA HIT THE GROUND, still feeling the grip of screaming darkness all around her. She gasped for breath, knees and elbows scraping against wood. She looked around the room expecting to see her uncle and Anton. Nobody was there. The lights were off, the room completely dark. She didn't recognize this place. It looked like her uncle's office. His books were here. Some of the furniture was the same. But it wasn't the same place. The room was bigger. There was a garden out the window with a large fountain that glittered in the moonlight. It looked like something from out of a dream. Familiar, yet far away.

A light in the next room flipped on. Footsteps began walking across the floor. Amelia tried to stand but tripped on the edges of the coat. She let out a grunt of pain as she hit the floor again.

"Amelia?" a voice called out curiously.

She straightened up. Uncle Ernest?

The door opened. "Amelia, what are you . . ."

His words were cut short by the impact of her flying into his arms. She held on tight, ignoring every word he said until he hugged her back, confused but accepting of her affection.

"Why are you up so late?" he asked when she finally pulled away. "And what on earth are you wearing?"

Amelia studied his face. Did he not remember . . . any of it?

"I couldn't sleep," she said at last.

"Okay . . ." Uncle Ernest said. "That still doesn't explain the coat."

"Oh, it isn't mine. I . . . I got it from the closet upstairs."

"You did?" he said with a frown. A glimmer of recognition flitted in his eyes so quickly she couldn't be sure if she imagined it. "Must have been your grandfather's," he said with a wry smile. "There's still a bunch of his stuff all over his house. I can't seem to get through it all."

Something clicked in the back of her head. The garden out back *was* familiar. This had been her grandmother's home. She remembered it from the funeral all those years ago. Uncle Ernest had sold it and bought a smaller house nearby, where they stayed each summer when she was home from school, the demands of his job making him unable to keep up with the maintenance of such a place.

"Come on," he said. "I'll make you some tea, but then you need to go back to bed. You've got school tomorrow."

He turned to go, and Amelia caught his hand, still reeling. "Wait. I need to ask you . . ." She hesitated. What if he had forgotten all of it? How would she explain?

"Could I have coffee this time?" she asked instead.

He laughed at her. "Oh, no. You're not going to talk *me* into letting you have coffee. Fifteen is too young. I don't care if your mother lets you have it when I'm not around."

Amelia froze in shock. "My . . . my mother."

"Apparently it's the German thing to do. But I'm putting my foot down. I'm your father, I should be consulted about these things."

He wasn't angry, not really, but his words stunned Amelia so much that he had to reassure her several times that he wasn't. He snuck an extra teaspoon of honey into her tea before giving it to her. As he slid the mug of tea across the table, Amelia noticed the familiar watch on his wrist, ticking away as if it was the most normal thing in the world.

Up in her bedroom, which looked like her normal bedroom, but also didn't, she paced back and forth, racking her brain for what could have happened. Could this actually be real? And if so, how was she supposed to know how this version of her life was supposed to have gone? It wasn't like she had any memory of it. Suddenly, she stopped pacing, remembering what Azrael had said. That she had shifted between two versions of the same memory. Moved along her own temporal plane. Perhaps she could do that again.

She held still in the center of the room and shut her eyes, waiting to hear the echoes of Time . . .

AFTER MAKING sure that Amelia had gone back to bed, Ernest returned to his own. His wife was sitting up awake, ever the insomniac, a book of poems in one hand.

"Everything all right?" she asked.

"Mm-hmm," Ernest said. He slid into bed beside her, leaning over to kiss her cheek. "It was just Amelia."

Lisavet hummed softly and leaned into his kiss. "What is she doing up so late?"

Ernest shrugged. "Couldn't sleep. Takes after her mother, I guess," he said, tweaking her nose playfully.

He had met his wife when they were children. Ernest's father had owned a prestigious watch company here in Boston and had hired Ezekiel Levy, a clockmaker he'd met studying in Switzerland, to come work for him in early 1938. The man had tried to put it off, but Gregory responded by offering him so much money that he couldn't resist, uprooting his daughter and son and bringing them to the United States just ten months before Kristallnacht.

Ernest and Lisavet had met when she first arrived, but even with just two years between them, neither thought much of the other until Ernest took over his father's company at twenty-four. By that point, Lisavet had grown into both a watchmaker in her own right and the most beautiful woman Ernest had ever laid eyes on. They married four years later.

"By the way," Ernest said, leaning his head against his wife's arm sleepily. "We need to talk about this whole 'coffee' thing."

Lisavet bit her lip, trying not to smile. "What about it?"

"Amelia is too young. I've been reading some of the research lately and . . ."

"Oh, are you a doctor *and* a watchmaker now?" she scolded warmly.

"I could be a doctor," he said bitterly. "I'd make a damn good one."

"Yes, I'm sure you would," Lisavet said patronizingly. "Amelia will not perish from a little bit of coffee every now and then. It's not like she's running around smoking. Besides, I drank coffee when I was far younger than her. And I turned out all right."

Ernest had to agree with her there. "That, my dear, is an understatement," he said, raising himself up to kiss her. He ran his hand over her moonlight blond hair, letting it fall through his fingers. "You are as perfect as the moon and every last star in the sky."

She laughed at him, abandoning her book as he pulled her down into bed beside him.

By morning, Amelia's mind had settled. As she visited each memory as a spectator, the memories of this version of her life came to her, crowding for space alongside her other memories. There existed two versions of her now. Both were true, and yet neither was more real than the other. Time was an illusion and memory even more so.

In this life, she was happy. Or at least happier than she had been before. This version of Amelia didn't understand how good she had it. She
still had a penchant for trouble, though not quite as much. She talked
back to her mother and father, not knowing until now that, in another
life, she had been an orphan. Her father was a watchmaker, heir to the
largest timepiece corporation in the country. Her mother worked for
the company, even though she didn't have to. They lived in this house.
He had never gone to work for the State Department and didn't need to
split his time between DC and Boston anymore. No longer overworked.

Everything was different. Incidents that had once been settled in the
time space were fought out in the real world instead, each of them coming to a slightly different conclusion than they had before. The world
was different. Amelia couldn't be sure if it was any better, but at least it
was free from interference.

She dressed for school in her bedroom, noticing the differences between this room and the one she had known before. Instead of towering shelves full of books, some of the walls in her bedroom displayed
photographs. Pictures of her and her parents when she was a child.
Downstairs, her father was cooking breakfast, the smell of eggs and coffee drifting throughout the house. He smiled when he saw her, dressed
in a sweater and a pair of slacks, red hair glossy and neat.

"Morning," he said. "How'd you sleep? No more late-night romps in
my office, I hope?" He set a mug of coffee down in front of her, looking
sheepish. "I talked to your mother last night," he explained, nodding at it.
"She seems to think that drinking coffee is an important part of embrac-
ing your German heritage, so who am I to get in the way?"

Amelia giggled in spite of herself. "Thanks," she said, reaching for the
cream and sugar. "Where is . . ."

"Your mother?" Ernest jerked his head to the window. "Out in the
garden." He set another cup of coffee down in front of her. "Take this out
to her while I finish breakfast, will you? Tell her it's almost ready."

Amelia took the cup and slipped through the back door, her feet knowing the way even though her mind was still catching up. In the garden, the air was chilly. The last warmth of summer was slowly fading. Amelia walked the gravel path, looking down at the neatly planted flowers lining either side of it. Bushels of Russian sage, catmint, and yarrow still clung to their petals. The trees were alight with early autumnal oranges and reds.

A little ahead, near the gate, a woman with golden hair was standing among the flower beds. Her hair was neither as long as Lisavet Levy's nor as short as Moira's. Some of the golden color was streaked with silver, just enough to be noticeable, but not so much that it detracted from the radiant, moonlit color. Amelia slowed her pace. The woman looked up, smiling when she saw her coming.

"Good morning," she said warmly.

Amelia handed her the coffee, feeling shy. Both halves of her knew who this person was, but the half that was less familiar didn't know how to behave. She studied the woman as she cupped two hands around the mug and took a drink. In her face, she could see traces of the Lisavet Levy from before. Of Moira, the woman Lisavet had become. But the whole of her was neither of those people. In this life, she was simply "mother."

"You're quiet today," her mother said. She still had the remnants of a German accent. She hadn't had that before.

"I was up too late," Amelia said.

"I heard. Your father thought someone was trying to break into the house."

Amelia smiled, letting herself slide into this life. A life where she could sip coffee out in the garden with her mother while her father cooked breakfast. But then she looked down and choked. At her feet, a clump of blue forget-me-nots with their bright yellow centers covered the flower bed. Blooming still in spite of the lateness of the season.

"Are those . . ."

"Forget-me-nots," her mother said, kneeling down to admire them. "They've been behaving so unusually this year. I thought we'd seen the last of them but when I came out this morning, here they were. Odd for a spring flower, don't you think?"

She looked at Amelia, eyes twinkling with meaning, a kind of understanding passing between them. Ernest called out the window for them to come in for breakfast. Lisavet stood up to go.

"Wait," Amelia said.

Her mother turned back expectantly.

"Is this real?" Amelia asked.

"Why would you think it isn't real?"

"I don't know. I just . . ." Amelia frowned. "What if this is just a dream? Or what if it's just some kind of memory and neither of us knows it?"

Her mother leaned down to kiss her forehead. "If it is just a memory, then at least it's a happy one," she said, squeezing her hand.

Ernest called again, accusing them of being slow. They returned inside together.

Amelia wanted to leave it alone. To embrace this beautiful new life and forget everything else. But the watch still called to her. She needed to know what had happened to that place. If it was really gone. If this was really happening or if it was all just a happy memory.

After breakfast, overcome by curiosity and unable to resist the temptation, she went to her room and retrieved Ezekiel Levy's pocket watch from her dresser drawer. With shaking fingers, she spun the crown three times and pushed it down. She held her breath and stepped through the door of the bedroom, squeezing her eyes shut. Nothing happened. The watch continued ticking. No silence. No stillness. Maybe it really was gone. Erased. Then she remembered that once, monks and prophets found the time space through little more than concentrated force of will.

That Azrael, who had never had a watch, had found it in the days when Time was just an idea.

She shut her eyes, turning the crown of the watch in her hand, and there it was. The whisper, just as it had been in the time space. She reached for it, the way Lisavet Levy had reached out to part the curtains of Time, and stepped back through the bedroom door again, feeling the very air shudder with indecision. There was stillness on the other side, invisible drafts giving way to absolute calm. Amelia waited for the impermeable quiet of the time space, but the whispers didn't stop. They got louder and louder, gathering, drifting, culminating around her. She opened her eyes and gasped.

There were no books. No shelves of any kind. Only stars that hung in the air, swimming in shapes that formed and re-formed in clusters, first in one place, then someplace else as smaller, more varied versions of the world were written and unwritten in an endless flow. Here, conscious thoughts came into contact, bounced off each other, and entwined in great swirling patterns that slowly became one light. Here there was no history, no confined past to be maintained. Here, there was only memory. Floating. Changing. Free. Each mind a world all its own, each memory neither reflection nor echo of any other.

For a long moment, Amelia stood, looking at the limitless expanse of possibility that was Time. The whispers all around her were ceaseless. Time had been silenced before, but now it sang. When she had seen all she needed to see, she turned back and stepped through the door, still open behind her. Back to the life that was both real and not real, that both existed but didn't, as with all memories. Amelia would hear that whisper for the rest of her life. The reminder that all of Time was a miraculous construct that gave shape to conscious thoughts and wrote a thousand versions of a single life.

The door to the time space closed behind her. She never opened it again.

AMELIA DIDN'T go to Pembroke anymore. Instead, she went to a different private school close to home where she came and went each day rather than boarding. Still snooty. Still prestigious. But different. Apparently this version of Amelia wasn't as prickly as the other had been. She had friends. Girls whose names she'd known her whole life. Girls who ate lunch with her each day and waited for her in the halls between classes. She was talking to one of them, a mousy-haired girl named Daphne, when she heard rambunctious shouting from down the hall, followed by a loud clattering.

Amelia looked up in alarm, watching a small crowd of seniors kicking some poor victim's books in all directions.

Beside her, Daphne sighed. "I really wish they wouldn't do that."

"What's going on?"

"It's Steven again. Harassing that poor Russian exchange student. They should leave him alone. It's not his fault he's a communist."

The bell rang. The crowd of boys gave their victim's belongings one final kick before dispersing. Amelia caught sight of a miserable-looking Russian boy hunched over, scrambling to collect his trodden books. A Russian boy with lanky limbs and hollow cheeks.

Daphne tapped her on the arm. "Come on, we better go. We'll be late."

"You go ahead," Amelia said, waving her off.

She watched the boy as the hallway cleared. It couldn't be . . . could it? She moved toward him slowly and bent down to pick up the last of the books. A Russian-English dictionary. She wondered if this version of Anton Stepanov spoke English as well as the last. He looked different somehow, and yet entirely the same. Still scrawny. Still dark-haired and hollow-featured. But some of the haunted look had gone from his eyes. He glanced up to see her standing there and pulled an irritated face she knew all too well.

"What are you staring at?" he snapped.

Amelia gave him an indignant frown. "Well, I was going to give your book back. But if you're going to be rude about it . . ."

"Oh, I see. Very funny. Take the dictionary from the communist boy so he cannot talk."

"I wasn't going to steal it."

"No? Then give it back."

Amelia held it out to him. He took it from her begrudgingly, turning back to swap some of the books from his locker.

"You could say thank you," she said.

"For not stealing? Okay, thank you for following the law. That is very nice."

"Wow. Are all Russians this rude?"

He shut his locker with a sigh. "Okay, okay. Thank you. Are all Americans so needy?"

Amelia couldn't help it. She giggled.

He scowled at her, muttering to himself in Russian.

At lunch, she saw Anton by himself on the outskirts of the cafeteria. His plastic tray of food had been largely untouched. Amelia picked up her own lunch and stood up, ignoring her other friends. She cleared her throat as she approached.

"Oh. You again," he said, frowning at her. "What do you want?"

"Want some company?" she asked awkwardly.

"You don't mind eating lunch with the communist?"

"No. But I think it means you have to give me half of your banana bread." She gestured to the plastic-wrapped loaf on his tray.

Anton frowned at her. "Why?"

"Don't communists believe in sharing?"

He pointed to the slice of chocolate cake sticking out of the top of her open lunch box. "I will trade you for it. After all, we are in America. Don't Americans believe in trading?"

"I hardly think chocolate cake for banana bread is a fair trade."

Anton cracked a smile. "You're right. It isn't. That's what makes it American."

Amelia smiled back and slid it over to him. They didn't say much else to each other that day, but Amelia didn't mind. She knew it took time for him to get comfortable.

The next day, she arrived before he got there and sat at the same table. Anton approached her but didn't sit down. She looked up at him expectantly. He held up his dessert plate. Today it was a blueberry cobbler. Amelia had brought a whole Hershey's chocolate bar in anticipation and offered it to him.

"You know, I think you're starting to get the hang of this whole being American thing," she teased as he sat down and peeled off the wrapper.

"Then maybe we try this instead," he said, breaking off the top quarter of the chocolate bar and holding it out to her.

"What country does this?"

Anton shrugged. "No country. Just friends."

Amelia smiled and took the offering of chocolate and friendship.

24

Somewhere and Nowhere All at Once

LISAVET LEVY WAS ONE with the stars. She lived in an endless memory, the realest thing she had ever known, making and remaking versions of her life. Versions where they were safe. Where they were happy. It didn't matter what was real and what wasn't.

All that remained of the place that had once been the time space were the stars that hung in the sky above it all. Living thoughts and dead ones, swirling together in the endless tapestry of memory. And she was among them, the girl who was untethered from Time, shining brighter than everything else around her. The moon at last.

Acknowledgments

To BEGIN TO PROPERLY say thank you, I first have to call upon a few spectral memories of my own, starting with my grandfather, Ernest, whose name and memory grace every page of this book. To every person who came before me upon whose histories my own life has been built, thank you.

As for the living, thank you first and foremost to my agent, Jennifer Weltz, who has been more ardent a champion of the book than I ever could have hoped for, and whose initial notes were integral to getting the ending right. Without you, none of this would have been possible.

Second, of course, to Kaitlin Olson, my editor at Atria, whose love for Lisavet, Ernest, and Amelia is second only to my own, and whose guiding edits helped make them truly shine.

Thanks also to the entire team at Atria and Simon & Schuster Canada, whose work to bring this book into the world has been nothing shy of a tour de force, including Brittany Lavery for bringing the book to Canadian readers, Ife Anyoku for fielding my questions and keeping all the details in order, managing editors Paige Lytle and Lacee Burr, marketer Dayna Johnson, publicist Gena Lanzi, and production editor Jason Chappell. Thanks also to Laurie McGee for helping to make sure all my dates and timelines were in order (no small task), and to Sara Wood and Esther Paradelo for their amazing design work. A million forgot-me-nots to the whole team.

Additionally, I'd like to thank the many publishers and editors around the world who have worked to bring the book to as many readers as possible. Your love and excitement for the story, felt across borders and oceans, has meant everything to me.

I also have to thank a litany of people who gave their time and expertise, and whose thoughtful notes helped to shape the final story, including Tara Singh Carlson and Gabriella Mongelli.

On the home front, all my love and gratitude goes to my family (both of origin and the one I married into) for your love, advice, and support along the way. Special thanks to my sister, Cassidy, my first-ever reader, who once tried to use a story I wrote for her fifth-grade reading project—the highest of honors. Also to my mother, who gave me a childhood full of library trips, and for being one of the few who saw this book in its earliest, messiest drafts.

There was much research required to make this book come to life, and I am forever indebted to Andrew Pettegree and Arthur der Weduwen for writing the book *The Library: A Fragile History*, from which the first threads of this story were spun. I would also like to thank everyone at the St. Charles Public Library for helping me track down obscure title after obscure title as I worked my way through decades of history at once.

Most significantly, to Angelo, whose enthusiasm for watches was the thing that helped me pull the idea for this book into sharper focus, and who has patiently read every draft, revision, and edit along the way. Thank you for letting me bring you along into dream after half-formed dream, for every long, rambling walk we took while I sorted out the details, and for believing in me more than I ever believed in myself.

To everyone who has dedicated their time and energy to fighting against censorship and to preserving the stories of those that history has rewritten, whitewashed, or forgotten, this book was written for you.

And lastly, to my son, who at the time of writing this is mere days away from being born, and to whom I would give the moon and every last star in the sky. All of this has always been for you.

About the Author

HAYLEY GELFUSO is an author and poet who works in the environmental nonprofit sector. As a writer, she is drawn to stories of the wild and wonderful that are rooted in real world history and science. Her poetry about her experiences working in the conservation field has been published in the *Plumwood Mountain Journal*. She lives in the Chicago suburbs with her husband and son.